ADVANCE READER PRAISE FOR *FIELD OF BLOOD*

"Wilson rises far above most in modern fiction and portrays the fight between good and evil in an innovative, refreshing way."—RED, rock group

"In a market flooded with 'perfect' heroes and squeaky clean Christian characters, Wilson gives us a healthy dose of reality. It's realistic and accurate where it should be and pure entertainment where it should be. It's everything you could hope for in a Christian book—something for the lost to contemplate and for the believer to never forget."—Meli Willis, www.inside-corner.com

"Ahhh! That was utterly amazing."
—Mara M., a fan

"Not only Eric Wilson's best novel to date, but easily one of the most powerful and inspirational novels I've read in years. This is intense and edgy writing to be sure, yet nowhere will you find the redemptive power of Christ's blood explored so brilliantly in fiction. And the best part? There are still two more books to come!"
—Jake Chism, www.thechristianmanifesto.com

"*Field of Blood* was wonderful! I loved the ending . . . it left me wanting more, more, more! Gina is the perfect representation of the human condition . . . a mind blow-ing story!"—Julie P., a fan

"Ridiculously topnotch!"—Jeremy M., a fan

"A classic genre seen through new eyes. The book was well researched and . . . I was blown away by the story."—James N., a fan

"Eric Wilson reveals his full potential as an extraordinary writer with *Field of Blood*. Characterized by a tightly woven plot, unforgettable characters—living and undead—and an overall remarkable sto⸱ ⸱⸱⸱ ⸱⸱⸱ders of all kinds."—Brandon V., a fan

JERUSALEM'S UNDEAD TRILOGY

FIELD
OF

BLOOD

ERIC WILSON

THOMAS NELSON
Since 1798

NASHVILLE DALLAS MEXICO CITY RIO DE JANEIRO BEIJING

Published in Nashville, Tennessee, by Thomas Nelson. Thomas Nelson is a registered trademark of Thomas Nelson, Inc.

Page design by Mandi Cofer.

Excerpt from *The Vampire Book: The Encyclopedia of the Undead*, © 1994 by J. Gordon Melton, reprinted by permission of the author.

Thomas Nelson books may be purchased in bulk for educational, business, fund-raising, or sales promotional use. For information, please e-mail SpecialMarkets@ThomasNelson.com.

Scriptures taken from the *Holy Bible*, New Living Translation. © 1996. Used by permission of Tyndale House Publishers, Inc., Wheaton, Illinois 60189. All rights reserved.

Library of Congress Cataloging in Publication Data

Wilson, Eric (Eric P.)
 Field of blood / Eric Wilson.
  p. cm. — (The Jerusalem's undead trilogy)
 ISBN 978-1-59554-458-2
 1. Vampires—Fiction. 2. Jerusalem—Fiction. I. Title.
 PS3623.I583F54 2008
 813'.6—dc22

2008019837

Printed in the United States of America

08 09 10 11 12 RRD 6 5 4 3 2

A NOTE FROM
THE AUTHOR

I love stories full of grit and emotion, especially when I find them sniffing around history's unexplored corners.

A few years back, my Romanian travels piqued my interest in the legends of the undead. Later, I came across this passage in J. Gordon Melton's *The Vampire Book: The Encyclopedia of the Undead:*

> an increasing number of novelists . . . possess no understanding or appreciation of any power derived from Christian symbols. For the foreseeable future, new vampire fiction will be written out of the pull and tug between these traditional and contemporary perspectives.

The words were a challenge to me, a flag waved before a bull. There were powerful concepts at work here: life, blood, and memory; evil, redemption, and immortality. I knew I had rich soil in which to plant a story.

The soil deepened when I read of two separate events from 1989.

The first involved a mysterious outbreak among thousands of Romanian orphans, an epidemic of subtype F HIV-I that started with a single infectious source.

The second was a discovery of unplundered burial caves on Jerusalem's outskirts. The tombs contained one sarcophagus and thirty-nine ossuaries—stone boxes built to hold the bones of the dead. Archaeologists determined this place was the *Akeldama*, a cemetery for foreigners and the site of Judas Iscariot's death. They also found that a number of the boxes were empty.

Okay, now I knew I was onto something.

As I headed to Israel for two blistering weeks in the summer of 2007, I had no clue how sharply my experiences would hone the concept for a trilogy.

I visited historical locations, made new friends, took hundreds of pictures, and reveled in how much could be done on a shoestring budget and a prayer. The highlight was Jerusalem, with its collage of cultures, religions, and history.

There was, however, a lingering frustration.

Where was the excavation site for these ancient tombs? I couldn't pinpoint the spot, and it was absent from any tourist maps.

The day before my return to the States, I was making a final drive around the Old City when I looked back over my shoulder and spotted the Rockefeller Museum, the building that houses the Israel Antiquities Authority. I made a U-turn into the angled driveway and stopped at the gate.

"I am sorry," the guard said. "The museum closes at three."

My watch read 3:05 p.m.

Disappointed, I reversed onto the road. Then, in a stubborn moment, I parked the car and jogged back. I bypassed the gate and went straight to the guard booth, where a different man was seated. He asked how he could help me.

"Is there a museum bookstore?" I said. "I just need some research materials. Please, I'll pay for them."

"Too late. There's no one there. Here, you come with me."

Unsure of his purpose, I followed along. He led me into the closed museum, past exhibits and three-thousand-year-old relics. Circular stairs took us down a level, where I saw chain-link storage areas full of artifacts. The smell of history hung in the air, and my heart pounded in my chest.

We reached an archive room tucked into the back reaches of the lower level, where I was introduced to a kind-faced, dark-haired woman. Her desk was barricaded by towering shelves on rollers.

"You want to know about the Akeldama?" She pronounced it with a guttural sound. "I suppose I can help. I was the one who drew the cave diagrams and most of the tombs' inscriptions."

"What? You've gotta be kidding me."

"Why are you interested? I've never had anyone so excited to meet me."

"Well," I told her, "I'm writing a book."

"I hope it's scary."

"Why?"

"Because," she said, "it's a *very* scary place."

The very words I hoped to hear!

She went on to describe her own experiences of crawling into the subterranean site, through tight spaces and piles of bones.

"Do you have any reports or maps?" I requested. "Anything that might help me in my writing?"

"It's been many years, but let's look here." She pointed at shelved files.

With her gracious and enthusiastic help, I amassed page upon page of information. I found inventories of the ossuaries, including the Hebrew and Greek inscriptions identifying nearly all of the dead. I read about the Houses of Ariston and Eros, two distinct groupings within the burial site, and it was from this research I found many character names: Ariston, Erota, Shelamzion, and so on.

I was thanking God and making final notes in the cramped copy room, when the dark-haired woman returned from a fact-gathering jaunt to the museum library.

She was beaming. "Eric, are you sitting down? I think today is your most lucky day. Come and meet one of the men who led the dig at the Akeldama. This is unusual that he is here. But very good for you."

Incredible was more like it.

At a table in the library, I joined the softspoken and internationally recognized archaeologist. He spread out a topographical map and pointed to the Akeldama's precise location, confirming that it was indeed where Judas hanged himself, the land bought with thirty silver shekels by the high priests.

An hour later I found myself alone in the spooky quiet of the Akeldama, where olive and almond trees clung to a dusty slope. I saw rugged holes reaching into the ground. I even found the old Charnel House, a boneyard used twelve centuries later by the Knights Templar.

My mind was on overdrive with scenes, ideas, and characters. Already, the story was coming to life . . . so to speak.

—*Eric Wilson, March 2008*

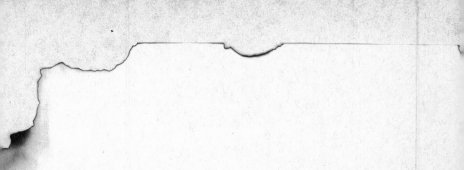

To my uncle, Frank Guise:

You didn't live to read this one, but I do believe we'll see each other again and maybe even go mountain biking on some undiscovered trail—*if* I can keep up.

And to my grandfather, Alan Wilson:

Long before I was published, you inspired me with criticism and praise in equal measure. You carried yourself to the end with quiet strength.

The news of his death spread rapidly among all the people of Jerusalem,
and they gave the place the Aramaic name Akeldama,
which means "Field of Blood."

—ACTS 1:19

PROLOGUE

AD 30—City of Jerusalem, Israel

The Man from Kerioth dangled over hard earth. His breath was ragged, his fingers grasping at the noose that clung to a gnarled olive tree. His larynx, nearly crushed by the short plunge, worked against the rope.

Air. One gulp, that's all he needed. Just one.

Despite this struggle for oxygen, he could not quell the whispers in his head: *There is a way back, even still . . .*

Impossible.

The sun rose orange and pregnant over the Mount of Olives, giving birth to purple shadows. His lungs heaved. He kicked in desperation, and his body twisted on the rope, providing him a glimpse of the city walls along the opposing ridge.

Those walls, they were were infested with Roman swine. He'd longed—oh, how he had longed—to join an uprising that would restore this city to the Jews. He had even aligned himself with a band of dagger-men, the *Sacarii*, but when their zealotry floundered amid internal rivalries, he'd hedged his bets instead on the aspirations of a Nazarene.

All for naught.

If he felt any remorse, it was that he'd squandered three full years on empty promises. He'd given himself, heart, mind, and soul, to the cause of the rebel king. He had collected donations for the Nazarene, even dispersed them to the needy, then watched a woman dump costly perfume over the man's feet. An utter waste—and the Nazarene had *allowed* it.

In the end, the supposed king was nothing but a shortsighted simpleton. Innocent, yes. But a fool.

Last night, the Man from Kerioth had made his decision. He refused to play the puppet any longer. For thirty shekels, the price of a common slave, he'd led an armed mob into a garden where the Nazarene kneeled in prayer, and he'd kissed that life away—quite literally.

"My friend . . ." The Nazarene had looked him in the eye. "Do what you have come for."

And he had done just that.

Yet here he swung. From the end of a rope.

Well, what was he supposed to do? Beg forgiveness? Grovel on his knees? He'd rather rot like the garbage brought out through the nearby Dung Gate, rather burn here in the Valley of Hinnom. Gehenna—wasn't that the Greeks' name for this valley? Children had once been sacrificed here to Moloch, and even now death licked at the air.

A way back . . .

Never.

Coarse threads drew blood from the abrasions on his neck, and his eyes bulged. As his throat convulsed against this restriction, something sulfuric seemed to crawl from his esophagus.

Bile? His departing spirit? Or perhaps the fierce presence whose malice he'd welcomed in these last few hours.

Sudden panic overtook the Man from Kerioth. As spreading sunlight tore his resolve into strips, he clawed at his robe. Where was the dagger? The one he'd swiped from the ground after the Nazarene's arrest. He would grab hold of the dagger, lift it to the noose, and cut himself free. Whereas Peter the disciple had failed to protect his master with this blade, the Man from Kerioth would put it to good use.

Live by the sword, or die by the sword.

Yes, if he could only . . .

His fingers found the hilt.

If he could . . .

The dagger slipped from his grasp and clattered onto the ground below. For the second time in one day, it'd betrayed the intentions of the one who had held it. He knew then he was finished.

Coated with a salty paste, his tongue ballooned in his mouth and his lips expelled a red-black mist. He kicked, spun back around. Heard a splintering sound. Felt his body lurch. Even as his mind grasped what was happening, the branch holding him surrendered to his weight in a prolonged crack that reverberated over parched ground.

For one moment, one blessed second of weightlessness, he tasted air—sweet, golden wine—sliding over his tongue.

Then his own bulk worked against him.

And he plummeted.

His knees buckled against the earth and pitched his torso forward, where it tore over a jagged stone. Like a street vendor's ripe fruit, his belly split and gushed open. Landing across his back, the broken limb shoved him further down upon the rock.

Agony exploded from his center, coursing through his extremities. He let out a raspy cry as his sour juices trickled into the field. So this was how it would end? With only dust and blood to mark his time on Earth?

Alongside his head, he saw a beetle scramble through clods of dirt—attracted, in all likelihood, to the stench of entrails. Soon the flies would be arriving as well. Minions of Beelzebub. Of decay.

A way back, even still . . .

Too late for that now.

Curse the Nazarene. Curse him and his loyal fools.

The Man from Kerioth began to curl and convulse in the wash of daylight. As his energy ebbed, the field's throat opened beneath him and drank of his blood in long, thirsty swallows.

THE FIRST DROP: REVENANTS

There was dust that thick in the place that you might have slep' on it . . . an' the place was that neglected that yer might 'ave smelled ole Jerusalem in it.

—BRAM STOKER, *DRACULA*

I remind you of the angels who did not stay within the limits of authority . . . but left the place where they belonged.

—JUDE 1:6

Journal Entry

June 21, 2010

The envelope showed up yesterday, brought over to Lummi Island on the ferry. Inside there was an old map marked with Hebrew writing. No return address, just a stamp and a Romanian postmark.

Have Those Who Hunt already found me? I thought this place was safe here in Puget Sound, worlds away from Seattle and all its hustle and bustle. Long as I can remember, this house has been my home. I've got shelves of books to read, great views of the sunset, and fresh crab on a daily basis. Still, sometimes it feels like a prison.

I've read in the Mosaic Law that the life is in the blood, and even Abel's blood cried out from the ground after Cain killed him. As soon as I saw the four red stains on the map, I wondered: could there be memories in these droplets?

Part of me said I should be disgusted by the idea. This morning, though, I couldn't help it. I put my tongue on that first crusty spot, and waited. I thought maybe I'd find a reason for my exile here, or at least more about Those Who Hunt. Was it wrong of me to at least try?

Within seconds, my saliva was working like lemon juice on invisible ink, bringing all kinds of stories into focus—secrets, and dark mysteries; a Romanian girl's face, and the fangs of some hellish beast.

I grabbed sheets of paper and started writing it all down.

CHAPTER ONE

Summer 1989—Cuvin, Romania

Gina's dog gave a sharp yip, rose from the front step of the whitewashed cottage, and hobbled forward on the three legs with which he'd been born. He sniffed the hot afternoon air and growled, his copper-colored fur rising like bristles on his back.

"Hush, Treia," Gina said. "It's only me."

He met her at the step and set about investigating her shoes, her shins.

"It's okay. That smell, it's just Teodor." She set down a sack of red potatoes and patted her dog's head. "Look what he got me."

Treia's attention turned to her hand, where the juice of fresh blackberries stained a brown paper bundle. He caught the first offering from her fingertips and chased the second across the stone pathway.

"And all it cost me was a kiss," Gina whispered.

A kiss that had tasted like goat's milk on Teo's lips, like cut grass. Not unpleasant. Not at all. The flutters in her tummy had told her she was becoming an adult, and it was true that she would be turning twelve in a matter of hours. A woman, by Jewish standards.

"Gina," her mother called from inside. "Bring the sack here. How am I to make *ciorba* without potatoes?"

"Sorry, *Mamica*."

"Why the delay? I hope you weren't talking to that boy again."

Gina pushed the bundle into the pocket of her handmade dress, then carried her burden into the kitchen area where Nicoleta was bent over the oven. Scents of parsley and celery root laced the air. Lunch would be stuffed cabbage and vegetable soup.

"Set it down."

She obeyed. Took a moment to scratch at a bite below her ear.

"I can't do it all," her mother said. "You must shoulder your responsibilities, you know this?"

"*Da*, Mamica."

"You'd think you were from Bucharest or Timisoara, a regular city girl, spoiled and soft." Her mother dumped potatoes beside a mound of sliced carrots. "Take a look at me. I travel once a week to study at the university, but you certainly don't see me neglecting my duties. Time to grow up, you hear?"

The words stung. Though she admired her mother's commitment to education, that grasping for knowledge seemed to have weakened her hold on tenderness.

Locked in this young girl's body, Gina was ready to break free, to pursue her own dreams. She loved the village children, adored their innocent, grubby faces, and her heart yearned to be of some use in an orphange.

Not that she had much to offer.

But weren't there constant cries for workers at the centers—in nearby Arad, in Cluj, even as far away as Constanta on the Black Sea? Stories circulated about urine-soaked mattresses in steel cribs, babies with bedsores, and abuses best left unnamed.

Gina scratched again at her neck.

"What is that?"

"Nothing."

Nicoleta yanked her hand away. "A mosquito bite? I told you to use the ointment before going out."

"It's fine."

When her mother pulled at her dress collar to sniff her skin, Gina giggled at the touch. She pulled away, and her mother's palm came flying across her cheek.

"It's no laughing matter, Regina. We're susceptible. Do you wish to die, babbling incoherently while some blood disorder turns your brains to mush? As God's servants we must be ever vigilant, or we'll be overtaken by evil."

"It was a mistake. I'm sorry."

"Sometimes I wonder. You're my angel, yes, but a silly girl."

"You know tomorrow I'll be turning—"

"It means nothing. Who has time for such frivolity? Making yourself useful will take you much further in life. Are you listening? There. If it's a gift you're after, I've just given you one."

Gina thought of goat's milk and kisses and said nothing.

"Now tell me," Nicoleta pressed. "Did you kill the creature? That's the only way to avoid the disorder. It robs the beast of its power over you."

"The beast?"

"Stop your quivering. The mosquito, of course."

"Didn't you tell me those were only wives' tales? The talk of gypsies and—"

"Honesty, child. Shush your mouth."

Gina had witnessed this cycle before, from religious hysteria to cold logic to hysteria again. There were so many taboos in this home, things that went unsaid. Perhaps university was her mother's way of fighting off years of misplaced guilt and superstition.

"Quick now," Nicoleta said. "Get me the knife. You know which one."

"Da."

Gina moved from the kitchen to a small sweltering alcove, where tight window mesh kept out the bugs. Though most Cuvin residents went without such screens and looked upon this household with distrust, she didn't question her mother's eccentricities. She could only hope one day to acquire some of her intelligence and good looks.

Her fingers pushed beneath Nicoleta's bed mat and found the black walnut box with the bronze clasp. The hinged box gave a melodic chime, spreading into a chessboard of blonde and ebony squares. On the under-side, glistening chess pieces—*piese de sah*—waited in red-felt niches for their deployment.

The set's simple elegance sparked her creativity. Honor and warfare. The royal game. Even her name . . .

In Romanian, *Regina* meant "queen."

"Child, I told you to be quick."

Gina peeled back the felt and took hold of a concealed dagger, a crude and ancient-looking weapon. This wasn't the first time she would go under its blade to be cleansed of infection. Tonight, as on previous occasions, she would find a way to hide the scar.

"Gina."

She hurried into the kitchen.

"Whatever took you so long? Did you find it?"

"Right here." She surrendered the knife, then squatted on the floor and tilted her head. "I'm ready, Mamica. I promise not to flinch."

CHAPTER
TWO

Jerusalem

He was a Collector of Souls. An inky smear in the ether. Borne along by shadows, he and the others had waited on this field's fringes, longing to access the caverns hidden beneath the hard soil, hoping to inhabit the dead.

Millennia had passed. For centuries, this slope had been silent.

Would today be their day?

The Akeldama, as it was called in Aramaic, was no ordinary place. Here, blood had been spilled. Here, on the south edge of Mount Zion, the Man from Kerioth had taken his own life.

Judas. That was his name in the Christian Bible.

He alone, in all of history, had played host to the Master Collector, and it was this potent infusion, this bitter life force, which had seeped down into tombs full of age-old bones.

The Collector trained his attention again on the work crew now populating the Valley of Hinnom. He wondered if these humans, with their modern machines, might crack open the earth for him and provide entry to the necropolis.

As a cluster leader, he thought of summoning the others, but he'd done that too many times before. Premature hope led to stillborn desire, and it only poisoned them against him.

First, he would take a closer look. Perhaps, cause a distraction.

Mortal minds were so easily turned.

The Collector released his fragile hold on a pitted tree trunk and slipped toward the workers and their heavy machinery.

Lars Marka brought down the bulldozer's jaws and watched them chew into stubborn Jerusalemite rock. He enjoyed this job. With a foreign work permit, he was making his own money for once, saving for the next leg of his travels while trying to stay one step ahead of his father.

Today was hotter than usual. The operator's cabin had become a sauna, wringing sweat from his pores, and he was about to request a break, when echoes of the past filled his head: *You're lazy, son. What else do you want me to say? I offer you a secure job, and you refuse me.*

He decided to push through the discomfort.

To prove his father wrong.

Earlier in the year, he had fled the man's domineering presence and, in the grand tradition of his Norwegian forebears, crisscrossed Europe on his way to warmer climates. No doubt his father had already sent out a search team formed from his own security personnel. A prodigal son was an embarrassment not to be tolerated, and—

Shuddering metal shook Lars from his thoughts. The black control knob vibrated from his grip, and the bulldozer screeched forward so abruptly that chips of stone exploded against the Plexiglass, followed by billows of dust. The machine plowed ahead another meter before he could bring it to a grinding halt.

He peered through the cabin's scratched panels. Had anyone seen his mistake? He needed this job if he was going to keep hiding out in Israel.

A voice, from his right.

"What's wrong with you?" The foreman hopped onto the bulldozer and yanked open the door. "Another late night at the bar? Or were you chatting up that French clerk at the youth hostel?"

"No. No, sir. There's this one girl, back in Oslo."

"Kid, you listen to me. Women'll steal your heart and then your soul. Trouble, every last one. Now, pull your head together or I'll relieve you of your duties."

"Sorry," Lars said. "The machine just got away from me for a second."

"Let's hope you haven't destroyed anything."

Lars's gaze followed the man's outstretched finger. Where the bulldozer had bitten into the slope, the detritus of the years had fallen away to reveal a square opening hewn by human hands. Though such findings were not uncommon on the Old City's outskirts, this gave coworkers in dusty hard hats an excuse to gather and gawk, poking at the rubble with shovels.

"Leave it alone," the foreman barked at them. "Step back."

"Just an accident," Lars said.

"Stop your mumbling."

The foreman snatched the flashlight from behind the cabin seat and dropped to the ground. Lars climbed down to join the others. Together, they watched their boss stretch out in the dirt and stab a light into the unknown.

The Akeldama was open for the first time in eons.

The Collector breezed unseen past the work crew, relishing this momentous event as he slid through the opening. To think that mankind—at long last—had come up with an apparatus capable of peeling away layers of rock.

And the one at the controls had been so susceptible. Weren't they all?

Most Collectors had learned through the ages to manipulate human emotion and will. A whisper of insecurity or temptation. A tender spot in the memory. Yes, preying on weakness was as easy as sifting larvae from sacks of rice.

A shape solidified before him. He floated toward it, tried to identify it, but this was no easy task.

Minus tangible form, he had only the crudest use of the five senses. To him, the cave's coolness was imperceptible. The object-strewn floor was a monochromatic landscape at best. He could detect only the barest whiffs of jasmine and diesel fumes from outside, mixed with these stale odors of death, and the workers' voices were little more than atmospheric vibrations that buffeted his shimmery frame.

This, he admitted, was his curse.

The Separation.

As a result of the Master Collector's defiance, Collectors everywhere had been stripped of the ability to indulge their physical faculties. They'd been left to wander, subjected to this planet's wretchedness. Hollow and lifeless, yet alive, they were parasites. Always on the prowl. Seeking habitations through which they might find perverse and vicarious pleasure.

Man. Woman. Beast . . . Any host with a beating heart would do.

Or, in the case of the Akeldama, any skeleton sprinkled in blood.

The Collector brushed over the shape and recognized it now as an ossuary, a repository for the dead. Ages ago, through previous hosts, he had explored Gentile and Egyptian tombs where organs and fluids had been removed from the deceased. Here, he sensed an ambient clarity instead. The Jewish practice of leaving the blood in the corpse meant he would soon be able to smell—almost taste—the wispy afterglow of life and human recollections.

He counted three burial caves, each with adjoining chambers, and a total of forty stone boxes. Would there ever be more powerful revenants than those buried in this unholy ground? Fused with the Man from Kerioth, the Master Collector had allowed a portion of himself to stain this soil deep red; and all around, these bones were waiting to be knit back together by his dark ambition.

The hovering Collector decided it was time to summon his cluster.

A worker knelt beside the hole. "Anything in there?"

"Hard to tell." The foreman grunted and slithered further into the recess, leaving only feet visible. "Some old cooking pots and vases. I see containers that could be coffins."

"Big enough to hold an adult?"

"A child, maybe." The man scooted back and sat up. "They might be ossuaries, which would mean they're very old."

"Great." The worker rolled granite-colored eyes. "Another history lesson."

"You're a foreigner, Thiago. I don't expect you to appreciate this."

"I'm a Brazilian, sir, but a Jew. I respect my roots."

"In that case, you'll find it interesting to know that it was our ancestors' custom to dig up bodies after they'd been a year in the grave, then to rebury the remains in sealed containers. Usually an ossuary was no bigger than the dead person's longest bone . . . the femur."

Thiago muttered an off-color remark, which earned a censoring look from his boss and a round of raucous laughter from the crew.

"Lars, come here." The foreman offered the flashlight from his sitting position. "You found it, so why don't you have yourself a look?"

Accepting this token of forgiveness, Lars lowered himself to the ground. He ignored his coworkers' gibes and ducked his head into the opening. Beyond the cone of white light, he saw only blackness.

He worked himself forward and felt the entryway dip, feeding into a square chamber cut from granite. He noted arched niches built into the walls, limestone boxes, relics, and skeletal remains. On the ceiling, red-black stains gave the impression that blood had seeped down through the ages from above—a possibility, considering the generations that had built here upon previous ones.

Hairs lifted along Lars's arms. This place was creepy, murmuring to him in sybaritic tones. His thoughts jumped to the mythological sirens who'd beckoned men toward their dooms, and he felt both fear and desire tingle through his loins.

He popped back into daylight. Took a large gulp of air.

"What do you think?"

"It's amazing," he told his boss. "Mind if I go in all the way?"

"Not gonna happen, kid. First, we notify the IAA."

Based near Herod's Gate, the Israel Antiquities Authority was zealous about preserving the land's history, and Lars knew construction would be postponed until archaeologists could study and catalog the cavern's contents.

Thiago spoke up. "So, boss, does this mean our workday's over?"

"Looks that way."

The crew roared their approval.

"Go home," the foreman said to the group. "Go on, get out of here, and for your families' sakes take good, long showers. You stink, every last one of you."

"You." Thiago pulled Lars aside. "You earned us some time off. Come along, and I'll buy you all the Maccabee beer you can drink."

Lars Marka was hero for a day. If only his father could see him now.

Grinning, he said, "Sounds good."

"Of course it does, of course." His coworker gave a nod and a wink. "And while we're at it, maybe you and me, we can talk."

"About what?"

"A friend of mine, he owns a bar just a few blocks away. We'll talk there."

In the moonlight, the lead Collector watched his cluster gather round. He counted eighteen, including himself. Ephemeral wisps. Mere hints of the magnificent creatures they had once been.

"How was it opened?" one wanted to know, her words feathery reverberations in the night. "Are we certain the pact was upheld?"

"Rest assured, a human was responsible. A kid named Lars Marka."

"And his Power of Choice was never violated?"

"Free will, ever at his disposal," the leader said. "Oh, I'll take credit for distracting the young man—fatherly accusations and a measure of self-pity—but the results lie squarely on his shoulders. For us, this means the effects of the Separation end tonight."

The boisterous cheers of those present did little more than stir a breeze in the olive branches.

"Soon," he added, "we'll get to enjoy the Old City's sights and smells."

"And things we can touch," said one of the males, with a longing sigh.

"Don't forget. Pleasure and pain often come wrapped together."

"Some of us *like* pain."

"Not I," a female said. "But it's better than total deprivation."

The leader said, "More than anything, I crave a good meal. All those delicious textures. Sugar cane and plump peaches. Cardamom, dill, and ginger."

The group fell silent, their pent-up desires pawing at the air.

"So what's in there?" another ventured.

"Three family caves. You'll have a variety to choose from."

"And you're certain this will work?"

"I have no doubt."

"Has it ever been done before, this reanimation of the dead?"

"Of course," the leader said.

"By Collectors?"

"Enough with your questions. We're here, and the earth is open."

He saw no reason to elucidate what his contingent already knew about the site. This soil was a stew of malevolent possibilities. While many of their number had lost patience and moved on centuries ago to different clusters—as permitted by the Principles of Cluster Survival—these eighteen had staked claim to this spot and settled in for a long vigil, joined together by a moribund hope.

Hope for access to indestructible hosts. To immortal habitations.

Jerusalem's undead.

"What're we waiting for, then? It's time to begin."

Another cheer.

"These tombs have been anointed for our purposes. I want each of you to taste and see so that you can judge the memories in the bones, but do your best to leave things undisturbed. Are you ready to proceed?"

"We're ready," came the joint reply. "*Facilis descensus Averno.*"

Beaming, the leader translated: "The descent to hell is easy."

He released his shadowy grasp on a tree and let a gust of wind herd him through the square opening. He was in.

CHAPTER
THREE

Cuvin

Gina ran a finger over the split skin beneath her ear, felt a flare of heat where the dagger had left its mark. It wasn't so bad. She could handle the pain, and she would wear high-collared blouses until a scab formed and fell away.

Was it normal to feel so lightheaded, though?

She wanted to pull the drape across her doorway and curl up on her bed, but that would only invite her mother's curiosity. It was best to do something productive. Not only would it placate Nicoleta, it would distract Gina from the dizzying emptiness in her mind.

More than the physical discomfort of the cuts, she disliked their effect on her thinking patterns. In the past, the tip of the knife had seemed to stab at the mirror of her self-awareness, leaving only jagged bits. With each incision, with each drop bled from her, she'd felt thoughts tumble and shatter. If only she could gather and fit those shards together, she had the sense they would create a tableau of mysterious beauty.

But that was one chore her calloused hands could not accomplish.

So, had Teo really kissed her this morning? He lived with his uncle Vasile, the village prefect, and they owned no goats. Maybe she'd imagined the whole thing.

And why would she have touched lips with him in the first place?

She eased through the screen door, past snoozing Treia, and reached for the laundry on the line between the house and the wooden gate. One by one, she removed clothespins and draped dry garments over her arm.

Clip-snap. Clip-snap.

She found comfort in the routine.

Once she had cleared the first of three lines, she hooked the plastic basket with her foot and dropped the load into it. Her arm brushed against her pocket. She reached inside, found a bundle of blackberries, and touched the juice on her fingers to her tongue.

Teodor . . . cut grass . . . an early birthday gift.

The kiss, then, had been real. She smiled as she moved to the second clothesline.

Clip-snap.

The visitor arrived unidentified and unannounced. Was the man here as an early birthday guest? His eyes were green, sprinkled with gold, and his hair was the color of wheat. In the afternoon heat that simmered over Cuvin's fields and bumped against the Carpathian foothills, he bore not one drop of sweat.

"*Buna seara,*" Gina greeted from behind the screen door.

"Good evening," he said.

Nicoleta stepped into view. "Go to your room, Gina."

"Can't I just—"

"Go."

"Da."

Gina left her mother with the handsome man on the front step, and flopped onto her bed. She kicked at the blankets. Pulled a pillow over her head. Then sat back up and stared at the wall.

She wasn't a girl anymore. Time to grow up.

With eyelids lowered and pulse slowing, she reined in her frustration and perked up her ears. She began to pick up their conversation through the window, along with the man's conspicious gum chomping. He was young, maybe ten years Nicoleta's junior.

The words had nothing to do with Gina or her birthday. He was discussing politics, of all things, and she decided he was a provocateur. At least that was the name the communist schoolteachers would give him.

A rabble-rouser. Up to no good.

Yet the things he was saying made sense . . .

"I'm worried about the people of Romania. About you and your girl. That was your daughter, wasn't it? I'm telling you, President Ceausescu's a vampire, sucking the life from this country."

"Keep it down," Nicoleta cautioned.

"Look around you, Nikki . . . "

How did he know her mother? What gave him the right to use a nickname?

". . . I mean, orphanages are overflowing while he builds monuments to his own immortality. Tell me that's not a man possessed?"

"Shush."

"Things're about to get crazy," the Provocateur said. "You'll see."

There was unrest in this land of theirs, it was true. A few days ago, Gina had seen a slogan spray-painted on a city bus from Arad: *Jos dictatorul!* "Down with the dictator!"

Nicoleta said to him, "I dearly hope that you're wrong."

"Well, you heard about Tianamen Square, right? Students protesting and getting gunned down? The whole world's been watching, and revolution is in the air. There are forces in motion, evil forces—which you should understand better than most—and we can't just sit by. You think you're safe here in this village? Holding on to superstitions? Wrong, Nikki. Wrong. For centuries, Romania's been a battlefield, and that's not about to change. It's time to get outta here."

"Lower your voice, won't you? Gina might hear."

• "Yeah, there's the answer. Close your eyes and it'll all go away."

In her room, Gina already had her eyes closed, and she visualized the Provocateur's face to go along with his smooth tones. Her father had died when she was a baby, and she wondered if this was what a dad was supposed to sound like—confident and strong. Was this how a dad looked—wide shoulders and dreamy eyes? American movie-star looks? Her cheeks warmed at such imagery.

"I want you to leave," she heard Nicoleta tell him.

"Come with me. You and your daughter. Before things get—"

"Enough."

The Provocateur's volume dropped so that Gina questioned if she was hearing him correctly. "At least let me stay till midnight."

Midnight? Gina's heart jumped. Maybe he had come to mark her birthday after all.

"You know you shouldn't be here," Nicoleta said.

"Please don't be this way."

"It's my house. I'm asking that you leave."

"Can't I just see her for—"

"No."

"Well then, maybe she'd like these. Could you give them to her for me?"

"What is this nonsense?"

"One little present's not gonna hurt anyone."

"Hmmph."

"Take them, at least."

"Very well," Nicoleta conceded, and for a moment Gina thought her mother's voice cracked with emotion. "Now leave."

"Nikki."

"Go."

Don't listen to her, Gina thought. *She's scared to trust anyone, that's all.*

But the Provocateur complied by vanishing down their rutted street.

Jerusalem

"Come on. Don't tell me you're losing your nerve."

"I'm not sure it's a good idea," Lars Marka said.

"You told me you'd go in there, don't you remember? Or maybe"—Thiago rapped large knuckles against Lars's head—"maybe the beer's wiped your memory clean."

The hard *thummp* caused Lars to sway. The return trek from the local bar to the Valley of Hinnom had required his full attention, one foot in front of the other, arms swinging to keep him vertical.

Ahead, a pile of rubble marked the grave site. The moon hovered low and blotchy now, a translucent amber sac ready to burst with some vile creature's offspring. The notion was ludicrous, of course, like a tale Lars might've concocted to scare his childhood schoolmates, yet he couldn't deny the mood of this place.

Jerusalem. The Holy City—for Muslims, Christians, and Jews.

These days, exiles came from around the globe to reclaim Israel as their home, and how many over the ages had given their lives attacking and defending her ramparts? Surely ghosts of the past inhabited every cranny and nook.

"Listen," Thiago said, "you're the one who broke into the tombs. You, Lars. Even had yourself a peek already. Don't you think you deserve a souvenir?"

"Well, maybe. Just a little something."

"That's right, that's right. And I know you'll share a trinket or two with your drinking buddy, won't you? The way we talked about."

Thiago had kept the drinks sliding to Lars along the polished counter.

The Norwegian tried to remember how many he'd downed. Three? Four? He'd lost count, entranced by the bar's neon colors and the attention of his coworker.

"I . . ." Lars planted his feet. "The ground's spinning."

Thiago winked a gray eye. "Maccabee beer. Told you it was good stuff. They're the ones who freed the Jews from oppression and put a stop to foreign slave drivers, back in the second century. Well, look at us now. Ha-ha. After a long day's work, we've still got them looking after us."

Lars meant to join in the laughter, but the sound stuck in his throat the moment he spotted the specter in the trees. What was that he'd just seen?

He rocked back. Perhaps it was *Gronnskjegg*, a ghoul from the lore of his native land. But no, that particular beast was solid and sported a green beard.

Whatever this was, it was less tangible than even the shadows pinned to the dirt. It floated over bristly vegetation. Writhed through twisted tree limbs. He sensed that if he grasped hold of it, the shape would squeeze like sludge between his fingers, then pool at his feet and rise again with malicious intent.

Okay. Definitely one too many beers.

He took a step back as a brackish breeze wafted over him.

CHAPTER
FOUR

The lead Collector felt enlivened. Passing through a narrow breach, he willed himself into the darkness of the third family's cave. Earlier he had selected the box he wanted, a limestone fixture in the back reaches.

There, between the gaps of a pivoting stone door . . .

There, past burial troughs and skeletons and a spatulated oil lamp . . .

He entered the final chamber and found the medium-sized ossuary. It bore Greek and Hebrew inscriptions—which he discerned with great effort—and was surrounded by other boxes, some chipped, even broken, but all of them subordinate to their patriarch.

Carved into stone: *Ariston of Apamea.*

This was to be his identity. As Lord Ariston, he would guide his horde as they ranged the earth once again in physical form. Their goal: to feed, breed, persuade, and possess.

Feed upon wayward cravings.

Breed despair.

Persuade weak wills.

And possess this world, into which they'd been banished.

It was theirs anyway, was it not? Only measly humans stood between them and ultimate domination, and resistance could not be tolerated.

Like fog settling over a meadow, the Collector descended upon Ariston's remains, a time-consuming process. He was inhabiting a dead man, after all, and this presented a new challenge, drawing vitality from the defilement of old blood.

Soon his host was regaining sight. Over the course of a few minutes, the eye sockets filled with ocular fluids and he began to imagine what it would be like to see again. His muscles and cartilage were also at work, connecting joints and bones, layer by layer.

The process was laborious, even painful, yet he knew it would be rewarded. Plus, didn't pain indicate life?

Ah, the irony of mortal existence.

The Collector wished he'd had more say regarding this human's bodily condition, but other factors had weighed in the being's favor. Personality and temperament, natural talents, the general state of the soul—these were key. They would serve as a foundation, a template, without which the Collector would be nothing.

I am a merchant, he told himself. *A man of means.*

He drew up more details, siphoning memory from the very marrow in the bones. He was Syrian. Relocated from Apamea. He was shrewd in worldly matters and generous in religious dealings, when there was something to be gained—and who didn't have something to gain in such contrivances? A father who demanded obedience from his sons. A husband who expected the same from his wives, in household dealings as well as matters of intimacy.

Shelamzion, his first wife. She was at rest in this tomb.

Would she, too, be chosen? Collected? Did Lord Ariston . . . did the Collector . . . even wish for that?

The answers were here within, predilections woven into the human fabric. He was alive again. Or undead. Either way, he'd found a vessel by which to maneuver this earth.

The Collector, the cluster leader, was now Ariston of Apamea.

The gamble, as with any habitation, was that he was subject to Ariston's physical and psychological makeup. Beyond energy-sapping bursts of activity, a Collector was at the mercy of his host. If Ariston was short and fat—which he was—then the Collector within would be unable to force him into an act of Herculean strength. If Ariston was prone to parental impatience, then the Collector, too, would be a candidate for fatherly vents of rage. While some gained more control than others over their hosts, this internal struggle was a never-ending one.

Ariston let out a groan. By the sails of Sicily, he had only moments before he would outgrow these stone confines.

He coughed, causing dust to swirl into his eyes. He winced. With lips stretched as tightly as dried animal hides over his jaws, he felt grit crumble onto his teeth.

He had to get out of here. Determined to escape, he lifted his head.

Thu-whackkk.

The lid proved a formidable barrier, and the force of impact dislodged his left arm, still under construction. The limb dropped, making a soft splat that reminded him of market day and vigorous bartering for sustenance.

Speaking of which, this corporeal shell was famished.

He wiggled downward, teasing the appendage to return. *Come, my estranged arm. Your father welcomes you home.* Sinews popped and twanged. Layers of skin stretched over sharp elbows and hipbones.

Assured that things had pieced together in proper order, he made another attempt to free himself. His palms thrust upward, and he kicked out against these cramped quarters.

Brittle with age, the ossuary fragmented, and its lid tumbled to the ground.

Through Ariston, the Collector was now free to roam.

He sat up, peeking through functioning eyes for the first time in ages. He'd dwelt so long in shadow that even the nocturnal light seeping into the chamber seemed to blind him. He squinted. Picked out angles and shapes and shades of color.

He also noted that his corpulence seemed to be swelling with a mind all its own. He would soon be a round-bellied temple of flesh.

Bah. It was better than the Separation.

Or a stint in the Restless Desert, that place of unending torment and barren heat. He knew of Collectors who had been sent there never to return.

At his feet, an inscribed fragment of red stone reassured him of his new identity. He found comfort in that. He, Ariston, had arranged for his family's burial here. And he had amassed riches. Soon, he and his brood would be walking with heads held high and fingers once again studded with jewels.

He stood. Swayed as his equilibrium adjusted. Whereas his hosts of long ago had always been alive, warming him with their beating hearts, this time he was occupying the dead. It was . . . different. He felt chilled, even empty.

He needed blood.

Lars Marka took another step back from the opening in the earth. How old were these graves? Should they even be scavenging through these bones? The whole thing felt wrong, very wrong.

"Retreating already?" Thiago's eyes narrowed. "You can't do this to me now, not when we have potential riches right at our fingertips. You think I'd fit through that hole? Ha-ha. Not a chance."

"What if we get caught?"

"I'll keep an eye out," Thiago said. "Get going. I'm counting on you. In and out of there, a sixty-second man."

"I can't do it. I . . . I won't."

"Hmmm." The Brazilian coworker pressed his lips together, nodding as though he had expected this. He lowered his chin and moseyed forward. In a flash, one hand clapped around the back of Lars's neck and yanked him off balance. "You think you're a big man now, do you? Making your own decisions?"

Lars breathed in short bursts.

"You come to Israel," said Thiago, "to play in the sand. And then you have the nerve to turn your back on this country's history."

"I'm . . . trying to protect it."

"Of course, of course. Because you think you know what's best, don't you? Just like the Americans and the bloody Brits."

Lars's thin plea for mercy only fed Thiago's viciousness. Steel-hinged fingers pressed him down till both knees hit the ground. As the sound of a loosening belt buckle reached his ears, he began to shake. He had run away from home to prove himself, to become a man on his own terms, and now that was about to be taken from him.

His father had been right all along. He was nothing.

CHAPTER FIVE

Cuvin

Gina scanned the night from behind the safety of the window mesh. Heat still simmered over the fields, and from high in the sky the moon white-washed the cottage and its blue flower boxes.

She could stand it no longer. "Mamica, did you know that man?"

"What man?"

"The one who came to the door earlier."

"He was simply passing through. There's no reason to speak of him."

Gina touched her fresh wound, wondering if she should press the issue. She assumed her mother was oblivious to her eavesdropping, which meant it would be better not to ask about the gift the man had left.

What could it be?

"He had pretty eyes," Gina heard herself blurt out.

Nicoleta lifted her chin, blinked twice.

Gina knew then she had pushed too far, nudging up to another off-limits subject, thus risking an angry backlash.

"I'll go get water for dinner," she said.

Minutes later, she stood at the village well with small, roughened hands clutching the crank. Though towns such as Ghioroc, to the south, offered indoor plumbing, this age-old chore still played out here in Cuvin. She planted her feet, leaned back, and strained against the metal bucket's weight.

Hard work was always rewarded. Wasn't that what she'd been taught?

The crank tore open a blister on her thumb, and a moan escaped from her lips. She clamped her mouth shut. What would her widowed mother think if she caught her daughter making a show of such menial labor? Wasn't a woman's job to serve without complaint?

Gina rocked back to maintain the crank's circular motion. Her dress tugged against her thin rib cage.

Although she embraced this task, she wasn't deaf to rumors of other countries where water flowed from spigots all day long, where electricity was reliable and food was plentiful.

Pebbles shifted behind her. Footsteps.

Jolted from her thoughts, Gina let the crank slip and the rope unspooled in a wild rush. The bucket's *spaa-looosh* echoed up through the shaft.

"If that's you, Teo . . ."

No reply.

Well, she wasn't going to let that boy get the better of her. He'd won a kiss, but that didn't mean he could sneak up to frighten her. She grabbed the crank again. "You made me drop it. I hope you're happy. Now leave me alone while I finish my chores."

"Young lady, that's no way to address an elder."

The voice belonged to Teo's uncle and made Gina uneasy. Vasile was known for meandering between Cuvin's brick-and-mud homes with ears bent for dirty secrets and eyes angled for female flesh. Though he was a communist prefect, Nicoleta had warned Gina about this one, told her to stay clear.

She looked back over her shoulder. "Forgive me, comrade. Buna seara."

"Go on with your work, young lady. Of course, considering your age, I suppose you could use my help."

"I'm a woman."

"Yes." The word rattled in his throat like the purr of a sickly cat. "I can see that you are. I still think you might be grateful for a hand."

"No, I—"

Concealed by the night, his arms wrapped around from behind and large hands moved over hers. He smelled musty, like damp animal fur. Gina's throat tightened but she made no sound, and together they drew water from the well.

"See there? Much easier."

She lowered her head.

"What? No thanks?"

"I must go," she spit out. "My mother's waiting."

"Nicoleta? A severe woman, that one. Very proud. She'd be disappointed to think that her daughter needed my assistance. I won't tell, if you won't."

The prefect's odor clung to Gina. She felt sick to her stomach.

"*La revedere,*" she said in farewell.

She tossed her hair and turned, grabbing the bucket from the rim of the well and deliberately banging the metal load against his arm so that bone-cold water doused his sleeve.

Vasile's expression stiffened before melting into sly approval. "*Bine.* Very good. Cuvin has enough weak women as it is."

Gina marched off, letting the sounds of her dress swish away his words.

"Da," he called. "It's good to see this toughness from a little girl."

Her eyes narrowed. Next time she would let the bucket swing lower, harder. Next time Vasile would see just how tough a *little girl* could be.

Later that evening, she happened upon the Provocateur's gift.

She'd delivered the water to her mother and gone out to offer a bowl to Treia. She ran a hand over her dog's head, scratched behind his ears. Earlier, with her own money, she had picked up a tin of oil-packed mackerel at the market, and she peeled it open now so that Treia could dig in. She listened to him snuffle with excitement while eating. He needed her, and she liked that.

When he was done, Gina moved around the corner of the house and dropped the tin into the half-full garbage can.

Moonlight reflections caught her eye. Something small and metallic. And glimmers of red.

A matching set.

She reached down and pincered the objects between her fingers.

Though she'd never seen them before, she was convinced they had been left for her by the afternoon visitor, only to be tossed out by her mother.

A stranger's kind gesture? Or did the Provocateur know tomorrow was her birthday?

She looked away as she wiped the items on her sleeve. It was only right to wait. Just a few more hours. She clutched her discovery in a bronze-skinned fist and slipped back inside.

After midnight, she would take a closer look.

CHAPTER
SIX

Jerusalem

Lord Ariston's spine crackled as he rose to full height. How were the other cluster members faring?

The cavern's dim light gave no immediate clues. On the floor beside him, he noticed sections of a large, orange-painted ossuary, and he remembered selecting that pigment from a Negev artist's palette, in the days of Herod and Vespasian. The bright color belonged to the box designed for his brute of a youngest son.

Natira . . .

The boy had lived well into his thirties before falling victim to a Roman sword. He'd never married. He'd fought bravely under Josephus at the seige of Jotapata, and been lain to rest with only sentimental tokens in hand.

Where was Natira now? No sign of him.

Ariston scooped up a coin from the rubble. Its unfamiliar lettering circled the shape of a cross. Very peculiar. It was like no currency he'd seen during his days in Jerusalem. Had someone else managed to infiltrate this space?

He set aside his musings and watched as the others began climbing naked from their chosen ossuaries. Among them he noted hook-nosed Sol, his oldest son, and two of his daughters, demure Shalom and darling little Salome. Then he was joined by his first wife, wary but submissive Shelamzion.

Glorious as the sensation could be, touch was also capable of turning one's stomach, and he cringed from the brush of her arm. Oh, how he hoped his second spouse was in the adjoining chamber.

Helene. Mother of Natira.

She'd known how to stir his desires, and already he was anticipating the moment when they could indulge in pleasure once more. Or was that solely the yearning of this Collector within?

As if it made any difference. Either way, their actions would be as one.

Such activity would have to wait, of course. They had things to do.

The majority of his cluster had already repositioned the lids on their graves, per his instructions to leave things undisturbed. As for his own burial box, it was decimated. What of it? He was their leader, and he'd done as he saw fit.

"Follow me," he said. Or at least he tried.

His jaws and tongue worked at the words, but his vocal cords were in need of wetting. He sucked on the insides of his cheeks until saliva formed.

The others waited. In their collective memories, he was the figure-head and they would defer to him. With hazel eyes round and desperate for approval, Salome, his youngest daughter, picked up a jewel-encrusted armband from the floor and offered it to him. When he slipped it over his wrist as a sign of the family's allegiance, she flashed a smile that was made all the more adorable by crooked teeth.

In the silence, a whiff of blood flitted through Ariston's nostrils.

"Hmm," he grunted. "Let's go find ourselves some nourishment."

They crawled through the passageway into the next chamber, which was adorned with geometric designs and delicate pilasters carved in relief.

Helene was there. She rose, smiling and ready to go. She was from the House of Eros, the clan occupying the second cave, and his marriage to her had formed a tenuous bond between the two families. Ariston felt an urge to embrace her, to slide fingers along that stately neck, but the others were watching.

"You sleep well, my doe?" The old term of endearment was still there on his tongue.

"The sleep of the satisfied," she said.

Her voice, raw from disuse, sent a shiver of delight through him as it had in years gone by, and he made no effort to hide his reaction from Shelamzion. The first to die, Shelamzion should've expected he would move on in a second marriage.

Invigorated, he led the way through the maze of burial chambers, gathering the others around him. Eighteen total. He wished Natira were here to fill a nineteenth spot, yet that was not to be.

First, the servants joined Ariston. Then olive-skinned Eros and his household, gliding along with sensual ease. Finally, a henchman with a grizzled red beard, whose ossuary guarded the opening into the land of the living.

"Barabbas," Ariston said.

"Sir."

"I'm glad to find you again at my side."

In his first-century existence, Barabbas had been an insurrectionist, a murderer, the type who could be handy with the seedy side of a merchant's dealings. While the man known as the Nazarene had been sentenced to crucifixion, the local crowds had demanded Barabbas's release, and he had become an indispensable part of Ariston's business, even earning a spot in the family tomb.

"I smell fear," Barabbas said.

"Oh, I'm not afraid. It's just good to—"

"No." He waved a grimy hand. "I smell fear out *there*."

Ariston followed his attendant of old, squeezing through the opening and joining him on a slope. Before them, a young male was kneeling at the feet of an older specimen. The pair's tangy scent took root in Ariston's head and seemed to grow with succulent promise.

"Lord Ariston," said Barabbas, "I'm thirsty."

"I think humans have ripened. We came at a good time."

"Sir, I don't like the way that one's eyeing me."

"Then you'll have to do something about it, won't you?"

"Upon your command."

The ground quivered beneath Lars's knees, and a teeth-rattling percussion kicked in nearby.

Click-clackkk . . . Click-clackkk . . .

He sensed the approach of something otherworldly—or maybe it was his imagination still toying with him—and then, from the corner of his vision, he realized it was a person. Unclothed, bearded, and sickly white, this strange individual was moving toward him. He looked unfinished, somehow. Like cement that hadn't yet hardened.

Others issued from the cave behind the towering man, spurred along by the drumming of two children with bones in their fists.

Ariston enjoyed the clattering in his ears as his daughters, Salome and Shalom, played with charred bones lifted from the front burial chamber, cremated remnants from a civilization after their own.

"Hello," Ariston called to the humans.

They remained motionless. Around him, Collectors awaited his signal.

He told them, "We're all in need of blood, are we not? Let's say we enjoy a good *mikveh*, a ritual baptism, to cleanse us on this night of our release. Blood instead of water. Death instead of life."

They uttered their support for this violation of a sacred ritual.

Very well then.

In a gesture meant to show respect for those who might soon provide sustenance, he turned to the humans and raised a hand in greeting.

Head still down, Lars caught a glimpse of the wave. It was followed by rusty words that sounded as though they could be Hebrew.

"*Shalom,*" Lars responded. *Hello. Peace to you.*

At least these intruders had spared him from his coworker's threats.

"Shut your trap," Thiago growled at him, then aimed his impatience at the others. "What were you doing in that cave? Get out of here. Now. Well, the ladies there, they can stay. But you men, spare us the details and go put on some clothes."

The man who had waved mouthed a single word.

Time slowed.

Click-clackkk . . .

Then, as though given an order, the towering individual beside him was advancing, muscles taut as steel bands along his upper arms and hairy pectoral region. With each step his fingernails elongated, intensifying in color, curved and pale green.

"What the—"

Thiago's gruff curse was chopped short. His fingers relaxed on Lars's neck, and the belt dropped from his other hand to the ground.

An odd sense of relief tempered the Norwegian's terror. Had this group been summoned to his aid? Protectors of the weak? Now the squat man was coming his way, perhaps to drag off the bullying coworker.

Then something moist landed in the dirt by Lars's knees.

Although the single eyeball stared up at him with the undeviating attention of a Cyclops, there were no signs of life left in Thiago's granite stare.

Lars tried to yell.

A clawed hand choked off the sound, and the fingers that wrenched through his blond hair tilted his head back like the lid on a beer stein.

Needlelike sensations pricked his neck, then sank deeper, injecting pleasure and pain in a heady concoction that had him believing, if only briefly, he was back at the bar. He was in one of those strobe-light TV commercials, the life of the party, with men feeding off his jokes and women lapping up his silver-tongued flatteries. He felt wanted, appreciated.

His lips spread into an eerie grin.

CHAPTER
SEVEN

Judean Hills, Israel

The Houses of Ariston and Eros traveled through arid darkness. They had given a speedy burial to the first victim of their feeding frenzy, and they carted along the second with the intention of dumping him far away, thereby diverting attention from Jerusalem.

Barabbas shifted the bloodless body over his shoulder. "Lord Ariston, where are we taking him?"

"The place I have in mind still exists," Ariston said. "I'm quite certain."

The eighteen revenants continued through the night. By inhabiting bodies from a previous age, they again had full use of the five senses yet only limited ability to categorize their findings.

They detected peculiar hums and chimes as they skirted townships. They walked along black roads smoother than Roman thoroughfares. Occasionally, metal chariots whipped by without horse or donkey, and at the front of each vehicle, lamps shone forth brighter than any of them had ever seen.

Civilization had advanced. That was to be expected. Nevertheless, Ariston knew his cluster would have to make quick adjustments if they were to function in this strange new era.

Another vehicle roared by.

"Toyota," Eros said, fumbling with new lettering and sounds.

"What's the word you speak?"

"I saw it on a passing chariot. The owner's name, maybe?"

"No." Ariston came to a stop beside an acacia tree. "I've seen it on others as well. It could be the name of the current king. The chariots might all be part of his fleet."

Eros furrowed his brow. "King Toyota?"

"Sounds reasonable to me."

"I suppose so. It's clear we have much to assimilate."

Like the rest of his household, olive-skinned Eros carried himself in a manner that bespoke physical prowess and grace, and his words fell from his tongue with lush confidence. Ariston couldn't help but notice that the females of his own family reacted with keen interest.

Now was a good time to point out the obvious . . .

"Speaking of assimilation, we all need to acquire some clothing."

A few of the revenants groaned.

"It's the only way we'll be able to blend in."

Barabbas spoke up. "There were robes draped over a line on the out-skirts of that last city—Hebron, if my memory's correct. Would you like me to gather them up, sir?"

"Your hands are already full."

"We can do it." Salome wore a crooked grin. "Me and Shalom."

"Very well," Ariston said. "But be sure you're not spotted. And don't delay."

He clapped them on the backs of their necks and found himself awash in fatherly pride. He blanched at this show of emotion. How revolting. Who had time for such hereditary human concerns? Whenever Collectors tried to nullify the Separation's effects, this was the challenge: the struggle between them and their hosts.

"Shalom, you watch after your younger sister," Shelamzion inter-jected, as the girls wandered off into the darkness.

Even more pathetic.

Ariston tried to hide his sneer from his first wife.

When their daughters trudged back into view twenty minutes later, the moon had pulled wisps of cloud across its face as though veiling itself from the coming shame.

And shame there was.

"Look at this hideous garb." Ariston spun once, scowling at Shalom. Not only was his new robe tight across his belly, it lacked sleeves and reached no further than his knees. His beefy arms, his plump calves, were there for all to see. "Have garments digressed this much during our time away?"

"There weren't many choices, Father. We grabbed all we could before a dog's barking drove us away."

"It's not your fault."

"It's certainly, uh . . ." Barabbas coughed into his hand. "Colorful."

Ariston glowered. "It's decorated with red and yellow circles."

"Maybe it's to be worn while at the reins of one of their shiny chariots."

"Ridiculous. I'd look like a moving target for some Babylonian horde. Even worse, I could be mistaken as a Bedouin woman displaying clothes for sale."

The henchman choked. Hammered his fist into his chest.

"Are you okay?"

"Yes, sir. I'm . . . I'm fine."

"At least your tunic and leggings have a more masculine look."

"Thank you, sir."

From the side, Ariston heard Shelamzion huff as she smoothed a beige robe over wide hips and eyed the more attractive drapings of Helene's attire. The rivalry between his two wives was yet more evidence of the earthly obsessions with which they were all saddled. He'd forgotten how difficult it was to set aside such matters.

"Come around," he called to the cluster. "Come close."

Still squirming into clothing, they shuffled and hopped his way.

"If you find this annoying, or even—in my case—humiliating, remember that we're here with a shared purpose. Isn't that so?"

"Lord Ariston, please reiterate it for us," Eros said. "Let's be sure our two houses are united."

"Certainly. Have some of you forgotten the wrong we suffered? We were two thousand strong. Our cluster was dominant, enjoying the infestation of a single human host. And then—quite rudely, I might add—we were banished by the Nazarene himself. Sent forcefully away. Squealing like swine into the depths."

He had their attention now, each word a splash of paint from a haunted brush, flung across the canvas of night.

"We lost most of our companions in the aftermath. In one fell moment, we were chopped down, belittled, and discarded."

Another splash.

"Separated even further from this land of the living."

Splash.

"Yet," he said in a whisper, "we did not die."

"Really? After two thousand years of inactivity, what's the difference?"

The objection came from Sol, his firstborn. Offspring of Shelamzion. Husband of Auge. Father of little Kyria. Without blinking, Ariston allowed the tension to crackle between their eyes. Best to stare down his son's rebellion here at the onset.

"We all know," Sol continued, "what brought us to this point. The question is, what will we do now that the Akeldama's been opened?"

"We're not here to do nothing."

"Agreed."

"To do nothing is to be nothing, which we are not. We are the Akeldama Cluster. In our stillness, we watched and waited, and we now have a chance to reestablish ourselves."

"By tracking down the *Nistarim*," Megiste said. She was the former priestess for the House of Eros, a comely woman with auburn ringlets and features carved from pure alabaster.

"Yes, the Nistarim. The Concealed Ones."

Sol folded his thick arms. "Seeking and finding are two different things."

"Son, we're not the only ones who know of them. They've been spoken of in legend, and they've wandered the earth since the final days of the Nazarene. Others surely seek them even as we speak. Such obstacles will not stop us from pursuing our purpose, though."

"Which is?"

"To bring them down," Eros noted over steepled fingers. "Rabbinical wisdom says that if even one falls without being replaced, they all fall— the human race, included. The entire thing collapses like a house built on sand."

"And where do we find these Concealed Ones?"

Ariston grinned. "Sol, your curiosity pleases me."

Cuvin

Gina crept from her bed.

The midnight hour had ticked past, meaning she was now twelve years old. In a few hours Nicoleta would pat her on the head and prepare a favorite breakfast for her, but that would be the extent of the celebration. This grim approach to such high-minded affairs was meant only to prepare her daughter for womanhood. Gina understood that.

Nevertheless, it didn't keep her heart from skipping in anticipation.

She closed the bathroom door, lit the candle over the toilet. She unfolded her fingers slowly, as though removing ribbons from a box, and she imagined the Provocateur's eyes bright with encouragement. In her plam lay a gift meant for a lady: modest earrings with dangling ruby orbs.

Her heart quickened. These were for her?

But what would her mother say? Nicoleta had thrown them out, hadn't she?

Gina decided she would wait a week or so before testing them in public. For now, she would enjoy them alone and in reflection. She held them to her ears in the mirror, where they seemed to capture the flame's dance in their deep red centers. She tilted her head, flicking back long chestnut strands for a better view.

And that's when she came upon a more jarring discovery.

A mark on her forehead.

She leaned closer to the glass, traced fingertips over her it.

After scrubbing at it with her hand, then trying again with soap and water, she decided the faint symbol was part of her skin. It looked like a splash of ink, a translucent blue x with curled tips.

Was it a bruise? A stain? Did it have any significance?

Her mother's words: *Do you wish to die . . . babbling incoherently while some blood disorder turns your brains to mush?*

If Nicoleta were to spot this mark, Gina suspected the knife would come out again. Maybe if she just left the thing alone, these thin lines would fade away. It was the best she could hope for.

She tugged on a lock of hair to shield her forehead, thankful for the first time for this unruly, thick mop of hers.

Judean Hills

"We will find them," said Lord Ariston.

In the broadest sense, Collectors were body thiefs. They sought out vulnerable creatures for vicarious thrills, any who might surrender their wills. Of course, he knew that some preferred nonhuman hosts—no questions of morality or ethics, and none of the archaic burdens of guilt or restitution.

It was survival of the fittest in its most twisted form.

In Greece and the Balkans, Collectors favored the fangs and claws of lycanthropic beasts, which humans called *vyrkolakas* or *loup-garou*: werewolves. Collectors in Russia, India, and the Arabic world often disguised themselves as *eretiks*, *rakshasas*, and *ghuls*.

Some chose more innocuous forms.

Always, though, they leeched off the life force of others. Always, they started with mortal hosts.

Until tonight.

Beneath the branches of the acacia tree, Ariston concluded his address to the Akeldama Cluster. "I believe those of us here have an unprecedented opportunity. By escaping the prisons of death's darkness, we've been equipped like no others to hunt down the Nistarim."

"It won't be easy," Eros said. "They're only thirty-six in number."

"Thus the meaning of their name. They've been concealed for quite some time. Oh yes, other Collectors know about the marks borne by the Nistarim, but they're blinded to them by their own hosts' limitations. Such things are dark to mortal eyes. We, on the other hand, are the first Collectors to be looking through the eyes of the undead."

"We can see beyond."

"That's right, Megiste. Their marks will give them away."

"Upon your command, of course, Lord Ariston."

Ariston gave his firstborn a hard stare. "All in good time. We'll first need a secluded place from which to forage and gather our strength. Meanwhile, with our victims in two separate locations, the governing authorities will be kept busy trying to understand what took place."

"Hunt us all they want, they can't cause us harm."

"But they can," Ariston pointed out, "alert the Concealed Ones to our presence. For now it's better to maneuver stealthily. Sol, since you seem full of energy, I want you to shoulder the corpse the rest of the way."

"Lord, I can carry on all night," Barabbas said.

"No, I want my son to share the burden."

"Yes, sir."

"It'll be mostly downhill from here anyway. Can anyone else smell the salt in the air?"

Sol let out a defiant breath, glanced around the cluster, then acquiesced. Grunting, he hefted the body over his back and set off over hard-packed sand.

CHAPTER
EIGHT

The Dead Sea, Israel

Benyamin Amit found and radioed in the dead body on the beach.

Male. Eighteen years old. Norwegian, judging by the passport fished from the deceased's belt pouch. Tattered clothes. Features shriveled beyond recognition. Skin covered with sores that'd festered and turned yellow-green.

What'd happened to the poor devil?

With orders to wait here for an American, Benyamin returned to pacing the gritty sand in shorts and a tan tank top. The temperature hovered at 104 degrees. With an M-1 carbine slung from his shoulder, he was on patrol for the *Mash'az*, a volunteer division of the Israeli Police, formed in 1974 in response to escalating Palestinian unrest.

Where was this Cal Nichols? Why were the Americans involved?

The patrolman waved off a young Russian-speaking couple. "Not today," he said. "You'll have to go further up the beach."

"Is something wrong?"

"Official police business. Move along."

Benyamin's fingers curled around the rifle stock. He felt irritable from lack of sleep. He lived in a city twenty minutes west of here, but he and his son Dov had camped last night in a *wadi*, a dry streambed, that sliced from the Negev toward the Dead Sea. Twice they'd been awakened by unearthly sounds. He'd told Dov it was the bleating of Bedouin goats, though he really wasn't so sure.

One thing he *was* sure of: he'd been bitten.

By a desert ant? A spider?

He stopped to scratch at the shekel-sized wound on his heel, then looked up as a tour bus braked at the nearest hotel and emptied its passengers onto the pavement. Vacationers had been surging to this Ein Bokek resort area, and international investors were taking notice.

But still no sign of the American.

"I won't wait here all day," Benyamin complained aloud.

He took another look at the corpse. Had the boy been shot? Stabbed?

Until this morning, weekly patrol shifts had never diminished Benyamin's appreciation of the Dead Sea. More than thirteen hundred feet below sea level, it was the lowest spot on earth, part of the Rift Valley. Fed with therapeutic minerals from the Jordan River, the dense aquamarine water glittered in the sun.

The sea's high saline content made it virtually impossible to drown here, and swimmers often bobbed along while reading paperback novels or newspapers. The few who did perish were victims of panic.

This region did, however, have its history of woes.

According to the Torah, Lot's wife had been turned to a pillar of salt just south of here, and the city of Sodom had been destroyed by brimstone and sulfur. Those same fumes continued to linger, and salt deposits crystallized along the shores, delivered by the lapping waves as though reminders of God's wrath upon those who looked back.

Old stories. Nothing more.

Benyamin Amit considered himself a modern man, a secular Jew. His grandfather had perished in the *Shoah*—the Holocaust—and he questioned the existence of a God who would allow such atrocities.

He rubbed at the itchy spot near his foot. Flipped open the dead man's water-bloated passport again. The name was indecipherable.

Just one more example of the Almighty's seeming apathy.

"Mr. Amit?" An American voice at his back. "Sorry I'm so late, man. I got held up at a West Bank checkpoint. Whew, it's a scorcher. Or is this just normal weather to you?"

The patrolman turned. "Nothing is normal, Mr. Nichols. Not today."

Cal Nichols was a billboard on two legs. Wearing Nike running shorts, athletic shoes, and a black T-shirt that said *Just Do It*, he bore a JanSport daypack on his back. His shoulders tapered to narrow hips. With lean ropes of muscle stretched across his quadriceps, he looked no older than one of the Israeli Army's mandatory enlistees. A European might've called his nose Romanesque, yet it seemed proportional beneath a tan forehead topped with wheat-colored hair.

"Mr. Nichols," Benyamin said. "Black absorbs the heat."

"What? Oh, the shirt. Yeah, didn't think about that."

"You need to, with your fair skin."

The American pinched his nostrils and eyed the deceased.

"Even with salt water to cleanse and cauterize the wounds, a corpse still stinks," Benyamin said. "Some days the sea's odor isn't much better, but one gets used to it."

"Sulfur and death."

"I hardly notice anymore."

"And that's a good thing?"

The accusatory tone annoyed Benyamin. "Please, explain to me your jurisdiction here. My superiors insisted that I not only wait for you, but that I also give you every liberty necessary to carry out your duties. Can you tell me why they would do such a thing, Mr. Nichols?"

"Call me Nickel, just plain ol' Nickel."

"Like the metal."

"Sure. That's one theory."

"Nickel, I find you exasperating. Are you capable of a direct answer?"

"I'm working for a very rich individual. He sent me. Does that help?"

"Hardly," Benyamin said.

The American stepped past and lowered a bare knee to the earth. He tapped fingers against his cheek, while green eyes flecked with gold roved the leathery corpse. The tapping came to a stop. Unblinking, he stared at the wounds that circled the Norwegian's throat—a necklace of round, puckered sores.

"Been a long time," he muttered.

"Yes, I would guess two or three days."

"A long, long time," he repeated, as though referring to something else entirely. He wiped his forehead with the sleeve of his Nike shirt. "Poor kid. Looks like a stinkin' Capri Sun—you know, right after all the juice has been sucked out."

Benyamin frowned. "Capri Sun?"

"Somebody shoulda called sooner. Why the wait?"

"I radioed it in this morning, the very moment that I—"

"Not you, Mr. Amit. I'm talking about the kid's father. No, you've been a big help, keeping your eyes peeled for trouble. Thanks for doing your job."

The Israeli shifted the M-I on his shoulder. "It's my . . . Well, it's my job."

"Exactly. And mine's security. An intel broker, you could say."

To Benyamin, it seemed a vague title for this puzzling individual. "And what exactly do you do, Nickel?"

"Oh, you know, nothing too glamorous. I get the call, and off I go. Gathering and processing data for different clients. Getting more, uh . . . more personally involved when the situation calls for it. Been to spots all over the globe, on all sorts of assignments. Work alone, mostly." Nickel eased his pack onto the ground, pulled out a Polaroid camera and clothespins. "Still kills me every time I lose one, especially a kid like this. Man, not even nineteen."

"You don't look much older."

"Good genes." A quick snapshot. "Often works to my advantage."

"Have you told me yet who you're working for?"

"Right now, I'm on payroll at Marka Shipping. Omulf Marka's the owner."

"Based in Oslo, if I'm not mistaken."

"You know your stuff." Nickel circled the corpse, clicked another photo. "And take a wild guess who we've got here. Lars Marka, his son."

"Have there been any ransom notes or calls?"

"Not jack-diddly. From the moment that Omulf—sounds like something outta *Lord of the Rings*, doesn't it?—the moment he learned his boy might be in Israel, he started pulling foreign diplomats into the loop. With his money and influence, he was able to get round-the-clock access to your commissioner's office. One more day, they told him, and they'd have Lars pinned down."

"Instead he vanished."

"Gone." The young intel broker snapped his fingers. "Lars never showed up for work, and neither did one of his coworkers, some guy who'd been in and out of local medical clinics. Name of Thiago. Whaddya think of that? Sounds like a hobbit."

"It's Spanish, I believe. Maybe Portuguese."

"He was Brazilian, yes," Nickel said. "According to the police report. But his name hasn't shown up on any of the flight manifests out of Tel Aviv, so I think he's still in the country."

"He could be an Israeli citizen, one of the Jews who've made *aliyah* —a return here to his homeland. Every day our nation grows stronger in this way."

"Yeah. Part of some prophecy, right?"

Benyamin shrugged with disinterest. He considered the quagmire of Zionist thinking a distraction from his country's more pragmatic concerns.

"Anyway," Nickel said, "their boss reported all this to the Jerusalem police, said he figured Lars had gone missing due to his embarrassment over some snafu."

"Snafu?"

"Bless you."

"Please," Benyamin said. "I'm not familiar with the American way of speaking."

"Snafu . . . a mistake, a screwup. Like when you've royally blown it."

"Royally?"

"History's biggest blunders, done in the names of gods and kings."

"On that, we agree. So what was this particular . . . snafu?"

"That's what I gotta find out." Nickel took two more pictures and handed over the set. "You mind clipping these to the pack's flap? On the shaded side. Yeah, just use those little plastic thingies."

"It's like hanging out a dead man's dirty laundry," Benyamin said drily.

"Hey. That was funny. It's not easy cracking jokes in a second language."

"I must say, Nickel, for this sort of occupation you seem very . . . cavalier."

"Just a big softy. Ask all my friends."

"You said you work alone."

"I did? Yeah, well—print me, cuff me, and lock me away."

Final snapshots. Another hand off.

"You know," Nickel said, "Lars ran off back in January, but I didn't personally get a call to start tracking him down until a few days back."

"Why the delay?"

"Long story short, Mr. Marka thought his own security guys would be able to locate Lars and keep the whole thing quiet. Save face for the ol' man, if you know what I'm saying? Now that's all down the tubes."

"The tubes?" Benyamin asked.

"The crapper. The WC, as the English like to call it."

"The water closet. Yes, yes, the British terms are ones I've grown up with."

"So." Nickel plucked the first developed photo from a clothespin. "We have a homicide victim on our hands. Seems strange, though. I mean, why dump this guy in the one sea where you know he'll keep floating? It's like begging for an investigation."

"Perhaps his killer was in a hurry, forced into a mistake."

"Still, wouldn't ditching the body be priority number one? Hiding it. Burying it. You know, running it through a meat grinder or something."

"Hmmph," Benyamin said. "I see why kosher is recommended."

"Another joke, Mr. Amit? Now who's being cavalier?"

"You're a bad influence, you Americans."

"Man, don't I know it. I get that a lot."

Nickel dug into his pack for graph paper, a syringe, glass vials, a scalpel, and a zippered bag. There were other items less familiar to the Mash'az patrolman, including a mallet and long, crude spikes that tumbled onto the sand.

"What're those?" Benyamin asked.

"MTPs."

"Forgive me, but perhaps in Hebrew we call them something different."

"Metal tent pegs. Come in handy, especially when you're on your own."

"Are you a camper? My son and I go sometimes."

"Uh, right. Camping." Nickel pointed at the pegs. "In a tent, of course."

The Israeli furrowed his brow, silenced by this strange reaction.

Nickel bundled the spikes, returned them to his pack, then fixed his attention on a laminated checklist. While Benyamin warded off passersby, Cal Nichols completed his tasks. At last, he eased the corpse into a body bag and paused for a moment of respect.

Sneaking glances, the patrolman felt grudging admiration. How proud he would be to see his own son proficient in such work. He flashed back to last night's camping beneath the stars—and to the obnoxious bite on his heel.

Benyamin reached down and touched the spot.

That was odd.

Instead of easing away, the poison seemed to have knotted around his tendon and flared into something malignant.

CHAPTER NINE

Cuvin

Gina pressed her face against the window's mesh. Low clouds had dumped rain earlier in the evening, and sunflowers stood with drooped heads in the fields. She'd left a jar of homemade jam on a neighbor's front step. Had the elderly man discovered it before the blue satin bow got drenched?

"Gina." A voice barked from the front gate. "Call off your dog."

She swiveled on her toes. *Vasile again? Why not his nephew Teo instead?*

At the screen door, she found her pet keeping the prefect at bay in an aggressive, three-legged crouch. Even with Treia's protection, she hoped her mother's bus from Arad was not delayed.

"Comrade, I think he likes you," she said to Vasile.

"He's growling at me."

"Maybe he smells another animal on your clothes."

"Make him leave." Vasile was on the stone walkway, his right hand latched onto the clothesline stretched between the house and an elm sapling. His grip made the towels and embroidered tablecloth quiver. "If he bites me, I swear that your mother'll pay a hefty fine."

Gina cracked open the door, snapped her fingers. "Treia, over here."

The dog ended his watch and loped back to his owner. Around his left eye, a sliver of white fur looked almost like a wink: *Don't worry. I'll ward off this evil man.*

"Keep a tighter rein on that creature," Vasile said. "We must take pride in our village. No more of these wild beasts roaming the alleys and relieving themselves wherever they wish."

"But, comrade, he was in our yard."

"Even so, he's a danger. He should be kept indoors."

"He's never hurt anyone."

"What about that bandage on your neck? I suspect the mutt bit you."

Gina cupped her hand to the wound, shook her head. She would never divulge to him the humiliation of the antique blade as it cut away the infection. So she was vulnerable. Weak. None of that was for him to know.

"You are impossible," he said. "Let me talk with your mother."

"She's been at university. She'll be coming around the corner any minute."

"Education is a waste of a woman's time, a modern conceit. And what sort of mother leaves her daughter alone with all the chores?"

"I'm capable."

"Of course you are, Gina." He flicked a glance in both directions. "But perhaps there's something you need done in there that requires a man's strength."

"My mother says I should shoulder my own load."

"You know, even adults need a bit of help now and then." Vasile's low chuckle matched the spookiness of his hooded eyebrows. "Tell me, are your mother's sights set on that fellow she's been seeing? He was here just a few days ago, was he not?"

"She's not seeing anyone." Gina eased back from the screen door.

"You wouldn't forget him. Young, fit, with wheat-colored hair and bright eyes."

The Provocateur's handsome face played through her mind.

"Don't you ever wish that you had a father around? A man to look after you? Let me come in. I'll bring in an armload of firewood."

"No, thanks, comrade."

Vasile moved up the path, but Treia poked back outside and bared his teeth. This time, in a sudden rage, the man returned the snarl, then snapped his gaze to Gina. A hard, yellow fire blazed in his irises, fed by oil-black pupils.

"Call off your dog."

"No."

"He may be a cripple, but I'll hurt him if I must."

Gina's heart thumped at her ribs, and her cheeks burned. Even stronger than her fear was her instinct to look after the defenseless and the outcasts. She said, "You should never underestimate a survivor. My mother taught me that."

"How pertinent. Since you're also a survivor."

"You should go. She's on her way."

"She's told you tales of the Nistarim, has she not? Do you know where they hide, these thirty-six? You know, I've . . . Well, let's say I've overheard talk from this very home." The flames in Vasile's stare flared through his voice. "Look in a mirror, young lady, and tell me what you see. Do you see the proof of your role in this grand scheme?"

"Go away."

"Do you?"

She spun inside, slamming the door with her elbow.

What did this repulsive man know? What had he seen? Yes, she'd heard talk of the Nistarim from her mother. What family of Jewish heritage hadn't? Who didn't wonder if, in fact, there was one of the thirty-six, a *lamedvovnik*, within their own family line?

But certainly this had nothing to do with the faint mark on her brow.

Unbidden, her fingers reached to trace the lines on her skin, the ones she'd tried so hard to conceal since their appearance a few weeks ago.

Arad, Israel

With only one leg under his bed sheet that evening, Benyamin listened to the wind come howling through the Negev Desert. It scraped cypress branches against the house and rattled window slats. Despite the oscillating fan on the dresser, the oppressive heat still leaned into his chest.

"You awake?" His wife touched his calf muscle with her foot.

His back was to her. His heel still bothered him, and he pulled away.

"I hear something," she said.

"Nothing but the wind, Dalia. Go back to sleep."

At times, Benyamin thought of moving away from this weather. Perhaps somewhere north, someplace cooled by the breeze of a river and stands of deciduous trees.

"There it is again," Dalia said. "It's outside our window."

"Don't be silly. Your mind is playing tricks."

Then he heard something else. It was the drone of a mosquito, and it unnerved him. Caused his ankle to throb. He thrust aside the sheet and padded to the bathroom, where he locked the door and leaned against the sink.

His mind traced outlines of the vodka hidden in the cabinet.

A few sips, maybe.

Just enough to blur the images from Ein Bokek.

A sudden gust toppled a shampoo bottle from the window ledge. It struck the tiled floor, rolled in a half circle till it pointed at him, and he kicked it away.

"Benyamin?"

"I'll be out when I'm done," he said.

Dalia Amit was a decent woman, if a bit tiresome. A clerk for the Israeli post office, she walked each day to her job in the city center. She came home, cooked, and cleaned. Brought in the laundry. She went to the synagogue on Shabbat, her head covered, silent and somber. She was a woman of routine.

With eleven years of marriage behind them, Benyamin saw only a plodding, predictable future. Today's events, however, had knocked him off that path, and he welcomed the disruption. He liked the fear that'd rushed through him when he came upon the body. He liked the disgust, the dread.

His own needs also filled him with disgust. And he liked that too.

One swig was all he wanted. The wife couldn't disapprove of what she didn't know. Plus, it might relieve the itching of his ankle bite.

What was this venom anyway? The wound had been burning with ever-increasing heat since its infliction, and he wasn't his usual self.

He reached beneath the sink, found the liquor tucked behind the cleaning supplies, and glugged down what he could—washing away the itch, for now.

"I hear it again," Dalia called from the bedroom. "Someone's out there."

Would she give him no rest?

"Oh, very well." He shoved the vodka back into its place. "I'll take a look."

He marched through the hall to the front door. Five-year-old Dov stirred in his bed, but that didn't stop Benyamin from bellowing out: "Better steer clear of the Amit household, you gutless thieves. My wife sees what you're up to."

It was all for show. He knew there was nothing out there.

Just as he figured: each and every person, all alone.

Cuvin

Only after the prefect had wandered off, after Treia had celebrated with a strut of superiority, did Gina succumb again to her curiosity. The mark hadn't faded away, as hoped. So where had it come from? It'd appeared soon after the Provocateur's first visit. Was it the reason he had expressed a desire to see her?

Certain her mother must be hiding things from her, she was determined to know more.

From the top kitchen shelf, an earthen teapot beckoned.

More than once, unaware of her daughter's spying eyes, Nicoleta had tucked treasures into this pot. It could very well provide insight.

Gina ignored the soiled dishes and climbed onto a chair. Her mother would be home any moment now, so if she was going to do this she needed to hurry. She could only imagine the fury that would be unleashed if she were caught snooping.

The very thought of the blade caused her mind to reel.

Hurry, she told herself.

With fingers stretched to their limits, she nabbed the narrow spout and lowered the object into her arms. She felt something shift within, but the weight was insignificant and gave no clue as to the contents.

Maybe it was best to do this another time.

No. Now that she'd proceeded this far, she would take a quick peek. What harm could there be in that?

She was turning to dismount when footsteps scraped along the path outside.

Mamica?

Oh no.

In her panic, Gina's weight shifted, and the chair tilted suddenly onto two legs. Caught in space, she hovered for one agonizing second, then felt the entire thing give way. As if in slow motion, she fell.

The only real pain in the landing was the sight and sound of pottery shards bursting against the floor. Then even that was erased. Before her, freed from concealment, the pages of a small photo album opened like flower petals.

Her mother's shoes stabbed into the room. "Child, what've you done?"

Gina couldn't tear her gaze from the nearest photo. Hypnotic and vivid, Jerusalem's Dome of the Rock gleamed golden in the background. She'd studied this in school, heard her teachers rail against the dangers of Islam while praising the wisdom of socialism, but her eyes were drawn now to the photo's foreground, where a body lay stretched flat across a boulder.

Clods of dirt and clay clung to the man's crimson-stained T-shirt, as though he'd been dug from the ground. He was swarthy, solidly built. Sores dotted his arms. One eye socket was a gaping hole.

Across the image, an official-looking stamp read: *HIV-positive*.

Nicoleta stomped her heel down on the album. "Fetch the broom this instant, you hear me? Clean this up."

"Da. Right away."

"And enough with your snooping. I catch you at it again, and you'll receive a beating to be heard throughout the whole of Cuvin."

Gina set about removing the evidence of her wrongdoing—*whiskk, whiskk*—but the questions crept back in.

Who was the dead man in the picture? And how had her mother gotten hold of this photo, all the way from Israel? Had the Provocateur slipped it to her on a more recent visit? Maybe this was evidence of the evil he said was coming.

Enough of this.

She told herself she was done causing trouble, done for good. Nicoleta needed for her to carry her load instead of shirking it at every turn.

Whisk, whisk, whiskkk . . .

She applied herself with renewed fervor, sweeping back and forth—every broken shard, every speck of dirt—working off her mischief until the only goal remaining was the mind-numbing beauty of a job well done.

CHAPTER
TEN

Ruins of Kerioth-Hezron, Israel

"How do you like this place, Barabbas?"

"I feel a definite connection here, sir."

"For good reason. This was the Man from Kerioth's hometown." Ariston waved down the hillside, where moonlight pooled between crumbling walls. "It's nothing but a haunt for jackals now—a haunt for us, too, of course. Miserably desolate."

"At least we're hidden from sight. I like this place."

"Hmm. Well, you might say this region is in our blood. Further back in time, Sisera—remember that name?—he was the commander of this region's armies. Folktales spoke of him being so large that he caught fish in his beard, which caused some to speculate that he was a giant of demonic origin."

"One of the 'sons of God'? The *Nephilim*?"

"A relation of ours," Ariston confirmed. "Of course, that was before Sisera was . . . destroyed. Something as innocuous as a tent peg through the head. And attacked by a woman, of all things, while he was sleeping."

"He's not the first man to have suffered such a fate."

"Oh? And what do you know of these things? Were you married once?"

"No," Barabbas said. "I had no time for such distractions."

"Well, look at what it did for me. I had first Shelamzion, then Helene—and now the two of them are back from the dead to plague me."

Both men laughed.

Ariston turned his thoughts to the other Collectors. How were they faring, led by Eros on this evening's foray into nearby Arad?

A few nights prior, Ariston had spearheaded their hunt just east of here. They'd feasted on goats in a wadi. Caused lots of bleating. Ariston and Sol had even tapped the heel of a human, an adult male, sleeping in a body-length bag of some sort beside his young son. Disguised, Ariston had gone back for seconds the following evening, finding the man at his house.

"Lord, do you think it's safe here at these ruins?" Barabbas said.

"I've been wondering the same thing."

As if to underline the risks of staying in this vicinity, a shriek sliced through the evening air. Ariston glanced into the valley and realized his first wife was the source of the distraction.

"Hail Hades." He sighed. "We're trying to remain covert here."

Shelamzion's actions were hardly surprising, considering her habitual whininess. Accompanied by Collectors and a bearded man in black robes—who was this stranger?—she rounded Kerioth's old winepress and stumbled beneath the weight of something in her arms.

Or some*one*.

Ariston's ribs tightened. He took a step forward. His wife's cloth-wrapped load was small, no larger than—

"It can't be," he breathed.

She shrieked again, and this time the sound snaked up the incline and around his chest. The Collector within told him to remain detached. His legs, however, were driven by old emotions that burbled up from his host's marrow, and he found himself rushing down the hill to Shelamzion's side.

She fell, wailing, clutching her burden and rocking on her knees. He pulled back the cloth and saw the face of his youngest daughter, hazel-eyed Salome.

She was dying. A smoldering mass.

As the Collector watched, his perceptions filtering through the eyes of Ariston of Apamea, the child shriveled away, like a corn husk splitting over an open flame. Her skin blistered, blackened, and gave off sulfuric fumes that dried the lining in his nasal passages until it seemed his face would ignite.

"What is happening?" he shouted.

Eros looked nonplussed. Shelamzion's high-pitched cries verged on hysteria.

"Who is responsible?" Ariston said. "Who did this to her?"

His wife squeezed the cloth bundle, and the corpse finished its rapid decomposition. Ashes spilled onto the sand. Bits of bone. Then even those disintegrated, and Salome was no more.

Ariston snorted. Tried to shake off his surge of rage.

She was his offspring, sure, but she had been a Collector first and fore-most. That could not be forgotten. She had come here to inhabit and possess, and somehow she had erred—an understatement, to be sure—and lost her host. If she'd simply left the habitation behind, or been banished, she might've had a chance of returning even stronger than before. Instead, she'd given up the ghost and the mortal casing that went with it.

Salome was gone. Cast into the Restless Desert.

What a waste. He scuffed his foot at the dirt. One hell of a way to go.

Shelamzion was still whimpering at his side, and Ariston was suddenly out of sympathy for such theatrics. The cluster was here to subjugate their hosts, not the other way around.

He slapped his wife once, hard, and told her to keep perspective. "You're not human," he reminded her. "You never were, and Salome never was. A long time ago, maybe, but that wasn't us. We're the undead. So now she's one of the *dead* undead. What's it matter?"

His wife swiped at her tears. Melted back into the group of Collectors.

"Talk to me. Who's going to tell me how this happened?" He looked over the cluster. "I'd like to think we can learn from our mistakes. Eros? Anyone?"

The fellow in the black robes stepped forward. "I've witnessed this type of thing before."

"And who might you be?" Ariston said. "You don't seem shaken by this."

"I'm Mendel."

"Ariston."

"I'm an ultra-Orthodox Jew, though I prefer the name some have given us: the *datim*."

"Datim?"

"The 'righteous ones.'"

"And what of this garb you are wearing?" Ariston gripped the bearded man by the sleeve and drew him away along a stone wall. Curled side locks swayed beneath a black hat, while stocking feet shuffled along in black shoes. "Perhaps things have changed, but this is like nothing I ever saw worn by Pharisees or religious leaders."

Mendel became indignant. "These robes are exactly as prescribed."

By the Almighty? By the rabbis?

Ariston chose not to argue the point, although it seemed what was prescribed was as capricious as the minds of mere humans. The religious garments had been quite different during his last stroll through the streets of Jerusalem, nearly two millennia earlier.

As Ariston weighed these things, the other man's skin turned icy in his grip. Not in the way a Jerusalem winter's morning could leave patches of ice on the ground. Not even like the chill of packed snow, which Ariston had experienced once in his mortal life. No, this was a stabbing sensation that drove deep and spread outward through the limbs.

More accurately, it was a physiological reaction, two like creatures repelled or canceled out by one another. He'd seen the same principle in nature, in mathematics.

He dropped the appendage.

"What?" Mendel said. "What is it?"

Ariston hesitated to respond. He sensed the presence of another Collector, one burrowed deep beneath this fellow's artifice. Some of history's most accommodating habitations had worn the cloaks of righteousness, providing disguises worthy of any opportunistic Collector. Usually, the hosts in these scenarios were blind to their own duality.

Carefully, carefully . . .

Ariston knew that with circumspect words he might draw out the creature folded up within Mendel's framework. If, however, Mendel was alerted to something subversive, he might halt the unveiling before it was complete.

"Forgive me," Ariston said. "I'm still shaken by my daughter's death."

"She's not the first, I'm afraid. As I said, we've witnessed this before in our town of Arad."

"Are you . . . ?" Carefully. "So you are part of a larger group?"

"Yes. A number of us are clustered there."

"Clustered."

"As datim, we take no small measure of satisfaction in our growing numbers." Mendel tilted his hat, and a cold spark ignited in his dark eyes. "Of course, not many are capable of treading our path of humility and uprightness."

"Humility."

"Not all are blessed with it."

The man's shrug caused long curls to sway, and Ariston caught whiffs of something acidic. The man's facade was giving way to an inky essence within.

"Well, Mendel," he said, "you can see that I have my own cluster. As their leader, I'm still seeking a place where we can tread out our own path, a place where this sort of . . . tragedy is less likely to occur."

"I don't know that any one location is immune to hardships."

"Of course not."

"But we do seem to have our disproportionate share of them here in

Arad. We've experienced an upsurge since the arrival of these Nazarenes."
Mendel spit out the word, his saliva black and glittering in the play
between shadows and moonlight. "In fact, we've centered many of our
efforts around harassing them, hoping to drive them away."

"What does this have to do with my daughter?"

"Hear me out." Mendel bent forward at the waist, eyes widening
beneath the brim of his hat. "See, they follow the ways of the Nazarene,
trying to deceive the city's poor and the destitute, the youth too. They dis-
tribute clothing and food. They befriend the lonely. With lies, they strip
away what little dignity these people have left."

"And you spend your time harassing them for this?"

"Shut up, shut up. What business is this of yours, I ask?"

Ariston raised a hand. "Pardon my intrusion. Perhaps you should
explain these 'lies' to me. My cluster and I, we've been Separated too long
from such matters."

"Separated?"

The word was a notched key, turning the final tumbler in the lock
upon Mendel's being. His mouth gnawed at the air and his tongue pushed
at his lips. Canine teeth shoved down from his gums, sharp, and tinged
crimson along the grooves. He bobbed on stockinged legs, side locks
swinging, his eyes hooded by his hat so that only his fanged mouth caught
the nocturnal light with each backward sway.

"These Nazarene lovers," Mendel hissed. "They speak always of him
and his sacrifice. His blood. After three days, he came back from the
grave—so they say. He conquered death."

The words flooded Ariston's mind with vestigial memories: a radical
and a blasphemer named Yeshua; a trial before the Sanhedrin; a crucifixion
and a . . .

It was enough to make him sick.

"They're still talking of this man?" Ariston was incredulous. "He's
still beloved?"

"His same sad tale is still spreading."

"I'd hoped time would erase some of that . . . well, that nonsense."

"It's disgusting." Dark spittle pooled behind Mendel's lower lip and dribbled down his chin. "There are many humans who go through the of drinking his blood, sipping grape juice or wine. As a formality. A duty. Nothing more. But others—these Nazarene lovers—drink to remember and identify with him. It's different. I don't know. Regardless, that's where your child slipped up."

"She's gone now. Speak plainly."

Mendel wiped his hand along his mouth. "See, she appeared while I was outside the home of Arad's head Nazarene. We hound this man's family, hoping to frighten them away, and tonight I was slashing the rear tires on his Toyota."

"Ah. One of the king's chariots."

Mendel snickered. "This man probably thinks so."

"So what was Salome doing there?"

"You must believe that I didn't see her hiding. When the family's son stepped through the gate, I shrank back so as not to be caught at my work, and that's when your Salome charged from behind a white broom bush. She sank teeth into the boy's shoulder and started drinking before I could stop her."

"She was thirsty," Ariston said. "Foraging with the others."

"Naturally, she was drawn to the scent of his blood, but I'm telling you, Arad is a dangerous city for it. That little runt of a boy pried her loose and commanded her to leave. When she rushed him again, he simply dodged her and walked back inside. Fearless, I tell you. Like his parents, he drinks the Nazarene Blood, and now he's transformed into one of them."

"Them?"

Ariston bristled at the idea. Felt his own tapered incisors swelling from their roots. He knew, of course, the power of the Nazarene. He and his cluster had been expelled from their habitation by a mere touch, sent into a herd of pigs. He could still hear those beastly shrieks as they plunged into forlorn waters.

Now, after centuries, he was abhorred by this persistent influence of the Nazarene, as well as by his own self-delusion that had convinced him to expect anything otherwise.

"Explain yourself," he growled at the black-hatted man. "Who are they?"

"They are Those Who Resist. Their blood has a tantalizing aroma, very rich and pure. So I can't fault your daughter, see? But it goes down like a fire." Mendel wagged his finger. "A flame that courses through the veins, raging, scouring. One taste, just one mouthful, and it'll destroy you where you stand."

"As we just witnessed."

"Yes."

Still unsettled, Ariston stared off over the crumbled ruins of Kerioth-Hezron. Long ago, their mentor had brought down the Nazarene with a kiss, yet the Nazarene's reemergence from the grave had only fomented deeper admiration and interest. It appeared that his influence had done anything but fade.

"Ariston?"

"What?" he snapped at the robed man.

"I think perhaps . . ." Mendel lifted the brim of his hat. His stare collided with Ariston's and, like one icicle jabbed at another, glanced off in a shower of black splinters and chipped courage. He cleared his throat. "I have a suggestion. You said you seek a place to settle. Perhaps a city such as Arad? And why not? We all tire of roaming, don't we?"

"I'm open to suggestions."

"I only want to help, of course. And if I may be blunt, I've . . . we've already established ourselves here in this region."

"Infantile rivalries. I see they still exist."

"That's going too far, Ariston. It's only a matter—"

"Please, just speak your mind."

"Are you aware that Romania, once home to the Dacians, has a city by the same name? It's true," Mendel said. "And some whisper of its regional link to one of the Nistarim."

"Is that so?" Ariston's interest was piqued.

"There's even a low-ranking, small-town Collector who says he'll divulge all the details—for a reward, of course."

Could it be this easy?

"Hmm." Ariston kept his tone flat and his eyes level. "I'm sure there's no shortage of glory seekers who throw out such claims. Sounds like a low-ranking ploy to me. Hardly worth a grain of salt."

"I suppose. And if there were any truth to it, you'd be biting off more than you could chew. Not that I mean to jest," Mendel said with a sly gleam in his eye, "but it's dangerous business dealing with the Concealed Ones. Even the most elite would have their hands full, so I'm sure you and your cluster would want no part."

"There are less perilous pursuits, I'm sure."

"My apologies," Mendel said. "I shouldn't have mentioned it."

"Oh. I'm sure you were only trying to help."

Already, Ariston was making plans. His cluster had spent the past few days regaining vitality and spying out this new civilization.

The time to hunt was upon them.

CHAPTER
ELEVEN

Cuvin

Broom bristles cleared leaves from the stone path. Gina worked her way from the door to the front gate, hoping to finish before her mother returned from the market. Always a list of chores. Same routine, day in and day out.

Whisk, whisk . . .

Gina understood that in this world she wouldn't be given a single *leu* coin unless she did her part and did it well. She knew it in the same way she knew the ointment she slathered on her arms was scant protection from life's true hazards. Things worse than mosquitoes were out there, on the prowl.

"Hello there." Teodor approached on his bicycle.

She looked up through straggles of hair. Why couldn't she get it to comb flat, sleek and shiny, like her mother's?

Teo braked outside her gate. "You hungry?"

"Nicoleta is on her way home for dinner."

"That doesn't answer my question. Here, Gina." He leaned the bike against the lamp pole and extended a paper bag. "These are for you."

"Red grapes. Did you pick them?"

"You're even smarter than you look," he said.

"How much do they cost?"

"Don't be silly. Do you want them or not?"

"You don't have to be rude about it, Teo."

"If you don't, that's okay. I'll eat them myself."

"Take them, then," she said, "if you're so hungry."

He snatched a grape from the bag, plopped it into his mouth, and bit down. The movement of his lips reminded Gina of that first kiss. She wondered now what he would taste like—sweet juice or tart wine?—and then chided herself for this schoolgirl daydream. Love could not be decided with one kiss. That was a notion found only in songs, books, and films from Hollywood.

"Delicious," he said, catching her eye. "You should try one."

"I need to finish sweeping." *Whisk, whisk.* "See you tomorrow."

"You're all dusty."

"Because I'm working right now, you oaf."

"Look." Teo mussed his straight hair. "We match."

"Well, if that's how I look, I shouldn't even be seen outdoors. Anyway, my mother would be upset to know I was talking to a boy in public."

"What about in private?" he teased.

"*Ciao*, Teo."

He winked, unfazed by her exasperated tone, then straddled his bike and pedaled off, leaving behind the bag of grapes.

Later, she spent her evening replaying that moment. Why had she been so abrupt with him? Sure, he was Vasile's nephew, but he was his own person. And cute, at that. As she chewed on the last of the grapes, she had the disheartening premonition that she and Teo wouldn't be talking again for a very long time.

Late Summer—Constanta, Romania

The Collectors entered through an east-wing window of the Constanta Regional Orphanage. They found themselves in a narrow room with shelves full of assorted containers and supplies. To their newly revived senses, the smells were medicinal and pungent, and Ariston was reminded of a Syrian physician he had visited in the months before his own earthly death.

He opened the far door and poked his head into a corridor. Stale odors and muffled cries assured him they were in the correct building. According to Mendel, this government-run orphanage was a handy layover on the way through this communist enclave, a chance to fill depleted veins.

To Ariston, this place was much more.

These children represented an opportunity. They were throwaways, victims of Romania's latest regime. This man—Ceausescu, was it?—he was only one more in a long line of history's ruthless leaders. With such a man at the helm, who would take time to investigate the orphans' misfortune?

Across the way, Ariston saw a larger room, darkened and vacant. There he would be better able to marshal his forces.

First things first.

He poked through the supplies and found a stack of transparent bags inscribed with numbers and lines. They were similar to old wineskins or animal bladders, with puckered funnels and corks the color of pomegranate.

So much was different in this new era, and yet the basic principles of most items seemed rooted in ideas long ago comprehended. With a little dedication and time, his group was already finding some of its bearings.

"Barabbas."

"Sir?"

"Take an armload of these bags." To the others, Ariston said, "Follow me, quietly."

"We're thirsty," Sol complained.

"You'll have to wait a little longer, son."

"In a building full of sustenance, you can't expect us to hold back."

"That's exactly what I expect. A modicum of restraint."

With the henchman bringing up the rear, the Collectors glided across the hallway into the larger room. With Salome gone, the group was down to seventeen. Nearly bloodless, they were all feeling the effects of the long voyage—from Israeli Arad to Romanian Arad.

Last week, diesel trucks had carried them through Syria into Turkey. Thirty hours ago, stuffed into the hold of a Turkish fishing vessel, they'd left the beautiful port at Zonguldak and ridden Black Sea waves toward Constanta. Here, they'd been dropped south of the shipyards, where they griped and cursed as jellyfish stings chased them from surf to shore.

Hadn't Ariston warned them?

Pleasure and pain, all part of this mortal life.

Each day was another lesson in how times had changed. Cuisine lacked the wholesome flavors they remembered. Transportation, though a marvel, still brought with it physical wear and tear. Most surprisingly, twentieth-century clothing indicated an impoverished civilization, unable to afford modest bodily coverings.

Not that Ariston was complaining.

In his mind, fine women were objects deserving of display. With bare bellies, swollen cleavage, and lips sweet as honey, they also made useful hosts. A female Collector might have even more leeway than in ages past.

"Barabbas." Ariston took hold of the big man's arm. "I want you to scout out our meal. We were told there should be only one guard in the place, but make sure that you're not seen."

"I'll be careful, sir."

"No marks. No fatalities. Slow and easy, you understand? Tap the first infant, just enough to regain your own strength, then siphon small portions from the others into the bags, one by one. We'll drink what you bring back."

"Yes, sir."

"Lord Ariston, we should go as a family," Megiste said. "Fresh is *sooo* much better." She was a willowy creature, a former priestess over the households and former mistress to Eros. Auburn curls blazed on either side of her stark white countenance.

"Seventeen of us traipsing through the halls? We'd be sure to draw attention. No," he said. "We'll dine together when Barabbas returns."

"Alone, he might be caught while drinking."

She had a point. Ariston recalled that first attack outside the

Akeldama—the deafening roar in his temples, the heady rush as nutrients flooded his mouth and throat.

"Megiste, did you drink alongside Barabbas at the tombs?"

"We all did. We—"

"Did you tap the same victim?"

"I did. And while I don't mean to gripe, the man tasted sour—if not horribly diseased."

"Barabbas told me the same thing."

"One of the vilest contaminations I've ever experienced, if you must know. And until I have a more substantial feeding, until that initial partaking has been entirely absorbed, the taste still lingers on my lips." She pouted, bringing attention to the soft lines of her mouth.

Ariston was unmoved. "Good."

"Good? You know, I *sooo* wish *you* had tried a drop or two."

"Enough of this. You may go with Barabbas."

She arched an eyebrow.

"Why not share the contamination?" he said. "With the children."

Her pout spread into a grin. "My dear Ariston, you are a cunning man. I love that about you."

"Go on, then."

The hulking henchman and the willowy priestess slipped into the corridor. Together, they would send infection marching through the ranks of the young, and from here throughout the whole of Romania. Anyone with connection to these infants would suffer along with them, emotionally, if not physically.

And the orphanages would never know what had hit them.

"The Akeldama Cluster begins to make its mark."

"If we don't wither away in the time being," Sol grumbled.

Shelamzion, Ariston's first wife, shivered and clutched her blouse to her breast. Like the rest of them, she was functioning on minimal blood flow. In the starlight at the window, she sulked and sighed, as though performing for theater patrons below her class.

Ariston faced the others. "Listen, I believe we're getting closer to the

Nistarim. We have a link to them, anyhow—if that man Mendel was to be trusted. Isn't that what we're after? Their destruction? Please be patient. By sundown tomorrow we could be in a position to wreak some genuine havoc."

Sol peered down his curved nose. "What if we've been tricked?"

"Speak your concern plainly, son."

Ariston found himself accepting these familial terms, since they worked as well as any. If the Collectors were to carry on in mortal shells, it was to their advantage to appear as normal as possible, with histories and relationships intact.

"What if," Sol said, "there is no village prefect named Vasile? That silly man—Mendel, in his holier-than-thou disguise—what if he only meant to chase us away from his sandy little realm? Perhaps we were too close for comfort, feeding around Arad. It's not as though there's a long history of goodwill between the clusters."

"True. Yet I'm willing to put his claims to the test. And if Mendel lied, so be it. No matter how long it takes, whatever it requires, our aim is to bring down one of the Nistarim. Considering our previous vigil, even another decade or two would be inconsequential, don't you think?"

"Another decade, father?"

"Or two."

"What would we be doing all that time? Redesigning the abacus?"

"Don't be ridiculous. Even in this room, there are things"—Ariston gestured at the four-legged shapes with flat wooden tops—"that go beyond our understanding."

"Seems obvious to me. We're in a place of education."

"How can you be sure?"

"Look." Sol stabbed his finger at a dark gray board marked with chalk letters. "A teacher's slate. A very large one. I recognize some of the Latin words from my days among the Romans—and we are in Romania, are we not?"

"I once knew a Roman soldier or two," Erota said.

Nineteen years of age, this dark-haired nymph and her younger sister were the daughters of Eros. At one time, they'd served under Megiste as prostitutes at the Grecian temple.

Not to be distracted, Ariston sucked in his gut and responded to his son. "Believe me, we will hunt. But this modern culture is new to us, and the Concealed Ones are known to be as wise as serpents." He lifted a book from a table. "We should study. Like good hunters, we may need to learn the terrain first and then explore the best uses of camouflage."

"I disagree. We've gone unseen long enough."

"Yes, well—you always were worried about being noticed, weren't you?"

Sol glared out the window, gnawing on his cheek.

Shelamzion shot Ariston a look of chastisement, which he deflected. She had sided with her son since their days in Jerusalem, and she was still reeling from dear Salome's loss. Tonight, he figured, there was no room for such parental anxieties.

Helene was the voice of reason. "Let's keep our egos in check, shall we? It's been said that 'a house divided against itself will fall.' We are one—the Houses of Eros and Ariston. Joined together, there's no reason we can't make all other Collectors squirm at our success."

"A worthy sentiment, my doe."

Discord and division had long been the bane of Collectors everywhere, and Ariston had to wonder if the seeds of such turmoil weren't rooted in that first cataclysmic revolt by the Master Collector himself.

"While we wait," he said, "let's each of us select one of the flat scrolls here from the room, something to further our understanding of these new times we find ourselves in."

Too thirsty and weak to argue, the others complied.

Sol said, loud enough for all to hear, "Judging by these drawings, father, I don't think your yellow- and red-dotted robes were meant to be worn by a man."

For once, Ariston and his son agreed.

Thirty minutes later, Barabbas and Megiste returned with sealed bags in their arms. The cluster drank together, slurping, staining their lips dark red. Color flowed back into faces and necks, eyes brightened, and the mood lightened.

"Come," Ariston said at last. "We have only a day's journey to Arad."

The others faced him with renewed purpose and respect. It helped, of course, that he had changed from his seam-popping, polka-dotted, white robe into something more befitting a leader. He now wore blue leggings and a matching cotton jacket pilfered from the storage room. Even Eros, eternally suave, looked impressed.

"And once we make it to Arad, it's but a short jaunt to the village Mendel told us about. Cuvin, I believe he called it."

CHAPTER
TWELVE

Cuvin

The Provocateur reappeared the next morning, this time in a dented red Dacia that sputtered outside the gate. Gina recognized his gum-chewing and level voice. His tapered silhouette at the front door stamped itself into her mind even as her mother scrabbled about the kitchen and the alcove, packing items into a soft-sided suitcase.

Gina tried to catch his eye. To read his intentions.

His dispassionate gaze made her wonder if the earrings had been from him, after all. She'd started wearing them last week, with nothing but a skewed glance from Nicoleta, and she was wearing them now.

Yet he showed no reaction. Maybe because her mother was here.

"I'll be back, my angel." Nicoleta had pulled up her hair in a yellow ribbon and her lips were full and pink. "Treia will keep an eye on you."

"Can't I come along?"

"No, you stay and take care of the house."

"I won't get in the way."

"You're staying, while I go to find you a better life."

Gina glanced toward the Provocateur, eyes pleading. "What if I—"

"You're staying here, is that clear? Now take this." Nicoleta pressed their dagger into Gina's hand. "Keep this with you. If anyone tries to break in, you stab them through the heart. Am I clear?"

"Mamica, I—"

"You do it."

"Okay." She grasped the weapon's handle. It was a crude artifact, yet effective, its blade sharpened on a grindstone. "What if something happens to you?"

"Don't talk nonsense, child."

And they were gone.

Gina waited till the car puttered off, then laid the weapon against her mother's pillow and eased the wooden chess set from under the bed. She thought of putting away the knife since it had brought her nothing but grief. Instead, she found herself enraptured by the stately chess pieces.

Treia hopped up beside her, nose twitching as Gina arranged the piese de sah on the board and played against herself, shifting light pieces and dark.

"*Sah mat*," she said at last. *Checkmate.*

Who had taught her the rules? She couldn't remember.

At least when it came to chess, her mind was sharp. Despite the complex maneuvers of gallant knights, promoted pawns, and doubled rooks, the game of kings seemed as natural as stacking clean dishes or slicing potatoes for dinner.

Honor . . . duty . . . combat . . .

Those words resonated in her bones.

Storing the carved figures back in their niches, she imagined them as her comrades-in-arms, as ones she could trust at her side in battle. She would need them. She was a young woman and nothing more. A nobody. Of course, the great master Philidor had proclaimed that pawns were the very life of the game.

A queen. A pawn. What did it matter? In chess, noble titles were never as important as a role nobly filled.

Where, though, had she learned that quote from Philidor?

It was yet one more mosaic, another fragmented piece of her memory.

Steps on the walkway shook her from her reverie, their sharp staccato rhythm like the sound of gunfire bursting into her thoughts. She snapped the chess set shut and grabbed the dagger.

Vasile was making late-afternoon rounds, spying through windows as he slipped along an alleyway, when he came face-to-face with a portly fellow wearing blue workman's trousers and a jacket.

"Buna seara," the prefect said. "Can I help you?"

The man cocked his head.

"Can I help you?" Vasile repeated.

With nut-brown eyes fixed straight ahead, the man tried to say something through fleshy lips. It came out as garbled nonsense. Another man stood behind him—a younger, thinner version. Father and son, perhaps.

"I'm afraid I don't understand you, comrade. What is it you're after?"

In response, the heavier man's hand thrust forward and clasped Vasile's arm in an ice-cold grip. The numbing sensation sent a warning through his body, which he shook off as he fielded another laughable attempt at communication.

Except Vasile was not amused.

He took pride in the beauty of his mother tongue, a Romance language, and if he was going to be accosted on a street—okay, in an alleyway—in his own village, then this man should at least pronounce things properly.

Vasile tried to pull away. The cold of those fingers was penetrating his skin. It reminded him of the sort of contact he hadn't experienced since . . .

"Let my arm go," he said. "I insist. I am a communist in good standing, and you'll pay dearly if I discover you have any criminal dealings. I hold the reins around here. Don't you squabble with me."

The thinner fellow stepped up, brown eyes set close together over his nose. His speech was halting. "This man is Ariston, my father. I am Sol. I was trained in Latin, so I hope you understand what I say. We mean no harm, but my father will do what he must."

Vasile considered this. "If he'll release me, we may have something to discuss."

Words were exchanged between father and son, and the clench loosened.

"We know who you are," Sol said to Vasile. "You are a host."

"A host? But of course. As a communist, I try to share and share alike."

"I think you know my meaning. You are at work with a Collector."

Vasile's stomach twisted, an inferno roared behind his eyes, and he thought for a moment he might vomit. Though bitter loneliness had accompanied his decision to abandon his cluster, he was free from the cluster's petty concerns and bureaucracy. Unless these men, these Collectors, were here regarding his claims, he had no use for them. He'd survived in this village on his own, and he could do without interference from whip-cracking superiors.

"What is it you want from me?"

"We need answers, straight and true. We seek the Nistarim. You, we hear, have knowledge that could help."

"I might." Vasile's queasiness began to subside. He did indeed have information, and this put him in a position of power—a position he craved yet rarely experienced in this backwater town. "As you may know, they are the Concealed Ones. Very difficult to find. I don't suppose you've ever located or even seen one?"

"No," Sol said. "But we will."

Vasile had no proof that he'd seen one, either. He'd heard things from the home of Nicoleta and Regina, and through the bathroom window, he'd spied the twelve-year-old running her finger in a specific pattern along her forehead.

Even so, he did not know for certain.

"Are you two familiar with the signs to look for?" Vasile said this with the manufactured conceit of a man who had viewed such things infinite times. "It's been fabled that they bear a seal, so as to be spared when Final Vengeance comes."

Ariston, jowls wagging, muttered something to his son.

"Enough," Sol said to Vasile. "You are going to help us now."

"I'm considering it. Naturally, there are things I expect in return."

"You misunderstand. It's not a question, but an order."

"Well, well, comrade." Vasile sneered. "There's only one way you'll get the details you want, and that's to play by my rules. Don't push your luck."

"You are a poor host. My father is displeased."

"What does he know, huh? He understands not a word."

"In just one moment," Sol said, "he'll understand more than enough."

At that, Ariston's head reared back, his eyes narrowing to slits, his gums appearing from behind peeled lips. With a puff adder's swiftness, he struck.

Punctured skin. Latching fangs.

And images collected from the hot, pulsing flow of life.

Despite brief stiffening along the skin as Vasile's own Collector tried to guard the premises, Ariston had no trouble accessing a vein. It was a Principle of Cluster Survival: *For the sake of consolidated fortification, the strong Collector is encouraged—nay, commissioned—to prey upon the weaker Collector.*

He disengaged from the prefect's forearm. A greasy residue ringed his mouth. The taste was passable, yet the blood itself was thin and diluted, and he'd stopped the moment after filtering out the necessary pieces of evidence.

A girl with chestnut hair . . . a faint Hebrew mark on her forehead . . .

Where Vasile had stolen a glance through a young girl's window and conjectured on what she saw in the mirror, Ariston was able to witness the memory through undead eyes and see clearly.

The letter *Tav.*

As for the girl's awareness of the mark . . .

If she could see it, was that not proof of her own link to immortality?

Task accomplished, Ariston set his hands on Vasile's shoulders and turned him back down the alleyway. The man lurched away, unblinking. A sleepwalker. Since times unknown, Collector saliva had worked as a memory-distorting coagulant. When Vasile regained awareness, he would be groggy, somewhat euphoric, with only dreamlike recollections of those who had stolen from him.

"That was not pleasant," Ariston said to Sol.

He'd been annoyed by the prefect's flippancy and by his own struggles to communicate. Clearly, language lessons were a necessity. While hitching rides to this western edge of the country, the cluster members had familiarized themselves with maps and colorful, flat scrolls borrowed from the orphanage classroom, but there was still much that was alien to them, much that stood in their way.

"Did you get what we're after?" Sol inquired.

Ariston wiped a hand over his mouth, licked the sticky smears from his palm. "A woman and her daughter. Here in Cuvin."

"Two females? They can't be our link, then, can they?"

"I saw men also. One in particular. But he wasn't Lettered, only the girl."

"That can't be right. The Nistarim are comprised of males only."

"Where, my son, do you think all menfolk come from?" Ariston swiveled on thick legs, eyes panning, nostrils flaring. "Call the others. Their house can't be far away."

The Akeldama Cluster neared the dwelling with caution.

This was it, the location Ariston had sifted from the prefect's memories—the same red roof and whitewashed exterior, the blue shutters, the flower boxes. He detected no signs of life, no lights from the screened windows. Large-winged raptors wheeled overhead, and a clothesline shivered in a breeze that swept down from the Carpathian foothills.

Ariston motioned Eros and Megiste to lead their household around the back, and they did so with a smooth elegance that belied the purpose of their visit. With his own brood posted at the gate, Ariston moved with Barabbas up the stone path, where they found a sweet aroma wafting about them.

An indicator of the Concealed Ones' presence?

"Let's introduce ourselves," Ariston said.

His acolyte's knuckles boomed against the front door. Each knock seemed to shake another serrated section from his fingertips, till the same nails that had scooped out an eyeball at the Akeldama were tapered tools primed for disemboweling.

Only silence from within.

Another knock.

Nothing.

"Let's go take a look," Ariston said.

Barabbas barreled forward, and the door frame splintered.

CHAPTER
THIRTEEN

Gina was afraid. And angry. Here she was, in the back of a car, speeding away from her birthplace. What was she to make of this?

Only minutes ago her mother had burst into the house—*"Didn't I tell you I'd be back?"*—with urgency etched into her face. They were leaving, she'd explained. Immediately. Romania was in turmoil, a storm was approaching, and they had to flee. A new life would be theirs across the border, and beyond.

Gina suspected there was more to it than that, but what could she say?

She packed her things into a burlap sack, then tucked Treia under her arm. Her mother took away the dog and set him down on the street. He would make do, she said. He was a survivor, after all.

Though Gina trembled with indignation and grief, she knew protest was futile. Outside, Treia whined. He hobbled back for a view of Gina on the Dacia's weather-cracked backseat, and Gina pressed her nose to the glass with eyes misting over.

Her mother said, "You stay down, angel. Out of sight."

Nicoleta then slid into the front beside the Provocateur. He was stone-faced, wearing a threadbare suit jacket, with tufts of his wheat-colored hair curling from his cap. He pumped the gas pedal until the engine kicked over.

As the car accelerated, leaving Treia back on the walkway, Gina lifted her head and spotted Teo beneath the streetlamp.

He looked up. Waved.

She debated mouthing the words she'd always wanted to say to him, and yet over the years she'd learned that her desires were secondary, and so she tucked her head between her knees and closed her eyes. Even though one teardrop hit the floorboard at her feet, she never made a sound.

I'm sorry, Teo. Please . . . Save another kiss for me.

When she at last dared another peek, Gina glimpsed road signs pointing to Lipova. She was being uprooted. Torn from her home. Farmlands and plains were changing to hills and forests, and birds of prey patrolled the valley from high above.

Where was the Provocateur taking them?

Like the grinding of the vehicle's gears, Gina felt something shift inside.

Next time, she decided—if there was a next time—she would not sit silently, docilely, obediently. Regardless of the consequences, she would let her feelings show. She would not be treated forever like a young girl.

The Akeldama Collectors swarmed through the humble dwelling, through the living and kitchen areas, the alcove, the windowless bedroom. Although olfactory markers stimulated their saliva glands, the place lacked the warmth of human inhabitants. Mother and child were gone.

Ariston swore in disbelief.

Where were they? On an errand? A visit to a friend?

He perused a handful of old mail and saw the family name of *Murgoci*. He wondered how hard it might be to track down others with that name.

"We missed them, didn't we?" Megiste draped herself across the scarred wood of the kitchen table, arched her back, and moaned as though intoxicated by the scents. "I'm *sooo* disappointed, and after an entire day in the backs of trucks and old buses and that farmer's smelly wagon."

"I'm sure they're close," Barabbas said. His eyes were glued to her.

"You're wrong. I'm telling you, they've taken flight."

"How do you know?"

Megiste let her tunic slip from one shoulder, exposing the curve of her breast. With Helene at his side, Ariston tried to ignore the woman's fluid gyrations—no use in stirring jealousies. He did notice, however, a shared look of disgust, a rare moment of alliance, between his wives Helene and Shelamzion. Shelamzion cupped a hand over demure Shalom's eyes to shield her from this wanton display.

"I'm *sooo* very thirsty. Where will I drink next? Hmmm, Barabbas?"

"Megiste, enough of this," Eros said. "How can you be sure that they've fled? There are clothes still here, cushions and blankets. Even food."

"And that scent," Ariston noted. "I'm sure they were here not long ago."

"Oh, but *nooo* woman would pack up all her facial powders and perfumes unless she intended to stay away for a while. Am I wrong?" The priestess lifted herself to her knees at the table's edge, auburn curls framing high cheekbones. She traced two fingers down Barabbas's beard. "And please, *pretty* please, no comments about my own lack of ornamentation. I *will* find a way to make do again."

She was right, Ariston admitted to himself. The Murgoci mother and daughter were gone from here. He should've known it wouldn't be this easy.

The search was still on, as it had been for ages.

Collectors down through the centuries had entrenched themselves in countries and cultures. Sniffing. Stalking. Ferreting out hosts and sources for blood. Many clusters dabbled in their own delights and pastimes, caught up in the snares they meant to set for others. Others, in territorial disputes, tore at each other's throats.

But always, there were those committed to the cause.

Those Who Hunted.

Their ultimate prey: the Nistarim, the thirty-six who carried the world's sorrows upon their backs. Three dozen men commissioned to protect the faithful, to hold up the weary, the widows, and the fatherless. Yet who was the leader of this ragtag crew? The Nazarene, as some claimed?

Bah. Ariston of Apamea had been there, in Jerusalem, as a man. Encoded in his memory, before the infiltration of any Collector, he'd heard the eyewitness accounts of the Nazarene's death upon a tree—thus cursed by Mosaic Law, a victim of Roman torture. The Nazarene had died.

Ariston had also heard the rumors of an empty tomb.

In the Negev, Mendel had confirmed those rumors, and the Collector within had grudgingly accepted this reality, overriding Ariston's limited recollections with his own knowledge of the Nazarene's defiant act. Where others had given way to the grave, the Nazarene had bridged the Separation. He had risen up from his resting place.

The entire thing gave Ariston a headache.

Or was it the Collector who was now subjected to splitting pain?

Always this struggle . . . Two wills battling for dominance while relying on one another in twisted symbiosis.

At the moment, it was immaterial. The young girl was the issue. Brushed across her skin, the letter Tav had convinced Ariston she had some connection to the Nistarim.

And, by the sails of Sicily, he was not going down without a fight.

He whirled into action, delegating cleanup and guard duties to his own family and commanding the House of Eros to gather information from the locals. Barabbas was left to repair the front door.

"What about you, Ariston?" Megiste purred. "Come join the fun."

"I've got my own task. When I return, I may need your help, so see to it that things are made right."

He peered into the sky, where feathered silhouettes were blurred by the encroaching dusk. Though nonhuman hosts were at his disposal, he knew utilizing one was a tenuous affair. Not only would he be dependent on animal instincts and proclivities, he would face serious depletion upon return. Collectors who dared to partner a human host with animalistic tendencies—in the guise of a werewolf, for example—often faced the added threat of the creature's capture or death. A time-consuming setback.

One the Akeldama Cluster knew well.

Eons ago, hadn't they drowned in the sea while at the mercy of a herd of pigs? The Nazarene himself had overseen that little fiasco.

Yeshua . . . There it was again. That name.

Ariston rubbed his temples, miffed by this convergence of human memory and much broader undead experience. He thought of the Nazarene's authority, as displayed there at the Sea of Kinneret and also in his abandoned grave. Perhaps Those Who Resist hoped to gain similar benefits through the intake of his blood: power and regeneration, as well as protection against the forces that sought to destroy them.

Nazarene Blood.

Ariston thought of Salome, his daughter. She had suffered the consequences of attacking such a person—a dry husk, a withering corpse, and sent back as dust to the Restless Desert.

Bah. None of it was original, not one bit. Collectors knew all about such vicarious survival, tapping the life, the talents, and the memories. If anything, these thoughts only galvanized his zeal to destroy the Nistarim and the fools who aligned themselves with the one called the Nazarene.

Ariston pulled back his shoulders, stared into the firmament, and honed in on a raptor, a black kite with a forked, brown-tipped tail. Through visual coupling, he called the bird to himself and found it receptive, even eager. The kite circled lower on outstretched wings, its sharp whistle changing to staccato chirps.

By the time those talons reached him, the Collector had emerged as a shimmying haze. He rose. Took possession of his temporary vessel.

Looking down through avian eyes, he saw the plump human frame of Ariston, wilted and lifeless, propped against the back wall of the house. Even now, vacant from his host, he felt the tug of Ariston's hereditary memories and inclinations. The longer a Collector maintained possession of a host, the weightier such things became.

It was not uncommon for a Collector to seek relief by switching to a temporary host, sometimes even for days or weeks at a time. To do so, however, was a risk. The temporary host might dilute and confuse the Collector's mind-set. If, for example, he spent time in a stray dog, he might come back to his human host with a tendency to scratch himself in public or to lounge for hours of mindless inactivity. More troublesome, he might find that the original host had become resistant to his return.

I must do what's necessary. I have to find the girl and her mother.

The black kite lifted on powerful pinions. Effortless in flight, it rode the breezes above Cuvin's patchwork fields while the Collector began his search.

North of Cluj-Napoca, Romania

The driver downshifted. "You haven't told her yet, have you, Nikki?"

"I will," Nicoleta said. "When the time's right."

Into the night, Gina had been fighting off sleep. The rattling engine made eavesdropping difficult, but the conversation up front was becoming more agitated.

"You know that whole 'ignorance is bliss' thing?" the Provocateur said. "It's a crock. If you keep her in the dark, that's right where those things'll find her. Your superstitions won't be worth squat. They'll track her down, and I've already seen what they can do. They'll suck her dry."

"Not where we're going," Nicoleta said.

Where? Gina touched the fresh scar on her neck. *What things?*

"I don't even wanna know where," the man said. "Safer that way. I'll drop you in the forest near the Ukrainian border. My friends from Kiev will meet you on the other side, then hide you away for a couple of nights. They'll help you find menial jobs and learn the language. Soon you'll blend right in. From there, you're on your own."

"No one's going to find us."

"There is one other possibility, you know. I could go with you."

"And draw more attention our direction? No," Nicoleta said, "we already discussed this. And to be honest, I'm not sure I can trust you ever again."

His tone softened. "You're trusting me now."

"For one night, that's all."

"Which," he said, "is how all this trouble started in the first place."

"Shush, Cal. Just drive."

The Provocateur turned toward Nicoleta with a censoring expression, and in the dash's glow his green eyes reflected gold. She breathed an apology. He turned his attention back to the road as a string of lights indicated passage through a town.

Cal . . .

So that was his name.

Gina studied the man's strong profile. What did they mean, that one night had started all this trouble? Could Cal be her father? Had her mother lied about her husband's death?

Yet these suspicions didn't seem to mesh with the Provocateur's age. He was ten years older than Gina, at the most.

"Here," Nicoleta said. "It has to be done."

The man braked, turned off the headlights, whipped down an embankment.

Gina held her breath. Had they heard her thoughts?

Cal pulled beneath overlapping branches of evergreen, switched off the engine, then without a word climbed out and came around to Gina's side.

He was opening her door, allowing in a rush of alpine air. He was looming over her, exhaling the crisp scent of mint gum. He was tying one of her blouses around her forearm. Her mother was twisting around and handing him the dagger from the black walnut chess set. She was nodding, mouthing for him to proceed.

A sense of panic. "Mamica?"

"You've sinned, Gina. You kissed that boy and allowed lust into your heart."

"Teodor? But it was only—"

"Sorry. You gotta sit still." The cap shaded Cal's face.

It was pointless to argue against such fanaticism. In her mother's mind, the world was an evil place, a battle arena, and even children were vulnerable to sin's wretched blackness. Better to cut away the gangrene. To spare the soul.

The part Gina dreaded most was the disorientation that followed these episodes, the way the knife seemed to slice away memories and leave gaping wounds in her mind.

She bit her lip as the blade drew a scarlet line across her arm.

CHAPTER
FOURTEEN

Borsa, Romania

Swooping through a mountain pass, the cluster leader sighted the town of Borsa below. These concentrations of modern lights still impressed him, white diamonds and red rubies, dazzling in the darkness. He lifted a wing tip, slid down a thermal, and leveled out over frost-speckled treetops.

He screeched. He empathized with the bird's exhaustion, its hunger. Above keen eyes, its black plumage was stiff with cold.

Still operating with the residue of Ariston's intellect, the lead Collector had delivered instructions throughout the night, while relying also on the kite's instinctive behaviors. The bird resisted him once, stopping for roadside carrion—strips of flesh from a rotting fox, as well as some live grasshoppers—then mounted up again to resume pursuit of the Dacia that now threaded through the center of Borsa.

Mother and daughter were in there. And a fair-skinned man at the wheel. Their faces matched those he'd found floating through the prefect's blood.

Only the girl bore the letter, though.

Initially, from high above Cuvin, the Collector had spotted the lone vehicle fleeing southeast toward Lipova. Calling upon his memory of local maps, he'd cut over the hills, past the medieval fortress of Soimos, and intercepted the car as it threaded along the Mures River. Although he struggled to match its prolonged straightaway speeds, he was able to cut distances while it negotiated curves and steep drop-offs. It was one of only a few traveling this late, save the sporadic gypsy caravan.

His goal: determine their final destination.

Though a skilled predator, his feathered host was not equipped to take on a trio of healthy humans. The cluster leader would have to gather the other Collectors, then return for a quick strike—to rip the limbs from man, woman, and child, in an effort to learn more about the Concealed Ones.

On the far side of town, the Dacia slid away toward the east, where slopes of trees formed a corridor of darkness. Time for him to close the gap.

Instead, the black kite slowed and began a spiraling descent.

No, the Collector directed. *Don't stop. Keep following that red car.*

The weary bird continued downward toward Borsa's perches and residual heat. The Collector plied the creature's will with promises of fresh flesh ahead, but soon he'd lost sight of his prey beyond the spire of an Orthodox church.

Keep going. You need food, don't you? A little bit further.

The kite lifted its short, black beak, emitted a whistle, then caught an upward draft that was swirling through the town. For now, it would remain compliant.

The car, however, was nowhere to be seen.

The Collector's frustration came out as a shrill shriek. His eyes roved over the landscape—the ribbon of road, forested peaks, patches of snow. He beat at the wind, racing along the lonely highway for kilometer upon kilometer.

Nothing, nothing.

At last, the bird revolted and cut back in the direction of town.

Had the car outdistanced him? Where could it have gone?

Dawn's glow crept over the timberline and gave the Collector his first clue. The moment the tire tracks leaped into shadowed relief, he flattened his wings and dove. Flakes of red paint against a stump suggested that the vehicle had eluded him beneath this copse of trees. A stained, rumpled cloth fluttered from a nearby bush.

The black kite couldn't resist.

It lighted on the foliage and tore into the still-tacky material, extracting what little energy it could from blood-soaked cotton. To the Collector's surprise, myriad images and voices washed over him . . .

Mentions of Kiev.

A striking, raven-haired mother.

A young lady bleeding out her sins.

This was Gina's shirt? Why had it been left here?

There'd be time for riddle solving later. Most likely, the car had backtracked through town and angled north toward the border, meaning Ariston would have to act now or his quarry would vanish into Ukraine.

The kite, however, was uncooperative. It flapped heavy wings and found roost in a spruce tree's upper boughs.

Wait. No, you can't do this. I need to rally the others.

The bird of prey aired its feathers. Started to close its eyes.

Frantic, the cluster leader scanned gaps in the branches. He required visual coupling to switch to another host, and he saw nothing but nocturnal creatures settling and the movement of insects along the forest floor. What could he accomplish through a carpenter ant? Only something larger, quicker, could help him get to—

The curtains closed. The kite rested.

As day broke, the Collector was taken hostage by slumber.

THE SECOND DROP: REFUGEES

Thus are we ministers of God's own wish: that the world, and men for whom His Son die, will not be given over to monsters, whose very existence would defame Him.

—BRAM STOKER, *DRACULA*

They are not only dead but doubly dead, for they have been pulled out by the roots.

—JUDE 1:12

Journal Entry

June 22

Even though I'm tired, I feel sort of excited. It's like I've lived through the stories contained in that first red stain. At first it confused me. Why, for example, were there scenes from multiple sources? Is there a collective memory that connects everyone?

I finally realized that first droplet must've come from Ariston. He'd been marked in the grave by Judas's blood, and grabbed the memories of others by drinking from their veins—or, in Gina's case, by wringing blood from her tattered clothes. He's among Those Who Hunt, but is he the one looking for me? Is he the one who sent me the envelope, trying to flush me into the open? Still, I'm not sure about the purpose of the old map.

Even though I'm told I'll be in danger if I leave Lummi's shores, I am considering it. I want answers. Sure, it's beautiful here. I mean, I love to watch the storm clouds that roll in from the Pacific, and there's nothing better than gathering shells and driftwood from the beach. But I'm lonely all on my own.

After a dreary walk through today's rain, I decided to taste the second drop. Whose memories would I find?

It wasn't as revolting this time. It was almost sweet, in fact. But that didn't last for long.

CHAPTER
FIFTEEN

Early October 1996—Chattanooga, Tennessee

"Look all you want," said Gina Lazarescu, "but I'm taken."

Tall and slender, she slipped into the line at Rembrandt's Coffee House. She avoided eye contact with the alpha males at the corner table. They sat back, arms crossed over their UT–Chattanooga T-shirts, and traded remarks that were meant to attract her attention yet only underlined her negative evaluation of them.

She sighed and grabbed a menu. Despite the occasional annoyances, she liked the new look and the attention it garnered.

Seven years had gone by . . .

In late 1989, mother and daughter had escaped before Romania's bloody revolution and bunkered down in various Eastern European safe houses. With the help of one of Cal's ambassador friends, they'd arrived at Chicago O'Hare Airport early the next year, valid visas in hand, and migrated south to Chattanooga's warmer climate. They seemed to have eluded whatever forces sought their demise.

Of course, they had abandoned the last name Murgoci and now bore passports with the name of *Lazarescu*.

A new name for new beginnings.

Despite the fear of discovery—which had at last begun to ebb—they still used the nicknames Nikki and Gina. With Gina's interest in such matters, she had learned that even the Federal Witness Protection Program left most peoples' first names intact. In a country of three hundred million citizens, chances of detection were minimal.

But it wasn't until last year, until her graduation from Lookout Valley High, that Gina had cut loose of Nicoleta's hold with a symbolic makeover.

Gina's unruly chestnut mop, once her nemesis, was now trimmed to shoulder length, with one orange-tinted wave that swept across her forehead and half covered her left eye. Her thick lashes and bronze skin made makeup unnecessary. A webbed, black choker covered the scar on her neck, while black boots hid other scars and symbolized her militant approach toward any who tried to corral her.

Particularly those who used religion as their cattle prod.

She wasn't one for living in the past, and she refused to grovel in Nicoleta's mystical slop while continuing to "pay" for her own sins.

She'd been there, done that. Had the hip waders to go with it.

In a final show of emancipation, Gina had visited a tattoo parlor two weeks ago. Her lower back was still tender, and she'd been saving its unveiling for her mother's visit today. Only twenty-one minutes from now.

Ahead of her in the café line, a pair of tongue-wagging socialites carried on at full volume, staging a performance for the corner alphas.

Pink Tennis Visor: "Girl, you wanna know what I think? You need to dump him and find yourself a man who's gonna treat you right. I mean, really—he's still borrowing Mom and Dad's SUV. *Hello.*"

Blue Eyeliner: "Like, I'm so over him anyway."

"Are you gonna tell him that, or do I have to?"

"I'll do it. I'm not *completely* helpless, you know. But there's that thing Friday night, and he *is* paying my way."

"Unless someone else wants to step up."

Gina tried not to roll her eyes. Could these two be any more obvious?

She turned her gaze to the outdoor patio, where groups of students and businesspeople chatted at tables. A sedan was parallel parking on High Street. Down the hill, school buses would soon be lining up for the newly opened IMAX theater at the Tennessee Aquarium.

Years had gone by . . .

And still she could not shake free of her occasional dread.

Were there *things* still out to get her? What if they'd traced her movements across the Atlantic? She never spoke to her mother about such matters. In fact, they barely spoke at all. It all seemed so unreal here in this land of freedom.

What about Cal? Did he know where she was?

Gina touched her earrings, the ones with the red ruby orbs, and took comfort in the inane yet persistent belief that the Provocateur was keeping watch. He had made her a promise on that last night in Romania, and she clung to it. Most likely, it was nothing.

Regardless, as she shuffled forward in the coffee line, she caressed the memory with a glimmer of hope. One colorful shard from her jagged tableau.

Seven Years Earlier—Borsa

"I'll carry her," Cal was saying.

"No, I don't want her pampered. She can handle her own weight."

"Nikki, I said I'd carry her."

They were parked in a small garage, maybe a toolshed. After pulling off the road for Gina's bloodletting, they had returned to Borsa and rushed to this alley tucked behind a bakery. Gina was awake, arm still throbbing, eyes burning with tears that she refused to let flow.

"Don't worry," Nicoleta said to the Provocateur. "You did what had to be done, and I'm certain Gina won't blame you. She's quite impervious to it."

"Sure. I bet she is."

Cal came to the passenger-side door. His arms slipped beneath Gina's petite frame, cradling her.

She stiffened, bit her lip, and looked off over his shoulder as he trundled across a gravel drive and up three flights of stairs into an apartment that smelled of concrete and fresh wood shavings. He set her on a couch covered with a knitted shawl. His hand brushed her forehead, and gold-flecked eyes danced there with interest.

She felt self-conscious. She'd feared that the recent appearance of the translucent markings would elicit ridicule from the kids of Cuvin—though it hadn't happened that way—and she'd been wearing her hair long to hide it.

As he withdrew his fingers, they caught in her long locks.

"Sorry," he said.

For this brief entanglement? Or for the inflicted wound? Gina wasn't sure, so she pulled the shawl over her arm and said nothing.

"You and your mother, you've gotta lay low here a coupla days," he continued. "Then a friend of mine'll take you guys someplace safe. I'm leaving now. Guess the dragon lady doesn't want me sticking around. But you're gonna be okay, you hear me, Gina? I know you feel small, like you're no one important, but that's not true." He leaned in, his breath a gust of winter cold. "Not a word of this to your mom, you swear? Just between you and me, I promise that one day, when it's the right time, I'll track you down again."

"How?"

"You like the earrings I gave you?"

She nodded. "Thank you. I like them."

"Just keep wearing them," he said, "and I'll find you. Somehow. Someway."

She tucked her chin beneath the shawl. There was no use in letting him see her emotion. Through that one simple gift she felt connected to this man, and wondered if he bore lines on his forehead, as well. What was the meaning of the symbol? Or was it nothing more than a strange skin permeation? She was afraid to ask, fearful of going under the blade again.

"Okay," she said.

"Atta girl. Now, grab a few winks while you've got the chance."

Chattanooga

Seven years had gone by. Not a word, not one.

Gina released her vain hope, letting Cal's features fade until she saw only the brass and polish of Rembrandt's Coffee House. She was still stuck in the line behind the socialites.

Blue Eyeliner: "Oh look, it's our turn. Like I have any *clue* what I want."

Pink Tennis Visor: "Omigosh. You have *got* to try the baklava."

"Is that, like, even American?"

Gina touched her tongue to the backs of her bottom teeth, counting, as a form of stress reduction. She figured it was healthier and cheaper than the random drags she took from friends' cigarettes. For each tooth, she had to think of one person upon whom she could bestow an act of kindness. She'd developed this method during later encounters with her mother's dagger. It'd also come in handy while living with Jed, her boyfriend of the past fourteen months.

Fourteen. The number of her pearly whites, divided by two. Also, the number of minutes till her mother arrived.

Let's see. Lower left molar? One act of kindness . . .

Gina resorted to the obvious: dropping dollar bills into the tip jar before pushing outside with her triple vanilla latte.

She found her attention drawn toward a man on the other side of the street. His hair was flaxen, almost the color of wheat. He was walking away. She hurried her strides beneath her ruffled skirt.

Could it be . . . ?

From the direction of the Hunter Museum of American Art, a dingy delivery van bore down on her as she crossed the pavement. Autumn leaves swirled in its wake, deep yellow and auburn.

The driver was squinting into the sun, and by the time Gina realized he couldn't see her, it was too late. The front grille caught and catapulted her up over the hood in a plume of coffee froth, sprayed crimson, and orange-streaked hair. She came down hard, skull cracking against the pavement amid the sprawl of contorted limbs.

She was wrapped for burial in strips of white linen. Her arms were pressed against her sides, and her ribs sagged. Like a rabbit tensed and motionless in the snow, in that moment before flight, her heart paused.

Everything slowed. Her pulse. Her breathing.

Cold. Icy cold . . .

A tingling, muted and far-off. Vibrations, felt only through the soles of her feet. Then a jolt, followed by the sounds of lightning and tumbling rock. Quaking earth. And fabric rending.

A cry of final release: *It is finished.*

That dying prayer on her lips,

fading,

fading . . .

Then a touch. Blood in her mouth. Moisture on a parched tongue.

Gina swallowed out of reflex, and began shaking, convulsing. Her eyelids peeled back, and light stabbed through her pupils. She thought she saw someone there, and she reached out—but the image faded.

Warmth followed. And sizzling heat . . .

Her heart squeezed within her rib cage, pushing life back through her arteries. Though she had no recollection of how she'd arrived at this spot near the curb, she knew she didn't belong here. She pushed herself up. Felt knuckles scrape the pavement, turning black with oil and grime.

She was on her knees. She tried to stand.

Collapsed.

She wobbled back to her feet and faced an unknown figure.

The Grim Reaper? Coming to steal her away?

She pushed and clawed at him. The man cried out, begging for her attention, her forgiveness—*I swear, I didn't see you there*—and insisting that she sit and wait for the paramedics.

But she wasn't going to succumb so easily, no.

She shoved away from the delivery driver and stumbled down High Street. Habit propelled her across an overpass, up a slight hill, to an apartment building. She stood in the lobby and stared at elevator buttons. Numbers ran from 1 to 7, and her eyes narrowed upon one in particular.

Was this where she lived?

Maybe it was a clever facade, a halfway house for the dead. This could be the tour's starting point, leading from an earthly residence and working forward—or upward, downward, whatever—to a more permanent location.

Hi, my name is Gina. I'll be your guide as we descend into the bowels of the earth. If you have any questions, don't hesitate to ask.

"Where am I?"

She got no answer from her reflection in the metal doors.

Swaying on the heels of her boots, she felt her head swim. Twin jets of hot water seemed to course down her spine, massaging the lower curve of her back and easing vertebrae back into place. Her muscles turned mushy. Everything blurred.

"Regina?"

The hand on her shoulder startled her.

"Stop the tour," Gina said. "I want to get off."

Nicoleta pushed the elevator button. "You're hurt. Let's get you upstairs."

CHAPTER
SIXTEEN

Arad, Romania

The Collectors met in the calm of dusk.

Erota, true to form, had done her homework about this meeting place: the *Cetatea Aradului*, the Arad Fortress. For ages, Arad had been a passageway between east and west, and this site had been completed in 1783 with Vauban-style embattlements. Shaped like the Star of David and situated in a loop of the Mures River, the Cetatea's six points formed a prickly line of defense.

Ariston shot Erota a look. "Are we all here, ready to begin?"

"Let me double-check."

She peered over fashionable sunglasses, shifting her eyes between the Collectors and the list in hand. With her calculating mind and attention to detail, she'd been assigned this evening's secretarial duties. Attendance was mandatory at these biannual gatherings—seventeen remaining revenants, from two houses, the entire cluster.

House of Ariston:

1. *Ariston*—cluster leader, Syrian household leader, husband, father
2. *Shelamzion*—Ariston's first wife, mother of Sol, Shalom, and Salome (deceased)
3. *Sol*—Ariston and Shelamzion's adult son
4. *Shalom*—Ariston and Shelamzion's teen daughter
5. *Helene*—Ariston's second wife, mother of Natira (whereabouts unknown), sister of Dorotheus (House of Eros)
6. *Auge*—Sol's wife, Kyria's mother, daughter of Dorotheus (House of Eros)
7. *Kyria*—Sol and Auge's young daughter
8. *Nehemiah*—Ariston's brother, Shabtai's father
9. *Shabtai*—Nehemiah's teen son
10. *Matrona*—Nehemiah's young daughter
11. *Barabbas*—Ariston's attendant

House of Eros:

1. *Eros*—Grecian household leader, father of Erota and Domna
2. *Hermione*—Eros's sister
3. *Dorotheus*—mother of Eros, Hermione, and Auge (married into House of Ariston), sister of Helene (also married into House of Ariston)
4. *Megiste*—Eros's former mistress, household priestess
5. *Domna*—Eros's youngest teen daughter
6. *Erota*—Eros's oldest teen daughter

She ticked off her own name. "All accounted for."

"Come along then," Ariston said. "Beneath these bunkers are underground bulwarks, where we can speak without inviting notice. *Facilis descensus Averno.*"

As Erota echoed the cluster motto along with the others, she visualized those words snapping like storm flags against the bruised apricot sky, signaling trouble and turbulence and the tenderizing effect of gale-force winds upon the unsuspecting.

In the years since their release, this cluster had relished their activity as revenants—dead bodies reanimated and dependent upon blood for survival.

After ascending from the Field of Blood, the House of Eros had immigrated to Ukraine, and the House of Ariston had settled here in Arad.

Ariston, taking the lead, had sold his jeweled armband from the tombs as down payment on a forsaken vineyard just east of Lipova. Erota and the others had immersed themselves, too, in cultural, financial, and linguistic dealings. All had managed to procure for themselves nondescript lodgings and functional false identities.

Erota still found it remarkable what could be done with the aid of Collector-hosting humans. Though armed with the Power of Choice, some seemed willing and even eager to sell their souls for any semblance of significance. Such hosts were particularly easy to come by in bureacratic circles—busy little bees, swarming to the sticky sweetness of money and power.

All of this made it easier, of course, for the Akeldama Cluster.

They embodied those long-fabled traits of the vampire: pointed incisors and unquenchable thirst; a narcissistic disregard for other life-forms; a chill in the bones, which, if not alleviated by ingested blood, left a chalky pall on the skin . . .

Erota had discovered differences, as well.

She loved garlic, for example—was there anything more tasty than a bowl of goulash? Her mirror was a close friend that never failed to reflect her beauty in all its undead glory. Her skin, her eyes, seemed sensitive to the sun, and yet with a modicum of caution she could function day and night as she saw fit. Some in the House of Eros even wore crucifixes as daily attire. Mockery was nothing if not a manner of declawing a fearsome foe.

As for holy water?

A cool beverage on a hot day.

Stakes through the heart?

Oversized slivers to be removed with force.

Through the centuries, certain other Collectors had cloaked themselves in vampiric guises and used compliant humans to great effect. What was the infamous Elizabeth Bathory if not a bloodthirsty and sadistic countess who reveled in her role as a hostess? Collectors had even bedeviled the Scottish lowlands as *Redcaps*, roosted in Malaysian trees as *langsuyaras*, and haunted nearby Carpathian villages as *strigoi mort*.

Erota had unearthed similar lore from nearly every culture. While some of the life-leeches were urbane, others gruesome and obscene, all of them reflected the Collectors' goals: to feed, breed, persuade, and possess.

However, only these from the Akeldama were truly undead Collectors.

So what if history had its spine-chilling tales based on a few corrupted souls? All of it worked in their favor. Fear was a catapult, crashing boulders through humans' psyches, launching diseased corpses into their palace courtyards to drive out all that was noble.

People—so malleable, susceptible.

Those who lived in fear saw demons behind every bush, while those who trusted in logic alone were blinded to danger by their self-congratulatory intellects.

Easy victims, all.

Erota sensed Ariston's frustration in his hurried steps, in the way he bit into his thick bottom lip. As they moved around the Cetatea's earth-covered casements, she drew alongside and handed him the roll sheet. "Sir? Is there some other task you'd like me to oversee?"

He shook his head.

"You seem preoccupied," she said. "Perhaps a few minutes alone?"

"Hmm?"

"With me?"

"No." His nut-brown eyes darted toward his wives, then caught a gleam of the setting sun as they turned back to Erota. "But thank you. I'm . . ." He cleared his throat. "I'm still baffled by our cluster's failures in Arad and Kiev."

"Failures?"

"We're still no closer to the Nistarim. To be honest, I thought I was operating under some sort of special guidance when I first escorted my household to this city."

"Special in what way?"

"I'm not sure. The coincidental nature of it all, I suppose. From the sands of Arad in Israel, to Romania's Arad. From Jerusalem's Golgotha, to—"

"The Hungarian Golgotha."

Erota called up the fortress's alternate name from her research. Now empty, these battlements had once held troops and prisoners of war, and in 1849, thirteen Hungarian generals had been hanged for their part in a revolution.

"Exactly," Ariston said. "I took those as signs."

"From the Master himself?"

His brow furrowed.

"If it's any encouragement," she said, "we haven't given up in Kiev. Hasn't been easy, though. Many of the inhabitants still carry traces of Chernobyl's radiation in their blood—barely drinkable. And even though Eros pushes us to search the land, to rake through the streets, we keep coming up empty-handed. As though they vanished into thin air."

They: the mother and daughter from Cuvin.

"Did I misread the signs?" Ariston mused. "I ask myself that each day. Is it true that some among you are now talking of a return to Israel?"

"Well, the Nistarim's roots are in Jewish legend, after all."

"And you think some of them are hiding in the Holy Land?"

"Seems possible, sir."

"Bah. They've probably moved as far from there as they can. Why, even here in Romania we have a good number of Jews. Some meet at the synagogue only blocks away, near Avram Iancu Square."

"I've seen it. Still, the long Ukrainian winters are driving us batty, and the weather's a lot better down south."

"Bear with me awhile longer, if you will. I'm not deaf to the murmurings, and for this reason I have Megiste exploring new tapping methods for our repertoire. She plans to give a demonstration at our next meeting. An unsuspecting male. In the meantime, let the others squabble. We have work to do."

"And if one doesn't work, he doesn't eat."

"A functional phrase, to be sure. Good for heaping guilt on the lazy, and stirring arrogance in the industrious. Here," he said. "Watch your head."

Ariston and the other Collectors ducked into subterranean darkness and shuffled along stone-cold walls, stirring the susurrus of those who had given their lives for this land. With both the dead and the undead in attendance, the stage was set for a meeting of black sedition.

CHAPTER
SEVENTEEN

Chattanooga

Gina cracked her neck, used a handful of Kleenex to wipe away the sticky trickle from her ear. She felt only dull pain.

"Are you going to tell me what happened?" her mother said.

"What's there to tell, Nikki? I got hit by a delivery van, I think."

They sat on opposite sides of the frayed couch, a garage-sale bargain from the north end of town. Gina leaned forward to adjust the boot buckles that had come loose in the collision. Middle-aged Nicoleta sat primly, as though afraid of touching her back to the ratted cushions. Over the dining bar, track lighting revealed Count Chocula chunks in a half-empty bowl of milk.

Although Gina's boyfriend was down at the Chamber of Commerce, where he worked as a graphic designer, the scent of his CK One cologne permeated the apartment and provided emotional support.

This was her territory. Their territory.

"Where did this happen?" Nikki demanded. "Were you able to jot down a license plate?"

"You mean, while I was hurtling through the air? No."

Her mother's thin nostrils flared.

"I was coming out of Rembrandt's, okay? What's it matter? I'm tough. Didn't you used to tell me a story of how I walked away from some horrible bike accident?"

"That was different. Not nearly as serious as this."

"If you say so."

"Look, you're bleeding."

"That used to be *your* fault," Gina said. "But hey, I'm still here. I survived."

"Don't you think we should go down to the hospital and have you checked out? You never know with these things. Did anyone call the police?"

"Relax a little. Made it back on my own two feet, didn't I? Anyway, I can't afford to miss any work. I've got to be there in an hour."

"Work is important." Nikki leaned forward. "Please, though—allow me to at least bandage that ear for you. We should cleanse it to avoid infection."

"I've already had enough mothering for one day. Jed can look at it later."

Despite her mother's disapproval, Gina had moved in with Jed Turney after graduation. She'd never clicked with kids at school, always the outsider, the girl stuck between two cultures. Always stuck in Nikki's shadow.

Which was where Jed came in. A decent guy, a middle child, a creative sort, he understood her in ways few others did. He drew pictures for her. He saw life as a complex and beautiful thing, an enigma that spanned borders and nationalities. He complained every now and then that Gina stepped on his feelings, and she always told him to grow up and get a thicker skin.

They were good for each other.

Even with Jed's position and Gina's job as a tour guide at Ruby Falls, they barely scraped by. Rent and water bills were killing them. Satellite TV: canceled. Constant late payments on car insurance. Canned food and frozen vegetables.

They were making ends meet, though—on their own.

Nikki gestured at the bar. "Doesn't he clean up after himself?"

"The bowl? That's mine."

A flat-out lie. Gina harped regularly about tidiness, and this morning she'd even reminded Jed to clean up since her mother would be visiting.

"Why, child? Why do you do that? I fail to see the point."

"Because I like my cereal soggy."

"No," said Nikki. "Why do you cover for him? I warned you—quite emphatically, if I recall—not to tread this path of promiscuity. And yet here you sit, reaping what you've sown, surviving on generic foods and rice."

"Sowing rice. Not so bad, in the global scheme of things."

"Where do you get this contempt for the upbringing I gave you?"

"You're the one who moved us here, to the land of the free, home of the brave. What'd you expect? Gotta live with the consequences."

"Don't you see, Gina, how you're letting the gangrene eat at your soul?"

"Oops. Guess you missed a few spots, huh?"

"How is it that I'm incapable of reasoning with my own daughter? It's a mystery to me, a bona fide mystery." Her pink lips expelled a sigh. "And all the while, countless others come to me for enlightenment."

Nikki had flourished since their arrival in the U.S. of Make-a-Buck A. While serving as a housecleaner for the city's upper class, she had acquired a wealthy patron, a woman smitten with her stories of survival under communist hardship. Soon, she was on the speaking circuit, first giving inspirational lectures, then headlining seminars that sometimes netted her five figures in one weekend.

Releasing. Cleansing. Renewal . . . A Session with N. K. Lazarescu.

She used only the initials, to further avoid detection, and always addressed audiences with her raven hair pulled back in a purple-and-gold-threaded gypsy scarf. Not only did it disguise her appearance, it added to the impression of supernatural insight. They responded to her soft accent, the enviable beauty of this woman in her late forties, and her invigorating blend of spirituality and self-reliance.

How, Gina now wondered, was she supposed to combat her mother's success? She swiveled on the couch, looked back over her shoulder, and said, "Have I shown you my tattoo?"

"Your what?"

"My tat."

"You mean to tell me you've defiled your own body?"

"Just doing what you taught me, bleeding away the sin." The pattern tingled as Gina lifted her shirt. "You like it, Nikki?"

"I think it's bound to draw more trouble your direction."

"C'mon. You've used those fear tactics long enough." Gina hitched one leg under herself on the couch, then dabbed the tissue again at her ear. "I'm over it. I won't keep hiding from something that doesn't exist."

"But they're still out there, I'm afraid."

"They. Who the hell are the mysterious *they*?"

"Watch your tongue, young lady."

Gina bounded to her feet and moved into the kitchen.

Since the move to the States, she'd attended public schools and, to her mother's chagrin, learned to speak like an American, even think like one.

Of course, Chattanooga was worlds removed from Cuvin. Crouched between tree-spiked ridges, this city boasted shiny cars on most of its streets, bright clothes and current styles. Newspapers criticized the government openly. And, for young Gina, there had been a novelty: black men and women with wide noses and full mouths and stories chiseled into their frank stares. That was how she'd realized not all Americans were as carefree as she once believed.

Still, she preferred this culture to her mother's zealotry.

She had no interest in the tales that rumbled through Transylvanian villages, misguiding the uneducated, compelling some to drive needles into cadaver belly buttons so that bodies would stay in their graves, or to carve out and fry in lead skillets the hearts of corpses suspected of being vampires.

Or to bleed the insect bites of their only daughters.

Nope. Not her thing.

Yet she did recognize something humble, even honorable, in those who refused to lift high their own intellects as the measuring rods for all truth.

Her own physical senses had fallen short in codifying some of her experiences, and even though she would never admit it aloud—certainly not in front of Nikki—her attempts to reject the spiritual realm outright had failed.

A spark remained.

It flitted and danced, refusing to be snuffed out.

Gina dumped the bowl in the sink, then ran the faucet while scrubbing dishes with the coarse side of the sponge. Her body ached from the collision, but she saw no reason to make a show of her pain.

"Do you realize you're a target?" Her mother was talking again. "We all are. That tattoo, that despicable marring of your body—it only underlines your ignorance. There are creatures out to destroy you, and you've joined forces with them by painting one on your skin."

"Actually, it's ink."

"It's an angel."

"Like me, right? Your little angel."

"Fallen angels." Nikki's voice dropped to a whisper. "That's what they are. Since the beginning, they've plagued mankind. They're Collectors, here to steal as many souls as possible from the hands of the Almighty."

"What about the good angels? You know, those plump little babies with the harps and wings?"

"A misrepresentation. Greek mythology's pollution of Christianity."

Even with the strains of truth that seemed to play through Nikki's words, it seemed to Gina there was something out of tune, not quite right. She couldn't help but goad her mother along. "Are you saying only bad angels exist? We're just stuck here on our own?"

"There are more good than evil, don't misunderstand. But that doesn't negate the corrosive power of the Separated."

"'Gotta keep 'em separated,'" Gina sang.

"What?"

"It's the Offspring. From this song called . . . Never mind."

Nikki pursed her lips and shook her head.

Gina returned to the living room, where she feathered fingertips over warriors on her black walnut chess set. She still played, when she had the chance.

"So the good ones, the good angels . . . are they the Nistarim?"

"Darling," said Nikki, "the Nistarim are as human as you or I. According to Talmudic tradition, they're the *Lamed Vov*. Literally, the Thirty-Six. They walk in anonymity and humility, and it's their presence that holds back Final Vengeance. If even one of them perishes without another rising to fill his place, we all suffer."

"Yikes. Sounds bad." Gina's sarcasm was meant to disguise her interest. "And what's that whole deal about the signs on their foreheads?"

"Where'd you hear of such a thing?"

Gina could still recall Cal's interest as he'd studied her, and his vow to return: *I'll find you. Somehow. Someway.*

"Is it true?" she persisted.

Nikki rolled her eyes. "Something similar to Harry Potter's lightning bolt, is that what you mean? Or perhaps the mark of the beast?"

"Oh, here we go. Roll out the holy chitchat."

"One day you'll better understand these things you take so lightly."

"Explain *this*, Nikki." Gina shoved back a wave of hair to expose the symbol on her forehead. "Does this make me a devil child?"

"I don't see anything."

"I bet it's why you were always cutting into me, huh?"

"Introspection is for the weak, Regina." Her mother spoke the words in Romanian for emphasis. "A luxury we can't afford. You're a Lazarescu, born to work your fingers to the bone. Just as I teach in my seminars, you can only exorcise the darkness through the light of your own labors."

"Even if I'm carrying the big, bad, nasty mark?"

"You're speaking nonsense, I tell you. There's nothing there."

Irritated, Gina dropped her gaze to the chessboard. Was she losing touch with reality? She'd lived for years with the mark, even expended energy trying to conceal it, yet her boyfriend Jed had told her the very same thing: *Sweetheart, there's nothing there.*

CHAPTER
EIGHTEEN

A Truck Stop Off I-75, Georgia

Nikki Lazarescu sat in her Acura NSX, beneath signage that flickered neon through the pelting rain. She was en route to Atlanta, on a preparatory trip for some upcoming seminars, but her reasons for stopping at this diner were more personal.

Should she go in?

Behind large windows, rough-and-tumble men forked hash browns and scrambled eggs into mouths stained by Tabasco sauce. She knew they would turn to stare. Like leeches, their eyes would wriggle toward her and sniff out the wounds she had worked so hard to conceal.

She needed details, though, about what had happened. Who had smashed into her daughter outside of Rembrandt's Coffee House? How had Gina walked away with only minor injuries?

After earlier inquiries at the espresso shop, Nikki had called in a favor with a local policewoman, who'd pointed her to a specific freight company and the driver who might have some answers for her. His delivery van was now parked here in this lot.

Nikki had rolled past a few minutes ago, confirming the registration and the name painted on the door: *Zach Larkins*. The sight of the dented front grille and bent hood ornament had sickened her.

Her poor, precious girl.

Setting her jaw, she stepped from the Acura, gathered her jacket around her neck with one hand, and jogged through the downpour toward the diner. She wiped her feet on the doormat inside.

And here came the stares.

Wherever she went, these leeches managed to find her, attracted to her shame. She'd been shaped—or misshapen—by her encounters with guilt. Not only had she bedded down with it, she had borne its terrible offspring and then done all she could to sever herself from its clutches.

Could any good come from airing her wrongs?

No, not that she could see. Instead, she strode through each day with shoulders pulled back and chin jutted forward, attempting to hide all that was evil within by bettering herself and those around her.

Releasing. Cleansing. Renewal . . .

Her seminars gave her financial wings, while also providing the means to buy back that purity she had discarded. She reasoned that if she had the power to destroy, then she also had the power to heal. This was irrefutable in her mind, and she'd built the last few decades upon that precept.

"How you doin' today?" asked a man with an assistant manager tag.

"Good. How're you?"

"If it's breakfast you're lookin' for, you've come to the right place."

"I'm looking for a driver, actually." She tilted her head and met his eye. "If you don't mind, perhaps you'd do me the favor of pointing him out to me."

"Don't know that I can do that. We got lotsa people that pass through."

"His name's Zach. Zach Larkins."

"He in some sorta scrape with the law? I don't want any trouble."

"Has he been in trouble before?"

"Who? Zach?" The assistant manager's gaze scooted toward a corner booth, where a black man with curls of grey above his ears was cutting into a stack of pancakes. "Nah, he's a straight arrow. Keeps to himself most of the time, just eats his food and leaves. Always tips good, though—which my waitresses, they appreciate."

"So that's him?"

A slight nod.

"Thanks for your help, sir." Nikki threaded between the tables.

As she neared the corner, she found herself under scrutiny. The driver's gaze was steady beneath a weathered brow, and his broad cheekbones were dotted with freckles. He placed both hands on the table, perhaps a subconscious gesture from his past to prove that he was unarmed.

"Zach Larkins? My name is Nikki."

"How you do?"

"I don't mean to disturb you, but I have a few questions if you don't mind."

"I'm in no hurry to go back out in that rain. How can I help, ma'am?"

"I'm the mother of the girl you hit a few days ago, in Chattanooga."

"Ma'am?" He put down his fork and knife. "You mind repeating that?"

"My daughter's the one who put the dent in your grille. She was walking across the street from Rembrandt's, on High Street, and I'm told you were traveling down the hill from the museum."

"I don't want any problems. My record's been clean all these years."

"I'm sure it is."

"I reported what happened to the police, and that's God's honest truth."

"I know, Zach. I have a friend in the department."

With that established, the man's demeanor changed. He bent forward, pupils wide with concern. "Is your girl okay? I tried to help, but she wanted none of it."

"That sounds like my Gina."

"If there's a hospital bill or anything, I'll do my best to sort it out," Zach said. "But you're coming to the wrong person if you're hoping to sue me. I'm not a rich man. Wish I was, wish I could do something, but that's just the way it is and the way it's always been."

"Rest assured, that's not why I'm here. Gina seems to be okay."

"Not that I can make any sense of that." Zach looked down into his orange juice, swirled the glass. "She should've been dead. I was squinting into the sun, and then there she was, just like that. By the time I hit the brakes, she was up and over my hood, leaving a crack in my windshield." He took a deep breath.

Nikki took one of her own. "Go on."

"Well, it scared me to my bones. I was traveling a good thirty-five, forty miles an hour. I'm not a young man, and I remember a time when hurting a white woman—no matter whose fault—why, that could be a fatal mistake, if you know what I'm saying."

"Yes, I understand. So you stopped to see how badly hurt she was?"

"Did indeed. I slammed on my brakes and ran back up the street. Saw a person or two already ogling the scene. Well, your girl, she'd been tossed through the air and come down near the curb, twisted like a rag doll. She had blood in her mouth, just a bit. I wasn't sure what to do. Had lots going through my mind. I don't get to church as often as I should, but I know a miracle when I see one, and there's no way on God's green earth that girl should've survived."

"What'd she do? Was she conscious?"

"She stood up." Zach shook his head at the thought. "Got right to her feet."

"Were there any visible injuries?"

"Sounds strange, I know, but I swear I heard bones popping back into place. She straightened up, her eyes all out of focus, and I told her she should wait for an ambulance. Told her she should sit down, and said how sorry I was. I hadn't even seen her there. She didn't say anything, just looked at me like I was a ghost, then pushed away and went lurching down the road."

"And you let her go?"

"Tried to stop her, but she was having none of it. That's when I saw the angel tattooed on her back—not that I was staring inappropriately, ma'am, but there it was—and I figured it was best to just leave her in the good Lord's hands."

"If only it were that simple," Nikki said.

"I believe it is. Eternal life and salvation, free gifts from above."

Nikki had faced this sort of simplistic reasoning in some of her sessions. "Zach," she said, "that sounds a bit irresponsible. Don't you think we each ought to do our part?"

"Oh, I won't argue that. But anything I do, it's just my way of saying thanks to the heavens above. There's no need to go paying for a gift. Listen." He reached into his pocket and pushed a business card across the table. "You call if there's anything you need. I'll try my best to help, and I do mean that sincerely."

"That's thoughtful of you."

"And I hope you'll accept my apologies for what happened. Never seen anything like it. Just glad to know your daughter's all in one piece."

Nikki hurried back through the deluge to her Acura. She locked the doors, gripped the steering wheel, and sank into her seat. As a mother, she'd always known her daughter was unique, but what were the ramifications of this?

She should've been dead . . . a miracle . . .

Sometimes Nikki, in darker moments, imagined her daughter following in her footsteps, wielding that same awful Power of Choice, corrupting the world about her and ushering in Final Vengeance.

Long ago, Nikki Lazarescu had sinned. A mere teenager herself, she'd crossed boundaries and destroyed her relationship with the man she adored. A man with immortal blood. Twins were birthed from their forbidden love, but her son had been taken from her, and only Gina remained at her side.

Gina knew nothing of her sibling, of her bloodline.

For her own safety.

If the Collectors determined her identity and whereabouts, they might try to destroy her in hopes of cutting off the Nistarim.

To avoid detection, Nikki had moved Gina from Seattle and the Puget Sound area to Romania and now to Chattanooga. She had misled her daughter about certain facts—her birthplace, for example—though, again, it was all for her protection.

Was Gina herself immortal? Had she inherited an immunity to the grave?

Nikki had nursed the hope that such was true, yet never summoned the courage to test it. What was she to do? Poison her own child and wait for a recovery?

Except now, she had her conclusive answer.

Gina had walked away from a head-on collision with a moving vehicle. She had also demonstrated, through the decades, an anomalous aging process. She showed a clear resistance to the effects of time, physically developing maybe one year for every two that passed.

Nineteen sixty-five: Gina's birth date.

Not that anyone would believe it.

These days, Gina's peers were fighting the first signs of getting older, while she seemed to be growing stronger, healthier, and more mature. She looked fifteen, maybe sixteen, and her birth documents were forgeries based on a mother's lies. Even the unavoidable brushes with medical professionals had stirred no suspicions. Based on her own academic progress, she believed she was nearing her nineteenth birthday.

Some ironic humor there. Most daughters acted like they were older than they were, and expected to be treated like adults.

Whereas Gina really *was* older. Already thirty-one years old.

Safe, hidden by the droplets that sluiced down the windscreen, Nikki mouthed: "What else was I to do, my dear child? I *had* to cut you. It was my only means of bleeding away your memories and blurring the years. It hurt me every time I did it—you have to believe me—but how else could I pay the price of my own iniquities? What could we do but share in the pain together?"

Nikki got no response. No pardon. Only drumming rain upon the roof.

Anyway, wasn't introspection for the weak? Tickets for her Atlanta engagements were already selling out, and it would do no good to sit here, paralyzed with regret. By the light of her labors, she would forge ahead.

At least my daughter is alive. Doubly alive.

She tossed back her raven locks and turned the key in the ignition.

CHAPTER
NINETEEN

Late March 1997—Arad

Benyamin Amit had an itch to scratch.

Fixated on a TV advertisement, he gazed across a meal of bread, local cheeses, and meat set out by his devout wife, Dalia. The screen was his world, and there was his cure: a bottle of Orsus Beer in the hand of a Latin beauty.

She was the fantasy, the draw for the recreational drinker. For those more serious about their intake, she was a prop and little else.

"You think she's pretty, Ben? Is that why you stare?"

"No." He blinked. "That's not it."

Dalia lifted her chin and pushed away from the table. She wore a long flower-print apron over her dress. Her hair was pulled back in an austere bun. "I know 'pretty' when I see it, and that . . . that girl . . . she's pretty. So there's no reason to deny what I can see with my own eyes, you understand?"

He lifted a chunk of bread to his mouth. Took a bite.

"I know I'm not the woman you married, and I can accept that."

Another bite.

"Can *you*, Benyamin? Can you face the fact that I am older, with gray hairs showing and these wrinkles on my neck? I am your wife, and I've served you dutifully, as before my Maker. Yet you mock me."

"I do no such thing."

"You gawk at this Romanian beauty and then say it is not so."

"Is that the real trouble?" he asked. "Or are you upset that I moved you here?"

"'From Arad to Arad,' you said. As though it were an epiphany. As though you'd be a happier man. I followed you for that reason and no other, but now our son's behind in his schooling. They treat Dov no better than a gypsy. All for what?"

He answered in monotone. "I needed a change."

"If you were content, Ben, these sacrifices would be justified. Instead, you sit here moody and restless, ogling those younger bosoms."

"Don't tell me my own mind, woman."

"Your eyes tell me more than enough."

"After all these years, you think you know me? You don't."

Dalia snatched half-empty bowls of *supa* from the table. Her footsteps shook the floor as she moved from the kitchen, to the bedroom, to the bathroom, and back. She got this way when she was upset, pacing away her sanctimonious anger. It'd become a pattern as far back as Israeli Arad, when she started adhering to the decrees of the datim, the ultrareligious, who fancied themselves ultrarighteous.

Benyamin didn't doubt their sincerity, but he wondered what it accomplished. Either way, he knew this much: in a minute, Dalia would return to the table, mumble something about the garbage needing to be taken out, and he would do it to appease her for another day.

She was right about one thing. He was restless.

That itchy-itch-itch.

With the Amit family's move three years ago, Benyamin had hoped to break up the routine. He knew their savings would stretch farther in Eastern Europe, and his volunteer experience with the Israeli Police had gotten him a job guarding a high-profile Romanian official here in Arad. He was paid well, with an occasional bonus in the form of premium Russian vodka, and he liked the prestige, the respect.

That all changed the first time he was ordered to kill a man.

In the ashes of Ceausescu's regime, bribes were commonplace, dalliances and indiscretions. And he was expected to play along. The last individual who had refused found his wife dead the next morning, jostled from a crowd into the path of a city tram.

Seeing no escape, Benyamin did as he was told—with a Makarov pistol and a double tap to the target's head.

And the little itch grew.

"There." Dalia plopped into her chair, wiping her hands together.

"Have you calmed down?" His voice was patronizing.

"See for yourself. I know you better than you think, my dear husband. In fact, I've removed the temptation."

"What are you up to?"

"You might understand if you peek into the kitchen." She gestured. "It's around that corner. I know you don't go in there often."

A grimace distorted his face. He folded and set down his cloth napkin, then strolled from the table. At the kitchen sink he found five bottles that represented his liquor stash from about the house, even the Grey Goose—a gift from a foreign diplomat, that he'd kept behind the panel in his closet.

Five bottles, emptied. Dalia had corralled them all.

Pain spiked through Benyamin's leg, and he peeled down his sock to get a look at the scar on his heel. Since its infliction years earlier, on the camping trip in the desert wadi, this wound had nagged him. Now it was discolored and puffy, the way it got when his need became great.

Who did Dalia think she was? What gave her the right?

Rage sparked between his ears, but it was nothing compared to the gnawing in his gut that demanded he find a way to douse this thirst. His stomach clenched, curling his body like a huge fist.

That itch. Unrelenting.

Only one thing to assuage his ills.

As if on cue, the phone rang, and he grabbed at it to silence the noise. He was relieved to hear the voice of his supplier, a low-level secretary from city hall.

"I have a case for you," she said. "Of *tuica*."

"Tuica."

"You must come quickly, and alone."

"Tuica." He fondled the word, touching his tongue to his teeth as he pronounced it like the locals: *tsweeka*. The very name conjured a flash of potent homemade spirits, plum brandy searing his throat with blessed heat.

"I'm sorry," she said, "but this time I need payment on the spot."

"Not a problem, Helene. Where?"

"The Cetatea Aradului."

"I'm on my way."

New tapping methods . . . a demonstration . . . an unsuspecting male.

Erota remembered the promises from the previous gathering at the Cetatea Aradului, and she could only hope their fulfillment would stave off the cluster's unrest. Some felt the move from Israel had been a mistake, and others questioned Ariston's decision to send the House of Eros off to Ukraine while his own household stayed in Romania.

With Domna at her side, Erota rounded one of the citadel's earthworks. The sisters wore matching sunglasses. Through personal experience along Kiev's riverfront, they'd learned the irresistible draw of two leggy brunettes in Ray-Bans. Ukrainian men had paid the price for such distraction. A few open-minded women, as well.

"Hello," Ariston said.

Though he stood in the darkness beside his wives Helene and Shelamzion, Erota picked him out with no problem. Her shades gave 100 percent UV-protection, and she wore them with the conviction of a monk bearing a crucifix. She'd read about the damage sun rays could do, and had chosen to preserve her eyes for superior night vision.

"How was the train trip?" Helene wanted to know.

"Long," Domna said. "Next time, we should all meet in Kiev."

"It wasn't that bad," Erota said. "I'm just thirsty and cold."

Helene rubbed her forearm like a mother soothing a child. "You'll be warmed soon enough, I can assure you."

"You should also be warm at your next destination," Ariston said. "Atlanta. Or 'Hot-lanta,' as I believe some call it. Of course, you'll be bringing your own form of heat, won't you, Erota?"

"I plan to, sir."

A week from now, she would branch off from this cluster and rendezvous with her husband-to-be, at Kiev's Boryspil International Airport. Hailing from Atlanta, Georgia, the man longed for a Ukrainian bride to parade before his high-octane business pals—and he was going to get one.

Rumors of late had filtered through other clusters to Lord Ariston, hints of a woman and daughter who had slipped into the United States in early 1990. Word was that they were living somewhere in the South, under assumed names.

It would be Erota's task to ferret them out. Or put the rumors to rest.

Either way, she spoke passable Russian and English, her papers were in order, her body statuesque.

A trophy wife?

The job was made for her. Or perhaps she was made for the job.

Dressed this evening in a tight silk top, a midnight blue jacket that barely reached her slender navel, and designer jeans that showcased her legs, she was eternally nineteen. This type of assignment was nothing new, considering the temple trade in which she and Domna had once indulged. In fact, she looked forward to being on display, even relished its irony. Hidden in plain view, she would have no difficulty finding trophies for her own Collection.

"We'll expect regular updates," said Helene.

"Absolutely. How'd we ever get by without telephones?"

"Can you imagine, dear?"

Ariston's stout arms folded over his belly. "Helpful technology, I suppose, but it also benefits Those Who Resist. At least we won't have to pass messages through rival clusters, letting them horn in on our strategies, seeking glory for themselves."

"Juvenile," Erota agreed.

From behind her, a set of high-pitched squeals caused her to jump. She turned and saw tiny Kyria and Matrona, arm in arm. They had hurried ahead of the other arriving Collectors, and they pretended to stumble in the shadows, milking the moment for attention.

"Kyria," Auge snapped at her girl. "Enough of that."

"She's just a child," Sol reminded his wife.

"She's a Collector, is what she is. Must we coddle her forever?"

"You may have to do just that."

Erota's smile was hidden in the darkness. Kyria would never age, would never grow taller. Even with years of acclimation, she would remain subject to her earthly temperament, which, in this case, meant that of an adolescent girl. As such, she would face certain physical hurdles. On the other hand, she would be less likely to raise suspicion from others and would have easy access to those of her own age group.

"Now where is Barabbas?" Ariston said.

As if on cue, the faithful acolyte appeared with torch in hand. His wiry beard and eyes glinted as flame hissed along a tightly wound towel soaked in kerosene.

"Speaking of technology, Barabbas, I had more efficient light sources in mind."

"The torch is warm and bright, sir."

"Very well. Yes, it is. Now lead the way, would you?"

The large man spearheaded their descent into a tunnel of curved ceilings and crude stone walls. The Houses of Ariston and Eros followed, merging into a single stream, and Erota had no problem picturing herself hundreds of years in the past.

This region had once been part of old Transylvania. Vlad Dracul, the father of Vlad Tepes, had traveled here during the fifteenth century with his Order of the Dragon. Later, his son had ruled with an iron hand, utilizing violent yet effective measures to curb crime and foreign invasion—and to mollify his own Collector's thirst. In Romanian, *Tepes* meant *impaler*, and he was known to have dined with hearty indulgence while his victims suffered nearby on sharpened stakes.

Some said the name *Dracul* could be interpreted as *devil* or *dragon*, while *Dracula* meant literally *son of the devil*.

Erota had never encountered the Master Collector personally, but she knew he had no son—not that she would dare whisper that fact. Like all Collectors, the Master lacked the creative spark, the intermeshing of spiritual and physical that enabled life. Incapable of producing his own progeny, he was forced to collect what he could from the loins and wombs of mortals.

Humans—these irksome beasts—they were the ones who carried the gift of life within. They misused it, abused, ignored, and polluted it. But it was always there. Glowing in their eyes, in their touch.

Even more annoying to Erota were the Unfallen.

The heavenly angels.

These were the ones who had refused to join the Master Collector's rebellion and thus remained in favor with the Nazarene. They served at his beck and call. They interacted between physical and spiritual, impervious to the Separation.

Though also forbidden to violate the Power of Choice, the Unfallen did not require hosts to interact with the earthly realms, and stories in Jewish and Christian Scripture showed them eating food set before them and even taking people by the hand.

Erota sneered in the torchlight.

Well, leave them to their fun and games. It'd all end soon enough.

Chattanooga

The first stab of discomfort caught Gina as she stepped into her work clothes.

A half hour ago, Nikki Lazarescu had left for her antebellum home in the St. Elmo district of town, her pupils dilated with disapproval and reproach. Things had been more tense than usual between daughter and mother, and even though Gina had no desire to hurt her mom—not deeply, anyway—it had been the purpose of her makeover and tattoo to spread her wings.

Wider than before.

The angel on her back was her statement of freedom, signed in ink.

She thought of the skin and blood that had curled up beneath the tattoo artist's machine last year, and was struck by the parallels between her adult emancipation and the childhood cleansings to which she'd been subjected.

Maybe her mother had been onto something after all.

The discomfort intensified, but Gina wasn't going to let a little tummy trouble keep her from work. In half an hour she was supposed to be at the entrance to Ruby Falls, the Cavern Castle, from which she would lead tours into Lookout Mountain's cave system. She'd never been late before. Why start now?

She pulled on tan slacks, a white shirt, and a tie. Attached and straightened her name badge. *Hi, my name is Gina . . . If you have any questions, don't hesitate to ask.*

The next stab came while she was tying her shoes. She'd survived last autumn's confrontation with the delivery truck—had only fragmented memories of it, actually—but this newest torment was undeniable.

It twisted in her belly.

Backed off.

Then drove deeper, to her core.

CHAPTER TWENTY

Arad

Ariston, it seemed to Erota, was mulling thoughts similar to her own. By firelight, he addressed the assembly. "The Nistarim," he said, "are the key to bringing down this dreary reality. After two thousand years of existence, they've managed to elude us. Other clusters have done their best to identify and destroy them, but here we all are, still trapped beneath layers of ozone. Is anyone else discouraged?"

A few grunts hung in the cold, smoky air.

"While rumors of the Concealed Ones have multiplied, they are by their very nature humble in spirit, which means they won't go about seeking personal accolades or exerting their own rights. It's their meekness that allows them to hide beneath our noses."

Erota folded her arms. Speaking of meekness, Ariston was not exactly the epitome of modern chic. He'd trimmed down his belly to a more manageable size, and he was better attired than those first days out of the tombs—*Please, strike that mental image from my mind*—yet he still seemed unremarkable.

Dressed in slacks, a collared white shirt, and suspenders mostly hidden by a rumpled suit jacket, he could stroll the city's avenues unnoticed. If the best Collectors were the least obvious, he was up to the task.

"Is there something you'd like to add, Erota?"

"Huh?" She caught his eye. "Oh, I was just thinking that we should be looking for people who are . . . well, who are dressed like you, sir."

"Like me?"

"No offense. You know, people who have the ability to blend in."

"Ah. I wish the Nistarim were that simple to identify. Unfortunately, clothing seems to be unrelated. Positions and titles, jewels and wealth— none of it guarantees an individual's humility, or lack thereof. The good thing is that we alone, through these undead hosts, have the ability to discern their markings. Where others can only guess, we can be certain with but a glance."

"Not that we can go through the earth's population one by one," Erota said. "Isn't there a better way?"

"Maybe," said one of the teens, "they've pulled an Elvis."

"A what?" Ariston said.

"An Elvis. Maybe they've left the building."

"No, Shabtai. They're still out there. Thirty-six of them. It's an infinitesimally small number from among the billions now crowding this planet, but believe me, they do exist. Don't let our setbacks suggest otherwise."

"Where'd they even come from?" the boy inquired.

"Good question. One we're still trying to figure out."

Shabtai hooked a thumb into a belt loop of his jeans. "Why don't we just go back to their roots, then follow the trail? I mean, really, how hard can that be? Like on one of those American detective shows."

"Been watching TV, I see."

"At our place here in Arad, we get some good channels. My dad says it's important to know pop culture."

"As a tool," said Nehemiah, his father. "To better understand your prey."

"Nothing wrong with a bit of cunning," Ariston agreed. "Certainly use

such knowledge to infiltrate your own peers, Shabtai. But keep your insolence to yourself, or I may be forced to ban you from future gatherings."

"Insolence? What does that mean?"

"It means you think you know what everything means."

"Well . . . I knew that."

Ariston gazed around the bunker and challenged any further interrup-
tion. "It's obvious," he said, "that we each face unique challenges through
our individual hosts. It's a headache—quite literally, at times—to exert
your knowledge through the limited education of a human, particularly a
younger one. But it's no excuse for ignorance, is that clear?"

Erota offered him a supportive wink.

"I am well aware," he added, pushing out his chest, "that you're all
thirsty. Please, bear with me a few minutes longer. Eros and I have been
in discussion with other cluster leaders, and we're told it's not uncommon
to go for generations without a trace of the Nistarim. Even if Collectors
from around the globe were to unite under the same goal, we would still
be shorthanded. That's why, as of this evening, our particular cluster will
be shifting strategies."

"We're giving up now?" It was Sol's turn to object.

"That's not what I said, son."

"The dismantling of the Nistarim is what I live for."

"An interesting statement, coming from the undead."

"I think," Sol said, "that you know my level of dedication. I want to
demolish this vainglorious empire of men. They're putrid, at each other's
throats constantly. My own brother was cleaved in two by a sword, a victim
of their warmongering."

"Natira was human," Ariston specified. "Don't confuse his sort with
us."

"His sort? What kind of talk is that? He was your son."

"Your half brother, as I prefer to think of him. From an era long ago."

Sol's nose was hawklike, his eyes ablaze. "What about Salome, my baby
sister?"

"I'll grant you, she came up out of the grave like the rest of us. She erred, though, didn't she? And she paid the price." Ariston panned to his first wife. "Sorrow will cloud your eyes, if you let it."

Sol moved to Shelamzion's side. "Leave my mother out of this."

Barabbas lifted the torch higher, until crackling flames outlined corded muscles and the thatch of chest hair at his shirt collar. His message was clear: he would not brook any trouble. His masculine odor clogged Erota's nostrils.

"Sol, hear me out. We want the same things," Ariston said. "It's just our methods that differ."

"I've heard the excuses before, father."

"Not excuses. Explanations."

"Semantics. You've spent too much time over these past few years dabbling in corporate courses."

"You'd be surprised. There's much in there that suits our agenda. And don't deride the human capacity for molding thoughts and belief systems. You think we know how to work them? Bah. They're experts are tearing apart the mind-sets of their own kind. Which," Ariston said, "is the tactic we're going to start focusing on. It's no mistake that we of the Akeldama have been given room to roam here at the end of this century, this millennium, and I believe this cluster is poised to make an undeniable impact. Our time is near."

"Let's hope so," Sol muttered.

Ariston turned toward Eros. "They're growing tired of my voice."

"Would you like me to handle it from here, Lord?"

"Do as you see fit."

Eros, Erota's olive-skinned father, was ever calm. He and his sisters Auge and Hermione took after their mother, Dorotheus—aristocratic, self-possessed, an almost regal air about them. Their very arrival was known to have stilled rooms of strangers.

The Grecian house leader faced the gathering and, with a level gaze, secured each revenant's attention. "Here's the deal, my friends. Ariston and I agree it's time for a complete revamping—if you'll pardon the terrible pun—of our methods. We are hoping to breathe some new life—"

A few groans.

"—into our cluster." He cocked an eyebrow. "I think we're all aware of the difficulties we've had tracking a lone mother and child. Their trail ran cold before even crossing the Romanian border, and years later we're no closer to finding which rock they scurried under. Naturally, we've gone on investigative treks into surrounding regions, sniffing for clues, but we've come up empty-handed. Does anyone else wonder if there wasn't some trickery in the clues they left us?"

"The thought's crossed my mind," Ariston confessed.

"Mine too," Eros said. "I feel like we were deceived. And I, for one, am tired of sipping on the Ukrainians' irradiated blood. If I *were* alive, I'd be dead by now."

"He'd be dead by now." Little Kyria snickered.

"That's right, cutie." Eros ruffled her hair. "So it's time we go about this more methodically. We do know that the Concealed Ones are meant to carry the sorrows of the world. Some of the legends speculate that when any one of them leaves this earth, he is so frozen with despair that he must spend a thousand years in heaven being thawed by God's own hand."

Kyria's exaggerated shiver earned a pearl-white grin from Eros.

He said, "Are any of you familiar with the Andalusian Jews, in Spain? Back in the seventh century, these people venerated a particular rock that was shaped like a teardrop. Do you know why? They believed it was one of the Nistarim, the Lamed Vov. In their minds, the rock was a humble soul petrified by humanity's suffering."

"If they were right, sir," Erota said, "wouldn't the world have already collapsed?"

"It should've. But sadly, another rose to fill his place."

"Will this ever end? I mean, how many of these people are there?"

"That's the very point of this discussion. We've been focused on hunting down individuals of the Nistarim—all well and good—but it's been ineffectual, hasn't it? Our new plan of attack is to add to their joint sorrows by shoveling trouble and pain upon humans everywhere. One by one, the burden will increase till the Nistarim crumble beneath the combined weight. It'll involve each of us on more personal levels, zeroing in on unique targets. Hunters and prey."

"A rousing speech," Sol said. "But how does it work in the real world?"

"Take my daughter as an example. Erota's upcoming trek to America will allow her to tap a whole new sector for long-term sustenance, exploring recent rumors, even while piling despair upon the Nistarim. Already, with her particular set of . . . uh, assets, she's brought grief to quite a few families. A quickie here. A jilted spouse over there. She makes it look easy."

"Dad." Erota arched an eyebrow. "Are you saying I'm easy?"

"Please," Sol fumed. "Is the entire Eros household so uncouth? I don't doubt Erota's abilities, but"—he took an elbow in the ribs from his wife—"I do have some logistical concerns. Drained corpses raise suspicions, and we've worked hard to evade notice, feeding in state hospitals, orphanages, alleyways, even upon farm animals. How will this new strategy make that any easier? What am I missing?"

"Ahh," Ariston cut in, smoothing his suit jacket. "It's a demonstration you want, son? Then a demonstration you'll get. Helene?"

"I called him earlier," his wife said. "He's on his way."

An unsuspecting male . . .

Erota wondered who this person was? What was planned for him?

Ariston nodded toward Helene and Megiste. "Go on, then. We'll follow along and meet you in the chapel in five minutes."

"Come thirsty," Megiste said.

The willowy priestess let the words trail behind her, and Erota registered the subtle charge of excitement that passed through the cluster. Yes, they were ready to drink.

There she was. Helene? Yes, that was her name.

Benyamin Amit had noticed her in city hall for the past year, an archivist at a small desk. Her movements were always fluid, her smile blithe,

but it was those doelike eyes that first got to him. There was none of that
fierce pride he saw in his wife, none of that sense of duty, of constant
obligation. Helene was a mellow spirit.

Of course, when it came to spirits, Benyamin was a connoisseur.

"Ciao," he greeted her.

"Ciao, Ben. You brought the payment? Good." Helene turned along
high earthen walls that formed one of the fortress's six points. "Well,
aren't you coming?"

He tried to push from his thoughts that old wound on his heel—pul-
sating, still infected with poison. He followed after her, shoes crunching
over frosty grass. He was watchful, comforted by the weight of the pistol
loaded and holstered beneath his jacket.

Helene led him through darkness toward the Cetatea's dilapidated
chapel with its dual bell towers. The place saw few visitors. The parking
area was now empty, and a breeze fluffed the branches of trees stationed
around baroque-style buildings. From a distant riverbank, music and laughter marked the location of the Neptun Strand, where locals gathered to eat
langosi and drink *bere*.

Though far-off, the familiar sounds reassured Benyamin.

Seemed safe enough. He and Helene had made exchanges here before.
This citadel was a convenient drop point—deserted, yet only a bridge
span from the city center.

Uninvited, a set of old images scrolled across his vision: Ein Bokek,
the waters of the Dead Sea, and that shriveled corpse . . .

And Cal Nichols. Nickel. Haven't thought about him in ages.

Benyamin could still picture those metal tent pegs—MTPs—tumbling onto the sand. Surely there couldn't be any metaphysical purpose
behind this recollection, though. He didn't subscribe to such rubbish.

Best to stay focused now. Pay attention.

He came to a standstill. The presence of an auburn-haired female
at the chapel doors gave him pause. Maybe it would be wise to go back
the way he'd come, forget the exchange, and apologize to his wife. He had
coerced her into moving to this land, pointing out Romania's rich Jewish

heritage and the fact that Elie Wiesel had been born here. Arad even had sister cities in Israel.

Dear Dalia. With nary a word, she had obliged and supported him. She deserved none of the distress he'd foisted on her. He would explain about this itch, and how it grew stronger at night when the loneliness worked as an irritant.

She would scold him. Perhaps lecture.

In the end, though, she would listen as she always did.

"You still want the case of tuica, don't you?" Helene was touching his arm. The night air smelled warm, almost salty. "This lady, she is awaiting her money."

"Helene, I'd like you to keep watch as I go in. Could you do that?"

"Expecting trouble?"

"My line of work dictates caution," he said. "I wouldn't put it past other black marketers to cut in on our private exchange."

"See?" Helene told the other woman. "A trustworthy choice."

The auburn-haired beauty turned her head. Poised, with shoulders back and bust pushing up against her blouse, she appraised him through the eyes of a jeweler. Her lips curled upward, and he took that as a sign of approval.

"*Intrati, domnule,*" she said, inviting him to enter.

"You have the case?"

"Just inside. I hope you don't mind us using the house of God for our indiscretions, but it does offer *such* good cover. Besides, if the dear Lord gave you this body of yours, don't you think He understands your need to address its fickle demands? It would be petty of Him to hold your weaknesses against you."

"Weakness? No, no, no. For me, this is a medicine."

"Oh, honey. I know all about such prescriptions."

"Either way, I don't worry over religion and old wives' tales. We should enable ourselves, rather than relying on mental crutches. I'm a man of learning."

"A man." She curled her hair around a finger. "Yes, you *certainly* are."

Benyamin was fit for his age, toned and powerful, and so he allowed her silky tones to strum his ego as his legs carried him onward. He would not concern himself with thoughts of Dalia just now, not after she'd taken it upon herself to drain his precious supplies. If these two women wished to fill his prescription, very well.

And if they thought it best to candycoat the prescription, he might be up for that too. Here a scratch, there a scratch.

Left, right, left.

"Ben, you have the money?"

He fumbled the bills from his pocket. "The case? It's in here, you say?"

"Through those doors."

His desire was a creeping vine, looped around his foot and reeling him in greedy lurches toward the token of temporary relief. He set a hand on his gun, but kept moving. Any apprehension on his part might cause these ladies to bolt.

It was best to keep walking, keep walking.

CHAPTER
TWENTY-ONE

Chattanooga

Gina gritted her teeth, grabbed her midsection, and rushed to the apartment bathroom. The toilet lid was down, and she—

No time. Hurry.

She brushed aside the ivory shower curtain and heaved into the tub. Her guts seemed to turn inside out as another spasm bent her over the drain.

Finally, she ran the water, sprayed the tub clean, then wiped her mouth and splashed her face. When she stood, she felt lightheaded and held on to the sides of the sink cabinet.

"What's wrong with you?" she said, peering into the mirror.

The girl in the reflection gave no reply. She looked haggard, but even here at her worst, she still looked like a teen. Men hounded her for this, drawn by the appearance of innocence and youth.

Innocent? Gina felt anything but. Weary and old was more like it.

Weakening fingers of pain clutched at her, then slipped away as she steeled her gaze in the glass. She'd removed her black choker for work, and her half-moon scar showed pale and thin. Her earrings dangled over the basin, and she had a flash of concern that they might wash down the drain.

Just like her thoughts and memories used to do, spiraling away from her.

All so complicated. Life on a chessboard.

In the apartment living room, her folding chess set reminded her of those days in Cuvin. When Gina moved out of her mother's St. Elmo district home last year, she had brought the set along. She'd removed the dagger from within, hiding the crude implement once used for performing surgeries of superstition.

True, she had inadequacies. But she would no longer submit to cleansing Nikki-style. No thank you.

She slid a hand down her right shin. There was the blade, beneath her clothing, sheathed in the leather her boyfriend had tooled for her last Christmas.

Faithful, forgetful, kindhearted Jed. He'd been good to her.

Another sensation moved through her belly.

Thinking it was the pain making a comeback, Gina prepared herself for the worst. This was different, though. A mere whisper of butterfly wings. It reminded her of Teo, of the flutters she'd felt from that first kiss back in Cuvin. Was there anything quite like young love—full of excitement, devoid of sexual politics and grown-up concerns?

Another flutter.

As though something were moving inside her.

Maybe she was a demon child, spawning something dark and hideous within. Back in Romania, her mother had seemed convinced of her defilement, yet Gina refused to buy into it any longer.

What had Cal said to her? *I know you feel small, like you're no one important, but that's not true.*

She hugged her tummy as a single tear rolled down her cheek.

Arad

The first sip of tuica darted down Benyamin's throat, then wound through the maze of his intestinal tract with a palpable heat.

Ahhh, yes.

If there was any mercy upon this lonely planet, it was no more evident than here in the magnanimous kiss of the bottle to his lips. This was his god, bestowing favor and strength. Benyamin was a disciple, paying homage in this twin-steepled artifice.

Helene came to his side.

"I thought you were keeping watch," he said.

"This is more interesting," she cooed, sliding fingers down his arm.

The willowy creature with the alabaster neck stepped into the chapel and pushed the door closed with her rounded buttocks. She glided to his other side, her hair bleached by gibbous light through the nave's windows. The two females eased him toward a pew and pressed him into a sitting position on the hardwood.

"You look to be a *delicious* fellow, Mr. Amit."

He fortified himself with another drink. It warmed him.

Helene squatted down and raised his ankle over her shoulder. She pushed back his pant leg, then traced one finger over his heel where the scar tissue was dimpled and red. "It's all swollen," she said.

"Right there," he pleaded. "If you could just scratch it."

She first brushed her lips over the spot—moist, very soft.

And then her teeth.

"One moment," said the second woman. "The others are on the way."

"The others?"

"Relax, Ben," Helene said. "Relax."

An icy heat swarmed through his ankle, his eyes trailed to the ceiling, and the chapel began to spin.

"Lead the way, Barabbas."

Ariston held the torch while his bearded henchman shouldered through a heavy wooden panel. Before them, the stone steps of a hidden passage curled upward. The design of these fortifications included underground escape routes, and this one fed from the vestry where Franciscan monks had once served.

Erota trailed the cluster leader, her olfactory senses detecting traces of votive candles and incense, of alcohol and . . .

Human blood.

Pulsing, pounding, pumping.

She thought of the promised demonstration, and she felt her own counterfeit heart quickening at the thought.

One by one, the cluster entered the chapel from behind the raised altar, their footsteps kicking up motes of dust that glittered in the moon-beams. The Collectors oozed through shadows and swaths of light until they'd reached the back pew where Megiste and Helene knelt like worshippers before a stone-chiseled idol.

The figure was male, grasping a bottle, his chest slowly rising and falling.

A real man, then. Not stone, after all.

"I told you to wait," Ariston said. "What've you done, Megiste?"

The hostage was in a cataleptic state, slumped back, eyes fixed upon the nave's high ceiling, his right leg outstretched with Helene as his footstool. In the darkness, the engorged skin at his heel resembled a blister about to burst.

"Helene's subdued him," Megiste said. "That's all. Meet Benyamin Amit, former patrolman for the Israeli Mash'av, present bodyguard for Romanian politicos. He's ready and willing, practically *begging* for our attention."

Ariston said, "It's him, isn't it?"

"Didn't I tell you?" Helene smiled up at her husband.

"This is the man, the one I found camping with his son in the Negev. I remember I'd inhabited a mosquito, as an experiment more than anything. A few drops, that's all I drew from him—but I felt glutted. It's too bad that in these human casings we don't have half the capacity of such an insect."

"A mosquito?" Megiste pulled a face. "Sorry, I'm not crazy about working with bugs. I don't know that I'd be able to choose one as a host."

"Your loss. A means to a most excellent meal."

"What'll it be next, Ariston? Leeches? Ticks?"

Erota thought the idea had some appeal.

"For their size," Megiste continued, "those're some *real* bloodsuckers, though still not equal to what Helene and I are about to show you. Apparently there's some truth in the saying that 'It's more blessed to give than to receive.' Mr. Amit here is the epitome of that. He's migrated with his family all the way from Israel to be near the one who first tapped his blood. I guess he wants to keep giving, Ariston."

"I don't mind receiving. Not at all."

Erota crowded in with the others, drawn by the *pumpity-pump-pumpity-pump* of the victim's pulse, by the sweet, coppery haze above his pew.

The haze seemed cleaner than the majority she'd seen before, devoid of the dietary impurities so prevalent in this modern era. She figured he must eat mostly kosher. If given the ability to swim through the air, she would be diving and bathing in this cloying mist. It would be her sacrilegious mikveh, her baptism.

"Helene, tell everyone what's going on here." Ariston folded his arms over his belly. "The things you and I discussed."

"Love to, dear."

Benyamin remained rigid and unresponsive.

"I first met this man," Helene said from her knees, "on the job at city hall. He likes to make small talk with me while waiting on his employers. He's decent enough, polite. Only when he thinks no one is looking does he allow himself to hobble along, and a few weeks back I began to suspect something was amiss when I asked him what tuica was. I'd heard other men mention it, and I hoped to increase my cultural understanding."

"As we all should be doing," Ariston said. "As a tool. A weapon."

"Absolutely."

Megiste nudged Helene. "Tell them what you saw."

"Well, it was clear as day. The mere utterance of that word, *tuica*, and Mr. Amit's eyes took on this intense, emerald gleam, like an ember coming back to life. I knew then he'd been compromised somehow, and it was his occasional limp that suggested to me the point of entry."

"Where I'd bitten him," Ariston said. "Back in Israel."

"That's right. In a moment of privacy, I asked to see his wound, and he obliged me. I noticed then the infection—the infestation, if you will—and later asked Megiste to help me discern its source. In a moment you'll see it with your own eyes. Mr. Amit tried to give me all the reasons for bringing his wife and son to Romania, but I believe he was drawn by our presence— yours, more precisely, Ariston. By allowing the bite to fester, he gave the poison time to permeate his body, and the very infection that's been eating away at him tells him he can only be soothed by more of the same. In his case, another drink."

"Fighting fire with fire, as they say."

"Father." Sol gave a protracted sigh and shook off Auge's censuring hand. "This is all very entertaining, as usual, but we were discussing the destruction of the Nistarim. Revised techniques and whatnot. Is this all you have to show us?"

"I think it's rather significant," Eros said.

Unimpressed, Sol huffed.

The Houses of Ariston and Eros fell silent. The flames of Barabbas's torch whistled and crackled.

The confrontation intrigued Erota. In light of her impending marriage to the man from Atlanta, she'd been observing interactions between husbands and wives, parents and children, siblings and cousins. What drove individuals onward? More important, what drove them apart? She'd seen all manner of discord among humans, in some of the lower organisms too. As a Collector, she drew perverse pleasure from this.

Yet the Principles of Cluster Survival were explicit: *When a challenge arises from within the cluster, the leader will determine its validity and, if necessary, banish any Collector that displays mutinous intentions.*

Ariston hooked his right arm through his son's. "Sol, Sol, dear boy."

"Don't start patronizing me now."

"Come, you two." Ariston hooked his other arm through Shelamzion's. "My first wife, and my oldest son. The issuance of my loins. You mustn't allow jealousy to blind you. Yes, I've always preferred Helene—a better wife, better lover. And so, it's only natural I would prefer the offspring I shared with her."

"Father, this is—"

"This is *necessary*. For your well-being." Ariston leaned forward, his joined arms forcing wife and son to bow with him toward the kneeling Helene. "By the sails of Sicily, look at her, look with me, and enjoy what you see. *Look*."

"I'm . . . looking," Shelamzion sputtered.

Sol only glared.

"Looook."

The torch flames wavered as Ariston drew in air. He did so slowly, intentionaly, sucking the color from the lips of his wife and firstborn and draining all semblance of vibrancy from their earthly habitations. On either side of him, they began to droop like deflated pig bladders.

"We're a small cluster, true. But," Ariston said to the incapacitated pair, "we are infused with traces of the Man from Kerioth and the Master Collector himself. This gives us potential never before explored. Now. I'd like it if we could share in this as a family. Would you be kind enough to give Helene your attention?"

Megiste held out slender arms. "Show them, Helene."

She looked to Ariston. "Now, dear?"

"Yes, show these loved ones. Show us all."

Helene's fingers moved over Benyamin Amit's heel, then squeezed and pulled upward in the movement of a seamstress drawing needle through cloth. The skin swelled, rose, reached a tented pinnacle, and finally collapsed as a large thorn punched through, as clear fluid gushed forth.

"Arrrgghhhh!"

The man on the pew snapped forward. The hiss that issued from his mouth reverberated between walls and chapel ceiling and awakened in each of the Collectors' eyes a peculiar glow.

Erota felt herself respond, felt her parched throat tighten. Her thirst was strong.

As suddenly as he had reacted, Benyamin fell back into a stupor.

Helene kept tugging, and the thorn—the *thorns*—kept unraveling from the wound, curved and glistening, mottled red and black.

CHAPTER
TWENTY-TWO

Chattanooga

Gina was in the employee restroom, with seven minutes before her shift. She stared into the mirror, ready to do her job. The facts, the anecdotes, the history—all there, committed to memory.

Over the next few hours, she would walk close to five miles as she guided groups through limestone caverns of flowstone and drapery formations, stalactites, and calcite crystals. Located more than a thousand feet beneath Lookout Mountain, the tour's highlight was Ruby Falls, an underground cataract plunging 145 feet into a shallow pool.

One more quick check. A personal matter.

She parted her dyed hair, studied her forehead. There, stenciled into her skin, stood the same crossed lines she'd seen in her apartment but which seemed to hide from view of everyone else. Everyone, with the possible exception of Cal.

And Teodor's uncle, the village prefect. *Look in a mirror, young lady, and tell me what you see. Do you see the proof of your role in this grand scheme?*

How had that revolting man known? To what role had he been referring?

She forgot these questions as a set of tools went to work again at her innards, scooping, scraping. She was a pumpkin, her guts hollowed out, her facial features carved by pain into something horrifying. A candle ignited in her core, more intense than before, and dribbling waxen tears.

She fell back against the wall. She felt empty. There was nothing left in her stomach to offer as appeasement.

I won't cry. I won't. I have to get to work.

She dry-heaved into the sink, felt the burn in her throat. Her mind flashed to the incident with the delivery truck, and the internal damage that she might've suffered. Were there injuries to her organs?

Another gut-wrenching spike of pain.

God, please. What's going on?

Arad

Erota found the spectacle both illuminating and delightful.

One by one, the thorns stretched the skin of Benyamin's ankle. One by one, they broke through the ruptured scar tissue. The stock upon which the thorns grew was crusty and cracked, in appearance like an ancient taproot that had fermented in worm-ridden earth. It rustled through the flesh's opening with the sounds of a snake passing through dead leaves. It writhed, as Helene pulled; it squirmed upon the chapel flooring, carving arcane shapes in the dust.

A tangled vine. A dragon's tail of spiked protuberances.

"Take one, dear heart." Helene snapped a thorn from its source and handed it to Ariston. "Try a taste."

He released his wife and son, who both stumbled to the wall.

Erota watched him cup the triangular shape and lift it to his mouth. He sipped. Moaned. Drank deeper. The burgundy liquid dribbled from his chin.

"It's been filtered," he said. "The fruit of the vine."

With his recent wine-making aspirations, Ariston of Apamea couldn't pass up the opportunity to present himself as a connoisseur.

"Exactly," Megiste said. "The vine starts as a minuscule seed, planted into a human soil with one *delectable* bite—an orally injected contagion, if you will. I believe these thorns started back in Israel, when you, Lord Ariston, first sipped from the man's heel."

"It's been growing in him all this time?"

"He's tried to fend off its effects with alcohol, with limited and temporary success. In ages past, we Collectors have always been able to pass on infections from other blood sources, but this is unique. It seems we have been enabled with a more *prickly* bite, shall I say? Could have something to do with the Man from Kerioth's betrayal and the thorns crushed into the Nazarene's skull."

"So this is unique to our cluster, is that correct?"

"It seems to be, Ariston."

"What is the method of injection? Is there anything special we must do?"

"The contagion's always there. We simply do what we do best, tapping sources for our own survival. If the host has any ailment or weakness, any unchecked susceptibility, the seed will have soil to grow. As it does, the vines will twine through veins and arteries until the thorns latch into place. Once in position, they tap the entire body. Each thorn filters and draws out blood for our enjoyment."

Erota's breath quickened. Her thirst intensified.

"The best thing," said the priestess, "is that we can come back for more." She gripped the thick twisted stem. "We simply snap off this entire portion and drink, but the vine keeps growing."

"You've verified this?"

"I've tested it on this man here for the last year. And still, as you can see, he is available for our nourishment."

"You mean to tell me, Megiste, you tested this without my foreknowledge?"

Erota caught a brief meeting of the eyes between Megiste and her father, Eros, and she felt her pulse quicken at the hint of intrigue. Had anyone else noticed the look?

"I do think," Eros purred, "that her actions in this case were warranted."

"Sorry, sir. I surely didn't mean to overstep my bounds," Megiste added.

Beside her, Ariston seemed to forget any perceived slight as he savored the remaining liquid from the pointed vessel, his irises gaining in emerald radiance with each lusty swallow.

Helene touched his arm. "It's beautiful, don't you think?"

"Better than I imagined."

"Instead of draining the mortals only once," she said, "instead of wringing them dry and moving on, we can drink for years to come. And, left unchecked, the seed can germinate in others, particularly any sickly family members or friends. Wherever the tiniest of openings presents itself, a thorn is sure to hook in. Sins of the fathers, as they say."

"All of this," Erota asked, "is initiated with one bite? One tapping?"

"*Wonder*fully simple, isn't it? Here." Megiste handed over a fresh thorn.

Erota was an unholy worshipper, receiving this emblem of communion from her priestess. Through the thorn's smooth husk, she felt the warmth of vitality and vigor. Then . . . she drank. By drawing the liquid over her own tongue, she was sucking life from this miserable being.

The invaaaasive,

creeeeeping

demise of a human.

She was spellbound. Loved every succulent drop. She was caught up in the blasphemy, the dastardly bastardization, of this most spiritual of experiences.

The Blood of the Host.

Of the Hostage.

In the end, wasn't that all these flesh-and-blood creatures really were? Hosts and hostages, habitations and infestations.

As Erota's vision painted the chapel in iridescent green hues, as the other Collectors joined in the experience with cupped hands and smeared lips, she reveled in the thought of marriage, where she would have her own prey upon which to feed. In the process, she could heap sorrow upon sorrow, grief upon grief.

The Concealed Ones, they could not hide from that.

Somewhere, already, the Nistarim were feeling the pain.

Chattanooga

Gina collapsed to her knees in the employee bathroom, spine bowed, shoulders sagging, while the weight of the world seemed to fall across her back.

CHAPTER
TWENTY-THREE

"Just one game of chess, Jed."

"Why waste my time? You always beat me."

"C'mon. It helps me relax."

Although the day's anguish had subsided, Gina was still sore around her ribs, still sensitive to rapid movement or bright light. She needed something to ease her unspoken concerns and assure her of a world unfazed by her earlier illness. Since girlhood, she'd found chess to be a glue that held her fragmented days together.

"Help you relax?" Jed said. "By beating me into the dirt? You're more twisted than I thought."

Even in jest, the accusation poked at something tender in Gina's mind. She began setting out the chess figurines on blond and black squares, banging down each one, a woman stamping her denial onto pardon papers.

"How'd it go at work today?" Jed asked.

Bang, stamp, bang . . .

"That good, huh? "

Stamp, bang . . .

"Great." He hit the Off button on the remote. "I'm gonna get my butt kicked."

"Want me to play blindfolded?" Gina said. "Then you *might* have a chance."

"Okay, now you're asking for it." Jed unfolded himself from the couch, grabbed a Pabst Blue Ribbon from the fridge, and joined her at the chess table beneath the black-framed Kurt Cobain poster. "Time to deliver the pain."

"Not on this—" She paused. "Not on this night, buddy boy."

"What's wrong?"

"Nothing."

"I just saw you wince."

"I did no such thing," she said.

"Did too. Look at you, Gina. You're gritting your teeth."

The discomfort was nothing she couldn't handle. A short stab.

From behind her back, she offered two closed fists. "Choose your color. Not that it'll make any difference."

Blue eyes studied her over thick-rimmed glasses. He touched her right hand, and she opened it to reveal a light-colored pawn.

"You're white," Gina said. Then, playfully, under her breath: "And getting whiter by the day, sitting in that office at the Chamber of Commerce."

"Hey."

"Joke."

"Sweetheart, you know I hate making the first move."

"Control the center of the board," she instructed. "Advance a few pawns, back them up with your knights and bishops, then castle quickly. That's it. Easy."

He sighed. Shoved his king's pawn forward two squares.

"There you go. Wasn't so hard, was it?" Gina's fingers played with her choker, then swung the queen's bishop pawn two squares ahead.

"What's that?"

"The Sicilian Defense."

"So now you're going all Mafia on me, huh?"

She whipped her dagger from its sheath. "Gonna feed you to the fishes."

"Not if I can help it." His knight jumped into the attack.

Gina, after pushing her queen pawn one space, went into the kitchen to grill cheese sandwiches. Jed called out each time he made a move, his thinking time increasing between turns even as his volume decreased. She responded to his attempts with constrictive maneuvers that set up a sudden counterattack.

He sipped his PBR and surveyed the battlefield. Realizing his imminent doom, he wrung his mop of brown hair while she poured tomato soup into mugs.

"I suck," he mumbled.

"Strange." Gina shrugged. "I'm starting to feel all peaceful."

"*You* suck."

"You, buddy boy, are a sore loser."

"Maybe," Jed said, "you should kiss me and make me feel better."

She sneered, bumped into him with her hip, then set mugs and small plates beside his measly trio of captive pawns. Her side of the table offered little space due to the number of slain chess pieces. She almost felt bad for annihilating him like this. Almost.

The perplexing thing, as always, was the ease with which she played the game. She knew that somewhere in her past she had received instruction, but she had no distinct memory of such.

She drank down the tomato soup, let the heat soothe her raw throat.

"Your mom hasn't called much, has she?" Jed said. "Since you showed her the angel."

Gina stared out the window.

"I mean, wasn't that the whole point of the tattoo? You, breaking free?"

"You know what?" Gina said. "I bet if she'd had a choice, Nikki would've never had me in the first place. Birth control was banned in Romania back then—so that way all good communist women could add numbers to the workforce, I guess. Born anywhere else I would've been a goner, guaranteed."

Jed thumped his chest with his thumb. "*I'm* glad you're here."

She met his blue eyes. Rewarded him with a half smile.

"Don't let that mother-daughter thing get to you," he said. "Here's a thought for you. What if we started saving up for a move to Florida, or Montana, or—"

"What about Seattle?"

"You serious? I've got an uncle named Vince, lives in the Pacific Northwest. He's a police sergeant, and he's always saying how it won't stop raining there, just year-round liquid sunshine. But he swears it's more majestic than you can imagine."

Gina bit into her sandwich, used fingers to remove dangling melted cheese. She had no idea where the Seattle idea had come from. She'd seen pictures, sure. Watched the Seahawks play on TV, listened to grunge. Something about the place appealed to her; more accurately, it called to something within her.

She changed the subject. "Did you get that project done?"

"For Mr. Carrington? Yeah, he seems stoked about it, so that's a good thing." Jed slurped from his mug. "What about you? How'd it go down in the salt mines?"

She'd fought off onslaughts of nausea most of the day, but she skipped over that tidbit. Instead she rattled off some of the silly questions she'd received from tourists and told about a woman's ear-piercing shriek as bats swooped by.

On the final tour of her shift, deep inside the mountain, Gina had basked near the plummeting crescendo of the falls, in the cool kisses of its artificially lit, ruby-red mist. While her group *oohed* and *ahhed* and took photos, she stood off to the side and closed her eyes. It felt safe there, underground. A cocoon.

It also brought back primal memories: *quaking earth . . . fabric rending . . . moisture on her parched tongue.*

Now, she had only a vague queasiness to remind her of the day's earlier turmoil. No use saying anything to Jed about it. Wouldn't help to complain, or to worry him. The upset stomach could've come from food poisoning or the twenty-four-hour flu.

What'd it matter? She always rebounded from this sort of stuff. Tomorrow, she was convinced, she would wake up healthy as ever.

The sickness returned at dawn. In a sheen of sweat, Gina stumbled to the bathroom and faced the toilet on her knees. She puked once. Then again.

The convulsive nature of her malady left her drained, and each movement was an effort that set her head spinning. She held on. Stared down at mauve- and cream-colored tiles, where shorn whiskers from Jed's electric shaver formed a haphazard dark-brown sprinkle.

Lovable Jed Turney. Messy, mind-on-other-things Jed.

He was at work already. She was alone, with a few hours before the start of her Wednesday shift. No one could see her here, hunched, with bedraggled hair, and knuckles white around the porcelain rim.

She felt insignificant. Humbled, and lowly.

What was going on? Was God punishing her for the tattoo, or the live-in boyfriend, or her myriad other sins—as listed in the Book of Nikki? Had last year's confrontation with the business end of a moving van inflicted damage to her internal organs? Or . . .

She did the math. Put the pieces together in her mind.

Is it even possible? Could I be . . . ?

Gina's whisper filled the bathroom: "I think I'm pregnant."

CHAPTER
TWENTY-FOUR

Arad

Collectors were unable to read minds. Sure, that presented some challenges, but who needed omniscience? Really. It was such a crutch.

Erota, after eons of practice, had little trouble discerning individuals' weaknesses. Follow their steps, their eyes, their hands. Eventually, actions betrayed a person's desires with all the clarity of that sign she'd seen on TV, the one in New York City's Times Square, scrolling thoughts and motives in blazing color for all who cared—or dared—to look.

"Let's have some fun," she suggested to her sister.

In three days Erota and Domna would be returning to Kiev by train, and soon after Erota would be on her way to the United States. To Atlanta. Maybe even with a chance to visit New York City someday.

Why not have one last hurrah together, here in Arad? Hunters and prey. Wasn't that what their father had spoken of?

Domna was a willing participant. "What've you got in mind?"

In the predawn hours, the pair of long-legged teenagers trailed Benyamin home. He was still woozy from the incident in the Cetatea chapel, knees wobbly, eyes watery. He closed the metal gate with exaggerated care, then disappeared inside.

The girls waited. At daybreak he reemerged with his son, climbed into a Peugot sedan, and headed off, presumably for work and school.

"Let's see what his wife's up to."

"She'll be out soon enough, Domna. Give it a few minutes."

Sure enough, Mrs. Dalia Amit appeared with empty canvas bags over her arm. She locked the gate, then shuffled along cracked sidewalks toward the corner market, folds of skin swaying beneath her chin. According to Megiste's assertions, this woman might already be victim to thorns of her own—perhaps a cantankerous vine of bitterness rooted in Mr. Amit's alcohol abuse—but that in no way dissuaded Erota from the pursuit of blood and personal pleasure. In fact, it might even simplify the procedure.

"There she is," Erota said. "As expected."

Domna tipped her sunglasses. "My, she's a plain woman, isn't she?"

"Good thing *we* don't get any older, huh?"

"I'd rather die than look like that."

"You," Erota said, "are so shallow."

"Look at her. It's no wonder our friend Benyamin drinks. You and I, we know how men are, and to be honest, I'm surprised that's his only vice."

"All it takes is one."

"True enough," Domna said. "What's hers, do you think?"

"We keep on her trail long enough, and I'm sure she'll give herself away."

They did. And she did.

It started at an outdoor bazaar. Dalia bought bulk paprika from a wizened woman in a thick wool coat . . . and made every effort to avoid contact with those dark gypsy hands. At the bakery, she told her afternoon plans to an acquaintance . . . while her eyes passed judgment upon the woman's revealing blouse and caked mascara. Dalia even angled her body away, separating herself from this obvious hussy.

To the baker, she grumbled: *"N-aveti piine proaspata?"*

The bread's freshness was not above scrutiny from insufferable Mrs. Amit.

Browsing a rack of fried donuts, *gogosi*, Erota and Domna listened and observed. They each selected a goody—why not indulge their taste buds, as part of the disguise?—then convened outside.

This would be too easy, they agreed. If any one foible offered more prospects for subversion and distortion, they couldn't think of what it was.

Oh, the potential in an overblown sense of piety.

Benyamin Amit chased two aspirin with a glass of water, smoothed back his hair, and jaunted down the marble stairway. His sidearm's reassuring weight shifted in the holster against his ribs. On the third floor of city hall, his superior was locked behind double doors for a committee meeting, leaving Benyamin unsupervised for the next forty-five minutes.

Enough time to visit his favorite doe-eyed archivist.

He eased into the file room on the building's lower floor. Aside from the dull throbbing between his temples, he felt better than he had in days. No limp. No itch. On his heel, the scar was nothing but a sunken depression beneath tan socks.

"Helene?

"*Buna zuia.*" She rose from her seat. "*Ce mai faci?*"

"And a good day to you," he replied from the doorway. He gripped the lapels of his suit jacket. "I'm doing well. Very well, in fact."

"Is that so?"

He gave a sly grin. "Last night relieved quite the burden, you know."

She checked the hallway behind him, then propped herself against the corner of her desk, with legs crossed beneath a long skirt. Behind her, a brass nameplate read *Helene Totorcea*. "I'm surprised you remember much," she said.

"I don't."

"Why so happy, then?"

"Today's a fresh start," he said.

In the Cetatea's chapel, Benyamin had experienced a groggy epiphany brought on by deep swallows and a mellifluous fire. He'd satisfied the beast within, bought off his demons, and today he felt like a man freed from chains. The coiled desire had abated, and he no longer needed the drink. Not now, not ever again. Of that, he was quite certain.

This morning, staring at his wife's rigid back in bed, he had decided to change his ways. Dalia deserved better. While she'd overstepped by dumping his liquor supplies, she had only responded out of hurt and frustration. Who could blame her?

"I suppose," he told Helene, "I'm happy to be starting over. The best tuica, it lays the memories to rest. So there it is. I have no more use for it. I apologize if I left you in an awkward situation last night, but I had to test the quality of the case. I must've passed out on the pew. When I awoke, I was curled up and shivering, all alone, but satisfied once and for all."

"Is that so? I'm glad you enjoyed it."

"*Multumesc.*"

"You're welcome, Ben. I make it my goal to deliver the best."

"There is one other thing, you know. A cloudy scene in my mind."

"Oh?"

"It's just that you're a single woman, quite attractive, and I can't expect you to remain detached from your feelings when we keep meeting like this. Yet, I am married. No way around the fact. And yes, if you don't mind me mentioning it, I'm quite sure you gave me a kiss before you left the chapel."

"On your foot, you mean."

"Your lips, Helene—they're quite soft."

"You were nursing a limp. I meant it as a friendly gesture."

"Good, then. We have an understanding." He drew up his shoulders. "Maybe in another life, there could've been something between you and me."

"Dear, sweet Ben." With eyes impish and round, she leaned forward and rested a hand on his arm. A trace of brackish odor reached his nostrils.

Was that him? He should shower when he got home this evening.

"You have only one life to live," she said. "Don't squander it."

Only one life . . . only one . . .

As he left her office, his ears rang with those words. They were barbs, hooked in and tugging. A warning, of course, but also an invitation to come away from the drudgery. What husband didn't wonder if he still had the goods to snag a desirable woman's attention? It was a survival trait, an aging male assuring himself he could still attract, still perpetuate his line.

One life . . . Don't squander it . . .

Had Benyamin done just that? Squandering what had been given him? True, he'd put a roof over his family's heads, but he had little connection with his son, Dov. It'd been two years since their last camping trip. As for him and Dalia, they functioned more as tolerating flatmates than loving husband and wife.

Dear, sweet Ben . . . only one life . . .

He paused at the end of the hallway, turned, then headed back toward Helene's office. He would go in, close the door, and make himself available.

One step closer. Two. Left, right, left.

He pulled up short. What was he thinking? How easily an epiphany could fall by the wayside.

He swiveled back around and darted up the stairs to his superior's office on the third floor. The boss was still in chambers.

Benyamin picked up the phone and dialed Dalia. He caught her as she was coming in from the morning errands. When he apologized for his behavior the previous evening, she broke down in tears. She was a stalwart woman. Never much of a crier. He fumbled with his response, better equipped to handle harsh exchanges than to soothe the sensitivities of a female.

It was a good sign, though. She still loved him, still cared.

"We should go out as a family," he said. "Every day you cook for us, putting hearty meals on our table. You know, I think it's time we dine out in style."

"Are you saying you don't appreciate the—"

"Not at all," he cut her off. "I only mean to give you an evening off."

"Please," Dalia said. "Don't kid around, Benyamin. Enough of this."

"I'm serious. We could go tonight, but I have an appointment, a possible side job to earn us some extra money. Perhaps Friday, then. Dov won't have any school the next morning, so we can stay out late. Even catch a movie if you like."

"Oh, I don't know."

"Come on," he said. "Live a little. It'll be good for Dov."

"A good example is what he needs, not some filth on the screen."

He lowered his voice. "It'd be nice to see you dressed up, with high heels."

"Heels? Honestly, Ben. Are you all right?"

"And maybe a dab of that perfume you used to wear."

"I . . . Well, it has been months since I let my hair down."

"I like it long."

"What's gotten into you?"

"Friday, Dalia. Six o'clock? Yes, six should work. I'll be sure to get off early and come by for the two of you."

She agreed; then emotion welled again in her voice.

Please, Ben thought, *not another outburst*. After making it this far through the conversation unscathed, he feared disrupting things with a wrong tone or misfired word. Best to stop while he was ahead. "Good-bye," he said. And hung up.

Predator and prey. The age-old dance.

"You say she was coming this way?" Erota double-checked.

"Chugging along on those stubby legs of hers," Domna said. "She's not fast, but the old cow's steady. She'll be rounding that corner any moment."

Erota and Domna had skipped ahead, anticipating Dalia Amit's movements. Earlier, the woman had unloaded her groceries at home, then returned on foot to the wide stretches of Revolutiei Boulevard. She was now heading toward this *piata*, this square, on the other side of the impressive State Theater.

The sisters were seated on a bench that faced the war monument, watching shoppers and businesspeople bustle by. On overgrown grass, lovers reclined with eyes only for each other, while a couple on the monument's concrete steps perused a tourist map and argued in English.

Erota couldn't place the accent. American? Australian? When she got to the States, she would practice to differentiate such things.

All in good time. Which she had plenty of.

Though time was a factor for any Collector, its importance was tempered by a patience unknown to their human hosts. Another few minutes? A week? A year or two? In the expanse of history, it was all relative. Ariston and his small cluster had waited nearly two millennia for an opportunity outside the Akeldama caves. Prior to that, each of them had spent time in restless wandering, each had blundered, even endured a brief porcine detour at the Sea of Kinneret.

Humans, on the other hand, seemed controlled by the clock. It measured their accomplishments and intensified their failures. It added worth to relationships, while sapping monetary value from most inanimate things. People were paid according to time clocks. Awakened by alarms. The city trolleys ran on posted schedules.

"Look at them," Erota said now to her sister. "Hurrying, always hurrying. Do they think they'll outrun time?"

"Don't waste energy trying to understand the way their brains work."

"But it's helpful, Domna. Anything for a peek into their motives."

"Who needs a peek?" The younger teen flaunted her legs and tossed back her brunette waves. "They're not half as complicated as they like to believe. Food, shelter, a good romp in the sack, and a few pats on the back . . . What else do they need?"

"Years of therapy, when we're done with them."

Domna laughed.

"There she is." Erota combed back her own hair. "Where's she going?"

"Stop already, stop."

"What?"

"You're trying to get inside her head again. You and your hunger for details. Just watch, Erota. She'll make her intentions clear. You'll see."

Thirty seconds later, the sturdy Mrs. Amit was standing before the window of Coandi's ice cream shop, on an avenue along Avram Iancu Square. She seemed to be debating with herself, pacing past the entry twice. At last, she nosed inside.

"What'd I tell you?"

"Okay," Erota said. "But what now, O great strategizer?"

"We'll wing it."

Erota rolled her eyes. As her vision swung back down, she caught slight movement in the lawn beside the park bench—a brown-black oval, crablike, no bigger than a peppercorn. She remembered Megiste's reference to ticks and thought back to the research she'd done on these efficient little bloodsuckers. Parasites, in general, were one of her most cherished subjects.

She propped sunglasses on her forehead. "I have a better plan," she said.

"Do I even want to know?"

"See that tick, on that blade of grass? In this cold season, I'm sure it's hungry. When Mrs. Amit comes out, I want you to drive her past this spot. I'll be waiting."

"You're kidding? That's disgusting."

"I'm thirsty."

"Any suggestions," Domna asked, "on how I get her over here?"

"Be creative. You want me to do all your thinking for you, little sis?"

Domna curled her lip and started to respond, then pointed out a dog that was panting on the steps beneath the statue. "What about him? I could use him to chase her across the square."

"Too mild. Look, he's not even worried about those pigeons there."

"I'll get him to do what I want."

"If you say so."

Domna did manage to catch the creature's eye, but he glanced away in bland rejection of the gesture. Even a witless four-legger had his standards.

"Fine." Domna flipped her hair. "What about that mutt beneath the trees?"

"He's growling, at least. And ugly as sin."

"Good."

"Once we've switched hosts," Erota said, "it's going to appear that we're just two teenagers snoozing in the sun. We'll be vulnerable out in public like this, so you'll have to return quickly. If you drape an arm over me, that should keep passersby from interfering with my abandoned shell. I'll be back in a few hours."

"I hope so. If not, I'll have to cart your body to the Cetatea for the night."

"You'd never make it."

Domna glanced at her sister. "You really think this'll work?"

"Sure. I mean, if Ariston can put a mosquito to use, I know I can work with a tick. They're active all over Romania, so I'm sure this one will know exactly what to do. All that's required of me is to hang on for the ride."

"Ughh. Erota, you really have no shame."

"One of my very best qualities."

Dalia examined the flavors on display in the glass case. Coandi was her favorite ice cream shop. She'd browsed along the boulevard, found an atomizer of the perfume her husband liked so much, and was now ready to treat herself. A mild winter day would not stop her.

"Cantaloupe and melon," she ordered.

The first nibble from the spoon waltzed with subtle sweetness on her tongue. After months of deprivation, it was a sensory overload. Fruits and sugars in a delightful blend.

"Mmmm."

Another, slower, more tantalizing taste.

"*Este foarte bun,*" she exclaimed.

Very good, indeed. Yet her own sounds of pleasure worried her. A woman in strict control of her urges, she considered diet a spiritual and practical reflection of her beliefs; thus, in her mind, this indulgence bordered upon carnality.

Perhaps if she had waited for her son Dov to get out of school, she could've brought him along and justified such enjoyment for his sake. She'd justified the perfume purchase with thoughts of her husband's appreciation.

But she had *not* waited. Her selfish desire was exposed for all to see.

She took three more bites before deciding she was done.

Heaven help her. Dalia Amit reminded herself that she was a woman of moral fortitude and that such indulgence was obscene. She wetted a napkin, wiped her lips, then headed for the door. As she escaped Coandi's tasty temptations, she took with her a bittersweet sense of victory. She was denying her flesh. Her walls were back in place, patched, so that few would ever know how close she'd come to crumbling.

Well, yes, she felt good about that. Rather smug, in fact.

That's when she spotted the dog, a mangy beast with a predatory stare above bared yellow canines. It crouched, hairs bristling and ears laid back.

"Good girl," Dalia said.

The creature snapped its fangs.

Dalia backed her way around a parked car, clutched the bagged perfume to her chest, and fled in a stiff-legged gait toward the nearby square.

CHAPTER
TWENTY-FIVE

Chattanooga

Gina stared at the pregnancy test, watched the indicator window respond to the hormones in her urine. Although these things could be inaccurate, it was hard to deny matching responses from three separate brands.

Knocked up? Check.

With child? Check.

El prego? Read the rosy-red plus sign and weep.

In this same bathroom where the little tyke had first made his or her presence known, Gina felt a gasp/cry/laugh catch in her throat.

Would she be a good mother? Or another Nikki?

She clasped a hand over the thin scar on her arm. Then, reaching down, she plucked her dagger from its sheath, let it rattle into the sink, where its blade bounced coins of light from the overhead vanity. She thought of hiding the weapon, even burying or locking it away.

What if being a parent made you go loony? What if you found your-self doing anything in your power to curb your child's negative inclinations? Could an infant's needs in the womb throw off your own chemical balance, until later, after the delivery, you found yourself capable of doing crazy things, out-of-control things, like those mothers you saw on the news, who caved beneath the expectations?

Nikki had been over the top in her attempts to shield Gina, to enforce religious extremes upon her. Gina knew she would not do that to her child.

Faith was to be shared, not shoved.

Though part of Gina wanted to toss out belief along with the superstitious ways of her mother, she could not deny a sense of the divine hidden deep within her. She feared embracing it. Would it burn her? Would it demand more than she was capable of? Would it corrode her mind and encourage an existence bereft of intelligent interaction?

Scarier still, would it mold her into a fanatic?

Gina knew she could never allow that, could never wield a knife and tell her child it was God's will. She would rather die first.

As of yet, no one knew she was pregnant. With a withdrawal from her savings and a "routine" doctor visit, she could sweep this away. Her stomach was still flat and tight, her breasts still small, with no indications of becoming milk wagons.

Would they ever get bigger? She seemed to be a late bloomer.

She braced her arms on either side of the sink and, despite the internal tug-of-war she'd anticipated, felt nothing. With so much at stake, she was immobilized.

She didn't have to rush, she told herself. She could just sit tight. For all she knew, this baby could be fated for greatness. Wasn't that a reason for keeping a child? Imagine if Bach had never entered the world? Or Shakespeare?

I could also be carrying the next Hitler.

Gina broke away from that thought, disturbing on so many levels.

She turned instead to the mystery of chess, where no two games were alike, where risk was involved at every turn, and brilliancy often revealed itself in the most desperate of moments. She pictured herself sitting at the checkered board, then toppling her king in resignation before committing to even one move.

But where was the adventure in that?

Nope. Not her style. The royal game, like life, was an act of calculated recklessness. Despite the best-laid plans, life surprised you. And when it did, you adjusted and made a decision and saw it through to the end.

A rule of chess: *If you touch it, you move it. No take backs.*

She ran her fingers beneath her shirt, resting her palm over her navel in hopes of detecting some proof of life. Her stomach was warm, expanding slightly as she breathed. Was there a baby in there? It seemed unreal.

"Hi there," she whispered.

Even though she felt nothing, she believed.

CHAPTER
TWENTY-SIX

Arad

Any moment now. Erota was on the alert. In most scenarios, predators were superior to their prey—stronger, larger, faster—but none of that applied here. If all went as planned, Mrs. Dalia Amit would be herded in this direction shortly, an easy target for a diminutive hunter.

Erota was a tick. A hard-bodied *Ixodes ricinus*. From the park bench, she had eyeballed this opportunistic little beast and found herself a new host.

She was now clinging to a blade of grass in the lawn that bordered the plaza. Her world had shrunk in size, her perch swaying in a breeze that seemed like a hurricane wind but was probably the draft of a passing truck.

Thunderous vibrations. Were those approaching footsteps?

Drawing closer, almost here.

She quavered. Her front legs contained sensory structures that were sensitive to every variance in thermal and chemical stimuli. She felt the ambient temperature rising, even as the tremors reached earthshaking proportions. She registered tart odors that could be signals of fear—from Mrs. Amit?—or the aggression of a dog.

Do your job, little sis. Herd her right past this spot.

Beneath Erota, around her, the host was tensing for an ambush. The timing would have to be impeccable. Erota was trusting the tick's natural instincts as much as her own. She knew these things could latch onto a victim's skin in fractions of a second.

She smelled blood now. Recognized it as human.

Pumpity-pump.

The tick let go.

Tiny legs found purchase on a passing giant of a person. From this vantage point, everything lost perspective. The massive mound of flesh swung through the air, then pounded down—swung, pounded, swung. Erota could only assume they had hooked onto Dalia's leg as she was chased by Domna's snarling host.

The tick was moving up, up, up. After weaving between fields of course thread, it ducked into a humid patch of black hair and fatty rolls.

The armpit. A favorite location.

Together with her host, Erota dove headfirst into her work. There was little else to consume their shared, primitive will.

Using tiny pairs of legs to hook into the epidermal surface, she injected a dose of anesthetizing toxin—similar to that in a Collector's saliva—and began her withdrawal. Erota knew a female tick was capable of absorbing one to two hundred times her own body mass in fresh blood, and she fed with glutinous abandon.

Drink till you're full, till you can take no more in, till you've reached the point of bursting, and then drink, drink, drink some more.

This was how tick-borne encephalitis found its way into the body. She'd read about it. TBE, a growing threat across Europe, incubated for days and then manifested itself in headaches, dripping sinuses, fever, and/or aching joints. Eventually, long-term neurological complications could arise.

Drink till you're bloated . . .

Warm and thick. Intoxicating.

Erota had supped from numerous sources over the years, and so she never took for granted a free-flowing stream such as this. It was a blessed reprieve from the contaminated veins in Ukraine or the chemical sludge that crept through the drug-addicted. She could still remember the acrid morsel of HIV virus that had filled her mouth during their first attack outside the Akeldama.

A mercy killing. She and the others had put the man out of his misery.

And already, thousands of Romanian orphans were rumored to have a rare strain of the same virus. All mysteriously infected in 1989. The reported epidemic was cause for the Akeldama Cluster's celebration.

Drink, drink, drink . . .

Erota tucked deeper into the pores of this Israeli woman. She discovered robust flavor. It was apparent that Dalia had taken care of basic nutritional needs and avoided artery-clogging cholesterol. Regardless, Erota knew she would leave here in an hour or two dissatisfied. Stretched to her limit, a vampire with flushed skin and distended belly, she would find herself longing for more.

She was insatiable, inconsolable.

Where was the cup that could quench her once and for all?

She'd found sickness, in subtle traces, working its way through the bodies of all she dined upon. Even from the healthiest of victims, sustenance was temporary, wetting the tongue, the throat, then hanging her out to dry.

The thorn's content in the chapel?

It had slaked her thirst for an entire day at best.

More fleeting still were regular meat and drink. She was no longer Separated from the physical rapture of flavors upon her tongue; yet each swallow funneled through a digestive tract that broke down and dissolved things in minutes. Food simply disintegrated within this undead vessel.

Thus, as a revenant, Erota had no need to excrete waste—for which she was grateful, considering her acute sense of smell—but her shell ran on eternal empty.

Only blood, that vital fluid, could be absorbed and put to use.

Whiffs of Nazarene Blood were the most torturous, hinting at something dense and rich, something fortifying for Those Who Resist. While for her and the other Collectors, that substance was anathema. Would she ever forget the crumbling remains of crooked-smiled Salome? Or Shelamzion's wails of grief?

These thoughts only added up to a migraine.

Well, it was no use ruminating on such matters. They were not open for discussion in the Houses of Eros or Ariston, and disgruntled members learned to keep their mouths shut. Except for when they were feeding.

The tick kept burrowing. Erota kept drinking, swelling.

She also injected a poison of her own. Soon, a thorny tangle would take root in Dalia's body, exploiting her flaws and filtering blood for the nourishment, albeit temporary, of the Akeldama Cluster.

Benyamin had twenty-five minutes till his off-hours appointment at Café Focsani, near Reconcilierii Park. During communism's heyday, men in high places and low had learned to take advantage of under-the-table opportunities, and such transactions continued to be business as usual.

Turn a blind eye. Shake hands. Pass along a wad of Romanian *lei*.

Why not? So long as no one was hurt.

He thought of Dalia and Dov. If he could skim off enough money from this exchange, he would take them to Sinaia for winter holidays. How remarkable it would be to ski the Bucegi mountains together or to stroll through Peles Castle's grandeur. Dalia would also want to see the town's famed monastery, and of course he would oblige her.

Farewell to his demons. He was making a fresh start.

Before departing city hall, Benyamin sat in the locked office and field-stripped his pistol. This Makarov PM was his companion, a semiautomatic with an eight-round magazine. The pistol's weight reduced recoil and provided greater accuracy.

Best to be prepared, he figured. Be cautious.

The truth was, people *were* hurt during such transactions. Why should he trust anyone willing to violate the established rules of democracy?

He dismantled the gun, removed the grips, and used steaming water from a plug-in coffeemaker to clean the components. The weapon was inexpensive and easy to use, but susceptible to corrosive salts.

It had other idiosyncrasies, as well. With a free-floating firing pin, there was the danger of an accidental discharge if dropped on its muzzle, and it was unwise to engage the safety lever while the hammer was cocked, since this action would cause the hammer to drop.

Stories circulated of men who had shot off their toes this way. Other parts too. Though Benyamin was sure those were only rumors.

He completed his task, loaded 9x18mm ammo, then pulled back the slide and engaged the safety. Ready to go. He holstered the Makarov, a grin splitting his face as he slipped his arms into his jacket. Already, he could taste that brisk mountain air.

Beneath Dalia's arm, lost in a near-microscopic world of survival, Erota was unable to judge the passing of the hours. She sensed voicelike vibrations along the ribs, a steady drone, and assumed the woman was speaking. Perhaps she'd stopped by the Arad Synagogue to utter *piyyutim*, penitential prayers, for her ice-cream escapade.

Beautiful guilt. A razor in an apple.

Didn't the Christian Bible speak of a guilt that led to death? It was a cancer that fed on itself, one that Collectors had tasted of and learned to nurture in others. Not that it needed much upon which to thrive. It was a resilient little beast.

Erota backed out from Dalia's pore. Time, she decided, to find her way back to her own slumbering body on the bench in Avram Iancu Square.

One problem: as a tick, she had no idea of her present whereabouts. Her sensory clues consisted of little more than hair follicles, pungent smells, and varying temperatures. Road signs were beyond her range of comprehension.

Where was she now?

At 986 Armpit Avenue, just north of Flab Circle.

To return to the park bench, she could always hop onboard another human, but there would be no guarantee of going in the right direction. From her tiny perspective, she could look for an animal—a squirrel, or a fluttering sparrow—and hope to guide it, using visual markers from her knowledge of the city.

But what if the squirrel was struck by a car? While it was only the loss of a permanent host that resulted in banishment, Erota would still be left floating in the ether, navigating shadows and capricious wind currents on her trek to the plaza.

This was why she avoided using secondary hosts. Too many drawbacks.

Since modern history's beginning on this pathetic celestial sphere, many Collectors had cashed in on the human species' advantages. There was nothing more efficient and flexible than a two-legger with half a brain.

It was settled, then. She detected nearing warmth, saw an outline that looked promising. Her legs gripped the cloth of Mrs. Amit's coat and prepared for the jump.

The tick showed no interest.

Now, she directed. *Go. Don't just sit here.*

The warmth faded as the outline moved on by. Maybe the gap had exceeded the tick's ability. Then the hard-bodied creature was descending, down, down, down, until Erota found herself on a vast expanse of cloth that tossed like an ocean wave, back and forth.

The fringe of the woman's dress? That had to be it.

Another figure approached, brushing alongside in splotched shades of rust and dark brown. The heat grew intense, as measured through Erota's sensory organs. She peered across the divide and decided this must be a cat.

She made visual contact with a pair of yellow feline eyes—*Please, let me ride along*—and found unreserved acceptance.

She was in. Good-bye, tick. Hello, tomcat.

Yellow Eyes needed no help finding his way through the late after-noon foot traffic. He padded along, slinking beneath parked vehicles, hissing at children who crossed his path. He owned the alleyways and low brick walls. At least one other cat showed signs of hosting a Collector, and Erota figured that the local cluster must be making good use of the numerous animals prowling the streets.

At last. There was the war monument, the square, the park bench.

And Domna.

"You're a pretty thing," Domna said, leaning down to scratch the cat's chin, her cleavage visible in a low-cut blouse. "Sis, I hope that's you. I've been fighting off these Latin lover boys for two hours now."

Yellow Eyes snubbed Domna's kindness and sprang instead into the lap of Erota's slouched body. Nothing like door-to-door service.

CHAPTER
TWENTY-SEVEN

Arad

"Cal Nichols?"

"Just Nickel."

"Buna seara." Benyamin switched to English. "I didn't expect *you* here."

He perused Café Focsani's seating area, where candles burned in bronze holders on lacquered tables, and dark chocolate and coffee aromas permeated the air. In the corner, a couple was deep in conversation, with eyes only for each other.

"Good to see you too, man. Thanks for showing up."

"You still look like a kid."

"The secret's in good hair products," Nickel said. "Buy stock now."

"Hmmph."

"Don't be a stranger. Here, take a seat. I won't bite."

Bite? The word triggered latent fears, heightened by a flare of pain in Benyamin's ankle. He transferred his distrust onto this foreigner with the flaxen hair and the face of eternal youth. He lowered himself into a seat, wary, yet comforted by the pistol nuzzled beneath his left arm.

After ordering, the two men faced each other over iced espresso drinks.

"Why did you come here?" Benyamin asked.

"Same reason as you. To work a deal."

"On the phone, you had me fooled. You sounded Romanian."

"Hey, in my line of work, you use whatever'll get someone's attention. You have any idea how hard it is to nab a minute of someone's time nowadays? Shoot, I'd speak Pygmy to an Eskimo if that's what it took."

"Everyone's busy trying to survive," Benyamin said.

"Survive?" Nickel snorted. "If people only knew how easy they had it. Hundred years ago, we didn't even know what a car was. Electric stoves? Forget it. A shower every stinkin' day? Not a chance."

"You Americans and your preoccupation with bathing."

"All part of our puritanical background. Cleanliness is next to godliness."

"Now you sound like my wife."

"It was a joke, Mr. Amit. A touch of irony."

"Ironing?"

"Always a good idea," Nickel gibed. "If you're dressing for success."

Benyamin furrowed his brow and took a long draw from his glass. What was the purpose of this rendezvous? What was Cal Nichols up to?

He noted a JanSport daypack tucked beneath the American's chair. The man had to be in his late twenties by now, yet he hadn't aged a day since their meeting on the shores at Ein Bokek. He was wearing Converse tennis shoes, Bugle Boy jeans, and a T-shirt that read: *All who wander are not lost . . . J. R. R. Tolkien.*

"I would like to know how you found me."

Nickel stabbed at his own chest with a thumb. "Intel broker, remember? I can track down just about any*one* or any*thing*."

"Tell me, does this have to do with our findings at the Dead Sea?"

"Wow. You're good."

"I want no part of it," Benyamin said. "Those are images I'd rather forget."

"Me too."

"Then why're you here, Nickel?"

"Forgetting is not always an option." The kid fetched a leather pouch from his pack, slid it across the table. "Go ahead, and take a look."

Benyamin loosened the drawstring. Removed a jeweled armband.

Hammered from gold, the thick, open-ended hoop had a dull gleam. Precious gems studded the exterior, capturing beams from the overhead track lighting and refracting them in prismatic shapes across the table's dark surface. Benyamin was no appraiser, but the vibrant colors and clarity indicated these were rubies and diamonds worth more than he could earn in a lifetime.

"It's stunning," he said.

"It doesn't belong here."

"I agree." Benyamin handed the pouch back, tossing a glance over his shoulder. The café was still virtually empty. "It should be locked in a safe."

"It *should* be back in Jerusalem. But where do you think I found it, huh? Any guesses? Right here-o in your own backyard-o."

"I'm not sure I understand. I live in an apartment."

"Ha! That's good. You're a funny guy."

Benyamin stared straight ahead.

"No." Nickel backpedaled. "What I meant is that the armband was used to buy an old vineyard near Lipova, maybe twenty miles . . . uh, let's see, thirty kilometers from here." He opened a folder of recon photos. "You ever been to the ruins of Soimos? You can see the property from up there. The purchaser's name was Mr. Flavius Totorcea, but I'd betcha that's a cover. I mean, how does a Romanian winemaker end up with an artifact like this?"

"Maybe he's into antiques. He could be a collector."

"A Collector." Nickel barked out a wry laugh. "Yeah, you got that right."

Benyamin scratched his heel against a table leg and wondered if the bar served anything stronger than this coffee concoction.

"I'm in places all around the world, my eyes peeled for certain things— well, one thing in particular." Nickel waved his hand, as though to wipe that statement from the air. "I've held Templar relics, Egyptian treasure, and trinkets of the tsars. But this baby here, it's unique. Experts took a look and dated it to the first century AD, even isolated clay and lime particles matching the soil's properties there."

"Where? What soil?"

"The Field of Blood. In the Valley of Hinnom. The very place that Norwegian kid bulldozed into before getting torn apart. His work buddy—you remember Thiago, the Brazilian?—he turned up the day after you and I talked. Even worse shape than the kid. Missing an eye. Throat ripped out. His body wasn't far from the tombs, buried under a coupla inches of dirt."

"Please tell me you apprehended the culprit."

"Culprits. With an s. There were eighteen individual bite patterns."

"Eighteen?"

"Pretty sick, huh?"

"There should be a separate chamber of hell for such people."

"Prisons of darkness," Nickel mumbled.

"Excuse me?"

"It's a passage from the book of Jude."

"Not familiar with it. Tell me this: have the killers been locked away?" The shake of the intel broker's head was nearly imperceptible.

"What?" Benyamin narrowed his eyes. "It's over seven years already."

"Longer than that," Nickel said. "We've been at this for ages."

"We?"

The American seemed to recede behind his words. His green-eyed gaze slid away, as though fleeing mistakes he would rather forget.

Chattanooga

Gina decided to keep her pregnancy a secret for now. She wasn't sure what Jed's reaction would be, and her mother could wait for the news. Much less complicated this way.

With that settled, Gina worked through her list of morning errands.

She picked up stamps at the post office, took a lunch to Jed—who, big surprise, had forgotten his bag on the kitchen counter—and stopped for an everything bagel and coffee.

No caffeine, of course. She was going to do this right.

No more liquor or beer, either, which was easy since she'd never been much of a drinker. But she would miss the occasional puffs on her coworkers' Camels.

With her chores completed, she walked onto the Walnut Street Bridge and propped one black boot against the lower railing. Beyond the next bridge, the *Southern Belle* riverboat was docking for another sightseeing cruise.

Gina tucked her skirt between her stockinged legs to keep it from catching the breeze and leaned out over the water. The Tennessee River flowed with a life of its own, curlicues and temporary ripples adding nuance to its personality. It wasn't particularly clean or clear, coursing as it did between miles of mud banks and clay, but it moved with an unhurried, unshakable purpose.

She stood straight and hugged her stomach, worried for the first time about the metal rail pressing into her middle. Her child was in there.

Did one more life really matter, though? Would it make a difference?

She gazed down in her search of an answer, mesmerized by the water's elusive swirls. Eddies were here and gone in seconds, mostly unnoticed, yet each adding to the dance, reflecting the river's essence. Each beautiful in its own way. Yes, each one mattered.

Gina's thoughts turned to Cal the Provocateur. Although it seemed illogical—maybe the hormones kicking in already—she found herself worrying about him. Cal was older than her, yet there was something boyish about him. He'd folded to her mother's wishes with childlike sub-servience, even wielding the knife upon her command.

After all these years, she still found herself going back to the moment in the Borsa safe house. Would he ever track her down as promised? What had compelled him to lead their escape from Cuvin?

Was he out there, still looking for her?

CHAPTER
TWENTY-EIGHT

Arad

The night was growing older. Benyamin drank from his iced coffee, then asked Cal Nichols across from him, "What're you implying, when you say you've been at this for ages?"

Nickel blinked. "It's a long story." The very thought seemed to tug at his countenance, to etch lines into the corners of his eyes and mouth.

And then something began to change.

Although Benyamin Amit took a rational approach to life, that didn't mean he had never faced incidents that eluded explanation. While some people carried their questions on the tips of their tongues, he preferred to shelve his until further notice. The most persistent ones he'd always dipped in alcohol, numbing them till they stopped kicking.

Now, sitting in an Eastern European cafe on a typical midweek evening, he was confronted with another of those inexplicable events.

Before his eyes, Cal Nichols began to transmogrify.

Nickel shrank back in his seat, ribs and chest collapsing between the jaws of an invisible vise. Arms curled and drew together. Wrinkles turned his smooth brow into the sun-cracked reaches of a drought-ridden land, and the gold flecks in his eyes melted and pooled into drops of quicksilver sorrow.

Except there were no tears. Only rivulets of shadow streaking his face, slices of anguish carving his cheeks.

Was this a nightmare? A premonition?

The former patrolman could come up with no logical explanation for what he was witnessing. The younger man had aged fifty years in a matter of seconds, and a loaded Makarov pistol was no protection against such alchemy.

Nickel's earlier words: *I won't bite . . .*

Benyamin figured he should wake Nickel from this ordeal. He overrode his fears and reached a consoling hand across the table, but as he did so, the man in the Tolkien T-shirt threw back his mop of wheat-colored hair, opened his mouth wide—so large and round that his teeth looked like the crenellated ramparts of a castle turret . . .

And screamed.

The tone was earsplitting, heart wrenching, pregnant with the groans of a dying planet and the horrors that washed across her shores.

It was raw, even primal, bellowing out an anguish that couldn't possibly come from one source, but perhaps from a thousand, tens of thousands—an entire generation's—indignant rage.

It was, Benyamin realized, the sound of a shofar. A ram's horn.

Despite his disinterest in religious matters, he'd heard the horn blown on numerous occasions in his homeland, for feasts and festivals. In times past, it'd also been used as a call to battle. That strident sound cut through everyday activities, awakening listeners from slumber, alerting them to coming judgment. Even now it gave him chills, and clawed at his old wound.

The shofar, as an ancient instrument, had symbolic ties to the ram that Abraham had seen caught in the thicket, just as he was going to plunge a knife into his son Isaac's heart. The ram was God's provision. A substitute. A sacrifice.

Benyamin peered around, expecting horrified or angry stares from the few people in the café, but no one seemed impressed by the Almighty's sleight of hand or the American's scream. There was no one looking this way. Everything was as it should be: the sound of steaming milk, the clink of glasses, and friendly chatter.

Café Focsani was a picture of tranquility.

Nickel, looking fresh and young, waved a hand. "You okay there, Mr. Amit?"

"Yes." Two short blinks. "I was . . . I was just thinking, I guess."

"And I haven't even got to the punch line yet."

"Punch line?"

"The part that really packs a wallop." Nickel's left fist smacked into his palm. "Usually, at the end of a joke."

"I'm not amused."

Benyamin finished his drink and pushed back from the table. He could feel his bewilderment turning to anger, and he questioned his own perceptions of what he had just witnessed. Was it a momentary case of insanity? Maybe it was drowsiness from the late night out at the Cetatea chapel. Perhaps the alcohol still in his system.

His religious grandfather would have reminded him of God's unfathomable ways and of the strange methods sometimes employed to get the attention of stubborn men.

Of course, his grandfather had died in the gas chambers.

Strange methods, indeed.

"Nickel, you misled me," Benyamin accused. "On the phone, you spoke of an opportunity that could be of great benefit to my family. That's why I came. Not for this mischief, these games, whatever it is you're playing at."

"It's no game. Your wife and son are in grave danger."

"Excuse me?"

"By working together," Nickel said, "we can minimize the threat to them. What could be more valuable than that?"

"Blackmail? Is that what you're up to?"

"I wouldn't stoop so low. Listen, I'm not claiming to be a saint. Sure,

I've got my own reasons for being here—not gonna lie to you—but I also wanna help you."

"Explain yourself." Benyamin slipped a hand beneath his jacket, fingers brushing over the holster. "Or I'll walk out that door and never look back."

"I believe there are nineteen killers, still on the loose."

"Nineteen?"

"Just listen."

Benyamin folded his arms.

Cal Nichols said, "Back at the Field of Blood, archaeologists checked out the tombs and reported a buncha ossuaries—stone boxes for the dead, reflecting burial practices from the Second Temple Period. We're talking *old*. Right around the time of Christ. All sortsa stuff in those caves. Pottery, jewelry—"

"Yes, yes. And that gold armband, Nickel. I understand."

"But of all the burial boxes, nineteen were empty. No bones, nothing."

"Grave robbers, I'm sure."

"Nah. That's just it, man. The archaeologists found no signs of plundering, not jack-diddly. I mean, yeah, there were some cremated bones tossed in by later generations, but basically these tombs had sat untouched for two thousand years."

"Tell me, what is your point?" Benyamin saw that the man and woman in the corner were still entranced by caffeine and candlelight.

"I think that the grave site was broken open, and that the two men who were there paid the price. I think we're talking about supernatural killers."

"The dead? The missing nineteen?"

"Undead. Just to be technical. One life is all you get, right?"

"What're you suggesting? Zombies from an American horror film? Vampires?"

"You tell *me*. You saw the bites on that Norwegian kid."

"You are speaking in crazy terms, Mr. Nichols. And, as you mentioned, there were only *eighteen* bite patterns on the Brazilian."

Even as Benyamin said it, he realized how far the conversation had veered from typical coffee chatter. It was all relative, wasn't it? You began talking of grisly deaths and empty graves—suddenly, numbers lost significance. Eighteen, nineteen: What did it matter?

"Yeah," Nickel confessed. "That part's got me scratching my head."

"Perhaps one of these . . . these undead went hungry."

"After thousands of years? I doubt it."

"Listen." Benyamin shook his head clear of this foolishness. "I don't want to know any more of this. I have my own life here, a good job, my family, and—"

"Your family. You cannot forget them."

"I'm not forgetting, Nickel. I'm trying to avoid whatever nonsense you are playing at. I want nothing to do with this. Why do you even waste your own time?"

"I wanna catch Lars Marka's killers, plain and simple. I'm all about bringing them to justice. And you can help me. You've seen the damage they're capable of, and you've had training from the Israeli Police."

"As a volunteer, mind you. In the Mash'az."

"Still, I gotta give it to you. You Israelis really know what you're doing."

"How else could we survive?"

"There. That's what I'm talking about. You're a junkyard scrapper, the sorta dog that grabs a person by the heel and won't leg go."

By the heel?

Benyamin tried to ignore the flare of heat along his scarred foot. There was no plausible reason Cal Nichols should know a thing about his private wound, and it was inappropriate for the American to be dragging him into this mess. Benyamin was starting fresh. He didn't need more worries.

But what if there was truth to this, that his family was in danger?

"You have one minute, Nickel. Give me your punch line."

"I believe the culprits are here, in Romania."

"You're serious."

"I wouldn't joke about it. My guess is that Flavius Totorcea—if that's even his real name—is the head of a clan that's been doing damage for years."

"Killers turned winegrowers?" Benyamin smirked. "A clever cover."

"An obvious mockery, more like. The whole thing smacks of sacrilege."

"How so?"

"In the Gospels, God is pictured as a vineyard owner. When the time comes for Him to gather those whose names are written in the Book of Life, they will feast and drink of the New Wine. In fact, Yeshua compared Himself to a vine that bears fruit, and when He was crushed for mankind's iniquity, He became that New Wine."

"You know I don't subscribe to such stories. After all, I am a Jew."

Nickel raised an eyebrow.

"A nonpracticing Jew," Benyamin qualified. "But born to a Jewish mother, so there it is, in my bloodline. A good woman too—may she rest in peace."

"Sorry to hear it. I'm out of contact with my mother."

"Life is this way. So, Nickel, now I understand the perceived sacrilege. How can you be sure, though, that these are the killers you seek? Perhaps you've watched too many of the old movies, *Nosferatu* and *Dracula*. Don't let these legends cloud your mind. They're rubbish. Harmless thrills and nothing more."

"Eighteen," Nickel said flatly. "Eighteen individual bite patterns."

Benyamin suppressed a shiver. "Okay. But why would they come here?"

"Why'd *you* come here, Mr. Amit? Maybe you followed after *them*. Drawn along without realizing it, and putting your wife and son in the line of fire."

"You are a madman. Who are you to make such accusations?"

"I'm nobody. I'm—"

"And why, exactly, would they come after *us*?"

"Because you came after them. Now, hold on a sec. I'm not saying it was intentional. Somewhere along the line, though, you got infected, and they feed upon that. They lap that stuff up. You're like the gate to your family, Mr. Amit. You've lowered the drawbridge and let the enemy in. You think they don't understand what that means?"

These indictments were ludicrous. Benyamin screwed his eyes shut, as his pulse throbbed in his temples.

"They're not your average killers," Nickel said.

Benyamin's mind flashed back: *skin covered with sores . . . yellow-green . . .*

"They want to suck the life from you," Nickel went on. "Bit by bit."

A necklace of round, puckered wounds . . .

"Even from kids. Babies." The American winced and lowered his head. When he looked up again, his face was chiseled from stone. "You know these HIV-infected orphans they've found? Thousands of them, all over Romania? No one's been able to explain why they all stem back to '89, but recent phylogenetic analysis shows that the virus had a unique nucleotide sequence and—"

"Please. This is too fast."

"Basically, it proves there was an unusual relation to a Brazilian strain of the virus, found in patients from Rio de Janeiro."

"Thiago. Was he from Rio?"

"Now you're tracking with me."

"So your theory is that Totorcea and his clan attacked Thiago in Jerusalem, became contaminated, then passed along the virus when they arrived in Romania?"

"By feeding from abandoned children," Nickel said. "That's right."

"Who *are* these people?"

"Already told you, I don't believe they're human. Or not entirely."

Benyamin huffed. "On that, we can agree. Animals show more respect."

"You're kidding, right? It's a harsh world out there. Flat-out cruel, all around. Up and down the food chain, you see the signs of a conflict raging."

"Is that so, Nickel? Are you going to lecture me on the Holocaust next?"

"Wow. Okay, I shoulda known better. My apologies."

"Just tell me, is there a way to halt the deviance of these . . . beasts?"

"Always." Nickel's eyes flashed. "I've got just the tools for the job."

"Your MTPs?"

"You got a good memory, man." Nickel fixed Benyamin in his stare. "Here's the deal. I know the methods of these undead, so I can direct you in making a stand. The catch is, I cannot intervene. For the sake of my other interests, so to speak."

"Oh? So I'm to do all the—what do you Americans call it?—the dirty work."

"Yes. While I supply weapons, tools, and intel."

"Metal tent pegs? I prefer," said Benyamin, "to leave my life as it is. I'll keep my eyes open, of course, but I think I'm smart enough to recognize if I'm being—"

"You're already working with one of them. Name Helene ring any bells?"

Benyamin swallowed. "Excuse me?"

He didn't want to hear this, didn't want to face the niggling suspicion—yet there it was. A simple nameplate: *Helene Totorcea*. He gulped at the air, reflecting upon those late-night exchanges at the Cetatea, his little deals with the devil. What had been Helene's motives? She was no killer. She couldn't be. He'd looked into her mellow eyes and seen nothing to give him pause.

"If there's any truth to this," he told Nickel, "you should take it to the authorities. The Israelis will know what to do. Present them with solid evidence."

"Evidence. Yeah well, that's hard to nail down."

"The police can help. Tell them what you know, and they can take over."

"I'm telling *you*, Mr. Amit. You used to be a patrolman with one of the finest forces in the world. And now that you're involved at Arad's city hall, you could come in handy accessing private records." Nickel folded his arms and leaned them on the table. "As for me, I'm not backing off. This is my life, or what's left of it. It's what I do."

"So far, it would seem you've failed."

"True." The American's eyes darkened. "Very true. But I can't go back and change what I've done. All I can do is try to change what's ahead."

"Let it go. That's my suggestion. Let someone else step in."

"Why not you?" Nickel shot back. "Every little contribution helps. And, what? You think if you just ignore that itch of yours that it'll disappear? Wrong-o."

The shape of Nickel's mouth around the last syllable made Benyamin think again of the shofar's blast. A call to arms. He looked off over the man's shoulder, afraid that if they locked eyes, he may reveal something of his own affliction. Even now, a needle seemed to be poking from his scar, threatening to puncture his skin.

"What itch? I'm fine," Benyamin said. "I'm making a fresh start."

"Sure. Except you won't get very far on your own. Think of your wife. And your son—he's turning into quite the little man, isn't he?"

"What do you know of my family?"

"I know they're important. The way I see it, you can sit back by yourself and act like everything's A-OK, or you can join me as part of Those Who Resist. The two of us? I'm telling you, we'd make a potent team."

Benyamin shoved away from the table, slapped down a bill to cover his drink. "I said it earlier, Nickel. I'm not interested in playing such games."

He strode from the café into the darkness, his holstered gun thudding against his chest. Statues commemorating martyrs and revolutionaries stood in silent evaluation and marked his escape from Reconcilierii Park.

CHAPTER
TWENTY-NINE

Two nights later, Dalia stood at the front gate and clutched Dov's hand in hers. She wore slightly elevated heels and a cornflower-blue dress. Light perfume wafted about the hair she had brushed out, each stroke a massage for a scalp accustomed to austere stylings.

"You look nice, Mama," her son said in their native Hebrew.

"*Todah*," she thanked him. "And you are a fine-looking boy."

He pulled his hand away. "I'm twelve."

"Don't take offense, Dov. In a few months you'll celebrate your bar mitzvah, and then you will be a man. A 'son of the law,' indeed."

She saw him straighten his shoulders, her little soldier boy. He wanted so much to spend time with his father, even went so far as to put on boots and hike through the house with tent and backpack strapped over his shoulders. She hoped this evening's dinner date wouldn't be another in a string of broken promises from her husband. Benyamin and his drinking. He'd strayed from the path early in the marriage—never violent, but rarely present. A poor example for their young son.

A sharp prickling ignited under her arm. She scratched at it.

Had she been bitten by something? That spot had been irritating her for the past day or two.

"There he is," Dov said. "He came."

Sure enough, Benyamin was pulling up in the family Peugot. Dalia checked her watch, saw he was only six minutes late, and rewarded him with a curt nod.

The evening began amiably. In the car, her husband gave her a wink and told her how much he liked the perfume.

She thanked him.

"And you're turning into quite the man," he said to Dov. "You and I, we need to go camping soon."

"Really?"

"Just like old times. I've been told there's some places in the foothills, north of Lipova. We could make a weekend trip of it. How would you like that?"

Dov nodded. Dalia smiled.

Dinner was at a Hungarian restaurant on Xenopol Street. The food arrived hot and on time, and the atmosphere included servers in traditional outfits and a trio of folk musicians. Dov was full of nervous excitement, vying for his father's attention. Which was fine, really, since Dalia and Benyamin had forgotten years ago how to carry on a conversation.

Trouble surfaced at the end of the meal.

An after-dinner liqueur was offered: Hungarian *palinka*. Benyamin's eyes perused the menu as he wrestled with the idea. Then, still looking down, he told the waitress, yes, he would like a drink.

"Just one," he said to his son. "To wash the food down."

Though Dov hadn't asked.

With lips pressed together, Dalia watched her husband imbibe. She tried to quell her rising ire. She rubbed a fingernail at the spot beneath her arm and figured Ben's response was to be expected, considering he walked this life alone, a secular Jew, jettisoning his trust in anyone other than himself and his beloved alcohol.

By the time he'd ordered a third glass, she was furious. She stood from the table, wrapped herself in a coat, and told him she would find her own way home.

She marched outside, past the proud columns of the Cultural Palace, to a path that meandered along the Mures River. Colored lights glittered on the water. She wound through the trees toward Eminescu Park. Named after Romania's national poet, it was a place she visited for periods of calm. She often sat here on a bench with a book, and while she adored Bet Bailik, father of Hebrew poetry, Romania's Mihai Eminescu offered his own unique take on the human condition.

She stopped. She heard a female voice. There, beneath a lamp stand, a long-legged woman with brunette hair was reading aloud from a leather-bound collection. Dalia recognized a stanza from *Luceafarul*, a poetic tale of Lucifer, the Fallen One:

> *There is nothing and yet there is*
> *a thirst which consumes him,*
> *absorbs him utterly, an abyss like*
> *blind oblivion.*

Dalia stepped into the circle of light, drawn to the relevance of these words. They pertained to Benyamin. How had she never seen that?

"Hello?" The reader looked up with almond-shaped eyes that complemented light olive skin. She seemed familiar. Perhaps they'd passed on the streets.

"I'm sorry if I've disturbed you," Dalia said. "Please, don't stop. You have a pleasant reading voice, and Eminescu's a favorite of mine."

"Some company wouldn't hurt, I suppose."

"May I sit down?"

"Of course." The woman pinned the book to her lap with one hand, reached out with the other. "My name's Erota."

"An intriguing name. I'm Dalia Amit." She planted her backside on the bench beside Erota, ignoring the discomfort beneath her arm and smoothing her dress over stout legs. Was that Benyamin's voice she heard in the distance?

She spoke in a conspiratorial hush. "If my husband wanders by, don't pay him any mind. I'm rather upset with him. He loves his drink, that man does."

"You poor thing. That must be rough on you."

"It's neither here nor there. Go on, please. I'd like to hear more."

An emerald glint showed in Erota's eyes. Probably a trick of the light, Dalia reasoned. The brunette returned her attention to the book of poetry and, over the approaching calls of a distraught spouse, read another stanza:

Would you have me come down to earth
and leave the eternal skies?
Remember that I am immortal
and you, condemned to die!

Benyamin stumbled along the walkway, warmed by the shots of palinka, and amused by his wife's dash from the scene. What a spectacle she had made of herself, and now here he was chasing after her. He'd given Dov strict orders to remain at the table in the restaurant till he got back.

So, what was the harm in one little drink?

Okay, two or three.

Benyamin caught a whiff of his wife's perfume and drew himself to a lock-kneed halt. She was nearby, hiding in the park.

"Dalia? Dear, let's go back inside."

When she failed to respond, he wobbled onward. His ankle pounded, his old wound burning with each step.

He heard a woman's gasp, one short cry, and he hurried toward it. That was his wife. She had taken a tumble, most likely, out here in the woods along the river. She was a stout woman, lacking in athleticism. One dip in the pathway could send her reeling.

"Dalia?"

Ahead, lamplight glimmered between the branches. There she was on a bench, her head lolling and eyes closed. That *was* her, wasn't it?

Who was the figure beside her, though?

And why did it look as though a thorny tangle bound them together?

As Benyamin stepped closer, the figure turned and gave him a languid smile. The other woman was young, beautiful, with a sensual mouth that glistened deep red. She ran her tongue along her lower lip and met his eye. In that moment, he felt the wound burst at his ankle and sensed something thick and crackly snaking forth.

Dalia appeared to be asleep, oblivious.

"Mr. Amit," the woman said to him. "Come join us."

"We can't stay out here," he said, thinking of Dov.

"You can share a little drink, can't you?"

"A little drink?"

"Sit down here. We'll all partake together."

His queasiness gave way to desire. The very sound of this woman's voice seemed to cool the heat at his ankle. He plopped down on the bench beside her, watched her run fingers down his leg, and then his thoughts were separating, spiraling away, carrying with them his worry and pain.

Chattanooga

"Dinner's almost ready," Jed called to Gina from the kitchen.

It was part of their agreement that he prepared the meals on Friday nights, since it was her longest shift down in the caverns of Ruby Falls.

Gina stood at the apartment window, staring over an array of city lights. She was still wearing her tour-guide uniform, and her name tag reflected her identity backward in the glass.

Her thoughts were on her mother. She loved Nikki. Always had. She'd learned from her a good work ethic and a sense of honor. She envied those high cheekbones, porcelain nose, and the shiny black hair—even if it *was* colored these days, to hide the wisps of gray.

The truth was, Gina was still a slave to Nikki's approval. Her tattoo, the black boots, and orange-dyed hair were all attempts to break free. Didn't take a shrink to figure that much out. Here she was, still worrying over Nikki's reaction to the pregnancy. Nearing her fiftieth birthday, what would Nikki think of becoming a grandmother? Not that Jed even had a clue.

"Why should I care what she thinks?"

"Sorry?" Jed turned off the stove's range fan, waved a dish towel through tendrils of smoke. "I couldn't hear you with that thing running. Guess the garlic bread's gonna be extra crispy tonight."

"My mom," Gina said. "Why do I care?"

"Uh, because she's your mom?"

"She's Nikki. I'm not sure that counts."

"You gonna come eat or not?" he asked.

"Or not."

He set down the towel and came up behind her. She caught a whiff of his CK One—it seemed so strong. Maybe it had something to do with her altered chemical balance. She felt his hands encircle her waist.

She pushed back against him. "I don't want you touching my tummy, Jed."

"What's wrong?"

"I don't like it. I feel fat."

"You feel cuddly." He tried to kiss her neck.

She turned and backhanded his chest. "I'm serious."

He caught her wrist. "Talk to me. What's wrong?"

"Take. Your. Hand. Off. Me."

He released her, raised both arms in surrender. "If you wanna be miserable, don't take it out on me. Since when do you let anything get you down?"

"I'm not down. I'm just . . . frustrated. Confused, I guess."

"Is it something I did? Did I leave my socks in the bathroom again?"

She met his eyes for the first time since coming through the door.

They floated large and blue behind his black-rimmed glasses. If Weezer ever needed a replacement lead vocalist, he would fit right in.

"What now, Gina? You're laughing at me, aren't you?"

She nodded and stifled a sudden bout of giggles. This whole hormone thing, it was quite a ride.

"What?" he asked.

"Yeah, it's something you did."

"Figures."

"I'm going to have a baby."

"You? You're . . . what?"

She looked up beneath her wave of hair. "Hey, you're partly to blame."

"I . . . Are you saying you're pregnant?"

She nodded and bit her lower lip.

"We . . . You and me, we . . ."

"That's how it usually happens."

He leaned back, his eyebrows jumping above the rims of his glasses.

"Are you upset?" Gina ventured.

"Are you?"

"I don't know, Jed. I mean, actually, I'm pretty excited about it."

"Well, you should be."

"And you aren't?"

"Of course I am, sweetheart. That's awesome. You'll make a great mother." He reached for her hand, and this time she let him take it. "Forget about Nikki and all that baggage. You're not her. You'll be amazing."

Gina dragged her lower lip between her teeth. "I hope so."

"I know so," he said.

CHAPTER
THIRTY

En Route to Kiev, Ukraine

Headed back to Kiev, seated in the blackness of an enclosed train compartment, Erota used her superior night vision to examine the snoozing pair of travelers across from her: a college-age girl in ripped jeans with a Union Jack sewn onto her backpack and an older woman with frizzled red hair, her head lolling, a pocket Bible lying open in her lap.

Their aroma was overpowering. Unmistakable. It filled the cabin with a haze of glittering scarlet jewels.

Nazarene Blood.

Erota felt aroused and tucked her hands under her legs as her nails began sharpening, extending. These unsuspecting women were cups brimming with the purest and richest of nectars. A forbidden elixir.

Lucky for them, Erota was full.

Lucky for her too. One sip and she knew she would suffer a grisly fate.

She contemplated finding a seat elsewhere, but there was something titillating about sharing space with Those Who Resist. The world was riddled with churchgoers in pious disguises, but many of them had only the stench of death. She'd never been this close, for this long, to the real deal.

She felt like a child, quivering with nervous curiosity, face pressed between the bars of a lion's enclosure. Except there was no zoo, no enclosure. Only taunting desire.

She was full, she reminded herself. She could make it through the night without another feeding. Her skin was already warm to the touch, tinged with color.

All thanks to the Amits. One unhappy little family.

An hour before the departure from Arad's central station, Erota had ducked into the nearby park for a few minutes of solitude. She'd read aloud from an evocative poem and found the words going out like strings of notes from the Pied Piper's flute.

Here came Dalia. Here came Benyamin, right on her heels.

Their son was left crying in a restaurant lobby.

Though the kid would be spared Erota's direct attention, she suspected—or at least hoped—that vines had already latched onto him as well. Loneliness was an easy opening to exploit. Of course, she'd noted through the years that certain children showed a resilience far superior to most adults.

For example, Mr. and Mrs. Amit were easy prey.

Erota fed off them there in Eminescu Park. In the darkness, she drew them closer, and her numbing saliva rendered them delirious, oblivious, donors to the ongoing Collector cause. She used the technique demonstrated at the Cetatea chapel and extracted knotted brambles from a throbbing heel and a swollen armpit.

So easy. She broke off each at its exit point. Supped from the thorns. Gorged herself to the point of bursting.

It was a fitting conclusion to her time in Arad, and a serendipitous sending off for her impending journey to the United States.

She'd been told Americans were skeptical of paranormal dealings, but that was of no concern to her; Collectors were given leeway to make adjustments within their environments, so long as the basic goals remained in place. In simplified terms, the Collector Procedure Manual listed three primary methods:

1) *Over-the-top*—Attack and feed in *ostentatious* ways, so that the population suspects unholy involvement in each and every misfortune . . . Example: A crowded boat catches fire, goes down, and the average person is convinced it's an act of evil spirits.

2) *Under-the-surface*—Attack and feed in *covert* ways, so that the population denies any and all unholy intervention in modern life . . . Example: A boat catches fire, goes down, and the average person is convinced it's another example of shoddy management and poorly maintained equipment.

3) *Behind-the-back*—Attack and feed in *subversive* ways, so that the population blames all things mournful and distressing upon a punitive, distant deity . . . Example: A boat catches fire, goes down, and the average person assumes God didn't act because He simply didn't care.

Erota rested her head against the curtain, as the rocking of the train lulled her toward sleep.

Then she sat up straight again, all efforts at relaxation rebuffed by the presence of the two females opposite her. Her temples pounded. Her nostrils flared at their stifling sweetness.

Oh, for one sip from the cup.

The red-haired lady stirred and opened her eyes. She squinted into the darkness and felt for her Bible, then turned her sights to Erota.

Erota sat motionless, sure she could not be seen.

"You don't really want to be here, do you?" the woman whispered.

The heavy curtain was cutting off all but the smallest particles of light, and Erota figured she must be dealing with one talking in her sleep.

"You can go," the woman said. "Just go."

"Are you talking to me?" Erota inquired. "Are you awake?"

"You don't belong here."

"This is my seat."

"I'm not going to waste my time." A dismissive wave of the hand. "Please, just find somewhere else."

Erota bristled. "Who do you think you are? You don't even know my name."

"I don't *want* to know it. I'm sure you'd be lying to me anyway."

Erota brought her hands into view, her nails curved and glowing green. She imagined bridging the gap and slicing through that sun-wrinkled neck. She fantasized about a crimson geyser erupting from the carotid artery. She would drink, a vampire at the schoolyard fountain, satisfying her thirst between activities.

One sip. Please, just one.

Through the blackness, the woman's watery eyes fixed upon Erota, and a stream of soft syllables rolled from her lips. Although forming distinct words, they seemed to be encoded so that their meaning remained hidden.

Erota's brain reached out, a skeleton key working at the lock and failing to find a match. Not even close. Gibberish, gibberish. The phrases were reminiscent of the mindless repetition heard from religious syco-phants everywhere: *Please God, this . . . Please God, that . . . If You will only answer me, I promise I will . . .*

However, this lady's words were pointed. They stung Erota's mind.

Ridiculous. She had no reason to put up with this mad blabbering. It was giving her a headache. Let the redheaded two-legger have this space if she wanted it so badly. Erota would look for greener pastures, thank you, and good-bye.

She fled into the passageway, where cigarette fumes and toilet odors embraced her like old friends—not always pretty, but familiar. She turned her mind to more profitable matters, such as her upcoming assignment as a desirable, vulnerable bride.

Atlanta. *Hot*-lanta.

Home to the Falcons and Braves, a thriving cosmopolitan city.

She'd been looking forward to the challenge of a new land, and in preparation she'd watched *Gone with the Wind*. Her father, Eros, had assured her that corsets and hoop dresses were no longer part of the attire. He impressed upon her, though, that a Southern belle was still expected to carry herself with a certain decorum.

How tedious. As if Erota wasn't tired enough of the vapid existence she had endured in Ukraine.

During the long wait outside the Akeldama tombs, she had hoped for much more. The Man from Kerioth had bled his traitorous soul into that dirt, and Ariston had promised something significant for those who accessed the hillside's dead.

She'd bought into his whole spiel. And this was all she got from it?

In a matter of hours, the House of Eros would be back in Kiev, filling nine-to-five jobs, attending schools, sweeping streets, and lounging in front of TVs. They would feign normality in hopes of going unobserved. Sure, there would be midnight forays for food. They might even—if they were fortunate—stumble upon a connection to the fabled Concealed Ones. Maybe a lone *lamedvovnik*, with the letter Tav imprinted on the forehead.

But such hope had made Erota weary. She wanted recognition. She longed for a place of prominence and power. How long till the fulfillment of her dreams brought such things about?

In the ears of this human host, time seemed to be ticking.

Which was ridiculous. She knew the passage of months and years was immaterial. Hadn't the Master Collector assured them that his Collection of Souls was an ongoing project, one that could span the whole of time? He guaranteed them eventual, eternal, everlasting, and ever-blissful success.

Yet she could not shake the *tick-tock* of this mortal clock. There were things to be done, and deadlines by which to do them.

*Un*deadlines.

She must remember to relax. To enjoy and prolong the inevitable. Sure, she would search for the missing mother and daughter; in fact, she had a lead on a coming seminar in Atlanta, conducted by a woman with Romanian heritage. But other Collectors seemed willing to pursue their own pleasures, momentarily setting aside the greater goals of their clusters, and she figured she could do the same.

Yes. Erota decided that when she got to Atlanta, she would pursue fresh adventures. Thanks to this shapely human vessel of hers, she was no longer Separated from physical capabilities, and she would put these senses through their paces.

Not for the typical Collector reasons, but for her own pleasure.

Touch, smell, taste, sight, and sound . . .

Along the way, she would censor her phone calls and reports to Lord Ariston. Who said he deserved all the details? Erota had no intentions of carrying herself like a lady.

CHAPTER
THIRTY-ONE

Mid-April—Chattanooga

Gina was on edge. Today was the day to spill the news, and if her mother disapproved, so be it.

She angled her '89 Camry through the city center, heading for Nikki's place in St. Elmo's District off Ochs Highway. A car with an out-of-state license plate cut in front of her, then screeched to a halt to parallel park. The bumper sticker said, *If you don't like the way I drive, stay off the sidewalk.*

Gina's tongue moved along her teeth. Stress reduction. Upper right canine. Time to think up a blessing for someone.

How about a mocha for her mom?

Fifteen minutes later, she was following the curved drive toward a stable-style, two-car garage on the left of her mother's house. White columns guarded the antebellum home's double doors, and magnolias shaded rows of yellow rosebushes in front. What a contrast to their life back in Cuvin.

Though Gina's memories of Romania lay in bits and pieces, she could still envision the small, red-roofed house of her girlhood, could still hear the creak of the crank as she drew water from the well.

People who thought of that as the simple life had no clue. Maybe they were confusing simple with clarity of purpose. Microwaves and remote controls—those were simple. Cell phones were simple. Village life was plain hard work, sunup to sundown, relying on the sweat of the brow to meet basic necessities.

Some days Gina missed that.

"At last," Nikki said, meeting her at the car door. "I was getting worried."

"Nice to know you care."

"Regina, I didn't raise you to be late to appointments."

"An appointment. Is that all this is?"

"You said you wanted to speak with me. I've been waiting all morning."

In her black boots, Gina climbed out and handed over the mocha without a word. She was determined to rise above her mother's belittlement. She had marked her nineteenth birthday last year, and that meant no excuses, no blaming her mom or the dad she had never known or the siblings she had always wanted. Chin up. Straight ahead.

Nikki accepted the drink. "Thank you."

"You bet."

"I see you've dressed for the occasion."

"Check out the hair," Gina said. "You like it?"

"A streak of purple. I suppose it does match the shirt."

Gina decided to take that as a compliment. She'd picked out this outfit carefully. She was wearing a dark purple cotton tank top, short enough to leave her lower back and angel wings showing. A silver-studded belt held up black zippered cargo pants, which concealed the dagger strapped to her lower right leg. Her boots, black choker, and ruby orb earrings completed the ensemble.

Keep wearing them. One day I'll find you.

She trailed her mother around the side of the house, where a pitcher of ice water and lemon waited on a doily atop an old apple crate. They took seats in wooden rocking chairs, and Nikki poured two glasses.

Gina tugged on the bottom of her shirt, trying to cover her belly.

"Are you feeling all right?"

"I'm fine," she said.

"Is your stomach upset? Would you like me to get you something for it?"

The truth was the pregnancy had been rough so far. Gina expected the morning sickness, but this life inside seemed to be a tormented, restless soul.

"Water's fine." Gina drained a mouthful. "Thanks."

"What's the purpose of this meeting, darling? I do have a session to prepare for, this coming weekend."

"Straight to the point, huh? Good. I don't want to waste any more time on this than you, so I'm just going to say it. Okay?"

Nikki rocked back, eyes leveled over the mocha as she sipped.

"The thing is, well, Jed and I have been together for almost two years now. He *gets* me. He doesn't try to fit me into a box. He just lets me be who I am. I know you're not a big Jed fan, but he's a good guy—"

"Barely out of his teens. Is he even legal to buy alcohol?"

"He's legal *and* responsible. What's your point? You want me shacked up with some dude in his thirties?"

"I think that, yes, you're mature enough to aim a little higher."

"When I'm around you, I don't feel mature at all." Gina tapped her boot against the chair. "It's like I'm this little girl, falling back into the old ruts of communication. I don't want to live in the past—that's the point. I have a future. A whole life ahead."

"More than you know."

"I can't live your life, Nikki, or the life you wish you'd had. I've got to follow my own path. You know, learn from my own mistakes and all that."

Her mother took another contemplative sip.

"True, Jed and I don't have a lot of money, but we're getting it done. I'm enrolled in the insurance at my work, and so far we've both been free of any medical issues. There's a lot that's on our side, even if you don't like the fact we're living together."

"There are consequences, Gina, when you surrender yourself to another person." Her mother's lips turned down, and she rubbed at her eyes. "You give a portion of yourself away. And take from them, as well. Sometimes you haven't the faintest idea of the repercussions."

"I understand all your reasons, but—"

"Understanding," Nikki cut in, "is a place from which a person acts."

"Profound. But do I look like a customer from one of your sessions?"

"Life students. Not customers."

"Nikki? Are you in there? I'm trying to talk with you, just mom and daughter."

"You have my complete attention."

"You've always disapproved of me," Gina said, "and I can't carry that weight anymore. It's too toxic. I don't mean to be disrespectful—okay, maybe a little—but how else am I supposed to shake loose from you? Seriously."

"You don't need my approval. You've made that clear."

"But I *do*. That's what's so sick about this."

"Darling, if you're referring to the cuttings—"

"What? Those? Nahhh, that was just healthy learning there."

"Perhaps I misjudged the effects they would have on our relationship. You were so acquiescent as a child that I assumed you were in line with my intentions."

"I was a little girl. What was I *supposed* to do?" Gina looked out from the porch, to a line of green-leaf trees sprouting along the steep ascent of Lookout Mountain. "You were my entire world."

"That, I will never be. That's what pains me the most."

"It's not like I don't love you. That's not what I'm saying."

"I'll be gone one day, an inescapable fact." Her mother seemed caught up in her own melodrama. "And you'll keep on, slowly forgetting that I ever existed. If you only had a child of your own, you might begin to understand how—"

"I'm pregnant."

Nikki froze.

"That's what I came to tell you. Jed and I are having a baby."

Brightness flickered in Nikki's eyes as they fixed upon her daughter, then dimmed until nothing but fearful determination remained. "You're certain of this, Regina?"

"*Yes.* For heaven's sake, yes."

Nikki indulged herself in another drink, then put the cup down, dabbed at her lips, and tilted her head back until her hair was a veil of black trailing along the back of the rocking chair. She aimed her next words at the roof over the veranda. "You have no idea what you've done."

"Who does?" Gina said. "Guess I'll make it up as I go."

"If only it were that easy."

"C'mon. It's what you did, isn't it?"

Nikki gave her a censuring stare. "Yes, and I ruined so much."

This admission was too broad, too nonspecific, for Gina to be moved. Confession was rooted in self-disclosure. In gritty exposure. What had her mother's statement revealed beyond a vague identification with the world's grief at large?

"At least my baby will have a father around," Gina said. "Jed's proposed. He says he wants us to do this together."

"Have you given him an answer?"

"We're thinking maybe sometime after Labor Day."

"Is that meant as a joke?"

"No. Would you listen, please? I don't want all the hype, just something simple. We both agree we're not starting this marriage in debt."

Nikki tilted her head. "I do have the wherewithal to lend a hand."

"Right. And you'd do that? Even for Jed?"

"I'm not certain. Then again, you haven't asked yet, have you?"

Gina tried to restrain herself. "Thank you, but we're going to do this on our own, free and clear, with nothing dangling over our heads. And we're going to have this baby. We're thinking we might even change locations. Find someplace else to raise a family."

"Somewhere close?"

"Maybe Seattle."

"No."

"I wasn't asking."

"Not there." Her mother shook her head. "That would be a poor choice."

"Again, Nikki—I'm not fishing for advice here. I'm trying to communicate, keep the lines open and all that slop. Forget it. I should've just left it alone."

"You mustn't have this child."

"What? How can you even say that to me?"

"There's too much at stake."

"Because you wouldn't be able to control it?" Gina chafed at the thought. "Is that what worries you? You're afraid it might be even more corrupt than I was?"

"Dear, it's for the best. Please believe me."

"You are *delusional.* I mean, off your stinkin' rocker."

"Gina! You think you're in any position to raise a child when you can't even control your own temper?"

Gina repeated herself, slower this time, with stronger and harsher words hammered onto the front end. She met her mother's eyes and funneled all her resentment and hurt and anger into one pupil-drilling stare. She felt tension crackle along that connection, felt it run down through her neck and stiffen the muscles along her lower back.

She whispered, "*Die,* for all I care."

With a sharp intake of air, Nikki Lazarescu lifted her coffee cup, peeled off the white plastic lid, and threw the remaining contents across the legs of her daughter's pants.

Cursing, Gina jumped from the rocking chair. The back of the chair slapped against the white siding on the house, careened forward, then slapped the house again. Though the mocha had cooled in the half hour since its purchase, she could feel the residual heat spreading down her thighs, over her knees, gluing the cargo material to her skin. Childhood feelings of dazed resentment roiled through her chest.

Nikki set the empty cup on the crate.

"C'mon," Gina growled. "Why don't you finish what you started?"

Her mother exhaled and pressed a hand to her cheek.

Gina stared at those porcelain features, framed by waves of raven hair. A jumble of recollections came together in her mind, a semicomplete picture of a toddler in younger Nikki's arms. On the child's leg, there were two fresh cuts. Matching the scars concealed by Gina's boots.

"You think I'm just *dirt*?" she said. "That somehow I'm not worthy?"

"Shush, Gina. You don't understand."

"*You're* the one who's got it all twisted in the head." Gina unfastened the sheath and dagger from her shin, found the ancient object wet with coffee. "Here you go," she said, turning the hilt toward her mother. "Take your last ounce of blood from me, if you want it so bad. Just *take it*. It's *yours*. Because after this, I'm done letting you carve your expectations into me. If you haven't purged the evil from me by now, then I guess you're out of luck."

Nikki let her eyelids fall shut.

"Here you go." Gina removed the knife and flicked the blade across her thumb.

"They'll come for him," her mother was muttering.

"For who?"

"Your child."

"Sure. Whatever." Gina was done putting any stock in the words from this woman's mouth. She watched pearls of blood bead down her own wrist, made a fist that squeezed red droplets onto the veranda's planking. "There, Nikki. You want it? You got it. Is that enough for you, or do you need more?"

No response.

"You can have your knife back too. Far as I'm concerned, that thing's cursed."

Her mother's eyes still closed. Not a word.

Gina sneered. "You could at least *look* at me while I'm talking to you." She let the dagger fall with a metallic clang, along with the sheath, then stepped forward and stretched forth her dripping hand. She pressed the thumb to Nikki's mouth and rubbed it once across, in a glistening smear. "That's all you get. One taste. You should've just bled it all from me while you had the chance."

Nikki opened her eyes, at last. They had misted over. Through red-painted lips, she said: "Darling, it was wrong of me to have ever had you in the first place."

Ukrainian Airlines, Somewhere over Europe

They left Boryspil Airport in the morning, headed for Atlanta via New York.

This flight aboard an AeroSvit Boeing 767 was Erota's first ever by mechanical means. Eons ago, she had tried flying by natural—or perhaps, unnatural—methods, inhabiting an Egyptian vulture and soaring upon its broad pinions. The sublime vision of aerial gliding had been marred, however, by the sheer stamina required to hold position in the air. Like most things, it was harder than it looked.

"What do you think, Erota?"

"It's so quiet up here. So smooth."

"You've really never flown before?"

"*Nyet.* I have lived a sheltered life," she said, lying to her husband-to-be for the very first time. She gave a shy shrug, and his gaze flitted to her pouty lips. "Look down there." She pointed. "The clouds are like lambs' wool."

Raymond leaned over for a view through the oval window, and she made no effort to avoid the brush of his arm against her breast. He mumbled agreement, then turned his attention to a current issue of *Fortune* magazine. When he wasn't drinking in her appearance, he seemed capable of tuning her out completely.

Despite his ordinary face, Raymond Pace was better looking than she had expected from the online photos. She wondered why he'd chosen a foreign woman over an American one. His earning power wasn't the problem, and he exuded a confidence mixed with bits of surly conceit that made him seem dangerous. Perhaps he had a taste for the exotic, the unpredictable.

If so, she would more than satisfy.

"Raymond?" she said a few minutes later. "Can I ask a favor of you?"

He inserted his customs declaration card as a page marker and closed the magazine. "Shoot."

"Uh . . . I do not understand."

"It means to proceed," he explained. "To say what's on your mind."

"I will learn these things. My English, I've studied only a few years."

"You'll get along fine, Erota. Just remember, when I'm reading, I don't like to be disturbed. You'll figure that stuff out about me."

She nodded. "Da. I mean, yes." The docile bride.

"What'd you want?"

"I am wondering, can I call you Ray-Ban?"

"Like your brand of sunglasses?"

"It sounds like Raymond, don't you think?"

"Sure," he said. "If that'll make it easier for you."

"One more question."

He rolled his neck. Swiveled his face toward her. "Yes?"

"We are going to marry in Atlanta, is this correct?"

He nodded. "You got your K-I visa, meaning a clean bill of health and no criminal record. Now that I know you're not a serial killer, I feel a lot better about tying the knot."

She gave him another pouty look. Though a hefty bribe had brought a Ukranian doctor's clearance, Ray-Ban didn't need to know that.

"Only kidding, of course," he said.

"Of course."

"Two weeks from now, we'll have a small ceremony with my close friends and family. My sister, she's been dying to meet you. Then there's a reception with some of my business partners invited as well. All you'll have to do is smile and shake hands. Some of the boys might try stealing a kiss, but don't let them intimidate you. They're just infatuated with your pictures."

She pursed her lips. "Ray-Ban, I think I can handle the attention."

"I have no doubt. If anything, a few guys in my office need to grow a pair."

"A pair?"

"I'll explain later," he said. "There's still a lot to learn."

"And I can teach *you* some things, nyet?"

"I'm willing to let you try."

Later, feigning sleep, she lolled her head against his shoulder. He reached over and brushed her hair back from her face. His fingertips were cool against her neck, lighting only for a second, but long enough for her to detect his steady pulse.

CHAPTER
THIRTY-TWO

Atlanta

Nikki Lazarescu had never struggled this much during one of her seminars. She tucked a stray hair back into her gypsy head scarf and referred to her notes on the glass podium as she addressed the congregation of twelve hundred life students. Here, in the Church of Universal Wellness, they followed her every gesture with round, bright eyes that were windows into impressionable minds.

She needed to get this right. Each of these attendees had paid $219 to be here, to see and hear N. K. Lazarescu in person, and her words were meant to sweep away their cobwebs of self-pity, to guide them toward the salvation of hard work and moral turpitude.

All she could think of, though, was her daughter—bred in a moment of irresponsible lust, yet infused with immortality. Was Gina the embodiment of her mother's malignancy? Or a conduit for redemption?

A miracle . . .

That's what the driver, Zach Larkins, had called her.

Gina had bumped shoulders with the Reaper there on High Street and kept walking. Had she gotten lucky, maybe landed just right? Had Cal been there, acting on her behalf? Or was Nikki's precious child all that her name implied?

Regina Lazarescu: *Queen of the Resurrected.*

On the veranda in Chattanooga, Nikki had wanted to tell all, but it would've meant delving into details of her own sordid deeds, and that was something she would rather avoid. Her shame was too much to contemplate, and she couldn't imagine revealing it for others to see. Especially her own child.

She'd decided instead to wash her hands of the entire thing. Gina wanted to do it her own way, walk her own path—and Nikki would respect that.

Not that any of it mattered now.

Three days ago, Gina had gone with Jed to the Hamilton County Clerk and filed for a marriage license. Obviously they'd chosen to forgo the plans for a late summer wedding. Her passport and permanent residence card proved she was old enough to marry without parental permission, a civil ceremony was performed, and Gina abandoned the *Lazarescu* to become *Mrs. Jed Turney.*

Nikki knew of this because of the photo postcard she'd received yesterday, showing Mr. and Mrs. Turneys' overlapped hands, with matching gold wedding bands. No signature, just printed names—and a date already passed.

A grandbaby was also on the way. Due in early October.

Would she be allowed to see the child? Would the helpless infant be safe from those who wished to terminate its life? Would Gina fall in the crossfire?

Now, in the Church of Universal Wellness, Nikki caught sight of herself on the big screen to the left of the podium. She saw her dark eyes, intent beneath the scarf's purple material. She saw her downfalls up there, larger than life.

The audience was waiting.

"Introspection is for the weak," Nikki declared aloud, reminding herself of this as much as anyone else.

The headset carried her accented voice across the auditorium, and life students scribbled down the phrase in white two-inch binders.

"I left my homeland with my husband and two children, escaping before the fall of communism." She changed the details here, for her own anonymity. "When my countrymen tell me of the violent days that led to the overthrow, they do not wallow in sorrow over the hundreds who fell. They understood there would be a price to pay. Instead, they rejoice over that moment, on December 25 of 1989, when our despot was executed by firing squad. They call it our national Christmas gift."

The huge screen behind her filled with a Romanian flag, its center cut out.

"You can see they waved our flag proudly after removing the corruption."

A pause. Anticipative stares.

"If you want a life revolution, you must be willing to get rid of the junk." She smiled at this point, to show she was a regular person like each of them.

Two girls in the front gave large, earnest nods.

Nikki wrapped up this portion of the event: "Even as a wound cleanses itself through the spilling of blood, your past bleeds out behind you and purifies your soul. It's nature's way—God's way, perhaps—of toughening you for future hardships. Find your place and be ready, because it's your turn on stage. As we say in Romanian, '*Se ridica cortina*' . . . The curtain is going up."

She was mobbed afterward by a throng of eager faces. She spent time with each student, signing books, posters, whatever might seal the event in their minds.

A tall brunette with almond-shaped eyes approached with pen in hand. "N. K., I have nothing for you to sign, but you are my first actual American celebrity."

"Really, I don't know that I qualify."

"Perhaps," the brunette said, "you can sign my arm?"

"If you'd like. What's your name?"

"Erota. Mrs. Erota Pace. Or it will be soon."

"A beautiful name." Nikki took the pen, a weighted writing instrument with a fine black point. Others were fidgeting behind Erota, anxious for their turns. "How far did you travel for the event?"

"From Ukraine."

"Aren't you a darling? That may very well be a record."

Erota pushed back a lock of shining hair. "Now, though, I live only a few kilometers . . . or, I should say, miles . . . away. My future husband came to Kiev for me, and he has brought me here to the States. We live in Buckhead."

"I know it well. One of my favorite areas of Atlanta."

"Much different than Ukraine. I've also been to Romania."

A pang of apprehension shot through Nikki. She gave a guarded laugh. "Yes, it's a whole different world here, isn't it? So, how did you hear about the seminar?"

"My future sister-in-law, she is a fan of yours. Kristine's been to your sessions before, and she said I must come with her so we could have a bonding experience. She's even more excited than her brother about my arrival in America."

The next student in line was pressing in, shifting from foot to foot.

"Thank you, Erota, for coming. Which arm did you want me to sign?" Nikki suspended the pen over the woman's olive skin. "Left arm or right?"

Erota bared her left. Nikki signed. She flipped the pen, so that it would not be pointed at her guest, and handed it back. As she did so, the next life student shoved forward for his opportunity and, in the blur of movement and clutch of bodies, the pen wedged between Nikki and Erota.

The sharp tip broke the skin along the top of Nikki's hand—a minor abrasion. She felt only a pinprick of heat.

Nevertheless, tiny spheres of blood dotted the surface.

Erota was horrified. She babbled in Ukrainian before switching to

English. "I am so sorry." She grasped Nikki's injured hand. "Please, you will forgive me?"

"Actually," Nikki said. "I believe this young man is the one who—"

She realized then that Erota was kissing her wound. She felt the woman's cool breath and the press of full lips. Despite the act's tenderness, she was nauseated by the thought of this stranger partaking of her life force, and was sickened even more by the expanding smear of crimson across the woman's mouth.

Those painted lips. A mirror image of her own, only days earlier.

Nikki sensed a siphoning away of her own thoughts, her memories starting to stretch and tear. The room was shrinking, zooming out. Was this the sensation Gina had endured as a child?

She grasped Erota's wrist and tried to disengage herself from the woman's hold. The skin was cold. Something about the woman's nearness, about her presence, caused Nikki's insides to quiver, and she thought of warnings she'd been given long ago.

Could this be a Collector?

Nikki had never knowingly faced a Collector in the flesh. She'd been told they could inhabit hosts of all sorts, anything that could facilitate the partaking of blood. She'd also been informed they were masters of concealment, capable of pulling far back behind the human facade.

"It's quite all right, Erota," she said. "Really."

"It was an accident."

"I know, I know."

"An accident," Erota repeated, eyes lowered.

Seeing how the poor woman was stunned by her own actions, Nikki questioned the suspicions she had begun to entertain. Erota seemed harmless enough, if not a bit strange. She'd kissed a wound, that was all. Surely, if she were a Collector, she would've hooked in with elongated fangs and lapped up blood with a sandpaper tongue.

"Thank you for your concern," Nikki said.

Already, though, the Ukrainian had pushed long-nailed hands into her jeans pockets and filed away through the crowd.

"Wasn't that just fantastic? So enlightening."

"Enlightening? Yes," Erota said. "Thank you for taking me, Kristine."

"Why, sweetie, this is so exciting. I've never had a sister-in-law. It'll be like having a new best friend. Mmmm." Kristine Pace lifted her shoulders and scrunched her eyelids together. "It's so wonderful, all the adventures we can have. We'll get along fabulously. That's just clear as crystal."

Kristine pulled her BMW 740i past a wrought-iron gate and parked at the scalloped stone entry to a grand Tudor-style home. Hickory trees and rhododendrons graced the landscaped lawns.

"Here you are. It doesn't look like my brother is home, which isn't surprising. Pharmaceuticals, you know. He's always busy, always working a deal or golfing with a client. Any excuse to hit the links, if you know what I mean."

Erota hoped a nod would stem the flow.

"He's given you a key, I hope?"

Erota patted her pocket.

"Oh, good. And you know the code for the alarm?"

Erota patted her temple.

"So how're you liking my brother's swanky digs?"

Raymond Pace's small estate was situated off of Peachtree Road Northeast, in one of Atlanta's most affluent areas. Buckhead, called the Beverly Hills of the South by some, was home to professional athletes, wealthy business and medical professionals. Even Elton John had a part-time residence here.

"Very much, yes," she said. "Ray-Ban is a rich man, I think."

"Honey, don't let that intimidate you. Some people might say you're lucky to find him, but it's the other way around. A dear like you? He should be thanking his lucky stars. Anyway, I just know we're going to get along, you and me. I've got this feeling down in my bones. Well, there I go again, talking your ear off. You poor thing. If I'm going too fast, you'll let me know, won't you? Because I do have a tendency to do that." Kristine winked. "At least now you see why Raymond's the way he is. He had me for a little sister, and I suppose I used up all of his words."

"That's okay." Erota winked back. "I like men better when they're quiet."

Kristine's laugh was effervescent. "I love it. Do all Ukrainian women think the way you do? Oh, I can't wait to help you pick out your wedding dress. I know this wonderful place . . ."

The babbling continued.

Erota's thoughts tiptoed back to that incident at the seminar.

She had succumbed to her impulses, reaching for N. K. Lazarescu's hand and seeking out the fresh wound. Although she'd refrained from latching on for deep, thirsty swallows, she had found enough upon her tongue to gain access to the Romanian's memories: *a young lady in black boots, and talk of the Nistarim, of the letter Tav, of a child on the way . . .*

The images could be distortions. Best taken with a grain of salt. Of the humans she'd inhabited or feasted upon, she had found that most had memories like trash receptacles, packed and polluted by time, resentment, and selfishness.

Oh yes, their waste was a terrible thing to mind.

But, what if?

It would be absurd not to explore the possibilities. If the images *were* accurate, Erota might soon be in a position to locate and destroy one of the Concealed Ones, thus ushering in Final Vengeance upon this gangrenous world.

A child on the way . . .

A male?

For now, this would remain her little secret. No need to rush. Surely, newlywed Gina Turney would have an ultrasound soon enough, and in so doing confirm for Erota what she now suspected deep in her undead midsection.

"Hello? Erota?"

A hand touching her arm.

"Look at you, you poor thing," Kristine Pace said. "I've talked your pretty little ear off again, haven't I? You might've noticed I have a tendency to do that."

Erota took Kristine's hand, running soft fingertips along her skin. She turned in the BMW's cockpit and faced her new companion. She felt a terrible thirst come upon her, a symptom of the many hours endured in an auditorium full of flesh-and-blood beings. Her head was aching. There was one way to shut this woman up.

"Kristine," she said, "what is your greatest desire?"

The woman, illuminated by the glow of the dash lights, opened her mouth to answer. She hesitated, bit her lip, then whispered, "To never be lonely again."

"Do you feel lonely right now?"

"No, I . . . I feel a little bit scared, but I'm not sure why."

"Fear can be exciting, don't you think?"

"Oh well, I suppose that—"

A sudden strike to the neck cut short Kristine's words. With lips peeled back, making way for incisors, Erota latched into soft skin and drank her fill. Anesthetizing. Spreading infestation. And loving every moment of it.

THE THIRD DROP: REVELATIONS

I am afraid of all things—even to think,
but I must go on my way. The stake we play for is
life and death . . . and we must not flinch.

—BRAM STOKER, *DRACULA*

Godless people have wormed their way in among you . . .
The fate of such people was determined long ago.

—JUDE 1:4

Journal Entry

June 26

I've put this off for a few days, wondering if I should keep testing these droplets. It's confusing. And I'm almost scared of what else I'll find.

This last drop must've come from Erota, with many of the memories hitchhiking from the wound on Nikki's wrist. I'm guessing Gina's memories were passed through the blood smeared on her mother's lips. I wonder how these drops came to be on the map, but I have a feeling I'll find out soon.

It's hard not to be caught up in these stories. While I'm reliving them, they seem so real. Like I could walk right into the scene and interact. How cool would that be? I'd stop the Collectors from sipping from those disgusting little thorn cups.

There's this other part of me, though—I don't even know if I should even write this down—a part that understands where they're coming from. My life's been pretty short and lonely, consisting mostly of books and education, and in that time I've read over and over again that it all boils down to survival of the fittest. Dog-eat-dog. Well then, why shouldn't Collectors take what they can get? Who's to say they're wrong? Sure, there's the common good to think about, but it seems a little too common. What if half of the people on this crowded planet were wiped out? It'd simplify things, all right.

I don't know. Maybe my brain's just a wreck from this rush of secondhand experiences. Not that it matters now. I may as well keep going and see how this ends.

CHAPTER
THIRTY-THREE

July—Chattanooga

Gina Lazarescu Turney turned away from the pandemonium on the TV set. She'd seen the footage before—the concussion of a pipe bomb in downtown Atlanta a year ago, a blast of light, people running, two dead with more than one hundred injured.

Pandemonium. A fitting description. If she remembered correctly, it came from Milton's *Paradise Lost*, his designation for the capital of hell.

"You mind turning the channel?" she said.

Jed had his feet up on the coffee table, the remote cradled in his lap like a pet meant to keep him warm. A reporter was discussing the FBI's ongoing investigation of that evening's attack.

"Jed," she said.

"Is your tummy bothering you again?"

"Please."

"Yeah, okay. Sorry." He hit the button. The scenes of last summer's Olympic tragedy gave way to an MTV video full of gyrating hips. He peeked over the back of the couch, caught her eye at the chess table. "Any better?"

She flicked her fingers, and he turned off the set.

"What's wrong, Gina?"

"I'm okay."

"Your *okay* is anyone else's *sick as a dog*."

She gave a weak smile. "I'm just going to assume that's no reference to the way I look right now."

"You look gorgeous. It's true, that whole thing about pregnant women."

"Having a glow? Give me a break."

"Well, not a glow. More like a—"

"Sickly green?"

The phone rang, and Jed checked the number. "It's your mother."

Gina shook her head.

"It's been what, a coupla months since you two talked?" he said.

"I've survived so far, haven't I? Much to her disappointment, I'm sure."

"She's gonna be our baby's grandma, though. Don't you think we should—"

"Hey, did you hear me asking for opinions?"

The phone stopped ringing, and Gina's husband of two months came around behind her. "Whatever she said to you, I'm sure she didn't mean it."

"She meant it."

"People say things when they're upset. She's just too proud to apologize."

"Whatever. I don't care. I'm looking ahead, just like she always taught me."

"You care," he said, setting his hands on her shoulders.

Gina propped her elbows on the table, resting her forehead in her hands. Her hair was a rag of pink-streaked black. Her stomach felt bloated, the size of a hot-water bottle shoved under her shirt. Though sensitive to touch, she let Jed gently massage her muscles and lower back. At least he was trying to help.

Any relief was appreciated. On a daily basis, arrows of agony came shooting through her womb. They arrived from all directions—the TV and radio, the grocery store newsstand, not to mention bits of gossip.

Sympathy pains, she called them. Her baby reacting to the sorrows that Gina saw all around. What was it Thoreau had said, about artists carrying the wounds of their generation? She was no artist. She was nothing really. Who was she, to bring a child into such a world?

"What'd the doctor tell you today?" Jed asked.

"Nothing's wrong, he said. Some women just get it worse than others."

"It's *your* body. What does he know?"

Gina shrugged a shoulder. The subject was getting old. She arranged the chess pieces and began moving them, deriving familiar comfort from their polished feel and stately presentation.

"You playing against yourself, sweetheart?" He was still massaging.

"Sort of," she said.

"You're, like, the only chick I know who plays chess."

"Chick?"

"How 'bout, 'hot mama'?"

"Hilarious, Jed. No, I'm going through the moves of the Immortal Game, this famous match played in London, back in 1851."

"Immortal?"

"Because it hasn't died. Even then, people realized it would go down for the ages as this example of brilliant sacrifice." She shuffled pieces on the board and tried to explain, but found little receptivity from the lunkhead behind her. "You don't get it, do you? Are you even watching?"

"I see it," Jed said. "I just don't *see*, if you know what I mean."

"Anderssen—he's the one playing white—and look at how he only captures three pawns from the other guy. But he gives up almost all of his own pieces to win. Both of his rooks, a few pawns, a bishop, and finally his—"

"Queen."

"Regina," she said, rolling the *r* in her native Romanian.

"Okay, sure, I get it. That's pretty cool."

"Yeah." She nodded, pink strands brushing her nose as her husband resumed his well-meaning back rub. "Takes a lot of courage, laying it all on the line like that," she said. "I don't know if I'd be able to do it."

"I betcha you would, if you had to. You're a pretty tough chi—"

"Chick. Go ahead and say it. I dare you."

They both laughed, and for the rest of the evening, the arrows of pain seemed to remain harmlessly in her quivers. She knew they would come raining down again soon enough, but she was a warrior.

Honor . . . duty . . . combat.

She was going to fight this pregnancy through to the end.

Atlanta

Mrs. Erota Pace stretched out her legs on a swatch of lawn. The air was cool, crisp. Around her, in this famed park, businesspeople ate lunches, while college students tossed Frisbees back and forth.

Her contact was three minutes late.

"You snooze, you lose, mister," she practiced her English aloud.

Centennial Olympic Park, a showcase for last year's festivities in Atlanta, had been the target of Eric Rudolph's bomb full of nails. Meant to undermine a government that allowed rampant unrighteousness, it was the sort of over-the-top act Erota would expect from a man as arrogant as he.

A few weeks back, here at this same spot, she had met a man of equal conceit. She'd spotted him—smelled him, was more accurate—and found he was host to a local Collector. A Collector more than eager to mete out his own destructiveness. Inspired by Rudolph's deeds, he, too, had bombed a nearby abortion clinic. In late April, with Erota tag teaming him, the man had wreaked similar violence on a lesbian nightclub.

All part of his reign of holy terror. Blame the media, the voices, the gods.

Of course, in lining up these missions, Erota was prepping him for her real target only weeks from now: Erlanger East Medical Clinic, Gina's hospital in Chattanooga.

Good-bye to the Concealed Ones. Hello to the End of the World.

"Okay," she spoke aloud. "Where are you?"

Erota tilted her head back, staring through sunglasses at a sky humans would say was gray and depressing but to her was a ceiling of marbled splendor.

This world was wondrous. A forbidden fruit, if you will.

Like all Collectors, she reveled in its beauty, longed for its pleasures, while despising the creative touch behind it. How could a loving being create such things, then place restrictions upon them? What sort of ego-centric creature would punish and Separate those who refused to bow at His every command?

Thank God—Erota snickered at this irony—for extending grace to these putrid two-leggers. Through them, she and her ilk could still sample pleasures.

Each day, while her husband, Ray-Ban, was playing at his pharmaceutical sales and golf, she tried to take it all in, a vampire exploring her five senses and doing her best to choose a favorite.

Touch.

Oh, the joys to be found here. She was a big fan of sexual temptations—had been since her temple prostitute days. With 1990s technology fast becoming part of her knowledge base, she saw unlimited possibilities. She'd already drunk from the libidos of her husband, sister-in-law, and a number of the business partners. She was a kid in a candy shop, as these Americans liked to say.

Smell.

This more subtle pleasure often caught her by surprise—the aroma of bacon cooking, Atlanta Bread Company, or the soft scent of roses. It was closely linked to memory too. One whiff of a lemon, and she might just as well be back in the Middle East, centuries ago, browsing the open-air markets they called *souks*. What better sense was there for dragging someone back to a place he wished to forget?

Taste.

Surely, this had to be a favorite. From the tannic plushness of a good cabernet to the sweet, coppery drops from a thorn cup, she adored the palette's ability to channel enjoyment. Her husband was a direct contributor in this arena, wining and dining her in Atlanta's superb restaurants. Flavors to be savored. No wonder obesity was a spreading problem—see, she knew how to use a pun—in this land of abundance.

Sight.

The world all around was a blast of color. Coming from the monochrome drudgery that had been hers without a host, she felt shell-shocked at times by the contrasts and lights. Other times she was moved to tears by something as blasé as the kaleidoscope of oil in a puddle. Her husband, like most males, seemed drugged by the curves and hues of female forms. Or by the ubiquitous movies and video games. Everywhere, blurs of motion and adrenaline.

Sound.

She found herself confused by her reactions to various rhythms and tones. Why she loved American hip-hop, she could not explain. Why certain men's voices strummed deep within her, she had no idea. Perhaps the sense's most rewarding elements were found in nature's symphony—a bird's bright chirp, the shushing whisper of leaves in a breeze, or the rattling satisfaction of a kitten's purr.

A favorite from these five senses? It was hard to choose.

And each had its drawbacks.

Some days, the continual barrage of sound gave her migraines. Touch could transmit heart-stopping pain, such as the time she'd brushed a hand over a stovetop's entrancing glow. Sights and smells could turn a stomach in seconds. And the taste of rising bile—was anything more disgusting than one's own foul juices?

Her journeys through the sensory world only underlined her fury.

The Separation . . . A hellish punishment, which had severed the Collectors' direct connections to the physical realm. It was inhumane.

And the Unfallen? They did not suffer its pain.

Such favoritism was just more evidence against the Almighty, All-Magnificent, Egotist who claimed to be in control.

As for the Nazarene?

The very thought of the man made her sick.

She had gathered with the other Collectors, forming a vast mob around the craggy edifice of Golgotha, and watched him scream out a question they all understood to their cores . . .

My God, my God, why have You forsaken me?

They had rejoiced in that moment. Gloried in his agony, in his death.

It is finished.

But it was a lie.

It was not finished. It was only the beginning.

He came out of the grave three days later. It was rumored he then broke bread with fellow Jews and let them touch his scars, then walked through walls like they weren't there. He declared his disdain for the Separation by moving between the physical and spiritual realms as though they were one.

The Collectors had been unable to stop his escape.

These disgusting, self-involved two-leggers would not be so lucky. They deserved what they had coming. The more Erota witnessed this world through their hands, noses, mouths, eyes, and ears, the more cemented she became in her resolve to cause them grief.

To feed, breed, persuade, and possess.

To tear these silly humans apart and bleed them dry.

She was on her own now, a warrior. She saw no reason to subject herself any longer to the Akeldama Cluster's oversight. Ariston was far, far away from this place in which she now lived. Here, in the land of the free—*ha!*—and the home of the brave—*double ha!*—clusters operated as part of a national syndicate called the Consortium.

Erota, like a few others, preferred her chances going solo. She saw no need to subject herself to the Consortium's instructions. Once she could confirm the sex of Gina Turney's child, she would wield the weapon of her own choice—and end this.

The reward? Unity and peace.

Wasn't that what she and other Collectors wanted, what clusters angled and finagled for across this overridden planet? Mrs. Erota Pace, former temple prostitute, onetime swine, and intermittent traveler of this mortal coil, wanted what had been promised by the Master Collector himself so very long ago.

Unity: the physical and supernatural brought together again, so that she could indulge in her senses without restraint, boundaries, or guilt.

Peace: to indulge herself, without these hoarding humans in the way.

"Erota?"

She turned toward the voice and saw a brown-haired man with an average build. "I was beginning to wonder if you would show up."

"I'm nervous," he said. "Meeting in this park, of all places."

"Relax. Nobody knows the things you've done. After this next act, though, I'm sure they'll be shifting their focus to you."

"I don't know that I want that."

"Sure you do. You want to be heard, right?"

"I have to talk louder," he said. "Nobody's listening these days."

Erota could see in his cagey expression that she had pegged him correctly. She saw the same self-righteous spirit that was there in Dalia Amit, Nikki Lazarescu, and some of the datim in Israel's Arad.

All of them, striving to be like God.

All of them, seeking heaven through their own efforts.

Well, they were in fine company, since it was the Master Collector himself who had made the first trek through that treacherous wasteland.

"Here's our next target." Erota passed over folded papers and a map. "This woman moved in with her boyfriend directly out of high school, and she's carrying a child conceived out of wedlock. A moral travesty, don't you think?" She kept a straight face as she said it. "You have five, maybe six weeks to familiarize yourself with the Chattanooga area. I've done some of the legwork, but you'll be doing the dirty work. Are you up for the task?"

"I'll blow up the clinic real good," he said.

"See? That has a nice ring to it. The exact date is still up in the air, so you must stay alert, and I'll be in close contact."

His eyes grazed up her legs, over the reclined curve of her hip.

"Hello?" She snapped her fingers. "Are we in agreement?"

He looked away and nodded dumbly.

CHAPTER
THIRTY-FOUR

August—Totorcea Vineyards, Romania

Due east of Lipova, Megiste and Eros walked the vineyard's hillside property. They'd made the journey down from Kiev to touch base with the cluster leader, and Ariston was now leading them on a personal tour, waddling between hanging rows of vines, many of which were still withered and dead. Megiste noticed that the soil was dry from the day's earlier heat, and scattered rocks indicated a site not yet cleared for steady production.

"The place has a lot of potential, Lord Ariston," Eros commented.

"It's coming along."

"Though I must tell you," Megiste said, "I prefer living amongst the denser population in Kiev. For the occasional tappings, you know—should the desire overtake me."

Below, the land leveled out toward the Mures River, where mosquitoes and gnats swarmed in the twilight. Guarded by a gate, a ribbon of dirt threaded from the main road to this modest place with its thatched-roof residence and decrepit warehouse.

Ariston had purchased the vineyard a year earlier, under his Romanian cover name: Flavius Totorcea. The alkaline in the soil had proven resistant to dependable grape harvests, and the previous owner's sons, who both resided in England, had shown no interest in the land. The estate's executor would have sold it to Ariston even if his name were *Beelzebub, Lord of the Flies*. The man's very words.

Ariston of Apamea offered his jeweled armband. The executor accepted. Then scampered off, probably hoping to auction the relic for additional profit.

Which, Megiste knew, was of no concern to Ariston.

"The place does need work," he told her and Eros. "A few years, though, and I plan to be bottling notable vintages under the name of Totorcea Vineyards."

"Why, it's the perfect false front," Eros said.

"I've been researching on the World Wide Web and found lots of information for making it into a legitimate business. I've e-mailed vintners from Bordeaux to the Willamette Valley." He noted Megiste's blank look. "In the state of Oregon. A Mr. Addison, from Addison Ridge Vineyards, was kind enough to send information on pinot noir grapes, one of my favorite varietals."

"You lost me, I'm afraid. Back at Bordeaux."

He puffed out his chest. "Wine talk, that's all it is."

"At least no one bothers you out here, do they?"

"Aside from my own family?"

Megiste peeked through her long curls. "Is Sol still giving you grief?"

"And the wives."

Eros chuckled. "Now you know why I've chosen to remain unattached."

"Some days I envy you that. With all of us under one roof, it gets tense at times. Bah. With two thousand years of waiting under our belts, you'd hope they could see past the petty differences of their hosts."

"Oh, you *foolish* man," Megiste said with a giggle.

"I can see why these modern grooms have it whittled down to one mate. So, tell me," he said. "How're things in Ukraine? Is the House of Eros having the same success that we've had with your slow-tapping method?"

Eros slid fingers down Megiste's arm. "I'll let our priestess answer that."

"Success?" she said. "Abso*lutely*. We've tapped hundreds, maybe more. The vines spread like weeds, creeping and crawling through every available crack. We've been focusing our energies on one person per household. Once the root takes hold, infestation progresses with only occasional nudges from us."

"We've found the same thing here. And the blood, it's much more concentrated than from a direct attack. I owe you my thanks, Megiste, for developing this tactic."

"As part of my training, I once used ritual sacrifice to see after the welfare of my congregants. Is this really any different?"

"I suppose not."

"We're all in this together," Eros said. "Two houses, one cluster."

Ariston's eyes snapped up. "You're sure of that? I'm having doubts about Erota. Do you have any contact with your daughter? The reports she's been sending me seem . . . sketchy, at best."

"She's an independent one, no doubt there, but I'll look into it. Any other trouble? Besides on the home front?"

"Hmm. Until recently I didn't think so."

Megiste came to a halt, pulling her fur coat tight as the evening temperature began to drop. "What's changed, Lord?"

"Little things. Maybe nothing."

"Do tell. It's our first trip back since the meeting at the Cetatea, and I want *all* the juicy details."

He confided to her and Eros that a recent nighttime intruder had been spotted several times near this property, yet never been caught. "I'm concerned by anyone showing interest in my family or this location. We've been careful to remain veiled in our activities."

"Probably just a thieving gypsy," Eros theorized.

"Hmm. I don't buy into the local prejudices. No, it seems that something's amiss, though I can't quite put my finger on it."

"Maybe we'll catch a farmer's son spying," Megiste said, "and then tap our own *private* vintage. What do you say?"

"I think you are insatiable."

"I've never denied it. We all want that one cup that never runs dry and satisfies our needs for all time. But it sounds so *droll*, don't you think? If such a cup exists, let those who want eternal boredom wet their lips on it." Megiste ran her tongue along the thin bow of her own mouth. "As for me, I'll keep sucking the juice from a variety of . . . well, grapevines."

Ariston chortled. "It's good to have you two here. Come. I'll show you the house."

On the way down the slope, Megiste offered a suggestion. "Considering this intruder, perhaps you should set out a guard."

"Do you think I've not done that?"

"Well, I'm sure you have."

"Barabbas is on duty even now."

"You think of everything, sir. He's not one to mess with."

Ariston grunted.

"I meant no insubordination," she said.

Though often mischievous, she believed in the chain of command as delineated in the Principles of Cluster Survival. In times past, Collector defiance had sent others packing, and she had no desire to follow in their tracks. She was Restless enough, without a visit to that scalding Desert.

"It's okay, Megiste." Ariston pressed fingertips against his forehead. "I've just been getting so ill-tempered, what with this intruder business and these migraines I've been experiencing."

"You too?"

"Nothing unbearable. Not most days, anyway."

"A dull drone?"

"Yes." He shot her an inquisitive look.

Eros spoke up. "Megiste and I discussed the same thing on the train. It doesn't seem to bode well for us, I'm afraid."

"The sensation grows," Ariston said, "until it would seem I have a thousand flies buzzing between my ears." He stopped at the entry to the farmhouse. "Hail Hades, some nights I can barely think. The longer I'm in this host, the more my focus seems corrupted by these human proclivities."

"I'm sure it's a passing phase."

"One can only hope." Ariston opened the front door, gesturing them inside.

Ruins of Soimos Castle, Romania

From behind a remnant wall of the hilltop castle, camouflaged by twilight, Benyamin Amit watched. He blinked. Refocused. He pressed his eye to the lens of his Swarovski scope, training the reticule on the woman's face down in the vineyard that hugged an adjacent slope.

She was new to the premises, yet he was certain he'd seen her before. The memory of that pale neck and auburn ringlets swam beneath his thoughts, shadowed and difficult to distinguish. As he imagined running a finger over her thin, shapely lips, his foot began to ache.

When she and the man called Flavius Totorcea stepped into the house, Benyamin was left with a sense of disquiet. Who was she? And why was she here?

What was *he* doing here, for that matter?

"Megiste and Eros," said Helene. "Why, how nice to see you. How is Kiev?"

Eros gave her a velvety kiss on the cheek. "Pleasant, this time of year."

"And your household—are they all well?"

"With Erota off in Atlanta, we're down to five, but we're fine, thank you. Dorotheus is managing affairs while I'm gone."

"Tell your mother hi for me."

"Certainly."

Shelamzion stepped in from the kitchen. "Welcome." Her greeting did not match her cold stare as she took Megiste's long fur coat and draped it from an antler rack to the right of the stone fireplace.

Megiste rubbed her hands at the hearth and chose to ignore the chilly demeanors of Auge and Shelamzion. These women and their jealousies. For good reason, she had followed Eros's lead by never marrying, and she found secret amusement in their trite concerns.

"Is there a meal underway?" Ariston said.

"Of course, dear heart. I'm serving *muschi* as a main course."

"Sounds wonderful, Helene," said Eros.

"And to think that I'll be missing out." Ariston still had on his overcoat.

"You're leaving?"

"You know I am. If you remember, my doe, I'm off on a visit with the vintner from Hunedoara. Need to leave right away, actually. I'm hoping to tap him for his every wine-making secret. My apologies for running off, but I should be back late this evening."

"Not *too* late, sir. We have *sooo* much catching up to do."

Though Megiste's words lowered dark veils over the faces of the House of Ariston women, she chose not to acknowledge their pettiness. As Ariston marched out to the vineyard's car, she let the tangy sweetness of pork in the air play through her nostrils, and she winked at Helene in a show of approval. Food would be a treat, even as she longed for something more substantial that her body could absorb.

The rumbling of the car's engine had faded by the time Sol came in from the slopes, his face flushed, his breathing labored. After abbreviated greetings, he said to Eros, "Listen, I meant to tell my father, but now that he's gone I think you should know. I noticed something odd on my way in from the fields."

"Oh, what is it?"

"Hypothetically, I wonder if the intruder he's seen could be a woman."

"Go on." Eros touched a finger to his chin. "I try to take everything into consideration."

"There was a city taxi that passed by not long ago, from Arad. It's not a common sight this far out, but I thought nothing of it until it passed back the other direction only minutes later."

"Is there anywhere to be dropped east of here?" Megiste asked.

"Not for many kilometers. Which is precisely what piqued my curiosity. And that's when," Sol said, "I saw her. This middle-aged woman ducked down, but stood straight again when she realized she had no place to hide. She shuffled by on thick legs and pretended she had no interest in me."

"This was along your property's fence?"

"Near the gate, yes. She had a boy with her as well. They're still out there, I'm certain, though I'm unclear as to their intentions. The woman's hair was pulled back in a bun, with features similar to ours."

"Jewish, perhaps?" Helene said. "Mrs. Dalia Amit, I would venture. She and Benyamin have a son, and she's come by city hall on a few occasions—to check on her husband's activities, if you want to know what I think."

Eros pointed Sol toward the door. "Go get the poor woman and child."

"And do what with them?"

"Is there some place we can question them in private?"

"The warehouse," Sol admitted. "But I don't think it would be—"

"You don't think. Yes, your father's told me of this problem of yours."

"I'm a grown man. I see no need for bowing to his every whim and fancy. I—"

"Go. Now," Eros kept his voice even and low, yet Megiste knew he was incensed with such insubordination. "We'll meet you in the warehouse in five minutes."

Megiste ran a hand along her neck as she watched Ariston's sniveling son stomp outdoors. "It's been a long day," she said. "Am I the only one feeling thirsty?"

CHAPTER
THIRTY-FIVE

Soimos Castle

Still vigilant, Benyamin repositioned himself against the remnant wall.

Months ago, Cal Nichols had tried to recruit him in a campaign against these killers, the undead from the Field of Blood, who had torn men to shreds and sucked every drop from their veins. Though Benyamin had tried to drown out those Dead Sea images, Nickel's reappearance had only stirred them back to the surface.

He'd rebuffed Nickel's offer that night. It was rubbish.

After fleeing the café, he had tried to repair his relationship with Dalia and Dov—and failed.

Dalia was barely speaking to him now, more condemning than ever of his misdeeds. Dov was almost thirteen, sullen in that teenage manner and wearing his hair over his eyes.

In an attempt to regain some fatherly respect, Benyamin had vowed to take his son camping this weekend in the mountains just north of these castle ruins. This time, Benyamin meant it. He even told himself it was part of his reason for being here now, checking out the terrain for their outing.

That wasn't his true reason, though.

Bugged by Nickel's assertions at Café Focsani, Benyamin had decided to investigate the claims on his own time. Using his position at city hall, he checked Helene Totorcea's records and found that she and her family, including her husband, were Romanian Jews who had returned here after a long hiatus. The only thing odd about their papers was the absence of anything odd. Even the most upstanding families had secrets buried deep in bureaucratic files, but this was a spotless bunch.

Curious, Benyamin had accessed the district property files next.

Which led him here.

This was his fourth random evening observing the comings and goings on the neighboring hillside, at Totorcea Vineyards. He'd even sneaked along the property's perimeter a few times to count the number of residents.

Eleven. As tallied through his scope.

Was Nickel right? Was this innocuous group responsible for the murders in Israel eight years previous?

But there had been *eighteen* bite patterns. *Nineteen* empty boxes.

He recalled Dalia's words, yesterday in the hallway: *Ben, what is it now? Is there another woman? Is that it? No. Please, I'd rather you not tell me. You'll do what you want, as you've made so clear. But your son, he needs his father. His bar mitzvah is close, and you are never around to instruct him. Can't you see this? One night you'll stay out late again, only to find Dov grown and gone when you return. Is that how you want it to be, Ben? Is that the Almighty's wish?*

This evening, racing east from city hall after work, Benyamin had watched the setting sun in his rearview mirror and promised himself this would be his last sortie to Soimos. If he found nothing conclusive, he would drop the entire matter. He would set aside the drinking. Apply himself to his marriage. Help his son prepare for the passage into manhood.

His earnest vows had sounded a bit too familiar in his own ears as he climbed the slope to the castle and took up this observation post among the ruins. But he meant them. He did. After tonight's action fizzled, he would start fresh.

All that changed when the strange—or not so strange—woman arrived.

How did he know her?

Goose bumps now rushed along Benyamin's arms beneath his jacket, followed by a buzzing in his head that was a companion to his old itchy-itch.

He double-checked the house through the scope, saw that the door was still shut, the lights glowing inside.

He had a moment.

He set down his scoped rifle—who said he needed Nickel's weapons or knowledge?—and propped himself against the wall. He rolled up his trouser leg so that he could get a look at his heel in the moonlight.

It was tender. The scar from years ago had become home to raging infection. The once glossy circle of pink was now a mound of crusty brown, and spiderwebs of blue-black ran up along his calf and down over the top of his foot. The entire leg hurt, and some days turned into a conflagration of unbearable pain. Other days, without explanation, he would wake up to find the tempest had died, the natural coloring had returned, and the swelling had subsided.

He tugged off his sock by its toe, airing the wound.

A sharp object moved beneath the skin, a shark's fin trolling blood-tinged waters. He hated whatever that thing was, despised himself and his sickness, and this world that turned a blind eye to misery.

Where was the God of his fathers, the God of Abraham, Isaac, and Jacob? Who had been there when his grandfather was facing the ovens of Matthausen concentration camp?

Dalia would scold him for such ruminations, as she did for everything else. But what did he care? He felt like barking his frustrations at the moon. This region's early dwellers had been called Dacians, derived from the word for *wolf*, and he imagined that werewolves lurked even now in these Carpathian foothills.

In fact, for a moment, he thought he saw glowing green eyes off to his left.

Nonsense, of course. All of it. This was 1997, and he was a man of cerebral means. He had no reason to rant at distant deities or to fear local folklore. He could find his own solutions to life's challenges, if only he applied himself.

The most immediate solution was in his jacket.

Benyamin was cold, buffeted by the winds that howled through the ruins. Time, he decided, to warm his old bones and prepare for the night watch.

He was tugging the flask from his inner coat pocket when an apparition appeared through the arched medieval entryway. The shape was gargantuan and bearded, its eyes pulsing—there was no way of denying it—with preternatural light.

One of the undead? A man-beast sent from the house to end his snooping?

"Hello." Benyamin said. "Like a drink?"

He felt calm. Here, at last, he would confront this slippery fear. One way or another, he would know where he stood between the worlds of the seen and unseen.

With the rifle just out of reach beside his bare foot, he switched his hand from his flask to his holster and drew the loaded Makarov into view. He pushed down the safety lever. Aimed the barrel at the apparition's abdomen.

"Don't you move," Benyamin said.

With eyes narrowed and luminescent, the figure advanced. In his wiry beard, flashes of moonlight became trapped like fish in a net, like the tales Benyamin's mother used to tell of mighty Sisera, oppressor of the Israelites, giant among the sons of God.

Weary and on the run from a lost battle, that particular giant had taken refuge in a woman's tent dwelling and downed a bowl of warm *lebben*, curdled milk, before falling asleep wrapped in a rug.

Only, Sisera never awoke.

The woman drove a spike through his temple. A metal . . .

Metal tent peg. An MTP.

Well, perhaps Cal Nichols was onto something there, toting around his daypack of rustic tools—the mallet, a few pegs, perhaps some bottles of warm milk for putting the bedtime monsters to rest.

Of course, that had all happened thousands of years ago, before readily available shotguns and pistols. Even a blunderbuss could do the job with more efficiency. There was no reason, in Benyamin's mind, to join Those Who Resist when he could deal with matters on his own by a few well-placed shots.

"I said not to move," Benyamin repeated.

The apparition stopped.

Some believed that the name *Sisera* meant *Servant of Ra*. Well, this modern-day counterpart looked nothing like a minion of the Egyptian sun god. He was wearing work boots and a thick corduroy jacket over a wool sweater. He was enormous, broad backed, but maybe a man after all.

"Don't shoot," the maybe-a-man said. "I'm just taking you to the vineyard."

"You're not taking me anywhere."

Benyamin remembered something else about Sisera. To this day, during the Jewish festival of Rosh Hoshanah, the shofar was blown a hundred times to represent the cries of Sisera's mother when she heard of his demise. In Benyamin's ears, he imagined that soul-wrenching wail now, the primal cry of the ram's horn. A call to judgment.

A 9x18mm judgment . . . Meet your Makarov.

"Not another step," Benyamin said.

"But I have my orders."

"Stay right there."

With eyes blazing again, the creature defied his command and charged ahead on powerful, driving legs.

Sisera, viscera . . . You're going down.

The former patrolman squeezed the trigger twice in rapid succession.

Chattanooga

"Did you hear that?" Gina said.

A throng of tourists milled at the railing, eyes fixed on a red-lit natural amphitheater of fluted stone formations and stalactites. A few cocked their heads, as though intrigued by what sounds might be trapped hundreds of feet beneath Lookout Mountain. The rumbling of an earthquake? Cries of the Confederate dead?

"Vat are vee supposed to hear?" a German man asked.

"Nothing. I'm sorry."

Gina stepped back from her tour group and cupped a hand over her stomach. In her ears—or was it only in her imagination?—she had registered two sharp thunderclaps. The baby inside had squirmed at the same moment, his discomfort radiating throughout Gina's body.

During this pregnancy, Gina had felt a heightened sensitivity of her physical senses that seemed to carry over into realms of emotion. It sounded crazy, even in her own head, yet she was convinced that her child had somehow dialed her in to others' turmoil and pain.

So had somebody been shot? Was someone in danger?

She grimaced. Rolled her neck. "It's okay, little guy."

"You're having a boy, huh?"

Gina glanced into the attentive almond-shaped eyes of a brunette. The girl was Gina's height, around the same age, with an unidentifiable accent, Ray-Bans pushed up onto her forehead, and slender legs and hips.

Gina hated her for that. Though Jed kept telling his wife that she hadn't lost any of her appeal and that he especially appreciated her swelling chest, one look in the mirror proved that her once shapely behind had turned to lard.

"Yes," she told the girl. "He's a constant mover."

"A little bundle of joy."

More like a ball of constant sorrow.

But Gina said nothing, afraid it might trigger abdominal cramps or hormonal sobs. She tried to keep tears to herself, hiding them from even her husband.

"Is it true," the girl inquired, "what they say about the ultrasound?"

"What do you mean?"

"You know, Gina—about determining the sex."

Gina fidgeted with her name tag, not sure she liked being addressed so personally. However, she had grown used to these questions regarding her pregnancy, particularly on the daily trips through the caverns. She was six weeks from her due date, toting a small watermelon beneath her uniform. What did she expect? But why did the promise of new life give strangers the right to rub her belly, ask what names she had picked out, and offer uninvited advice?

She looked into the upturned eyes and recalled seeing this same girl in previous tours, maybe a month or two back. That was strange. Never mind, though. The girl meant well, just wanting the best for mother and baby.

"Haven't heard that one," Gina answered. "Look, we better move along."

"There's no rush." Cold fingers touched Gina's arm. "The others are still taking pictures. From what they tell me about ultrasounds, males always have their hands down in their laps—yes, we know how those boys are, don't we?—and the females have their hands up by their heads, already primping."

"Sure. That could be true."

"So. A boy, huh? I bet you're excited."

Gina nodded.

"You look about ready to pop."

Gina gave her a questioning look, but saw nothing but reptilian disregard above the girl's pasted-on smile. "Still got a ways to go," she said.

"Have they given you a due date?"

"Hope it's soon, that's all I care. Okay, I've got to gather everybody before the next group catches up."

"You seem upset, Gina."

"About what? No, I—"

"Hello." The German man came alongside, voice booming and friendly, a daypack in hand. "Vee also haf places like this in my country, Gina. *Sehr schön*. You haf lunch break soon? Vee can sit down, I buy you Big Mac, and vee talk about it, *ja*?"

Hitting on a pregnant woman? What was up with that?

"I'm sure it's nice," she said. "C'mon, everyone, let's move along."

Gina eased from the girl's olive-skinned touch, but the chill of those fingers clung to her forearm for the rest of the tour, accompanied by a faint, briny odor. She checked her arm two or three times, thinking the brunette had taken hold of her again, only to find the girl standing ten yards away with a rapt, haunting stare.

CHAPTER
THIRTY-SIX

Soimos Castle

Benyamin watched the two rounds plow into the creature's gut.

At the shooting range, he'd witnessed the aftermath of fired 9x18mm slugs. They chewed through targets and left no doubt about their deadly intentions. Of course, he had never seen the projectiles' actual paths.

Now, in the gothic confines of this centuries-old Transylvanian citadel, in this moment of imminent danger, his senses kicked into overdrive. The human mind was a thing of wonder. Time became an abstract entity, sliced into segments, split again into thinner ones—frames to be studied from a reel of film.

The spent cartridges ejected over his right shoulder.

The rounds spit from the Makarov's mouth and spiraled forward.

The apparition that was a man, that wasn't a man, couldn't be a man, rushed forward in great clopping strides, while the fish tails of moonlight flapped in his beard, and the gleams of his irises intensified.

The pair of Russian-made rounds punched through his chest, lifting and slowing him, so that in this freeze-frame mode, it appeared he was vaulting, almost flying, over rock slabs and patches of grass. The skin sucked tight around the wounds, puckering, oozing blood. His bounds turned into a run, into a jog, a walk—

And then he stopped.

"Never been shot by a gun before," he said.

"Most people don't live to tell about it," Benyamin said.

He waited for the apparition to fall, a victim to the laws of physics and nature. But the man still stood there. Perhaps he was a steroid-riddled athlete, or a hyped-up drug addict, or a person of abnormal strength and pain tolerance.

Or, as Nickel had asserted, one of Jerusalem's Undead.

The man drove hairy-knuckled fingers with long tapered nails through one of the holes in his sweater, searched around in his chest cavity, then brought into view a flattened slug dripping with bodily fluids. He studied the object, sniffed at it, and touched it to his tongue.

Undead. Yes, Benyamin decided, that had to be the right answer.

The Makarov's magazine held six more rounds, and Benyamin fired them all with short trigger squeezes.

He thought about his wife and son—so many regrets. Would he and Dov ever get to go on their camping trip?

He thought about Nickel and Those Who Resist, and wondered how things might've gone if he had partnered with the man. A potent team? Surely, though, Nickel could find others to recruit.

I'm still here firing, still kicking. I'm not dead yet.

Benyamin turned to run. Forget the expensive Swarovski scope and rifle. Who cared if he was missing a sock and a shoe? He knew his only hope now was to outdistance this unholy manifestation, maybe hide somewhere down near the river, or find a place beneath the foliage or in a mud bank.

Keep moving, keep moving.

But his aggravated foot rejected his commands. The appendage dragged the soil like a rotted tree stump. He could barely move.

From behind came none of the unearthly growls or werewolves' howls or bat screeches that were supposed to go with this scenario. It was eerily peaceful.

Only thudding steps, closing in.

So Nickel had been right about these killers from the Field of Blood. Benyamin had no idea where the others were, but he knew eleven dwelled right here. Down this hill. He also realized the woman he'd seen through the scope, entering the Totorcea house, was a twelfth revenant. She was the one he'd met last year on the Cetatea chapel's doorsteps, the one who'd directed him inside for his case of beloved tuica.

Had she poisoned him then? Done something to the alcohol? Sure, his infection had started years prior, but was she the one who had triggered and turned it into something hideous?

It seemed they had been playing him all along.

Mammoth hands caught Benyamin by the upper arms, dragging him down. Fingers dug through his coat, latching into the skin with razor-edged nails. The beard scraped over his neck like steel wool.

"I never gave you an answer," the revenant said.

"About what?"

"You offered a drink, and I would love one."

"Here you go," Benyamin said, producing the flask from his pocket.

The assailant swatted it away.

Megiste had been warm in the thatched-roof house, with the crackling logs in the stone fireplace and the lingering smell of muschi. At Eros's bequest, she had trekked with him toward the warehouse and left her fur coat behind. She shivered in the moonlight, her skin more ghostly than usual, almost translucent.

"There it is again," Eros said. "Gunshots."

"Maybe Barabbas found the intruder Ariston spoke of."

"But he doesn't carry a gun."

"Doesn't need to, does he? He's a hulk of a man, if I've ever seen one."

Eros studied her expression. "He's been a faithful servant to the cluster."

"Faithful? Why, what a *tedious* word."

"Come. You look cold." He draped an arm over her shoulder, guiding her through the warehouse's wooden door in its sliding track. "Let's find something to take the evening chill off. I'm sure Barabbas will be along shortly."

"*He* can warm me, if he likes."

"I have a better alternative," said Sol, from inside the building.

Ariston's oldest son stood beside a wheeled hay cart, his hook nose and hooded eyes aimed at them. An electric fixture dangled from an overhead girder and spotlighted the middle-aged woman laid out in the cart.

Dalia Amit was motionless. Twin scarlet dribbles ran from her pudgy arm, indicating the location of Sol's anesthetizing bite and staining the pale-yellow straw that was to be her deathbed.

"What're you up to?" Eros demanded. "And where's the boy you mentioned?"

Sol ignored the household leader's questions, despite the fact Eros was the cluster's second in command. Already, Sol was preparing the emblems of blessed blasphemy—a scabbed wafer torn from the woman's armpit; a thorn extracted from the pus-filled opening.

"Where is the boy?" Eros repeated. "If he's here, it would be in our best interest to guarantee that he, too, is infested."

"This woman, she wrestled with me and allowed the little rodent to scurry off."

"Did I give you instructions to start tapping her?"

"She's sustenance for our families, collectively and individually. Is there a reason I'm beholden to your every whim as it pertains to my own feedings?"

"She's been visited before, on numerous occasions. If you take much more, there's the possibility it would kill her. We need only enough to erase whatever memories she has of this place."

Sol's finger flexed around the wooden rail of the cart.

"Sol," Megiste said, "I think the concern Eros has is that Mrs. Amit remain a long-term resource for the House of Ariston. We would all *adore* depleting these humans till there was nothing left, I understand. But we have to ration ourselves."

"I'm an adult. I'm tired of relying upon Ariston's or *his*"—Sol stabbed a finger toward Eros—"weak decisions."

"He's your superior. You would be wise to hold your tongue."

Sol wiped a hand over his mouth. With a deep breath, he took hold of the vine at Dalia's underarm and tugged—*thwapp, thwapp, thwapp.* The tangle of withered taproot popped loose, thorn by thorn, and coiled in the straw. He snapped off the first thorn, turned and glared into Eros's eyes, then gulped down its contents.

Megiste found her own desire stirred by this greedy display. Her nails began to elongate. She was thirsty—powerfully, *irresistibly* thirsty—after her overland journey to this vineyard. Her skin was cold, her limbs low on life force, and these joined factors spurred a bloodlust that seemed now to have a focal point.

"Eros?" she said.

"I think it's time," he concurred. "My patience has worn thin."

Far away, in Kiev, Megiste and Eros had weighed the options of striking out as a household on their own, forming a cluster independent of and unhindered by the House of Ariston's infighting. Sol's brazen disrespect only underscored their concerns. During the sudden banishment of Salome, they had also witnessed Ariston's capacity for distinguishing between his host's emotions and his Collector ideals. Surely, he would understand.

"Time for what?" Sol sneered.

Megiste took one step toward Ariston's insolent son and slashed his throat with her lethal set of nails. The wound reached through to his spine. Sol, reliant on his protected status as the cluster leader's firstborn, seemed stunned by this abrupt punishment, pulling both hands to the gaping incision, then sagging to his knees on the warehouse floor.

Blood pumped from the opening, geysers of stolen vitality not to be wasted.

Principle: *The strong Collector is encouraged—nay, commissioned—to prey upon the weaker* . . .

Principle: *The leader will* . . . *banish any Collector that displays mutinous intentions.*

"Will Lord Ariston question our actions here?"

"You heard him voice his frustrations," Eros said. "I shouldn't be surprised if he thanks us for doing him—doing the cluster, as a whole—a favor. Are you thirsty?"

Megiste smiled.

Eros, wearing his own silken grin, knelt to take the first drink, and the priestess joined in. She tasted the dreams and nightmares of those whose existences Sol had fed upon. She felt liquid spirits squirt between her teeth, warming her, working their way through her ashen frame. There was nothing but the pulsing in her temples, the hammering of the blood, soothing her migraine and shutting out all other concerns.

When she disengaged at last, she realized Eros had disappeared.

She widened languorous eyes and spotted the leader's feet dangling over the edge of the hay cart. He had dived into another meal, his hand clasped around Dalia's prickly vine, with depleted thorns dotting the straw about him.

"I guess Ariston's son wasn't enough for the two of us," Megiste said, still giddy.

No response.

She thought she heard the rustle of straw off in the shadows along the far wall, but she figured rats were to be expected in a drafty facility such as this.

"And to think, Eros," she said, "that *I* was the insatiable one."

Not a word.

"Where're your table manners?" she joked. "Sir, I'm speaking to you."

His feet didn't move.

Megiste let go of Sol's empty shell. He fell backward, his left shoulder cracking against, then sliding down the curved wagon wheel.

She grasped the rail of the cart and pulled herself up. She looked over the edge and found that Eros also had been relegated to emptiness, to the Restless wanderings that all Collectors feared.

A rusty metal tent peg had been driven into his skull.

CHAPTER
THIRTY-SEVEN

Chattanooga

"You are immortal, Gina."

"As in, 'I'll live forever' and all that junk?"

"Ja," the man said in German. "I mean, yes."

"Yikes. In that case, I should pay more attention to my diet." Gina swabbed a french fry through the ketchup on her paper plate. "Honestly? My mother's real big on that religious mumbo jumbo, so it's sort of burned me out."

"Some people, they never quite get it."

"Hey, you can't judge me by the—"

"I'm talking about her."

"Oh."

Gina nibbled on the fry, still bewildered by the identity of this man who had been down in the caverns, who had sounded like a German tourist, and who even now carried himself with a continental flair. Why had she agreed to have lunch with this Mr. Schaefer?

Earlier, he had stepped in and deflected the prying questions of the girl with the reptilian stare. That was a point in the guy's favor, right? And he'd asked only for a chance to share lunch with Gina at these public picnic tables by the Ruby Falls parking lot. Nothing too creepy about that. The hill here did offer some nice glimpses of Chattanooga below.

None of this had convinced Gina to accept his offer, though.

She had a husband. And a baby in the oven. And tour guides were discouraged against off-hours interaction with attendees.

There was one thing he had said that hooked her: *I have a message for you, from your friend in Borsa.*

Borsa? A message from Cal the Provocateur?

It was so outlandish that she had to find out if it were true. Gina took a slow breath and felt her baby settle inside. She would've discounted Schaefer's claim, except no one else would've even known to mention that obscure Romanian town.

Still, best to play it safe.

She hardened her gaze and said, "Mr. Schaefer, if this is your way of hitting on a married woman, you are out of luck, pal. I've got a good man, and he would tear you to pieces if—"

"I get it, Gina. Read you loud and clear."

"Okay, you've got the American accent going on now. Very smooth."

"Sorta like changing hats for me," he said.

As if to demonstrate, he removed his walking cap and set it on the picnic table. His hair was black, with tufts of gray in his sideburns. His skin had the tanned look of a wealthy European, one who spent winter months in Cairo or Eilat. Only his cerulean eyes hinted at Germanic heritage. Gina recognized such things from her overseas childhood, as well as her daily interaction with international tourists.

Schaefer shrugged. "I'm fluent in more languages than I can count. Enough to make your head spin. Let's see . . . Ancient Greek and Aramaic, Italian, German, Mandarin, a bit of Farsi—"

"Right," Gina said. "Because you *also* are immortal."

He said nothing.

"You've had lifetimes to learn it all, I bet. A real man of the world, soaking in knowledge like a sponge. Must come in handy with the chicks. I mean, you talked me into lunch, right?"

"Fast food?" He thumbed the soggy meat patty in his burger basket. "This hardly counts. You want the good stuff, you should visit a Brazilian *churrascaria*."

"Speak Portuguese too, do you?"

"Enough to get by."

"Okay, okay," she said. "Not like I can prove you wrong."

"Try me in Romanian."

"You think you're up for that?"

Cool and casual, he cupped his hand and waved it toward himself.

"Fine then." She asked him how he was doing. *"Ce mai faci?"*

"Bine." Good.

"Ah, too easy. How about this?" Gina planted an elbow on the table. *"Intoarce-ti fata la dreapta stinga pentru ca soarele sa nu-ti bata in ochi."*

He turned his head to his left, avoiding the sun as she had suggested. She'd intentionally steered him wrong, however, and he blinked as the mid-day glare off of a parked car stabbed at his eyes.

"You're wearing contacts," she said. "I can see the edges of them."

"But are you convinced? By my Romanian, I mean?"

"Are your eyes really blue?"

"Why so nosy? Can't a guy pass on a message without an interrogation?"

"You come talking and acting like you're German. Then you switch to English. You imply that you know friends of mine in Romania." Gina leaned forward. "And, as if that's not strange enough, you decide to take it up a notch and tell me I'm immortal."

"You are," he said. "That's what this is really all about."

"See, the thing is, I knew that already. Now I'm just bored by the whole deal. I mean, I regularly pass through walls and catch bullets with my teeth, but it's lost all its excitement. Skydiving's not as thrilling when you know you can't die doing it."

"Man, you gotta be kidding. That's what makes it so much fun."

"You, buddy boy, are out of your stinkin' mind."

"Yeah? I've been told that before."

Gina started to rise from her bench. "Nice chatting. Back to the grind for me."

Schaefer crossed one leg over the other, glanced at his slim-faced wristwatch, and said, "You've got twenty-one minutes left. You wanna hear this or not? And, oh, if you really wanna know . . . my eyes are green."

"Show me."

"Right here?"

"Or I'm walking."

"You're no pushover. That's good." He ducked his head, squeezed his fingers around his contacts till they popped loose from his corneas. He flicked them to the ground, then edged forward and lifted his gaze. From the side, sun rays highlighted every speckle of gold in his deep green irises. "Look familiar?"

That voice . . . his minty cool breath swirling over her . . .

Cal? In Chattanooga?

After eight-plus years without communication?

Gina rocked back from the table, her hand toppling the cup of Sprite. She grabbed napkins and started mopping up the mess, her downturned eyes wide and scared and confused. She saw liquid dripping onto the JanSport pack tucked by his seat, and she nudged it to the side with her foot. It was heavy.

"My hair's still yellow-blond underneath," he said. "But I look older like this. A little gray does the trick. Gotta keep changing up the look, you know."

"For all your different personalities? To fool the multiple wives?"

"Marriage isn't for me." Deep sadness in his voice.

This was crazy. Why should she believe anything he said? She shook her head from side to side, her pink streak cutting through the black like the coloring on a fifties poodle skirt. She thought of her own makeover. The tattoo. The dyed hair. Boots. Technically, she had no good reason to doubt his transformation.

"I promised you," Cal said, "that one day—when it was the right time—I'd find you again. Well, here I am."

"That was 1989. A long time ago."

"A matter of perspective. I've tried not to draw any trouble your way."

"Trouble, huh? Okay. Listen, Mr. Schaefer, Cal—whatever your real name is—thank you for helping me and my mom get to America. It's been awesome. It's been great. I'm glad I can finally thank you in person. Now I need to get back to work."

Cal touched her hand with his fingers.

"No. No, look." She pulled away and flashed her wedding band. "I'm married, okay? Whatever schoolgirl crush I might've had for a day or two, it's gone. I'm over it. I mean, every girl has those, and we all grow up eventually. As you can see, I'm having a baby soon, so that should give you a good feeling, knowing you had an early hand in my well-being. Maybe you should stop by on your way out of town, say hi to my mom."

"Already tried. She wasn't too thrilled."

"Don't take it personally. She and I aren't even speaking nowadays."

"We all do things we regret, Gina. I'm more guilty than most."

She used his split second of introspection to study his features, to verify what her heart had already confirmed. She saw the same nose, same cheekbones. Young face. Tanned skin, which he could've come by naturally or unnaturally. She visualized that mop of wheat-colored hair showcasing his gorgeous eyes.

This was the Provocateur. He was here. He'd come back for her.

Her throat tightened.

"Well, buddy boy," she said at last, touching the scar on her arm. "Just to keep the air clear between you and me, I want you to know I've forgotten about that whole cutting ordeal. Nikki's into that, and I know you were just doing what you were told."

"I am sorry about that, Gina."

"Like I said: forgotten."

Defying her words, the old wound on her neck seemed to swell like a blood blister about to pop.

"It was meant to throw them off. You know, a little misdirection. In the car, we talked about Kiev, then headed south to Belgrade instead. When they found your bloody shirt, they had only your memories to go on."

"My memories?"

"The ones I bled from you. It was so they wouldn't—"

"The mysterious *they* again."

"The point is, it worked," Cal said. "We had to get you outta there, because they were onto you. Until recently, I don't think they had a clue where you were. But now, this pregnancy of yours has them sniffing around again."

"I don't like the way you say that."

"You know that brunette in the cave? The one asking all the questions?"

"She gave me the creeps."

"She was a Collector. That's why I tried to butt in."

Gina rubbed the goose bumps from her arm. She thought about his earlier German tourist act. Cal, here in the flesh—for the safety of her unborn child.

"They're just waiting," he added, "till they know for sure."

"Know *what*? You throw out all these things, and I feel like that little girl again, back in Cuvin. You're losing me, Cal. Collectors, immortality, my baby . . . Give me something to sink my teeth into here."

He snapped his eyes to hers. "Don't even joke like that."

"Dang. It's just an expression."

"It's a reality. I've seen what they can do. They'll suck everything they can from you and leave you empty. Your time, money, creative energy—all of it, feeding into their Collection of Souls. The collective misery, piling higher and higher."

Gina's stomach contorted. Sharp, needling cramps.

Around the picnic area, parents and students were caught up in their activities, some milling in the parking lot, others yelling to get into/out of/off of the car. Gasoline fumes arose from an SUV idling near the Cavern Castle entry.

"They've been here," Cal said, "since the beginning."

"The beginning of what?"

"Of everything. Of history."

She scoffed. "As in Adam and Eve? That beginning?"

"Sure. Before then, after then. Collectors, out to drain your lifeblood. And I think there were more released a few years back. Without going into all the details, I believe we've got this new vampiric breed that's found a way to use dead hosts. Well, previously dead. Undead . . . Anyway, for a period, they'll wreak all the mayhem they can."

"This is lots of great stuff for a movie, Cal. You're, uh, just taking it a little too seriously maybe. Not doubting you. But, you know, stay tethered to the real world."

"Nikki hasn't told you much, I take it."

"About this? No. Only enough to justify each of her purgings."

"Yeah, she knows just enough to be dangerous."

"No argument from me."

He sighed. "Seems everyone's out for blood, in one way or another."

"Yum, yum."

Cal's eyelids closed for a moment over the gold flecks.

"Sorry," she said.

"It's okay, Gina." He put on a grin, tossed a cautious glance around the picnic area. "In fact, sometimes I joke about it too, just to stinkin' stay sane. But this is urgent. You're having this baby soon, and as you confirmed for that brunette today, you're having a boy. That makes him a potential target. In any given generation, there are one or two males born—for safety measures—to take the place of the Nistarim."

"The Concealed Ones." She patted her belly.

"You give the term a whole new meaning."

"Nikki's told me the basic spiel. I know they bear the world's burdens, holding back Final Vengeance, or the Day of Judgment, or whatever. And we should all want to be humble in spirit, right? Show care for others."

"A noble goal, sure."

"But, uh, if it's only boys who qualify for the Nistarim, then why're you talking to me about this?"

"You're carrying a boy, aren't you?"

CHAPTER
THIRTY-EIGHT

Totorcea Vineyards

The warehouse door scraped along its metal track, revealing a bulky silhouette. Megiste started at the shrill sound, then touched a hand to her cheek, relieved to see the stalwart Barabbas. Her thoughts, however, continued spiraling downward. In a matter of minutes, the cluster's very foundations had begun to crumble.

Sol: he was here and gone.

And about time.

Eros: he, too, was gone. How could this be? The head of the House of Eros was a hollow husk and nothing more. What would Ariston's reaction be to this devastation? Would she face repercussions for her involvement?

"*Facilis descensus Averno,*" she muttered in benediction to her former lover.

"Megiste?"

She sighed. "What is it you want, Barabbas?"

He stepped into the pool of overhead light. He wore a despondent expression to match her own. With the large form slung across his shoulders, he could've been a hunter returning with a stag, with another rack of antlers to adorn the wall beside the fireplace in the house.

"I didn't mean to do it," he said.

"What've you done *this* time, my dear? Who is that?"

"The intruder, I found him. Cornered him up in the ruins."

"Well, there's nothing wrong with that."

"But Ariston'll be mad at me."

"I wouldn't worry. I think he'll have more pressing matters on his mind."

"I tapped almost everything," Barabbas said. "More than my share."

"Sometimes the need overtakes us," Megiste said bitterly, glancing back at the shrunken form of her household leader.

"He'll find out when he gets back, though." The henchman flopped the victim onto the floor, and the priestess recognized the features of Benyamin Amit. The body was withered, entwined with crusty brambles that had issued from his heel. "I had him there in my hands, and I smelled the blood, and I just . . . I tried to leave a few at least. Here." He surrendered an untapped thorn, displaying his willingness to share while also making her complicit with his perceived wrongdoing

Megiste drank, smiling as she siphoned out Benyamin Amit's earlier and distant admiration of her appearance. Yes, the man was quite right. She *did* look good through a scope, although a bit pale.

"Do you think I'll be punished?" Barabbas was asking.

"What?"

"When Ariston gets here?"

"You're not comprehending what I'm saying. Look." She took a step toward the hay cart and cupped Eros's fractured cranium, lifting it into view. "Your victim isn't the only one Ariston'll have to worry over. It seems you and I may have both gotten ourselves into some trouble, don't you think?"

"Eros?" Barabbas tripped over Mr. Amit in a rush to see this for himself. He moaned, pulling the unresponsive corpse away from the dead woman and examining the horrendous split in his skull. His whisper was gruff. "How did this happen?"

"There's one easy way to find out." While Megiste snapped off the next thorn along Dalia Amit's infected strand, she reflected on the skittering sounds she'd heard earlier from the shadows. "But I already have a good idea which little rodent it was that tried to rescue *dear* old Mama."

"Who?"

Megiste sipped. Sipped again.

Searching for, and finding, answers from Dalia's fated last hours on Earth.

Two Hours Earlier—Arad

Dalia was incensed. Yesterday she'd confronted her husband about his nocturnal escapades and hoped to shame him into an act of contrition, but he'd given no response. Not that she expected any different. Long ago, he'd set off on his own path, with no intentions of returning to the more respectable road she traveled.

"Come along, Dov." She turned off the oven, put a lid over the supa. "We're going to find out what your father is up to. He comes home late. He has little time to spend with his own wife and son. When, I ask, was the last time you two went fishing together? Or hiked the trails?"

"We're going this weekend, Mama. He promised me."

"Phaw. Promises are nothing to him. When was the last time he even arrived home in time for supper, huh? You tell me."

Her son lowered his head until dark hair brushed thick eyelashes.

"When, Dov?"

"I'm thinking, Mama. Maybe a few months ago."

"Well, now—don't you think it's time he showed what a true father should be? You are nearly thirteen, nearly a man. How much longer can he put off such a matter? Fetch a coat and follow me." She removed her apron. "We're going to see that he listens to his family. Perhaps he'll give heed to your words more than mine."

Dov reappeared at the front door with a pack hanging from his arm.

"What is that?"

"Our camping supplies," Dov said. "Just in case."

"Hmmph."

"He made a promise."

"I wish I had your optimism."

Dalia tugged her son by the hand, down the stairs, onto the street. They hailed a taxicab to city hall, then parked a half block away from Benyamin's Peugot. He would drive from here, and they would follow at a distance. He was up to something, and Dalia intended to discover what that was. Or who it was.

"Don't worry," she told the cab driver. "You'll be paid."

Forty minutes later, they were moving through Lipova, chased by the day's lengthening shadows, toward a castle on a nearby peak. The Peugot had turned off somewhere just out of town. Had they lost Ben? Did he know he was being tailed?

"Slowly," Dalia said.

Her son tugged on her arm. "Just over the hill there, this is close to where he said we'd go camping. Maybe he's here to scout it out."

"Maybe."

They passed a smattering of farms, houses, and a sloping property with the name Totorcea Vineyards scrolled across a placard between two posts.

That name. Dalia knew it. On a number of occasions, she'd been to city hall to keep tabs on her husband's whereabouts and his companions. Helene Totorcea was an archivist on the lower level, a simple but pretty woman. Benyamin had always denied infidelity, but now the picture took shape in Dalia's mind, substantiating years of suspicion and accusation. She was about to catch him redhanded.

And if his son's presence brought greater shame, so be it.

"This is the place, driver." The rap of her knuckles against the window sent a jolt along her skin to her underarm affliction. "Here. Right here."

"You are sure?"

"Must you argue with a paying fare? Goodness." She flung a wad of lei onto the front seat, then turned to Dov. "Are you ready?"

"Yes." He patted his pack, producing a metallic clink. "I have it all here—the tent stuff, some food, and a couple pictures from our last trip. You could join us, Mama. It'll be fun. We can camp out beneath the stars."

She hadn't seen her son this animated in some time, and though she wanted to believe the best, she hadn't the energy to maintain such hope.

"If you need a pillow," Dov went on, "you simply wrap up your clothes in a coat. That's what Dad taught me."

The poor boy was in denial.

"Go." Dalia shooed him from the backseat. "Let's move along."

Megiste dropped the thorn.

"Who was it?" Barabbas said.

"Her son. A measly, *meek* twelve-year-old."

"Is he infected, the way his parents were?"

"I don't see how that's possible. Not if he could get away with . . . with this reprehensible violence against our own kind."

"Defending his mother—"

"Killing a grown man, Barabbas. Don't gloss over the details. Well, wherever you are now, little Dov Amit, you're an orphan, I'm afraid."

"He could still be nearby."

She pointed. "I believe he crawled off in that direction."

Together, Megiste and Barabbas searched the premises, in agreement that this was the first order of business before revealing to the Akeldama Cluster the horror that had befallen them. Later, much would have to be decided—a burial site for the Amits, and a new leader to guide the House of Eros.

At a gap in the warehouse wall, Barabbas found scuffs in the dirt that confirmed Megiste's suspicion that the Hebrew boy had gone out this way.

Probably entered here, as well. There was little else, however. No trail. No hiding place. He had vanished into the night.

"He could've gone up into the hills," the big man said. "Or down to the river. If you'd like, I can switch hosts and take a look from above. Or . . . I don't know. Maybe he hitched a ride from a passing motorcar. What should I do?"

Megiste, as priestess, felt sorry for the henchman. For so long he had followed orders that he was listless without them. Clear objectives would have to be set down to keep him on course until Ariston's return.

Or, perhaps . . .

Her conniving nature coiled into position, hissing of plots and machinations, preparing to strike a deal for the benefit of her household.

As things now stood, Ariston's foundations of strength were compromised. He was without a known successor; his wives and family members were weak-spined creatures, trained by his dominant nature to recede into subservience; and Barabbas alone showed earnest, if not half-witted, faithfulness to the pudgy chieftain.

"What *are* we going to do?" she asked of the bearded oaf before her. "The House of Eros is leaderless, and who are we but a handful of women? How *ever* will we survive on our own?"

"Ariston will—"

"Oh, Barabbas, don't speak of him now. He can be so . . . controlling. It's just you and me here, together."

"But he'll be back soon."

"Hours from now, if at all." She lifted her peasant blouse over her head, revealing alabaster skin. "Come here, you clumsy brute. Look at you, all messy from a *hard* night's work." She took his hand, used the blouse to rub away the grime and viscera of his feeding. "You really ought to wash beneath your nails, dear Barabbas."

"Each morning, I—"

"All in good fun, doll. Oh, look here. A spot on your mouth."

They had both supped already. They were both warm and sated. This need that overtook them was earthier than that, and Barabbas grunted in approval of her nibbling lips on his. His fervor grew. With one hand, he plucked the bodies from the cart; with the other, he pushed her back onto the straw.

"I like it when you take the lead," she said.

He groaned.

"My dear Barabbas, come away with me. Why, *you* can watch over our household."

"I'm not sure I—"

"Don't talk," she whispered. "Please, won't you give me time to convince you?"

A few minutes was all it took.

CHAPTER
THIRTY-NINE

Chattanooga

"Oh." Gina crossed her arms over her stomach, and glared across the picnic table at Cal. "Right. So, what you're saying is that my baby is . . . Listen, this is crazy talk. And since when does any of this make me immortal? I mean, are the Nistarim even immortal?"

"Not all of them."

"That sure clarifies things. Isn't it just legend anyway, a way of giving good Jewish families something to shoot for? How'd the whole story start getting passed around?"

"Heard of Sodom and Gomorrah?"

"Been years since I've read a Bible, but that's pretty basic knowledge. Sodom's there by the Dead Sea, isn't it? The Salt Sea?"

"A lotta history around the place. Some of it recent, and not pretty."

"Okay," Gina said. "Back to the legend."

Cal glanced at his watch. "You've got six minutes left."

"You say my child's in danger? The job can wait. Keep talking."

"I'll make it quick. You shouldn't break the routine, though. Act normal."

"Can you just get to the point?"

A butterfly flitted into view, landed on a drop of spilled Sprite, then flew off.

"Sure. The story goes that Abraham, he begs God not to destroy the wicked cities, and so he starts wheeling and dealing: 'God, if there are fifty righteous people, will you save the place? What if there's forty-five? Forty?' And so on. 'Yes, yes, yes,' God says. All the way down to ten."

"Must've been one bad place. They still got the brimstone, didn't they?"

Cal's eyes turned mournful at her flippancy. "The story," he said, "shows that the Almighty was willing to protect many for the sake of a few righteous ones. Which leads to the Nistarim, the Lamed Vov."

"Thirty-six of them, right? Guess that should be more than enough."

"Grace beyond measure," he agreed.

"Talk to Nikki about grace, and she starts sharpening the knives."

"She needs it more than most."

"What'd she do that was so awful?" Gina shooed flies from her plate of fries.

"I'll leave that for her to tell. She's sworn me to secrecy."

"Convenient."

"Actually, a real pain in the butt. There's so much I wanna say."

"Start with the whole immortal thing. You've already spilled the beans on that one. How can you even know? About me, I mean?"

"I was there, Gina."

"Where?"

"Last year. That morning, outside Rembrandt's."

"You . . . you were there?" Gina's heart wedged in her throat, her thoughts churning in reverse to that specific day in Chattanooga, in the Bluff View Art District. "You were across the road."

"Heading up High Street," he confirmed. "I've checked in on you over the years, but that day proved to me what I already suspected. Death by natural means won't be your biggest concern."

"Is there any other way?"

"You could have your very soul sapped from your veins."

"As in, the whole Collector-slash-vampire thing?"

"Something like that." Cal tapped his watch. "Two minutes and counting."

"Okay. But who says I should've died? Other people survive things like that."

"And just walk away? You had a broken back, a cracked skull—"

"There's no proof any of that happened."

"*You* know what happened."

Before her eyes, images swarmed from that horrendous collision between flesh and metal. She could still feel the cartilage and bone shifting back into place, still recall the sensations of heat, light, and moisture on her tongue.

"Did you . . . ?" She faltered. "Give me something to drink?"

"Just a little bit."

"It was blood."

"Yes."

"Whose?"

"Someone who cares about you deeply."

"Yours?"

"If it woulda helped, I woulda given it. But, no."

Gina's mind reeled with these continued questions and revelations. She remembered a shadow standing over her, her reflexive swallowing of warm liquid, the sudden quickening of her body. If she was immortal, as Cal claimed, and if she had been energized by a sip of the red stuff, what did that make her?

"Are you saying I'm a . . . ?"

"A what?"

"A vampire?"

Cal's burst of laughter was so lighthearted, so unaffected, that it washed her suspicion away. "No," he said, his shoulders still shaking with mirth. "You're no such thing, Gina. Unless, of course, you've been draining necks and sleeping in coffins."

"Not recently."

"Phew. That's a big load off my back." He chuckled again.

"Glad you think it's funny. But what're you saying, then? How'd I survive the run-in with the truck?"

Cal covered his mouth and tried to calm himself.

She investigated another angle. "What about you? Are you . . . ?"

"Go on. I gotta hear this one."

"Well, this is just as crazy, so don't laugh. Okay, here it is—and I don't even know if I buy into this stuff myself—but are you my . . . guardian angel?"

"One of the Unfallen?" Cal almost choked.

"I told you not to laugh."

"C'mon. Can you see me sitting on a cloud, playing a harp?"

"That's a misconception found nowhere in the Bible."

"Don't I know it."

"But you just—"

"I was messin' around, okay? And the last time I checked, vampires weren't sleeping in coffins either. That's a modern addition to their mythology."

A charge of anger warmed Gina's cheeks. "What if I *had* been killed on High Street? What if you were wrong about me being immortal, or whatever? You think then it would've been oh-so-ha-ha hilarious?"

"I knew it wouldn't play out that way."

"Right. Instead, you just stood by for the show. How sick is *that*?"

"But I knew."

"How?"

"Gina, since way back in Borsa, I've known you had a purpose. A destiny, if you wanna call it that. Because of that seal there on your forehead."

"This?" She pulled fingers across the spot. "You mean, you can see it?"

Southbound I-75, Georgia

Not even four p.m. yet, and cars were at a standstill on their way into Atlanta. Erota knew she should've left earlier, but after the visit to Ruby

Falls—and her favorite tour guide—she had swung through downtown Chattanooga for lunch at the Mellow Mushroom. Was there anything better than pizza stacked with meat, fresh olives, and herbs?

Now, staring down rows of vehicles, Erota felt tempted to hitch a ride on a winged insect or a feathered friend. Of course, there would be that little issue of abandoning her human host, in her husband's Jaguar, on the interstate.

She could hear Ray-Ban now: *You found her body* where, *Officer?*

Not that such creatures were the cure-all for her impatience, anyway. Take, for example, the Collector she'd crossed paths with in Decatur. He was a pedophile. One afternoon in a traffic jam, he'd left his living human habitation for a snappier ride in a passing dragonfly. Only to run head-on into a semi's headlight.

It was so pure, so beautiful, he told her later. *I couldn't help myself.*

There was his problem in a nutshell, and she bore him no sympathy.

The filthy Collector had found himself a hundred miles away, at a truck stop, before he could disengage himself from the splattered mess of his secondary host. Nothing more than a wispy tendril in the atmosphere, he had spent hours hopping wind currents and hugging shadows to find his way back to his usual dwelling.

Erota, in her husband's Jag, flicked on the AC, cranked the Bose stereo, and eyed the driver in the adjacent car. Through her sunglasses, she watched his look of surprise turn to sly approval, then winking flirtation. He'd be ready for a cold shower by the time she was done playing mind games with him.

Easy pickings, here in the Peach State.

Erota inched forward a car length, put it back into Park, and savored thoughts of a much greater victory only weeks away.

Did that German tourist think he'd fooled her during the cave tour? She knew what he was up to and knew just how to exploit him. She had her contact in place at Gina's hospital, she'd verified the unborn's sex and approximate due date, and she had a trusty helper at work in a basement not far away.

The components were all in place.

Once she could see the infant for herself, she would light the fuse.

Chattanooga

"Is this gonna get you in trouble?"

"Nope, we're fine," Gina said.

Side by side in her Camry, arms brushing with each bump in the road, Gina and Cal had driven down to the riverfront. They faced the water now, sitting on concrete steps near an historical marker for the Trail of Tears.

"My supervisor was cool about it. I used the old prego excuse—which is legitimate, in this case—and she said to take the rest of the day off, come back tomorrow with a fresh smile."

"I like your smile," Cal said.

"You do?"

"Melted my heart the first time I laid eyes on you."

"I was just a kid."

"Who knows how old you really were?"

"Oh, good point. Me being immortal and all. Very clever. Well, if you must know, I'm two hundred and holding."

"Uh, not even," Cal said. "So, do you wanna hear about the mark?"

She was still mulling all that he had revealed up at Ruby Falls. Her own childhood memories were a scattering of mosaic tiles—not quite matching, dazzling but jagged, hinting at a picture that seemed to never take shape. Did he hold the pieces that could connect it all? Sure, she could buy into the idea of the Lamed Vov. As a Romanian Jew, Nikki had raised Gina with stories of the Nistarim and of distant uncles or cousins who were suspected of being a *lamedvovnik.*

Still, to think that her own child might be involved.

"Let's hear it, buddy boy," she said to Cal. "Tell me what you see."

She'd been waiting for his explanation of the symbol on her skin. No matter his response, she was certain that immortality and the Fountain of Youth were concepts for fairy tales, not her own flesh-and-blood experience.

"Once I tell you, you'll be responsible for what you know."

"Is that a good thing, or bad?"

"It just is," he said.

Gina's gaze lighted again on the Trail of Tears marker, and she debated whether it was a bad omen or just a counterpoint to her recent struggles. "Well, Cal, I'm all for responsibility, and I'm tired of wondering. Plus, if it's my key to life eternal, maybe I can market it. Sell postcards and T-shirts, or something."

He turned to face her. "The mark has nothing to do with that."

"What do you mean?"

"You being immortal is a whole separate issue."

"So the mark's meaningless? What're you getting at?"

He brushed the hair back over her head, exposing the symbol she had long tried to hide—and which no one else, except a village prefect long ago, seemed to have had any awareness of.

She felt naked beneath his scrutiny. "Well?"

"There's these light blue lines, almost like veins."

"Yeah, I know."

Tracing her skin, his fingers were dry, yet smooth—the way leather might feel after years of wear and tear—and their touch caused something to swell in her chest. A bittersweet desire. She'd always been drawn to those with links to her homeland, but this seemed to go beyond that. It made no sense to feel deeply for a man who had shared only a few incidents in her past.

Confused by her yearning, she slipped back into sarcasm.

"Is it a tumor?"

He frowned at that.

"Kidding," she said. "Just a joke."

Even his reaction tugged at her, and she told herself to be cautious. She'd always had genuine concern for the downtrodden and the orphans, and she found herself susceptible now that the same concern was turned her direction.

Cal's green eyes were locked onto her.

"What?" she said. "Do I look like a charity case?"

"You look like a beautiful young woman."

She tapped the ring on her finger. "Married. Don't you forget it."

"I hope he's good to you."

"Jed? He's the best."

She meant it, and she tamped down any thoughts otherwise. Cal had information she needed, and that alone was her reason for being here beside him on the riverfront steps.

"So," Gina said. "We've established that it's not a tumor."

"I already know what it is. You've been Lettered."

"Lettered in varsity track and field, if that counts."

"The letter Tav, Gina. Or Tau. It's from the ancient Hebrew alphabet. Almost like an *x* with soft little curls on the ends. Over the centuries, it's been simplified and used by all sortsa people. Basically, a cross. Some call it the Roman Cross, or the *crux commissa*. Saint Francis of Assisi, he even used it as part of his crest."

"Okay. And?"

"You ever seen those people on Ash Wednesday, wearing the Sign of the Cross on their foreheads? It all comes from the same original story."

"This is sounding like Nikki now. Snoozeville."

"You wanna know?" he said. "Or you gonna make jokes?"

She stared off over the meandering river. "What's it mean for me, Cal? You come waltzing in to my work—after quite the long absence, I might add—and start making these wild claims. Like I'm supposed to believe you. Well, give me something real." She tapped his chest with her fist. "Something tangible."

"I'll give you what I know. You'll have to decide from there."

"Loads of fun. Hit me with it."

"First, lemme guess. This symbol appeared on your twelfth birthday."

"Hey. There's no way you could—"

"Gina, listen. There's all kindsa stuff that got lost in your past, jumbled up and bled away. I know how strong you've had to become. That's good. You're trying to move forward and put the old things behind you, and I admire that. But now you've got this wall of cynicism up, to keep anything else from getting in."

"I won't deny it. What? Is that a problem for you?"

His eyes softened, drifting down to hers.

"Sorry," she said. "It's just—"

"No, Gina. It's okay. If I wanna get to the bottom of things, I'm sure to stir up some mud."

"That's me. Ol' muddy waters."

"That's not what I see," he said. "Not at all."

As Cal spoke, he ran the pad of his finger up left, down right, up left, down right, over the mark. Gina felt cool tingling spread across her scalp—a cup of pure water, of snowmelt, emptying over her head and running down into her hair.

How else could she explain the sensation?

She resisted labeling moments such as these, although she'd had them before a time or two. She hedged against the fanaticism of her mother and ran screaming from anything that smacked of spiritual arm-twisting. Put enough people in a room—or an N. K. Lazarescu session—and a skilled communicator could work them into a blather over just about anything.

But could there be a seed of truth in all her mom's talk? Something unmarred and radiant that lay hidden beneath heaps of crusty religion?

In Gina's mind's eye, somewhere behind these lines etched into her thick skull, she watched colorful glass shards begin to float into place, bumping softly, easing, joining, becoming one. In Romania, she'd seen meticulous craftsmanship just like it, broken stone turned into works of art.

She stared off past Cal's shoulder. Lifting her chin. Afraid to blink.

"Can you just tell me the story?" she said.

"Sure thing."

CHAPTER
FORTY

"It's from the ninth chapter of Ezekiel," Cal Nichols explained. "God instructs this guy carrying a writer's case to go through the streets of Jerusalem and to start marking the foreheads of those who sigh and weep for the sins they see all around. Each of the ones that got Lettered, they were spared from the wrath to come."

"Final Vengeance," Gina said.

"A foreshadowing, maybe. These people, they were not to be touched during that particular day of judgment, because of the sorrow they'd carried with them, mourning for a world gone mad."

"Is that what you think of this place?"

"Me? I see beauty, and lots of amazing things. Everywhere I go, I'm running into people with big hearts and love that won't quit. That's why we need you, Gina. If this all pans out, I mean. We've gotta fight to protect others. We need your son. We need the Concealed Ones, who are like the solid foundation—humble and unseen, but without them the whole thing crumbles."

"Why me, though? I thought it was all a male thing."

"They have to come from somewhere, don't they?" He gestured to her tummy. "See there? Prego, in your own words."

"So the women do all the work, while the men get the glory? Typical."

"Well, with that attitude of yours . . ."

"Who makes these rules?"

"Hey, man, at least you get the Letter." He flashed a smile. "Not to mention that your son will have a portion of immortal blood—thanks to you, that is. In Jewish culture, heredity passes through the mother's side. Aside from the original Thirty-Six, the previous Nistarim candidates have always been mortal."

"If you ask me, it sounds like a flawed plan."

"We're all flawed."

"So I've heard."

"But it doesn't disqualify us from being Those Who Resist."

"Well, that's a big relief."

"It should be. Even though some people think this stuff I'm telling you is just legend, much of it comes down through revered rabbinical traditions. To a devout Jew, the Talmud's just about level with the Torah and the Scriptures. And of course, the male is seen as a covering or a protector, going back through thousands of years of culture."

"And you think my child is a part of all this?"

"You tell me."

She reflected on the past months of cramps and knee-buckling grief, of sympathy pains that seemed to torment her son within. What sort of life lay ahead for him? She felt a flutter in her midsection.

"My poor baby," she said.

"Yeah, there's not much glory in the job." A weary expression crossed Cal's face. "It's all about dying to yourself every day. Often a long, lonely road."

"That about describes it," she said. "From the moment I took the pregnancy test, he's been putting me through the wringer. Sure, it's painful.

But it's more of an emotional thing, a psychological drain. Does that sound totally whacked?"

"Makes perfect sense to me."

"Oh? You've been pregnant before?"

"Funny." He rested his hand on her arm. "I know that you, Gina, in your heart of hearts, care deeply about the world around you. What we've been talking about, this is your chance to carry on that concern through your child. And that's what's got these Akeldama Collectors all fired up. Through their immortal—no, they don't even deserve that word—through their *undead* eyes, they're able to see the Lettered. They know you must be carrying a special child, and that's what they're waiting on, to know if the kid's the real deal."

"So I pop him out, and there they are? Ready to snatch him away?"

"Probably not that simple. The Letter appears at adulthood. For boys, that's age thirteen. Until then they won't know for sure that your son's one of the Nistarim, but they'll assume that's the case based on your Letter. My guess is they'll wait to be sure you have a male, then make a move."

"Basically, we're doomed. Is that what you're saying?"

"I wouldn't put it that way."

"How *would* you put it? Thanks, Cal. Way to drop a bomb on my picture of domestic bliss. What am I supposed to do? Hire armed guards? Move to Timbuktu?"

"Want my advice? Stay put."

"What if I run away? Try to sneak off somewhere?"

"They'll follow. Predator and prey."

"No, thank you. I had enough running early on in life."

"More than you even remember, Gina."

"What?"

"Just ride this thing out," he said, "to the due date. I'll be hidden, but I'll be watching. You have to trust me on that part, no matter what."

"Like I trusted you to come find me?"

"I'm here, aren't I?"

Gina imagined laying her head against his chest, but that would open doors inside that were best left closed. She thought of Jed. She gave a nonchalant shrug.

"Thing is," he said, "I've faced these creatures before, even put down a Collector or two in my day. That's my job now." A somber tone in his voice, one of grim determination. "My vow to you is that I'll be here, keeping an eye on you, guarding your going in and going out—at home, the hospital, wherever. I'll make sure your baby's safe and sound."

"Right. Like you did on High Street?"

"Don't forget I gave you that drink."

"What drink?"

He fished a necklace of braided twine from around his neck, tapped the vial that hung from it. "Moisture on your tongue, remember? Reviving drops."

"But I . . ." Gina shook her head. "If I'm immortal, I wouldn't have died anyway, according to your wonderful theories. And for that matter, why worry about my baby? I mean, they can't kill him. Isn't that what you've been saying?"

"It's not that simple."

"Uh, news flash. Yeah, it is. In English, *immortal* means you cannot die."

"There are limitations. It's not a free pass, some *Get out of jail free* card. If the Nistarim are put to death, they must be revived within three days or their pilgrimage on Earth is over. It's a window the Nazarene opened by His own defeat of death."

"Well, the whole thing seems overrated, if you ask me. I mean, I take a bullet, I keel over, and then I get three days for some miracle to happen or I'm still toast."

"That's three days more than the average person."

"Whoop-dee-doo."

"And you come back good as new."

"Well, there's the real sales hook. Sign me up."

Cal's eyes met hers. "Gina, most people are appointed to live once, but your role is slightly different. You're a direct descendant of the original thirty-six."

"What do you mean, 'original'?"

"The first ones. Before any had collapsed beneath the burden. Before any others had risen to take their place. In Jewish numerology—this whole school of study called *gemetria*—eighteen is the number of life. So thirty-six is—"

"Let me guess: double life."

"Exactly. So, if you're tracking here, we have the doubly dead. More specifically, this new breed of parasites: Jerusalem's Undead. The good news is that there's the other set of Jerusalem's Undead: the doubly alive. They are the Nistarim, raised up to bear the weight and to strengthen Those Who Resist."

"Hold on. Time-out. So the original Nistarim are the ones who were Lettered in Ezekiel?"

"You got it. They lived thousands of years ago and eventually died natural deaths, after serving their purpose during the time of the prophets."

"But now they're back? I'm confused."

"They came back, yes. When Yeshua was crucified, there was an earthquake—it's all written there in the Gospel of Matthew, chapter 27—and three days later He was resurrected. Bam. Then, like it was some sorta proof of His victory over death, the saints from Ezekiel, they got up out of their graves and went wandering into Jerusalem too. They were seen by a buncha people."

"You know how insane this all sounds?"

"Wait, and here's the clincher. There were—"

"Thirty-six of them."

"Pretty smart."

"I think you mean pretty *and* smart."

"Sure, that too."

"Cal, I'm going to need time to process this."

"Gets one step wilder," he said.

Gina caught her breath. She was already walking through a mental hall of mirrors—reflections and shadows behind her, ahead of her, in multiples all around. She felt disoriented, strangely invigorated. She feared for her child.

"Those original Nistarim," he pressed on, "have been walking the earth now for the past two millennia. They were commissioned by Yeshua Himself to protect and comfort Those Who Resist."

"Oh. Well, *that's* good to know."

"Better believe it."

"And Those Who Resist are . . . those who stand against the Collectors?"

"They find their life in the Nazarene Blood."

"Everyone out for blood. Your words."

"The life is in the blood, so it's all a matter of which life you want to lead. By drinking from the Nazarene, you identify yourself with His life, His memories, His suffering. All of that. You can see why it'd be total anathema to the Collectors."

"Uh, excuse me, but when did we cross back into Nikki territory? She's drummed into me enough fanatical talk for a lifetime."

"She's missed the whole point. Have you ever seen her drink?"

"Nazarene Blood? Sorry, but that's just nasty."

Cal pulled a knee up close to his chest, let his gaze drift off over the river. "Gina, I know how strange all this has gotta sound." He cleared his throat. "Please don't blow me off, just because Nikki's mixed in her own brand of mysticism with good ol' brass-tacks truth."

"Mysticism? Oh, you mean like cutting a helpless child?" The old neck scar surged with a phantom pain.

"She thought she was protecting you."

"Boy, was *I* ever lucky."

"Still bitter, and I don't blame you. But you don't have to live with those scars, not forever. Yeshua, when He came outta that tomb, He left His blood to cover all the evil that your mother thought she had to cut away."

"Thank you, O wise one. Just not sure I buy into all that."

"You could never buy into it, Gina. It's a gift that was given, and all you have to do is accept it—just like the gift I gave you back in Cuvin."

"These?" She touched one of her earrings. "Would you believe I had to dig them out of the garbage? Nikki had thrown them away."

"Life gets messy sometimes, doesn't it?"

"All part of the deal."

"Did you know those earrings contain drops of Nazarene Blood?"

"What?"

"If you choose to believe, that's all it takes. One drop."

"Of blood?"

"A chance at being cleansed. A complete transfusion. Only the pure stuff, absorbed into every vein, every corpuscle."

"You know what? Gross. Disgusting." Gina lifted herself to her feet, holding her stomach in her right hand. "And I thought I'd escaped from this sort of thinking. Not to be rude or anything, but you've now wasted half of my stinkin' day with this crazy talk. I'm married. I'm having a baby. I've moved on, thank you very much. Now, go away."

Cal brushed comforting fingers across her dangling left hand, and—

"*No.*" Gina withdrew from his touch. "Don't even start. Whatever little game you're playing, count me out."

"The last person who said that to me, his name was Benyamin."

"What do I care, Cal?"

"He died two hours ago."

"While we were talking at the picnic table? And how would you know that?"

"I felt it."

"Oh. Right. Of course." Gina rolled her eyes. "Get *away*, you freak."

Cal sighed. "We're done, then?"

"You think?"

"I do have some things to take care of," he said, standing. "Someone to watch over."

"Good. Go. Good-bye."

"Don't worry about your baby. I'll keep him safe."

"Right. Sure, you will. If that's what this was all about, you could've skipped story time and protected him from behind the scenes. There was no need to drag me down into all this."

"Gina, I love you. Always have."

"Bye."

"It's not all that it seems."

"Doesn't seem like much at all." She leaned toward him, shoved aside his cap and his black-dyed hair, and studied his forehead. She rubbed the slate of tanned skin, found nothing there. No lines. No symbol.

Just as she'd figured.

She waddled back to the car, called over the door. "Cal, I'm going to let you find your own ride, okay? You just watch out for those pesky Collectors."

"My never-ending task."

Gina sought solace at her chessboard that evening, playing through the Immortal Game, analyzing moves, weighing risks and gambits and sacrifices. It was all so complex.

"Rough day in the caverns?" Jed asked.

"Mm-hmm."

"Coke." He handed her a glass. "Caffeine-free, for the little guy."

"Thanks, Jed. You're going to be a good dad."

"I hope so."

She continued staring at the board.

"Gina?"

"Hmm?"

"Did you know I called you at work today?"

"Mmm."

"They said you'd left early, not feeling good. Left with some dude."

The implication of Jed's words penetrated her chess calculations, and she swiveled in her seat. She realized now why he'd been so standoffish since her return home. "He was an old friend," she said. "Nothing to worry about."

"You sure?"

Cal's warnings buzzed in Gina's head. If there was any truth to his words, they had a *lot* to worry about. How could she possibly unload all that on her husband, though? She herself barely knew what to make of it all. He would think she'd gone over the edge.

"It had nothing to do with you," she said. "I swear it."

"And we're okay?"

"You and me? Yeah, sweetheart, we're good."

"I'm trying not to jump to conclusions here, Gina. Don't get me wrong. I just hope that whatever was going on, you got it worked out."

She nodded. "That makes two of us."

"Three of us," he said softly. And turned on the TV.

CHAPTER
FORTY-ONE

Early September—Chattanooga

Another day down. Three and a half weeks remaining till the due date.

With eight hours on foot every shift, and between four and five miles traveled through the Ruby Falls cave system, Gina was a regular workhorse. She figured at this rate she would be ready to run a marathon the week after her delivery.

Alone, leaning over the employee restroom sink, she tried to process again all that had been explained—and all that had not—seventeen days ago, on this very property. She hadn't seen Cal since, but he had promised to be nearby.

First, there had been that confrontation down in the caverns. She had felt something rise within as she faced the snooping, slender brunette—a need to fight, to protect her young. She'd told herself at the time that it was an overzealous burst of hormones. It had to be, right?

Because it would be schizoid to start going around thinking everyone was out to harm your baby.

Then came the revelations, from her conversation with Cal.

So there *were* killers after her child?

Maybe she *was* schizoid.

It was too much to assimilate, to catalog. Cal claimed he had reappeared for the sake of her baby, but it wasn't every day you heard talk about the doubly dead, the doubly alive, vampire hordes, and secrets of the Hebrew alphabet. At least Jed had been patient with her. She hated keeping him in the dark, but she didn't see any good that could come from revealing all that had been told her.

Gina scooped back her hair.

There it was, all the proof she would get: the letter Tav.

"You." She pointed into the mirror. "Yeah, you. You're one bad mama-jama."

Then she chuckled at herself. Which caused her baby boy to shift inside, pushing a foot, or maybe an elbow, up beneath her ribs until she was sure a lung would puncture. This was what you endured for your child, all part of the process.

She said, "I sure hope you get here soon, kiddo."

In response, pain barraged her belly and back, arrows streaking in from all sides and angles, piercing, tearing, pinning her entire being down to the bathroom floor in a quivering pool of thin, warm liquid.

Was this it? Had her water just broken?

The child inside of her was saying he'd had enough and that if he was going to feel the sorrows of the world, he might as well do so out in the open, where he could face them like a man.

Gina could respect that. Intense love welled up in her chest.

She dragged herself to her knees, fetched the keys from her pocket, and stumbled out into the parking lot. She would have the nurses call Jed from the clinic, but there wasn't a moment to lose. Her baby had dropped into position, exerting pressure between her hips.

Ready or not, the little guy was on his way.

Buckhead

Erota pranced into the vaulted entryway and greeted her husband. "Ray-Ban. You're home early for a Thursday evening."

"Long week already."

"Well, *I* had fun. I took a day trip to Chattanooga."

"Again?"

"It's so quaint, compared to Atlanta."

"Just be careful with the Jag. The insurance is through the roof."

"The roof?" She glanced upward, feigning ignorance.

"Lots of money," he said. He tossed his jacket over the knob on the banister, the expectation implicit that she would see to it for him. "Brutal day at work. I had a good-sized deal fall through—six figures—but the boys and I'll get it cleared up in the morning."

"You're good at what you do, aren't you?"

"Don't let 'em know you care. That's the secret."

She gave an exaggerated blink of her eyes, brushed fingers down his chest. "Is that why you are so often gone? To make me think that *you* don't care?"

"Is it working?"

"I don't care either," she said. "I think we're both happier this way."

"I'm going to check the news."

"I'm going upstairs." She pushed away from him. "For a shower."

"Now?"

"A long, hot shower." Pouty lips. "Not that you *care*, my husband. Now that you've got your Ukrainian bride to show off to your friends, you can carry on with your life with no one thinking you have other inclinations."

"Hold on there. Is that what you think, Erota?"

"Convince me otherwise."

She was in the middle of being convinced when the cordless phone rang. At day's end, Ray-Ban abhorred all forms of communication, and he swiped the offensive appliance off the night stand. The phone rang again. Erota rolled to the side of the king-sized bed—a circular affair with mounds of pillows—and retrieved the receiver from plush white carpet.

"Leave it." He swatted at her.

She checked caller ID. Her contact from Erlanger East Medical Clinic.

She felt her heart rate pick up and thought for a moment that her predatory side was about to manifest—the glowering eyes, the nails, the curve of long teeth. All of it, in anticipation of blood. The desire ran hot up her chest, into her throat, and—

She winced. There it was again, that stabbing pain in her temples. The tension between Collector and host grew more intense each day, as though sooner or later one of them would have to give.

"What's wrong?" Ray-Ban asked.

"I've got a headache."

"But," he said in a husky voice, "I haven't finished convincing you."

"Later, alligator."

"Wrong phrase, Erota. And no one says that anymore."

"I don't *care*. Remember?"

Phone in hand, she sashayed into the master bath and closed the door.

South of Atlanta, Georgia

He was a soldier. A demolitions expert, if you will.

Leaned over a wooden work bench in this College Park basement, he pressed his arms against the edge to keep his hands steady. No sudden movements. See? Just like that. Nothing to fear. The black gun powder was in the old plumbing pipe, and the nails were going into position now, each one a messenger of wrath.

Beside him, on his bedroll, his pager waited. He had pulled it from his belt so that he would not be startled in his task.

The call to duty would come, though probably not tonight.

True, too true, he had served in Uncle Sam's army—prior to being discharged. Uncle Sammy had spurned him, the same way others had misjudged and overlooked him in his thirty-plus years on this earth.

This nation, it paraded its lewd behaviors through the streets and tossed the by-products of its immoral couplings into alleyway Dumpsters. Just as Mr. Rudolph had done with his bomb at the Olympics, he, too, had tried to get their attention, hoping to expose their shame before the world.

But did they listen? No.

True, too true, he was in the Army of God now, winnowing out targets for maximum impact. A few more nails. A fuse. See? And when that was done, he would make another bomb to add to this precious package. Three, maybe four, would do the trick, with a timer and detonator added for the final touches.

He would hit the trail, a conscript on a mission. He would gather lives. That's what the instincts in his gut told him to do, his internal guides.

He was collecting souls for the eternal damnation they deserved.

He spent the rest of the night in the basement, finding release in his work. He had a stack of books about outdoor survival skills, which he pored over. He made notes on a legal pad. He liked these quiet hours— the alone, not-to-be-disturbed hours.

At last he grew too tired to go on, and he reached for his bedroll. That's when he realized the pager's beeper had been muted the entire time. There was a message from last evening.

From Erota.

He pushed aside thoughts of her toned form. He knew too well the weakness of man, and that's why he knew to stay fixed on his assignment. To punish. To teach. To purge the evil from others that he felt even now coiling within.

The text of the message caught him by surprise, though.

Chattanooga? So soon?

According to earlier discussions with Erota, the date for the bombing should've still been a few weeks from now.

Daylight was already feeding through the squares of cardboard taped across the basement windows. At this time of the morning, he would hit gridlock on his northbound journey through Atlanta. I-75 became a bottleneck, and it could be three hours, even four, before he reached the clinic and its birthing area.

Not to mention that Erota wanted him to pick her up along the way.

His exhausted body sparked into action, ignited by thoughts of media coverage and further embarrassment for those who called themselves leaders. These politicians and doctors, all of these fat cats purring with contentment while sin abounded.

He taped his supplies into a compact bundle, then set them in the bottom of his new pack—the one Erota had specified for this mission.

He was a soldier. Time to unleash the dogs of war.

CHAPTER
FORTY-TWO

Chattanooga

Gina stood with weak legs at the nursery window. Jed was at her side, his hand covering hers on the sill. The morning was sunny, the sky a robin's-egg blue scarred by thin gray clouds. The colors matched her initial joy and the intermittent concerns that cut through it.

Why had her baby come now? Why so suddenly?

Would he survive? Was he healthy, with all fingers and toes in place?

Count 'em: one, two, three, four, five. Same on both hands, both feet. A plastic clothespin still clung to the spot where Jed had cut the umbilical cord.

With the child out and the endorphins subsiding, she realized that her husband wasn't the criminally negligent madman she had seen at her bedside last night. He'd stuck by her through the whole thing and never even fainted—though that had been a real concern of his.

"Just look at him," Jed was saying. "You did that."

She twined her fingers in his. "*We* did it."

In an incubator behind the glass, their frail boy squirmed in a snugly wrapped blanket. There were two infants to his left, one to his right, but Gina and Jed had eyes for him alone. His head was covered by a cap the size of a teacup, his little fists working the air in tiny mittens. In the name slot: *Jacob Lazarescu Turney.*

"Don't you dare call him Jake," Gina said.

"J. L.?"

"Just Jacob."

"Kidding, of course," Jed said. "I'll call him anything you want."

"See how he never stops moving? That's how he was inside. No wonder he came early."

"A go-getter. Like his mama."

"That's a good thing, right?"

"A very good thing." Jed's blue eyes turned watery. "He's perfect."

"He's amazing."

"Definitely. And as far as I'm concerned, you're Wonder Woman."

"Thanks, Jed." She touched his cheek. "I sure don't feel like it."

By birthing standards, things had gone well. Still, her body was depleted, her hip bones made of wax and ready to melt, her lower section a knot of abused muscle. Contractions had rippled with insuppressible force along either side of her spine, seeming to push and pull through her very bones, as though the gravity of the earth's own mass was calling forth life with travailing groans.

Much later, Gina had requested an apple juice. Almost apologetically.

"Don't you be afraid to speak up if you need anything," the nurse told her. "You did as much work as anyone does here. Just packed it into a shorter period."

The delivery had lasted ninety-seven minutes, from the time she drove herself from the job and checked in at the clinic to the moment of Jacob's arrival in a gush of fluids and blood. He was almost a month early, small enough to fit in both palms, too weak to suckle at her breast. No one had expected him so soon, not even the doctor who'd examined Gina four days ago.

"Did your mother have a quick birth?" the nurse had asked.

"Don't know. She never talks about it."

"You must've given her fits."

"I'm sure that's what she would say."

Peering into the nursery this morning, Gina wondered what sort of life lay ahead for her newborn. Would he give her fits of his own? Would she turn into another Nikki?

Though the pregnancy had been an exercise in endurance, she felt today like she could breathe again. Physically, there was no longer any pressure against her lungs, or anything distending her belly. But the relief went beyond that.

Each day with Jacob in the womb, she had carried the weight of the world on her shoulders. Now, with that burden unloaded, she could begin to live again.

What was wrong with her? It sounded selfish to even think that way.

Her son was safe, and that's what mattered. No undead assassins. No signs of Cal, either. Just another sunny day in Chattanooga, Tennessee.

As if to demolish her tentative calm, as if to say he knew exactly what lay ahead, little Jacob let out a thin cry that escalated into a torturous wail.

Atlanta

He was in the cab of a rented Dodge pickup. On I-75 heading north out of Atlanta, he finally broke free of the tangled traffic, free of the tangled life. That's what he told himself. He was headed to Chattanooga with his messengers of wrath tucked into their beds in the daypack on the passenger-side floorboard.

See? Right over there, beneath Erota's satiny nylon legs.

No, he thought. *Eyes straight ahead, soldier.*

Nevertheless, he allowed himself to wonder for a brief moment what it would be like to zigzag the country with her, a modern-day

Bonnie and Clyde, robbing the lives of the unrighteous instead of banks. Zeroing in on the places where lawlessness reared its ugly head.

Not that the banks were lily-white. The fees they were charging nowadays? That was robbery in and of itself.

"Hey, mister."

"Huh, yeah?"

"You're weaving into the other lane," Erota said.

He jerked the pickup back onto the right course, the straight and narrow. He sneaked a glance her direction. She had those sunglasses on, so that he couldn't—

But wait. She was taking them off. She was looking his way, with a request in her upturned eyes.

Yes. That was his instant answer. *Oh yes.*

With that reaction, he felt something stir inside him. There was a visceral male response, true, but there was something deeper too. A presence, her very essence, bulging through his limbs and prying his ribs apart with an invisible crowbar. He could almost smell fetid earth and a gnarled vine creeping through the opening.

Then the image disappeared, and he was back in the real world, where cars were exceeding the speed limit on his left—lawlessness, everywhere— and Erota was asleep in the seat to his right.

He sniffed at his chest. He smelled sweaty, salty.

"Erota?"

She was sagged against the door, eyes closed. Nobody home.

He said her name again, then realized she was but a shell next to him. Yes, she was already here with him, *in* him. They were going to do this *together.* They would mete out justice as a team. As for those doctors who got paid to deliver newborn life during one appointment, then to take an unwanted child in the next . . . *they* would pay. The ones who funded such hypocrisy . . . *they* would pay too.

And if Erota wanted some collateral damage, he was all for that.

"Not much further," he said, watching a road sign pass overhead.

He was a soldier. A demolitions expert, if you will.

"I need to call my boss," Jed told her. "Let him know I won't make it in."

"Sure."

"Be right back, Gina."

"I'll be here, keeping an eye on our baby."

She watched her husband pad down the corridor, out of sight. She turned back to the cries of her child, her heart flayed by each note. Ignoring hospital guidelines, she eased into the room to console Jacob. She touched his hand, leaned down over the incubator to kiss his soft cheek.

A mother's love . . .

He only wailed louder. His slender lips peeled back, contorting into shapes independent of one another, red matching banners that curled and snapped in the blustery winds of his unspoken sorrow.

Between the closed eyelids, a sliver of color showed. Gina had observed Jacob's irises earlier, while cradling him in the birthing suite. She thought she'd seen flecks of gold.

She had also spotted faint blue splotches on his forehead, but she was reminded that the letter Tav would not appear until adulthood—if she even believed any of that. No, these particular markings were nothing more than bruises from Jacob's passage through the birth canal, sorrows endured for the greater reward of life.

"Just stop," she whispered to herself. "Stop being so philosophical about everything, and just try to enjoy this."

Jacob's continued cries made that difficult.

His hands were now grasping at the air, his body rocking in the tiny bed. The warble started again in his throat, his lips fluttered, and a scream rose with bansheelike persistence. Although Gina had always loved children, even dreamed of working in the orphanages of her homeland, this was more than she could bear. He was a miserable baby, and each shriek was an indictment against her.

Had she done something wrong? Was she inadequate, unable? Maybe he was just upset that she was standing so close and not picking him up.

"Sorry," she breathed. "Please don't be mad at me."

Gina slipped back out to the thick viewing window. The cries were muffled yet still audible, and she was struck by a disturbing vision of the months to come . . .

She would take Jacob home, armed with medical guidelines and cautions and what-to-do-ifs, but no one would have an answer for how to deal with his screams. She would rock her baby for hours on end, pace the floor, and try to feed him, hoping, praying, pleading, that he would fall asleep or find a few moments of peace.

None of it would help. Little Jacob had a burden to bear, a rare gift.

What had Cal called it? *A long, lonely road . . .*

The doctors and the neonatologist would examine Jacob and find nothing wrong. They would pat her on the back. Assure her all was in order. Even suggest that if she would only relax, then her son would too— like it was all her fault.

Of course, none of this would alleviate his misery.

Was this the plight of those who carried the weight of the world? Was Jacob truly one of them? Who could bear such a burden?

She imagined filling prescriptions for depression. She saw herself enrolling in one of the local postpartum support groups, then retracting her enrollment, mortified at the thought of soccer moms in pink, brushed-velvet pants, giving her advice through collagen-swollen lips.

She visualized walking through the mall, seeing accusations in strangers' eyes, hearing shushes from browsers in the bookstore. Everyone would know that she was a horrible parent. Who was she to argue with the evidence?

A screaming child.

A young mother, tagged on her forehead with a warning sign.

Cal had forgotten to mention how, back in the book of Genesis, Cain was marked for life after he killed his brother. Smack-dab on the noggin. And then there was the whole triple-six thing, in the book of Revelation. Gina had learned all that stuff from her mother, but rejected it along with the abuses.

Maybe Cal was wrong about the symbol. What if it didn't indicate an escape from wrath or from the jaws of death? What if it was the mark of curses and iniquity?

In the incubator, Jacob was still thrashing.

Gina touched her palms and face to the glass. She'd pressed through the last eight months, telling herself it would end on the day of delivery. She realized now, however, that this was only the beginning. There was much more to go.

She felt tired beyond words. Through the vivid reflection in the window, the fatigue was clear on her face.

Her brow was also clear. She pulled her hair back to be sure.

Yes, the Letter was missing, faded and gone. She pressed closer, but there was no doubt about the clarity of her skin. In delivering this child, had she washed herself of the identifying mark? Did this mean she'd done something wrong? Or was it the natural—supernatural—result of fulfilling her duty?

"I'm cleared for family leave," Jed said, touching her arm. He was back from his phone call.

"Oh." She stiffened. "Good."

"So whatever you need, Gina. I'm on it."

"I need to lie down," she said.

"I thought you were keeping an eye on—"

"Jed."

"You betcha, sweetheart. I know you're wiped out."

He passed the clinic, eyeballing it all the way, then parked the rented vehicle two blocks further down.

He eased the pack from under Erota's feet. She was motionless. He decided her empty shell would be fine where it was, enjoying a little nighty-night. Just to keep her safe, though, he locked the doors before heading back up the street.

He was a regular joe—walking to work, or taking an early lunch, or just another wandering tourist, or . . . an expectant father coming to offer support.

Yes. Yes, that was the image to project.

The idea came to him from left field, but now that it was here in his head, it seemed so obvious. Yes, that was good. He must stand straight and pull both shoulders back. He was a man rushed, and sure of himself, and not to be delayed.

CHAPTER FORTY-THREE

"Gina, darling."

"Hello?"

"Is he healthy? Where is he?" Nikki said, stepping into the room.

Behind her, Jed shrugged and rolled his eyes, like a man who'd fallen asleep on guard duty and didn't know whether to sound the alarm.

Did you frisk her for ancient daggers? Gina wanted to ask.

She propped herself up in the hospital bed. With the months of silence between them, she had no idea where to start. A part of her wanted to share this experience with her mother—the circle of life, a chance to bring things back to their proper order. On the other hand, she didn't trust this woman around her child.

"Nikki. Uh, hi, Mom. How'd you even know?"

"I should've guessed the baby would come while I was away."

All part of my master plan, Gina thought. But kept her lips sealed.

"Naturally, I hurried back as soon as I heard. *You* might not be answering my calls, but the clinic's been kind enough to keep me abreast."

"Who? I didn't give anyone permission to—"

"I am your mother, for heaven's sake."

"Yeah, you're right. Thanks for coming." Gina combed at her hair with her hand. "Sorry if I seem a little on edge."

"I'm sure you're exhausted."

Gina swung her feet over the side of the bed. "Jed took some pictures. We can get you reprints, if you like."

"Thank you. So how was the birth? Natural, I hope. I do believe that's best."

"She had to get some stitches," Jed said. "But you know Gina—she'd never tell you that herself."

"Too much information," Gina snapped.

"She's your mother. Not like she's never been through this before."

Nikki wrapped an arm around Jed's middle, the first ever display of her approval. "You should listen to this husband of yours. He speaks wisdom."

Gina flashed a fake grin.

Jed stepped forward and gave his wife a hand as she pushed her feet into slippers and pulled on a robe. "Sorry, I found her wandering down the hall," he said under his breath. Then: "Here, sweetheart. Let's go show your mom little Jacob."

"Please. I'm dying to see my grandson," Nikki said.

"Jed." Gina squeezed his hand. "Give us a minute."

"Now?"

"If you can just wait outside. I need to ask Nikki something, in private."

"Uh, sure." He inched the door closed, eyes begging for information.

The room was cheery, clean, dappled with sunlight. Gina rubbed her hands against her lower back, felt the floor tilt and sway. She braced herself by the bed.

"What is it, darling?"

"I . . ." Beneath her mother's scrutiny, she vacillated. "I'm not even sure what I want to ask. Did you get a visit a few weeks back from Cal?

You know, Cal from Romania—or wherever he's really from. He told me he stopped by the house, but you weren't too thrilled to see him."

"He stopped by, yes." Nikki crossed an arm over her stomach. Her hair was coiffed and colored. She was in a business skirt and pumps, with a pale pink top that matched her lips. "I didn't think it was wise of him to be drawing attention our way."

"Attention from who?"

"Regina, please. Let's not revisit the past."

"If it's the past, then what's the worry?"

"There's no reason to go digging up trouble. That's simply not for you and me now, is it? You have a son to care for, and we'll keep marching onward. We are survivors."

"Immortal? Is that what you really mean?"

"Excuse me?" Nikki crossed the other arm.

"Well, don't stand there trying to think of the right answer. True or false?"

"Wherever did you hear such nonsense?"

"You're avoiding the question."

"Dear, I'm—"

"Yes or no, Nikki."

"Yes, if you must have an answer. We all share a measure of immortality."

"As in, eternal souls. Heaven and hell."

"Of course. Now, may we return to the matter at hand?"

"My son's heritage, his purpose," Gina said, tilting herself away from the bed. "This *is* the matter at hand, don't you get that? Just tell me, are we descendants of the original Nistarim?"

"Cal put you up to this, didn't he?"

"Just *give* me an answer."

"This is a lot for an old woman to process."

"Old woman, huh? So you're denying that you're immortal?"

Nikki's pink top expanded beneath her jacket as she sighed. "The Nistarim," she said, "are sworn to celibacy. They were not meant to have genetic descendants. They were given an assignment, a God-given task, and after they rose from their tombs, there was to be no giving or taking in marriage. That stipulation was very clear."

"Cal left that part out."

"Yes, I suppose he would. Listen, dear, this is talk for another time." Nikki reached out a hand with painted fingernails, while tragic beauty carved age lines into her face—reminders that she might be human after all. "I can only wish I was something I am not. As you know, I turned fifty this year. Though I must say, I do have my ardent male admirers."

"I didn't mean to yell, Mamica."

"It's okay."

"Just tell me, is Jacob in some kind of danger? Are there . . . creatures out to hurt him somehow? Are they the same ones we were trying to avoid when we left Romania? Is that why you got upset with Cal for coming here?"

"Which question first?"

"Start with Jacob. Is he in danger?"

Nikki's eyes flickered to the side, and she gave a reluctant nod.

"From the Collectors? That's what Cal called them."

"Yes."

"Then," said Gina, "why didn't you—"

The bomb blast rocked the entire ward, shattering glass and deafening ears, shaking walls and temporarily knocking out circuits. The swaying floor that Gina had been standing on moments prior became the anvil for a mind-numbing hammer blow. The explosion's physical force lasted mere seconds, but the overload of the senses imprinted each damaging, nail-slicing, metal-bending sound into Gina's memory, where they would screech and roar for years to come.

CHAPTER
FORTY-FOUR

Mid-October—Chattanooga

The second-cruelest part of the whole matter was that the three other infants in the nursery had been gathered up for bathings and feedings, while Jacob Lazarescu Turney remained within the bomb's primary blast zone.

Drywall dust, and slivers of glass, and . . .

Gina had rushed to the nursery, brushing past a wounded nurse, kicking past a toppled gurney. She'd stumbled into a chamber of hell.

Buckled subwalls were surrounded by sparkling shards; blood was spattered across sections of mangled aluminum; scraps of shrapnel were embedded in wood and plastic. Panicked cries. Screams of pain. In the incubator, her baby was lifeless and punctured by nails, his teacup-sized cap still in place.

Five weeks had passed since that day. Media outlets still trolled the town for sporadic updates, hoping for new handheld video footage or anything else that might spike the ratings. Already, though, attention was shifting to the next spate of bad news.

Overwhelmed by constant calls for empathy, the public had turned pragmatic: *One dead? Eleven injured? What a relief. It could've been so much worse.*

It couldn't be worse.

Gina Turney hadn't slept more than two or three hours any one night since the bombing. Her imagination was her foe. It crept at the edges of darkness and painted images she wanted no part of. When she tried to make it her ally, it flitted off.

Engrossing novels? Creepy movies? Side-splitting sitcoms?

They had all lost the power to sweep her away.

Gina was now staked to good ol' terra firma, surviving from one moment to the next. That's what she did. At heart, she was a Lazarescu. She couldn't bear, however, the thought of meeting with her mother, and she was unable to meet her husband's eyes for fear of falling to pieces.

The cruelest part of the whole matter was that the earth continued spinning. Either Jacob hadn't been what Cal and Nikki thought he was, or there had been others already in place to fill the spots of any vanquished Lamed Vov.

Either way, her son had been killed for nothing.

She blamed the Collectors, and she didn't even know what they looked like. Were they fang-toothed beasts? Erudite Old World bloodsuckers? The only picture she could pop into the frame was the face of the almond-eyed brunette who had harassed her down in the caverns.

She also blamed her mother.

And Cal, who had failed her. What were his words? *I'll be there . . . I'll make sure your baby's safe and sound.*

Then again, she had told him to bug off.

Mostly, she blamed herself. She'd told Jed she would keep an eye on their baby, but she hadn't. She had planted a kiss of betrayal on Jacob's little cheek, then cowered from the vision of a miserable child and fled to the comfort of her bed. She'd stranded Jacob there in his incubator.

If only she had stayed at the nursery window . . .

If only she had heeded Cal's words . . .

In these weeks after the bombing, Gina asked for more hours at Ruby Falls, extra shifts. Anything to stay busy. The tourists kept coming, and she kept guiding them into the womb of the earth.

Womb? Not quite.

More like the bowels of the earth. A place for her to hide, to forget, to slowly process and digest. She was a survivor. She would press on.

Hi, my name is Gina. I'll be your guide as we descend . . .

CHAPTER FORTY-FIVE

First Week of November—Buckhead

It was a dark and stormy night.

Erota had always loved that well-worn phrase, and she thought of it now.

Lightning was arcing over the skyline of Atlanta, and thunder rumbled through black clouds like the sounds of Civil War cannons being rolled into position and fired at random. In the spacious Tudor-style manor, lights flickered, and Erota started setting out candles. For her husband's sake, more than anything.

She had no trouble with the dark. After centuries in the tomb, her eyes had ballooned back into their sockets with an unearthly clarity of vision. Her ears, too, were keen to sounds, especially as she'd been fine-tuning her senses to the pleasures all around.

Ray-Ban would curse her, however, if she failed to take this precaution—as if he couldn't do it himself, as if it was so hard to light a wick.

The man was too busy, of course, with his Internet distractions.

Well, there was something to be said for that. Erota had infested him with the thorns of her own lust, so why not allow him a few entangle-ments on the side. It gave her a sense of accomplishment. Anything to boost her confidence, after her failure at Erlanger East.

She was still baffled by that. She'd ridden along with the pipe-bomber, seen for herself the tiny infant who was wailing as though the world already sagged heavy upon his shoulders. Then she'd encouraged her host to set down his satchel of goodies. She could not control his mind—the Power of Choice was inviolable—but it had been a good test of her abilities to persuade and possess.

She'd heard the click as he set the timer on the bomb.

Fifteen minutes later, from the parking lot outside, they'd watched the building shudder, saw the eruption of light and smoke, and the shower of glittering glass that hissed down upon the shrubbery.

Why, then, had the world carried on?

She had done as planned, finding a link to the Nistarim and meting out destruction. Yet the planet kept rotating. Humans still scurried here and there.

Where was the Master Collector's promise of peace from these infer-nal beasts?

Though she could scarcely allow herself such impertinent thoughts, she saw no evidence of the new earth he promised—a planet seeded with the blood of dead two-leggers; a Collection of Souls producing vegeta-tion and sustenance for eons to come.

Erota would have to keep seeking out her own meals, thank you very much.

In the den down the hall, Ray-Ban was moaning. Erota moved that direction, drawn by his restrained, guttural sounds. Almost primal in their urgency, they spurred something in her own loins.

She turned the door handle, eased into the den, and glided toward him on tiptoes. His eyes were glued to the computer screen. She wrapped her arms around him in his office chair, becoming one with his desire and feeding off of it. As her lips grazed his ear, she found her own arousal growing, and then she was teasing his thorns from within.

The thick, crusted cord of netherworld brambles inched about his waist, down both legs. Triangular talons clawed over skin and cloth, restricting circulation while causing his muscles to tense. His right hand clutched the mouse. His other was entwined in that taproot of ancient venom.

Erota flashed back to her days as a temple prostitute. Men had come to exorcise their demons of the flesh, and she had allowed them that banal deception. She beckoned them one by one, enduring the midday heat and the presence of fleet-footed lizards on the stone walls.

Ah, but this was so much easier, was it not?

The cushioned chair. And his monitor, this rectangular device of lurid hues and sounds.

"What we do in our own home is our business," she purred into his ear. "As long as it's not hurting anyone."

He snapped his head back. "Erota."

"It's okay, Ray-Ban."

It wasn't, of course. Yet he seemed oblivious to the pernicious vine that now encircled his chest. He seemed unaware—or maybe just didn't care in this moment of mounting lust—that the dry, withered vine was rooted in a part of himself that he seemed to enshrine.

Erota was no longer able to resist the elevated heat from his body, the pounding *pu-tatta-putatt . . . pu-tatta-puttat* of his bloodstream. She feathered the pale-green daggers of her fingernails up through his hair and lowered tapered teeth toward the back of his neck where his tie still hung, rather loosely now.

She sank her fangs into his flesh. She drank.

The doorbell crescendoed, breaking through her singularity of purpose.

Ray-Ban started in his chair, pushing back and sending Erota reeling. He punched off the power on the monitor. The vine slithered back into its place of hiding. Erota windmilled her arms for balance, then slunk beside the armoire as her husband gathered himself and went to answer the still-clanging chimes.

She licked the blood from her lips and followed after him.

Megiste's arrival was unannounced.

Erota welcomed the woman into the house, took her fur coat and folded it over the banister—*Ha, if you would be so kind, Ray-Ban, to put that away?* There was no doubt in Erota's mind that her own days of philandering were about to end. Had Ariston sent the priestess after her? Was there a traitor here in the United States? A spy from the Consortium who had reported her renegade ways?

"Come in, come in," Erota said.

"Thank you."

Megiste eased into the vaulted entryway, her willowy form catching the eye of Mr. Raymond Pace. He was still red faced, his pupils still dilated.

"My friend Megiste, from Kiev," Erota told him.

"Hello. Good to have you."

"I'm sorry to drop in so unexpectedly," Megiste said. "But I simply *had* to see my dear, uh, Ukrainian friend while passing through your wondrous city. She's sent e-mails about this new husband and life of hers. To be honest, I'm rather jealous."

Erota saw her husband eating up every word. It was disgusting, in the extreme. She hooked her arm into Megiste's and told Ray-Ban that they would be on the screened back porch, watching the storm. His lascivious glances followed them with all the subtlety of a goggle-eyed teenage boy.

The female revenants sat with hips touching on the swing made for two. Wind curled through the yard, shaking leaves from the trees and spitting them against the fence, while the storm's electricity flashed above the quivering branches.

"What're you doing here, Megiste?"

"More appropriately, Erota, what are *you* doing, here in this new land of yours? Ariston suspects you've been busier pursuing your own pleasures than staying true to the goals of our cluster."

"I won't deny I've pursued happiness. It's the American way."

"Happiness. A fleeting concept, don't you think?"

"I found one of them," Erota said. "One of the Nistarim. That's what I've been up to, if you must know. I trailed the mother of this unborn male, after verifying the presence of the Letter on her head. She gave birth only last month."

"Why didn't you speak of this to us?" Megiste said. "I could've helped you."

"I took care of it myself." Erota pushed herself to her feet and let Megiste sway beneath the creaking chains. "I planted a bomb."

"And yet we're still here? I'm sorry, doll, but these excuses pale in light of the troubles to which I've been attending. While you've been playing at your charades, our cluster has fallen into disarray."

"What're you saying?"

"First, both of Ariston's sons are gone, and that means he is without a successor. Sol has been banished—deservedly so, I might add. It happened on a night back in August. And Natira, well, he would be next in line, but as you know, his ossuary was empty and his whereabouts unknown."

"If a successor becomes necessary, I'm sure my dad would fill that role."

"Eros? No, that's also out of the question."

Erota turned to face the swinging chair. "What?"

"For a short time now, the House of Eros has been without a leader."

"You mean . . ."

"Your father, yes. I'm sorry."

Megiste recounted for Erota that terrible episode in the vineyard warehouse. She told of the human casualties, which Barabbas had been quick to bury in the foothills—deep enough to evade not only digging animals, but the suspicious local constabulary as well. She told of the spike through Eros's temple. Of the child who had escaped.

Erota pressed her hands back against the screen room's white aluminum framing and swayed on her feet, her head split apart by the oppressive humidity and buzzing of insects. The pain was physical. Tangible. She clung to this undeniably human experience to avoid the even more cutting sensations of sorrow and dread.

Her father? Removed from this earth?

Yet he was only a shell, a carbon casing for a nameless Collector. There was no reason to be enslaved by any emotion. Give and take. Die and let die.

So why this knot of anger in her breast?

"I'll find the child," she said. "I'll wrap him in vines and tear him apart, thorn by thorn."

"This boy, Dov, he was only protecting his mother with the implements on hand. I don't believe he attacked with any foreknowledge of the specific devastation he could inflict."

"I remember him," Erota said. "Quiet. No backbone to speak of."

"Although he did use a mallet and spike with great effect."

"Hmm."

"Not that you should concern yourself with him. He's grown *very* quiet now. Barabbas and I found a tent a few days ago, in the forest five kilometers north of the vineyard. We believe he was hiding out, fearful and un*doubtedly* heartbroken. There was evidence of a struggle, perhaps with a wolf. Those mountains are rife with carnivores, the largest collection anywhere in Europe. Barabbas also found shreds of bloody clothing, a torn shoe, even a toe—a child-sized toe, mind you. Too grimy, in my opinion, to belong to a girl."

"It could've been a runaway. A gypsy child, perhaps."

"No," Megiste said. "We found an old photo in the tent. Mr. Amit and son Dov, side by side, holding up fish they had caught on the Sea of Galilee."

"Kinneret? Don't even mention that lake."

"We're now thinking of regrouping back there. In Israel."

"We? Meaning who?"

"Our household. We'll form our own cluster, free from the restrictions of Ariston and his paltry crew. Barabbas has agreed to come along and lead us."

"He's a mindless acolyte."

"A puppet, yes. What more could we ask for? Dear Erota, I know all this comes as a shock, but I believe it's for the best."

"I guess, then, you won't be any further away than you are already."

"You fail to see my point." Megiste stood and joined her at the screen, where flies and bugs were clinging to the mesh. Beyond, the storm was moving eastward, herded by high winds. "You will be going back with me tomorrow so that you can join us in our return to the Negev, in Israel."

"I'm married, Megiste. I'm established here."

"But this would've been your father's wish. Surely, you can see that."

"He's gone," Erota spit out. "He's nothing to me now, is he?"

"Think of the role you can play in the void he has left. In fact, when we return I intend to elevate your status within the household. You and I, we can enjoy the preening of others over us—*especially* the male Collectors. They're so simpleminded, don't you think?"

"What does Lord Ariston think of this decision to part ways?"

"Oh, well, he's not in *favor* of it. He's lost control, though, that's clear. A cluster leader is in no position to dispense judgment when he cannot keep things in order. Let him fume. It won't stop us from moving forward."

Erota wanted no part of Megiste's power struggle. Already she'd shown herself capable here on her own in the U.S., and she knew she could turn to the Consortium if the need arose.

"My father," she said, "would've told me to make my own choice as a grown woman. I don't plan to go back to Israel, or anywhere near those godforsaken tombs. They're all yours."

"I warn you: Sol met his end by voicing similar defiance."

"I'm sorry, Megiste. You're right, of course. That was out of line. It's just that I'm enjoying my life here, and I think I've added some nice specimens to our Collection too. Did you see Ray-Ban, my husband? I've got him wrapped around my finger, as the saying goes. And his sister Kristine? She's been putty in my hands."

"Then you should be free to move on. Trust your infestations to take hold."

"I don't think you—"

"They grow quite nicely, once the humans start tending to them. Trust that. With a sudden divorce, your husband'll find even more time to nurture the things. Really, I'm in no mood for such arguments. Not after this *awful* turmoil."

Erota watched the priestess push back her ringlets of hair and hold a palm to her head, showing a grimace of discomfort. Erota recognized the look from her own recent migraines. Even now, her head continued to throb, but this empathy did not change her feelings.

Put aside the goals she had set for herself? Out of the question.

"Are we in agreement?" Megiste asked.

"Sure."

"Glad to hear it." Megiste took her hand.

Erota's mind raced for a way out of this sudden change in plans. "You know, if you're going to leave tomorrow, I should really go start packing. I'll be in my room, but feel free to help yourself in the kitchen. Help yourself to Ray-Ban, too, if you like. Filthy males."

"I'm actually interested in knowing more about this Lettered woman."

"What? It's old news now. Just a silly mistake on my part, I'm sure."

"I suppose I'll see for myself, won't I?"

Before Erota could repel the attack, she felt Megiste's teeth latch into her forearm, pumping, anesthetizing, then sucking away memories like one of these Southern thunderstorms tearing shingles from a roof. She felt drowsy, disoriented. She had found her own Collector's item, so to speak, and she fought now to retain her mind's grip on it: *the link . . . the Letter . . . the Nistarim.* Erota might've miscalculated in Chattanooga, but she was still convinced that Gina Turney was a vital connection, one not to be lost.

Erota slowed her breathing, her heartbeat, and tried to tug free from the hooked fangs. She was a warrior. "Megiste, please."

Still draining away. Roof shingles, memories—fluttering in the storm.

"Megiste."

The priestess opened her eyes, mouth gnawing, rimmed with red.

"Why don't you come back to drink more later?" Erota said. "I won't stop you. But if you're wanting to know where the woman is, the one with the Letter, I'll tell you. You can go see her for yourself tonight."

Fangs unlatched. "I would like that."

CHAPTER
FORTY-SIX

Chattanooga

.

Gina lay in a tub of hot water and gardenia-scented bubbles, with a candle burning on the sink. Jed was trying to help. He said this would relax her. She did as she was told, settling back in the bathwater, thick chestnut strands drifting over her shoulders. Her hair had never been as silky or confinable as her mother's, and she hadn't cut or added color to it in two months.

Knock, knock . . .

Along her eyelids, she felt the sting of salt. Didn't go well with gardenias.

Knock, knock, knock . . .

"Gina?"

"Mm-hmm."

"You okay?"

"Mm-hmm."

"You need me to come in and help you with anything?"

"What, Jed? Am I on a suicide watch here?"

"I was thinking of something . . . romantic. You know, you and me."

"I'm still healing. The stitches and all."

"Yeah. I mean, what was I thinking? I knew that." His presence hovered there, outside the bathroom door. "Silly question," he mumbled, and walked away.

Gina pushed aside any regret for hurting his feelings. He was trying to comfort her, but it only stirred the pain further. She filled her lungs and let herself slip beneath the surface, the bubbles crackling in her floating strands of hair, the heat shifting back and forth across her bread-dough belly and breasts that had deflated after the buildup of the pregnancy.

This was what it was like to be immortal, huh?

Swell. Just great.

She wondered what, if anything, had been true in her conversation with Cal. Long ago he had tried to help her and her mother, then disappeared for years. What was his emotional investment in her life? Why had he been there in the first place? Finally he had come back, dumped a bunch of secrets on her, and promised to be there as guardian and protector. What an idiot she'd been to think he would put himself on the line for the sake of her child.

"Don't worry about your baby," Cal had said. *"I'll keep him safe."*

"They'll come for him," Nikki had tried to tell her months prior.

Gina's lungs were about to explode, and she resurfaced to the shrill of the phone. She let her arms float beneath the bubbles, her fingers already puckering.

Brrng, brrng . . . Brrng, brrng . . .

"You going to get that, Jed?"

No answer, but the phone did stop bleating. She could hear her husband's low voice, the words indiscernible from here in the bathroom.

Knock, knock . . .

"What now?"

"That was Mr. Felsner," Jed said. "From the FBI. You know how they think this bombing is connected to the three in Atlanta? Now they're not so sure."

"Mm-hmm."

"They've isolated a section of material from the package that contained the explosive device."

"The pipe bomb, Jed. The nails. Just say it."

"Gina . . ."

"I was the first one to see our son, okay. I know what happened."

"Can I come in?"

"I'm relaxing."

"Does that mean no?" he said.

"What'd they find? What was the call about?"

"All of the Atlanta incidents were perpetrated using matching packages."

"Perpetrated? Jed, stop. The fancy words won't make this any less real."

"Our incident . . ." He cleared his throat. "It broke the pattern. They're thinking it may've been just a copycat, so they're shifting most of the focus back to Georgia."

"Fine."

"I guess this package, it was just a regular old daypack. JanSport brand."

She inhaled the aromas of the candle and bubbles. From under the door, a horsefly buzzed into the bathroom. It explored the vanity, then came at her hand on the tub's edge. She batted it away, felt her fingernail catch and bend back against the corner of the adjacent countertop.

Ignoring a burst of pain and the red liquid that squeezed from beneath the injured nail, she said, "Jed, thanks for the bath. It feels nice. Listen, I'm sorry for being a jerk."

His footsteps shuffled off to the living room.

Flies had always disgusted Megiste. She detested the very thought of using one as a host, fearful she would be tainted by its diseased mind-set.

Sometimes, though, a Collector had no choice.

While still in her human host, Megiste had located the Chattanooga apartment without difficulty and taken the elevator to the seventh floor. From a thin gap beneath the locked door of the Turney residence: sounds of a phone, muted voices, then the blaring TV.

She had no time to wait for Gina Turney's morning exodus to work. She had to do something now. She imagined a brash attack, crashing straight into the apartment and taking by force what she wanted—memories, blood, any available evidence to substantiate the claims of the untrustworthy Erota.

Megiste decided against the direct approach. Already, Erota's streak of narcissism and violence had raised the ire of police officials and local clusters.

Bump, bumpp, bzzzz . . .

Along the seventh-floor hall, a horsefly bumped against the sconce lights.

No. Megiste really didn't like this idea. Did she have any better option, though? It was late, with no signs of activity in this hallway. Facing the elevator, two armchairs flanked a magazine table and a fake, potted palm. She took a seat, a safe place for a slumbering host, and pulled up her sleeve to reveal smooth, alabaster skin.

Luring the dreadful thing. Waiting for it to find her.

Find her it did.

Horseflies, she knew, could be vicious. The females fed on blood to foster reproduction and used razored mandibles to pick at the skin of their victims.

Bzzzz, bumpp, bummpp . . .

Megiste met its prismatic eyes and waited for a response.

Moments later, her Collector was in a world bombarded by multiple angles of vision. Thankfully, this female fly was an experienced navigator, coordinating the viewpoints and honing in on what she was after.

There: down and under the apartment door.

The buzzing wings matched the sound in the Collector's head. She tried to concentrate. Tried to direct her host toward what she wanted. The female hovered near a kitchen counter, looking for blood where someone might've cut themselves peeling carrots. She moved next toward the bathroom, where a woman might've nicked herself shaving her legs—an American custom she found fascinating, as well as sensually suited to her own brand of delights.

She heard water now, booming like ocean surf. And a sharp, hissing sound. Was someone running a bath?

Gina's blood, her memories, that's what the Collector was after.

It was the human scent, however, that drew the horsefly in a hurry.

She descended, tried to latch on for a taste. She was batted away, and in the moment that followed, the scent intensified. She zoomed down toward the drops of blood that splashed against the floor.

Gina pulled the bath plug with her toes. She listened to the *glug-glug* of the water as it sucked bubbles in a spiraling journey downward. She could hear the twenty-seven-inch TV blaring in the living room, manipulated by Jed's ubiquitous remote.

She replayed that moment again, at the Ruby Falls picnic area, when she had spilled the Sprite and scooted away the heavy pack beneath Cal's feet.

JanSport . . . Was she supposed to be surprised?

Cal . . . Had he come to track her down, to cozy up? To target her child?

Covered in fleeting bubbles, Gina started to shiver. There had to be a way to escape from the stark images of the decimated nursery. She thought of her mother's dagger—that old familiar therapy.

Speaking of her mother, had Nikki tried to stop Cal? Was that why she'd been upset by his visit? Or had her mother been in on it? That seemed unlikely, since Nikki was with Gina at the time of the explosion. Of course, Nikki could've planted the pipe bomb herself. Jed said he had found her wandering in the hall.

For that matter, why hadn't Jed done anything to stop this? Where had he been while the bomber was planting the package?

Maybe the FBI's Mr. Felsen suspected the baby's father of mischief, and that's why he'd called, fishing for means or motive.

Gina told her brain to stop. The thing just kept churning, contorting, a boa constrictor trying to crush its prey before swallowing it down. She was the prey, and these thoughts would devour her if she let them.

Her fingertip was throbbing. She looked down, saw beads of her own blood like ruby bath crystals along the floor of the tub, and was oddly pleased by her revulsion to them. She was done with her mother's cure-alls.

Beside her, the horsefly was leeching from Gina's spilled blood on the tub's edge, storing up to breed its pestilence.

"Shoo," she said. "Get away."

What was it Cal had spoken of? Forming a group of Those Who Resist? His words just didn't mesh with those of someone who would trigger the destruction at the clinic.

Gina decided she couldn't accept Cal's guilt, not till it was proven he'd been there that day. If she wallowed in self-pity, it would only drag down her husband and others. She would stand beside the Provocateur in his belief that this world was a beautiful place.

That wasn't to deny the evil.

It was here. It slunk in corners, staining lives.

Even hours-old Jacob had not been spared. Wickedness had stalked into that clinic and jabbed its penetrating nails into his chest.

Stop. Don't go there, Gina. Just . . . stop.

The tub was done draining. Gina climbed out and dried herself. As she slipped into jeans, she heard the horsefly hovering again, back near the rivulets of pinkish-red. She ran the water till the color was gone then twisted her towel with a shake of the wrist, and landed a shot that sent the big fly spinning, stunned, into the corner behind the toilet.

Though the fly was interested in laying eggs, the female Collector kept this temporary vessel fixed on the duty at hand. Drinking was a simple matter, an orgy of flavor, whereas siphoning memories was a wholly different function that required focus and mental energy. For a fly, it was a real stretch to add anything other than instinctive behaviors to the primitive brain.

The winged host was preparing for final cleanup when a typhoon swirled overhead, a sudden change in the weather system that buffeted and sent it reeling.

Buckhead

Early morning rays were peeking between the live oaks when Megiste got back to the Paces' home off of Peachtree Road. The fly experience was one she would rather forget, and she was disappointed by the information she'd filtered.

This Gina woman, she no longer carried the mark.

She was washed up. Of no use.

Which only helped sharpen Megiste's focus. She would return to Arad, to Kiev, enlist the loyalties of the shaken cluster members. There was no reason to continue following Lord Ariston. What a man could do, Megiste could do better. She would guide them back to Israel. There, they would partner with refugees, terrorists, the ultrareligious—anyone who could help in increasing the sorrows of this dying planet.

And let the Nistarim suffer with the putrid humans.

Let them crumble, one by one.

It might take time, but the House of Eros would soon regain its strength and continue in its quest to usher in Final Vengeance.

Megiste arrived at the doorstep of the Tutor-style home, expecting Erota to be ready to go. Her instructions last night had been explicit. She and Erota would be buying tickets out of Atlanta today, and by tomorrow they would be helping their household—Dorotheus, Hermione, Domna, and, of course, burly Barabbas—regroup.

The estate was eerily quiet, still illuminated by lawn lights, but with windows dark all around. The front door was unlocked, even open a crack.

The scent of death drew Megiste upstairs.

She knew before she'd reached Ray-Ban's desiccated body that Erota had broken away and abandoned the needs of her family back in Kiev. Ray-Ban had probably caught her in the act of packing and tried to put an end to it. A man of his money and position, proud of his trophy wife—he would not take a soft-handed approach to such ungratefulness. Plus, his business pals would see it as a sign of emasculation.

Oh, if only Mr. Raymond Pace could see himself now.

Barely a man at all.

As for Mrs. Erota Pace, she was nowhere to be found.

With a plane to catch and a household to guide back toward that sliver of a country squeezed between the Mediterranean and the shores of the Dead Sea, Megiste couldn't burden herself with such matters. Let the puerile Collector in the nineteen-year-old's body choose a path of rebellion. On her own, Erota would be ineffective. Inept. Certainly not worth fretting over.

THE FOURTH DROP:
RETURN

Good! It has given us opportunity
to cry "check" in some ways in this chess game,
which we play for the stake of human souls.

—BRAM STOKER, *DRACULA*

Rescue others by snatching them from the flames . . .
show mercy, but be careful that you aren't contaminated.

—JUDE 1:23

Journal Entry

June 27

I'm not sure what to think at this point. I have one drop left, and so far I've found mostly heartache. Each stain has come from a Collector, one of Those Who Hunt. The memories are full of dark things, and I'd like to believe it's all fantasy. Just some good stories to keep my interest.

Who sent me this map? Someone trying to help me escape this little corner of the world, or someone trying to flush me out of hiding? That's the part I can't figure out.

Megiste's blood did give some interesting viewpoints. I'm not really sorry to see some of these characters take the fall, but there's a part of me that . . . well, that likes the darkness. Maybe it's because the light can be so blinding at times. You just feel more—I don't know—at home, I guess, in the dark. It doesn't force you to wear a pretty face or look just right. You can let your hair down. I mean, who's gonna notice? Who's gonna care?

I've been taught to beware Those Who Hunt. That's all good. But no one's ever given me the scoop on Those Who Resist. Where are they? Do they meet secretly, or mingle in the open? Would they even accept someone my age?

Suddenly, it seems so obvious. I mean, what else could it be? I'm being screened and recruited. I bet they want me to join their cause.

CHAPTER
FORTY-SEVEN

August 1999—Arad, Romania

The orphans brought back her joy.

Gina's heart had been ripped out nearly two years ago in Chattanooga, and she had battled on through the dark months that tried to engulf her. She figured that if she kept even one *nostril* above water, it meant she was still kicking and alive. Alive was a good thing.

At the beginning of this summer, Jed Turney had announced his plans to head for the Pacific Northwest to live near his uncle, the police sergeant. *And to clear my head, you know, try to put things back in perspective.*

Without her. That's the part he had left unsaid.

There were a lot of things they hadn't put into words, and despite efforts on both sides and joint sessions with a counselor, it was time to reevaluate.

Gina understood this. She felt as though they'd been holding separate handles of the same baggage, trying to drag it through the mud while heading in slowly divergent directions. Jed was as torn up as she by the loss of baby Jacob, and their son's precious few hours on this earth had forever joined the two of them as a mother and father. That couldn't be taken away.

The whole wife-and-husband thing? That was less certain.

Jed left in a U-Haul, and Gina waved good-bye from the sidewalk. She wore a brave face, refusing to let her emotions stop him from going off in search of himself. He was still young, and his grief was as real as her own. His left hand out the window was the last thing she saw as he headed down the hill.

She gave her two-week notice at Ruby Falls.

Shared one last cigarette with her coworkers.

Earlier, she had e-mailed a private orphanage in Arad, stating her desire to help and explaining her own childhood in the region. They'd accepted her application with exuberance, after criminal and background checks. With the HIV-infected kids and severely abused, the need was great. They would take anyone willing to serve.

Gina figured she fit the bill.

She shared a tense but cordial lunch with Nikki and said only that she was planning to save money by living more communally. Nikki assumed hippies. Gina let her think what she wanted. Later, she could send a letter of explanation.

She put an ad in the paper and sold off her remaining things. Half of the items were infant related: a crib, mattress, stroller, and car seat. They were all brand-new, but she sold them for a pittance. She had no desire to profit from Jacob's death, and she hoped the items would be helpful to someone in need.

She kept only the black walnut chess set and a suitcase of clothes.

Using the name Lazarescu from her Romanian passport, she combined her final paycheck and her sale earnings to buy a one-way ticket to Bucharest—*Bucuresti*, as she called it in her mother tongue. She wondered how it would be to find herself inundated again with the sonorous flow of a Romance language. Would it all come tumbling back? Would the food and culture feel like old buddies, or like friends that had parted ways?

She arrived two days later at Otopeni International Airport, with only seven hundred dollars of savings in her front pocket, her dual citizenship in her back pocket, and the orphanage's address on the other side of Romania.

And she felt free.

Gina Lazarescu never felt sorry for the kids. The Tomorrow's Hope Orphanage staff members, *muncitors*, marveled at her connection with their young wards. Most of these children had played the "poor orphan/ poor HIV baby" act for so long they knew nothing but pity from others. Accordingly, their emotions were amplified, their behaviors unrestrained.

Here came Gina. She spoke their language and gave straight answers. She showed scars on her arm, neck, and legs that paralleled wounds that many of them felt, but which most only knew how to demonstrate through tantrums or withdrawal.

She had broken free, even lived in America. Then come back.

Now, she was one of them.

She learned that in 1989, more than a hundred thousand kids had filled orphanages across Ceaucescu's ravaged land. Inexplicably, many had become infected with HIV.

"No one knows how?" she asked a muncitor.

"There are theories, naturally."

"But no one's tracked down the guilty party? That's crazy. What if some irresponsible doctor was reusing needles for vaccinations? I mean, that kind of thing has to be stopped. Am I wrong?"

The muncitor wore an expression of disinterest. "You've been too long in America, with your naive notions of justice. Things such as this were commonplace during our days under communist rule. Really, who had energy to be concerned with anything other than survival?"

"These children, though. I mean, if I ever find out who—"

"You want to help?"

"Yes."

"Then get to work, Ms. Lazarescu. We have beds to make."

"Right away."

During her first few months at the center, Gina found out that many poorer families had seen no choice but to surrender newborns to the government. The catch was that they could retain legal rights to their offspring, so long as they came to visit once every six months.

With some of the children now getting closer to an employable age, parents made sure to show their faces, counting on future paychecks from their juvenile workers.

However, certain kids would never be employable.

The gypsy orphans, for example, were societal outcasts with centuries of prejudice that kept them from good jobs. They were destined to be street sweepers and garbage collectors. This only encouraged their thievery and cheating, which then reinforced the ugly perceptions of them.

Though Gina had grown up around this struggle, she boiled with indignance when she overheard a fellow muncitor berating one of the gypsy wards in the fenced play area: *Hai prostule!*—come here, you stupid one.

"He's only as smart as you'll let him be," she barked back.

Word got around that she was the big sister—the one ready to defend, while never showing too much pity. Building relationships with the kids took time, and she made many of her first connections as their sister through the love of games.

The boys were convinced she would be easy prey at the chessboard, a notion she dispelled in a hurry. She earned their respect through her no-gloating policy and her aggressive style of play.

With the girls she played *remi*, a game using numbered and colored tiles. The real focus during these sessions was unguarded girl talk around the rec room table. Many of them were victims of sexual abuse. At ages ten and eleven, they were showing interest in related topics, and she was a nonthreatening advisor who gave real answers, with hard-hitting cautions against the risky behavior in which some were already engaging.

Daily, Gina found herself smiling at the small victories.

Every night, Jacob's unmarred, beautiful face flitted before her eyes.

"Are you happy to be back?"

"Definitely, Petre."

There was no hesitation in Gina's response to the orphan boy. She loved the charm of the old buildings that lined Arad's Revolutiei Avenue, and the broad, gardened approach to city hall. Street and business names evoked nostalgia in her. Even walking into her new banking establishment, *Banca Transilvania*, conjured images of her childhood.

At the moment, the Tomorrow's Hope choir was lining up before city hall for a performance approved by the mayor. Public religious displays were frowned upon—in fact, many churches viewed Christmas as a pagan celebration—but this was a holiday leading into a new millennium, and some concessions could be made.

Gina quivered in the cold. The day was unseasonably warm for December, yet her blood had thinned after years in Tennessee's temperate climate. Even with chattering teeth, she decided she liked the bracing slap of the breeze. It appealed to something deep in her—a call to stand against the elements, to bend but not break.

Conscious of dehydration, she took a sip from her bottle of Borsec mineral water. She had missed this too. It fizzed with unsweetened delight on her tongue.

"Este extem de frig," Petre Podran said.

"Ahh, it's not that cold," Gina responded.

"You know, my brother thinks you're pretty."

"Really?"

"He says you might marry him one day."

Gina chuckled and looked down into the ten-year-old's round, black eyes. "I don't think that will happen."

"You love American men now? But Pavel is handsome, yes?"

"Stop it, Petre. I know what you're up to, and you're only saying this because you two are twins. I think maybe you're the one with the crush."

Petre changed the subject. "Why did you leave America?"

"Because my husband was gone, and I needed a boy like you to love."

Petre beamed.

"As a little brother," she qualified. "Or a nephew."

Pleased to be loved on any terms, he bounced across the walkway, trampled a hedge, and weaseled in among the choir members.

Minutes later they broke into their first number, a statement of national allegiance sure to win over the passersby. The song had been banned in 1947, after the communists' forced abdication of King Michael I. Gina had never heard it sung publicly in her homeland, and it caused a lump to rise in her throat:

> *Awake, you Romanian, from the sleep of death* . . .
> *It's either now or it never will be* . . .
> *that you create for yourself another destiny* . . .
> *It's either life in freedom or it should be death.*

When they were done, Gina tried to whistle without success—it was a skill Jed had never been able to teach her—and resorted instead to hearty applause with gloved hands. The children in the choir tried to hide their grins.

A destiny, Gina thought. That's what she wanted more than anything. It's what she hoped to give these boys and girls.

Much of Romania's soul had been drained in the seventies and eighties. In the same way, many of these orphans had suffered health issues that put them into constant survival mode.

Hepatitis B and intestinal parasites were not uncommon. Thousands of kids across the country were HIV infected. The World Health Organization had stepped in recently to help, providing antiretroviral treatment, but many were already dead. Conditions were not always sanitary in the state-run facilities, and a simple sinus infection could rage into a life-threatening illness for those with weakened immune systems.

The public mind-set was also difficult to change. Many shunned and feared these stigmatized kids. Thus, as the orphan choir switched to the joyful sounds of a Christmas carol, Gina was not surprised to see a few hecklers in the crowd.

She *was* surprised, though, by the man who stepped up to confront them. He had a chiseled chin, eyes hard as flint, and a mouth that—

Tasted of grapes and blackberries? Of goat's milk?

Was this her Teodor, from the village of Cuvin?

CHAPTER
FORTY-EIGHT

Teodor and Gina strolled along the Strand Neptun, an outdoor recreation area that usually catered to all ages. With winter upon them, the swimming and wading pools had been emptied, leaving only patches of ice that glinted in the afternoon sun. Lawns were forlorn, the trees naked and shivering. Clustered in the center area, restaurants tried to attract diners, while old men played remi at tables under Pepsi umbrellas.

"Langosi on me," Teo said.

"You don't have to do that. I have money."

"I've been with the tourist bureau for three years, Gina, and I'm sure my job pays more than the orphanage. Please. For old times' sake." He stopped at a small hut, leaned his arms on the counter. "How do you like yours?"

"With dill and grated cheese," she said.

"Coming right up."

The orphanage choir, after a half hour of lukewarm response, had been ferried back to Tomorrow's Hope, and Gina had been released for the evening. Later, she would take a tram, then connect on a bus to get back to her place—a one-bedroom flat in a complex adjacent to the center. Food and lodging were part of her salary, leaving her the equivalent of twenty-five dollars a week for personal luxuries.

"Multumesc," she thanked Teo.

The smell of the fried flat bread tugged Gina back to cozy recollections. She felt awkward here, now, with her childhood beau. She was married—on paper, at least—and had no desire to betray Jed in any way. There was an ember of love still there. Nevertheless, her heart was in a tug-of-war between what was and what could've been.

Here on Romanian soil, she felt rooted in reality. Life in America, it seemed far away. Almost unreal.

Or maybe she just knew it was time to forge ahead. She couldn't let the past bleed her dry.

With snacks in hand, Teo and Gina followed the meandering brick path around the curve of the park. He was tall and thin, his gait long and loping. He seemed at ease, and she hoped none of her anxiety showed. She tucked her free hand into her coat pocket and watched her breath turn to fog in the cold air.

"Do you know what happened to Treia?" he asked her.

"My dog?"

"When you drove off that day—why, I've played that over in my head a thousand times—I saw you duck down in the backseat. I could just feel it in my chest that you weren't coming back. I really liked you. You knew that, right?"

Gina finished her bite. "What happened to Treia?"

"I kept him."

"You did? Is he still alive?"

"That was ten years ago," he said. "If I'm not mistaken, he was with me for a total of four. It made me think of you every day. At least he died peacefully. I woke up one morning, and he just never responded. He was gone."

"I loved that dog. Thank you, Teo."

"What else was I supposed to do? He would've ended up roaming

Cuvin with those wild packs, and I'm not sure how long he would've made it on only three legs."

"He would've made it."

"Yeah," Teo agreed. "I moved to Arad soon after. It's nice here, especially in the summers. We'll have to stay in touch, don't you think? We can go to the lake, explore the Cetatea—a very interesting place. Maybe take some hikes or whatnot."

"Maybe. It's hard to say. I'm still adjusting to the center's demands."

"Tell me this. If you could have three wishes, what would they be?"

"*Teo.*" She jabbed a finger at his arm. "I'm not one to kiss and tell."

"You remember that? I was wondering. It was my first real kiss, you know?"

"Pretty obvious, actually. Mine too."

They laughed and looked in opposite directions.

Gina's gloves fumbled with the wrapping around the langosi, and she said, "To hear the national anthem. That would be right up there."

"One of your wishes?"

"I couldn't believe that was happening, and in downtown Arad."

"It was definitely moving to hear those kids sing it. You missed the revolution, didn't you? Well, we admire our martyrs of 1989. They bought back our souls with their blood, you might say. Forget about those hooligans who tried to disrupt things at city hall today."

"It happens. Thanks for speaking up."

"I would've spoken sooner if I'd known you were standing there."

"That would've been my second wish," Gina said. "Running into you again."

"Really? And that was number *one* on my list." He gestured to a park bench facing the Mures River, and they sat. "What about the third wish?"

"Don't know. I'll have to think it over."

She *did* know, though. Her unspoken desire was that one day she could enjoy a relationship built on unconditional acceptance. Not on her looks, or on any baggage from her past, or even on physical chemistry. Something deeper. Something more.

"Here," Teo said. "Let me get that for you."

He took her trash, balled it up, and made an arching shot that bounded off the rim of a metal receptacle. He was standing to retrieve the errant throw when a shape appeared from the huddle of foliage near the riverbank.

She saw the boy before Teo did. "Hello," she said.

If Gina could've compared her life to a thick novel, she would've pointed out that the most pivotal moments came in bunches—sharp peaks in the pace of the story. Of course, whole chapters had been torn from the spine of her biography, so she knew her perceptions could be flawed.

This did not negate, however, her ability to hone in on the details of a given moment. And this was one such moment.

The child was malnourished, eyes dulled by hunger and earlobes bluish white. He was the same size, maybe a year or two older, than most of the boys in the center. He had a small, dirty pack over his shoulder, and he wore a pair of shoes that were too large for his small frame and showed a smear of red around the canvas toe of the left one.

He stared down at the ground. Was he deaf?

It wasn't uncommon. Street urchins were a regular sight around the city, often sent out by poverty-stricken parents to rummage for change and old bread. Citizens were approached at outdoor eateries or at traffic intersections. This nuisance had overwhelmed and tired most people, who had their own daily concerns.

"Hello?" Gina ventured a hand wave this time.

The boy eyed her from beneath tangled hair.

Her motherly instinct said to rush to him, while her intellect cautioned otherwise. She'd seen the same sort in the orphanage, those with the mentality of cornered animals. They would react to an advance by: (a) fleeing for their lives, or (b) attacking first to fend off a perceived threat.

"Money?" he said at last, his hand outstretched. "Food?"

"We can get you something to eat," Gina said to the youngster.

"Money."

"We don't hand out cash, but how about a meal?" Teo said. "Come along."

The boy stood motionless. He looked from Teo to Gina, his wariness wrestling with his need. An icy gust rolled up from the river, combed over the foliage, and tousled his dark mop of hair.

Gina gasped at what she saw.

The boy's eyes darted to her, and he tensed. Ready to escape.

She inhaled, then let out a breath. She imagined warm calm melting down into her limbs, radiating across this patch of dead grass between them. She could not frighten this child away. Not now.

She looked to Teo, nodded toward the path, and said, "C'mon. He wants to be left alone."

Teo's brow furrowed, but he fell in step beside her on the trail.

"Money, food. Money, food."

"Keep walking," Gina whispered.

"Food." A tug on her coat. "Food." A tap on her back.

"I should be getting back to the orphanage," Gina said. "It's been great seeing you again, Teo."

Another tug. "Don't leave me, don't leave."

In an unhurried motion, Gina turned and kneeled. She looked into brown eyes locked between thick lashes. She lifted a hand, and the boy pulled back for a moment, gripping his pack in a grubby hand. She waited for him to extend his trust, then brushed back the bangs that hung in his face. Her gaze panned the letter Tav on his forehead, trying to fathom what this meant for him, for her, and for the story that threaded through the thick, yet torn, volume of her life.

"I want to help you," she said.

"I'm cold."

"What's your name?"

"Dov," he said. "My mother is Dalia Amit, and she is . . ."

"What, Dov? What is it? You can talk to me."

"I did a bad thing, and if they find me, I will die."

Gina knew in America this would be information warranting

investigation, corroboration, and a report to the authorities. This was Romania, though, where remnants of communist corruption under-pinned much of the political framework.

And he was Lettered. There was something else at work here.

"Shhh," she said. "It's okay, Dov. Don't say another word."

Gina had already experienced firsthand the deadly results of that sym-bol. This child was in imminent danger, and she wondered how he had avoided trouble this long. Her heart told her to wash her hands of the matter. What if she failed this boy? As she'd failed her own son. She could not endure another—

No. Her own feelings were not the issue here.

She had to protect him. Hide him. Fight for him, if necessary.

She started with Teo, swearing him to secrecy regarding this child's puzzling confession. She had her reasons, and he would have to trust her on this one. Teo reminded her that he had cared for her dog. Which was good enough for her.

A new year was upon them. A new millennium, in fact.

"Don't you see?" Gina pleaded. "This boy needs a fresh start."

The headmaster at the orphanage was unmoved. "We see this sort of thing every day, Ms. Lazarescu. It's always difficult for new munci-tors to comprehend, but we cannot take in strays off the streets. Now, please hear me out. It sounds heartless, I'm sure, to your ears, but it's for the best of those we're already treating. Medical supplies are low as it is, and we can scarcely acquire enough Fuzeon to inject the worst of our HIV cases."

Gina thought of Dov Amit, seated in the corridor outside. She'd looked into his past, verified his orphaned status. She could not allow him to be abandoned.

"You must understand," the headmaster prattled on, "the strain that even one more ward would put upon our staff and the other kids, not to mention the financial supporters of this institution. It's simply out of the question."

Gina stared straight ahead. Her tongue—working along her teeth, counting, counting. Upper left incisor? One act of kindness.

"I appreciate your concern, of course, but this is not like the United States you have become used to, where money grows upon trees."

"It's not like that there either," she said.

"Well, Ms. Lazarescu, I'm sure you see my point. Let me explain the history and purpose of Tomorrow's Hope . . ."

Gina tuned out the man's voice, running mentally over the city archives she'd checked during her off time. She had confirmed the identities of Dov's parents, as well as their unexplained disappearances two and a half years prior.

Records showed that a Mr. Benyamin Amit's Peugot was found deserted near the ruins at Soimos. His scoped rifle was entered as evidence from the site. No other sign of him was ever found. According to a detective's notes, his wife and son had traveled in a taxicab to the same area that evening, disembarking near Totorcea Vineyards. They, too, had vanished.

When the vineyard owners were questioned about this matter, Mrs. Helene Totorcea told the authorities she had known the Amits from her work at city hall but had no knowledge of their whereabouts. Mr. Flavius Totorcea authorized a property search, and the local constabulary found nothing to substantiate their suspicions. On the list of priorities, the case slipped to the bottom.

Nearly thirty months later? Here was the boy, scavenging the streets, and alive.

Gina wondered what Dov had gone through and how he had lost his left pinky toe. She and the center's nurse had already cleaned and bandaged the near-gangrenous gash, but it hinted at unspoken horrors. It also underscored Gina's worries that he would be next in line for a Collector attack.

Cal's voice: *The Letter appears at adulthood. For boys, that's age thirteen.*

According to the archives' dates, Dov had turned thirteen days after his parents' disappearance. Had he eluded observation since the emerging of the mark? Was he aware of it? What would happen if his identity were to be discovered?

"Sir, this has to work," Gina said to the headmaster. She was determined that Tomorrow's Hope was Dov's hope for today. "This boy, this young man, is fifteen now, and yet he shows all the signs of a psychologically scarred individual. Even physically, he's small for his age. I appreciate the job I see being done here. The orphanage does a great service, and I only want to continue in that vein."

"Of course you do. Any good muncitor has a heart for children, but—"

"I'll donate my weekly stipend," she said.

"Excuse me, Ms. Lazarescu?"

One act of kindness . . .

"My money. What do I need it for, right? I have a place to sleep, eat. I've got the kids. Take it. Use that to cover his expenses, and we have a deal."

"You will give a portion of your salary to sponsor this child's place in our center? A kind gesture, indeed. Though I wasn't aware we were in negotiations."

"We're not," Gina said. "I throw myself—and my money—upon your mercy."

The headmaster chewed on the inside of his cheek, his lined face doleful and judicial. "It's a deal," he said at last. "I like you. You do well with the children. Don't make me regret this."

CHAPTER FORTY-NINE

Gina's dread was a sliver lodged in her mind. She had to keep Dov safe.

There were days she helped in the center's kitchen or played volleyball in the yard with the kids and realized she'd never once felt that sting of fear. Other days, she would be jolted by the sight of a mother cooing to her baby, and it would set the sliver throbbing for hours.

One brisk day in March, while browsing outside a bookshop near the old Water Tower, she glanced up to see a reflection facing her in the glass. It was the slender brunette she had met down in the caverns, those almond-shaped eyes now glaring at her with malevolent intent.

What was she doing here, all the way from America? What were the odds? Maybe she really was a Collector, as Cal had claimed.

Gina twirled to confront the girl.

This was not the same person. Sure, there were similarities in face structure and skin tone, but the eyes were different, and the woman's expression went flat at the sight of Gina. Probably just a window-shopper, hoping for her to move along.

What now? Gina asked herself. *Am I'm turning schizoid again?*

As she headed home, she found herself jumping at shadows from the arched walkways that branched off of the cobbled side streets. Her imagination was on overdrive. How crazy could she be?

Still, she vowed to keep Dov hidden from public scrutiny.

The boy, with his reclusive ways, made this easy for her. He sat in the corner of the rec room and watched his fellow wards, rarely taking part in their activities. At the dinner table, he tore into his food and made wolfing noises that disgusted the others. He avoided going outdoors, though he often stood in the daylight at his window and flipped through photos he kept in a pouch.

"What've you got there?" Gina asked one day.

"Pictures."

"Of your mom and dad?"

"Yes."

"Can I see? If not, that's okay. I just thought—"

Dov handed them over. The prints were worn, yellowed and curled at the edges. Snapshots of the boy and his parents. Fishing. Camping. Floating in the waters of the Dead Sea.

"Are you from Israel? Your name's Hebrew, by the sound of it."

He snatched the photos back, slipped them into their pouch. The conversation was over, and Gina let it go at that. Aside from that initial confession of his at the Strand—given to ease his own mind, perhaps, or to elicit her protection—Dov clammed up when the questions became too numerous or too personal.

What was it he had done? Why would anyone want to kill him?

The letter Tav. That was all the explanation she needed.

As had happened with the other boys, chess became an avenue to friendship and communication. Dov had an analytical mind bubbling behind that inscribed brow, and he spoke of an Israeli grandmaster who had been his father's favorite. Others, such as Pavel and Petre, were jealous of Gina's time, and she had to approach things delicately in this communal environment.

A round-robin tournament one spring day brought Dov and Gina together for the final showdown.

"You're good, Dov. You try to explore every possibility on the board."

"I can beat you."

"I'm sure you can," Gina said. "But it hasn't happened yet. And for your own sake, I won't let it, unless you can do it on your own."

As she spoke, her fingers caressed the carved chess figures. She ruminated on the things Cal had told her of the Nistarim, those who were humble in spirit. This boy carried the mark identifying him as a candidate, and yet he exuded a quiet arrogance.

Or was it confidence? Maybe bravado masking insecurity?

Gina showed him no mercy. When the game was over and the other boys had wandered off, she said, "Would you let me teach you some things, Dov?"

He shrugged. Adjusted his rows of polished warriors.

"I won't waste my time, unless I know you're going to be all ears."

"Yes." He looked around the room. "Please, I want to learn."

"Have you ever seen the Immortal Game?"

He glanced up through shaggy black hair, intrigue dancing in his eyes. Gina took that as her cue to proceed. She explained the balance between calculated accuracy and artistry. Some people played the game by the book, by the numbers; others, she explained, played by intuition and gut instinct.

"You need both," she said. "See how Anderssen controls the middle of the board, how his knight's planted there on the fifth rank? How his pawn's in black's way? He built on the principles, then blew his opponent away with gutsy creativity."

"The queen died."

"A sacrifice, it's called. Setting up the victory."

Dov leaned forward and replayed the bishop's final, checkmating move. He slid the piece and slammed it down, jarring the others on Gina's black walnut board. "You see?" he said. "This is how it happened when I did the bad thing."

"What do you mean, Dov?"

"He was hurting my mother, and I . . ." The boy slammed down the bishop again for emphasis. "I ran into the hills. That's where the other man found me two nights later. He helped me hide."

"Who?" Only mild interest. "Your father?"

"No, he's gone. The other man, the one with gold in his eyes."

Gina's heart leapt. She knew a simple disguise could've been used to great effect, but she still had to ask. "Did he have yellowish-blond hair?"

"I think so. He wore a hat. He taught me how to use the tent pegs if I ever see them again."

"Them?"

"The ones with green fingernails and sharp teeth. He said to watch out, because someday they would come back."

CHAPTER
FIFTY

Early April 2000—En Route to Sinaia

The sound was meant to ward off evil spirits.

Thunk-thunk, thunk-thunk . . .

Along village roads, folks banged out the rhythm against planks suspended from fences and trees. This ringing of hammers upon wood was a Good Friday tradition meant to remind the spirits of Christ's crucifixion for mankind's sins.

Thunk-thunk . . .

The echoing pattern faded as the charter bus packed with kids and queasy muncitors wound up another road of switchbacks and mountain tunnels. Evergreens graced the steep ledges, and dots of white indicated sheep in the emerald valleys below. These views were the things of Gina's past, triggering thoughts and emotions long untouched.

Thunk-thunk . . .

"Okay, very funny." She turned to the twins behind her. "No more kicking my seat, please."

"It was Pavel."

"It was Petre."

"It was both of them," Dov said from his place across the aisle.

The Podran twins scowled at him. Dov turned his attention back to the magnetic chess set in his lap. Gina flashed a grin to let Pavel and Petre know they were forgiven, then returned to her enjoyment of the passing scenery.

She was thankful for this time away from the city. She had her chestnut hair pulled back in a clasp, and wore a thin spring dress that could double as an Easter outfit or the comfortable garb of a weekend visitor. On this, her first overnight excursion with the orphanage, they were headed to the tourist town of Sinaia.

Rhymes with Shania, as in Twain. That's what she told her friends back in the U.S.

They'd left Tomorrow's Hope at dawn, herded onboard by a surly driver with hunched shoulders, a drooping mustache, and a cap that looked like something a communist border guard might've worn years ago. He slid his belongings under the driver's seat and grunted.

Gina had seen the type before. The man put on such an act of annoyance that she suspected, behind his reflective sunglasses, his eyes were skipping with amusement.

Head now pressed to the window, she let her thoughts wander.

In February, she had written letters to both her husband and her mother. Jed's reply was courteous but guarded, with basic details of his uncle's place in Oregon, of the job he'd found at a local dairy, and of fishing with Uncle Vince—or Sarge, as Jed seemed to prefer. He described Sarge as overweight, down-to-earth, and decent. She got the feeling her husband was in good hands.

As for Nikki, she had not yet responded.

Gina wondered if her world seemed as unreal to the two of them as their worlds now seemed to her.

During the past few months, Gina and Teodor had kept in casual contact. They'd gone out for coffee a few mornings. Teo never pushed. He was a pleasant, familiar face—and yes, she had some lingering romantic feelings—but she wasn't sure love was her lot in life. There was no self-pity in the thought, only acceptance of other tasks.

She had a child to protect. This time, she had to get that right.

Gina still railed in her mind against Cal the Provocateur. She'd seen enough evidence to believe many of the things he'd told her. She had no other explanation for the Lettered foreheads or the bomb that targeted her firstborn.

Yet he'd failed her in the way that mattered most. He had not been there, as promised.

Had he been guarding Dov Amit instead, during that time?

Was it Cal's goal to train future Nistarim and to fight the Collectors?

Well, he'd been quick to abandon her and her own offspring as soon as she showed any signs of resistance. Forget him. If he was willing to sacrifice others' lives because of some fairly reasonable doubts on her part, then she wanted nothing to do with him.

Gina switched her thoughts back to Teo. Last week, her childhood beau had taken her to a display at the Cultural Palace so that she could see for herself the story of Romania's martyrs, those who had put their lives on the line eleven years ago to challenge ruthless tyrants.

That theme resonated with her.

She saw it in the sacrificial moves on a chessboard, in the lines of the national anthem, and here in the local traditions leading up to Easter.

Thunk-thunk . . .

After the *toaka*, the hammering of the wood, there would be silence from the church steeples until twelve a.m. Sunday. Then bells would ring in celebration across the land. Friends and strangers would greet each other for the next week or two with *"Hristos a inviat!"* Christ is risen. They would crack red-dyed eggs as symbols of death and new life, and they—

Thunkity-thunk . . .

Gina Lazarescu sat straight in her seat. What was that? She looked around, saw that most of the bus riders were beginning to snooze in the long shadows cast by a sun slipping behind distant ridges.

"Did you hear that?" Dov said.

"Yeah. That was different, wasn't it?"

He snapped his chess set shut, sending magnetic pieces tumbling. He said, "They're coming to find me."

"Don't talk like that. It won't help either of us, okay?"

"Ask *him*."

Gina followed the pointing finger toward the mustached man in the sunglasses. "The driver?" she said.

"He knows."

"You sit tight, Dov. I'll be right back."

Though unsure of what was going on, she had learned not to discount her young ward's cryptic claims. To date, everything he'd said had lined up with her own experiences and investigation.

Gina, who had once been Lettered . . .

Dov, who now carried the same symbol beneath scraggly bangs . . .

In the middle of this great big world, by mysteries greater than Gina could fathom, the two of them had been brought together. This was her shot at regaining a measure of peace and redemption, his shot at replacing a portion of the family that had been torn from him.

Thu-THUNK-ity, THUNK-thunk . . .

Gina grabbed at the seats on either side of the aisle, felt the floor rise and buck beneath her. She heard drowsy cries and a child's scream behind her, as the brakes squealed with rubber-shredding alarm. The driver, in his border-guard hat and sunglasses, spun the wheel to correct the vehicle's slide toward a guardrail.

Muncitors were barking out orders now to the children. A few overnight bags lurched from the luggage racks and plopped into the aisle, one of them careening off Gina's shoulder.

She stumbled forward, felt her bare knees buckle and touch the floor. She pulled herself up and said, "It's going to be all right," to a bug-eyed girl in the front row beside her.

The driver was calm but intent, his hands moving over the steering wheel. He corrected again, away from the precipice, easing off the brakes

and punching the accelerator so that the bus straightened and charged
ahead into the arched mouth of a tunnel.

"Stop this bus," a male muncitor ordered from the back.

The driver pressed onward.

"We have children aboard. We need to check that everyone's okay."

The driver was unperturbed, his glasses reflecting the headlights'
dull beams as they bounced between the tunnel's stone walls. The others
onboard had fallen into stunned silence.

"Stop," the muncitor said. "I must *insist*."

"You," the driver said, with such authority that it gusted down the
aisle and buffeted between the panoramic windows, "will take your seat,
watch over the children, and shut your stinkin' mouth."

Gina stared at the man behind the wheel. That voice. Could it be . . . ?

There's no way.

"You should get back to your place," he told her. "For your own
safety."

"What happened back there?" Gina asked.

"We hit something."

"We . . . Well, maybe we should've stopped. What was it?"

"Show no mercy," he said through his mustache.

"Was it an animal?"

They exited the tunnel into a purple and red-black twilight. Along
the aisle, muncitors spoke in low tones to calm those awakened by the
sudden lurches.

"You could say that," the driver replied. "Could say it was human too.
Now, back to your seat, if you don't mind. I'm trying to get us to Sinaia
in one piece."

The lights of an approaching car threw his profile into silhouette,
and Gina felt a spark of recognition. "Cal?"

"Go on back. Stay close to Dov."

"It's you?"

Green eyes peered over the rims of his shades, allowing her a glimpse
of gold flecks twinkling in the glow of the dash. "Shush." He said it the

way Nikki would have, with the same inflection—as if he had the right to be bossing her around. "Please, Gina, let's wait till I can stop this thing."

"But why're you—?"

"The train station just outside of Sinaia. We'll pull over and talk there." He braked, heading into a hairpin turn. A road sign indicated they were twenty-seven kilometers from their destination.

Gina seethed with questions the entire way.

On the asphalt where the tour bus had roared past moments earlier, the wolf whimpered for the last time. Playing temporary host to Ariston's Collector, the foolish creature had disobeyed orders and found itself snarling and wild-eyed in the path of hurtling metal.

Now, in the darkness, the Collector was left drifting.

He was joined by a female whose primary habitation was Erota. The nineteen-year-old had returned to him last year, offering her allegiance to the Akeldama Cluster and vowing vengeance on her father's killer. Though suspect of her human inclinations and the long-term effects of estrangement from her younger sister, Ariston had embraced her presence as a welcome diversion from the tedium of his wives. While Barabbas and Megiste had betrayed him, luring others with them, Erota's youthfulness could work in his favor.

Or so he thought.

Moments ago, just down the incline, her Collector had suffered a fate similar to his own and left behind the carcass of a small bushy-tailed fox. They were both stuck once more in the shadowy corridors of the Separation—imitations of life, at best; mere hints of physicality in the air.

Ariston's Collector tethered himself to the dead wolf's ear. "What now?"

"We'll have to make it back to our original hosts."

"I think that driver knew. I'd swear that he aimed for me."

"For me too," the female Collector said.

"Dumb animal instinct. The wolf tried to chase a rabbit across the road and ignored my every command."

He sniffed. His permanent human shell was in repose a number of miles to the north, in Zalmoxis Cave. Erota's was farther away, in the underbrush of a ravine.

Hidden in the steep slopes between Sinaia and Busteni, the cave was named after a semimythical character who had lived centuries before the arrival of the Nazarene. It was said the man had secluded himself for three years in the caverns of these Bucegi Mountains, along the Carpathians' eastern fringe, then staged his own "resurrection." The locals were so impressed that they hailed him a god.

Ariston had chosen the site months earlier as the final resting spot for Eros's and Sol's corpses, a place of historical and otherworldly significance. The location was a reminder to the cluster that he valued their fallen, that they were in this together. The bodies served notice that this world of humans was fraught with danger, and they would be wise to heed his commands at all times.

His Collector, now drifting over the carcass of the wolf, wondered what to do next. Why had he allowed a young woman to talk him into this? Unsure of the orphans' schedule, Erota had suggested they utilize creatures of the forest to spy out the approach of the tour bus, then to cut back over the ridge to Sinaia before the diesel monster could claw its way up the longer, more circuitous road.

"Now they're going to get there before us," he told her.

"Don't worry. We know their plans for tomorrow. After visiting the monastery and Peles Castle, they'll be taking the Busteni cable car up to the hikers' cabana that overlooks the valley. We can weed out the boy anywhere along the way."

"Or cut the entire cable car and send it plunging to the rocks."

"See? We'll adjust our plans, that's all."

"We do have a few others who can help."

"That's right," she said. "Plus, your daughter will be with us."

"Shalom, yes. She saw Gina in Arad, did she not?"

"While shopping."

"So she'll know what to look for."

"Absolutely."

Ariston's Collector found a measure of solace in that.

Earlier, they had discussed Megiste's attack on Erota while in Atlanta, as well as her decision to lure away Ariston's henchman—and all of it *after* cutting down his own son. The woman was inscrutable. She was crafty, he had to give her that, but who was Megiste to think she could take over leadership of the House of Eros instead of submitting to his cluster's oversight?

Word was that she had tucked her tail and scurried back to Israel. Well, let her rot, as far as he was concerned. Not that he would take anything for granted. Before making today's trip to Sinaia, he had posted a handful of his remaining cluster on the vineyard premises to ward off any unruliness. He could not afford any more defections.

"You ready to make our way back?" Erota's Collector inquired.

"I'm ready."

He released his slight hold on the expired wolf, elevating on a cold wind that scooped roadside leaves into the air. He let it carry him up over spruce and fir trees, past a grey owl and clumps of boulders where medieval battles had taken place. East of him, Erota's Collector was riding her own current, nothing but a wisp of evening vapor.

Gliding along, he sensed the ghosts of Romania's past below, the whispers of invaders and whiffs of spilled blood. This country had long been a chessboard of real-life intrigue. Marauders and armies, sultans and lords, had ravaged this land with their ruthless ambition.

Farther north, at Bran Pass, a fortress still stood as a reminder of such conflict, and Vlad Tepes, better known as Dracula, had frequented the area as he rallied the locals against all threats.

The feudal lord had never actually drunk blood from human necks, but it did make for scary tales.

If only he'd known what he was missing.

The Collector shivered in palpable anticipation of the coming showdown. He drew vitality from the determination of those who had remained true to the Akeldama Cluster—Shelamzion and Helene; his daughter, Shalom; Auge and her young daughter, Kyria; Nehemiah; teen-aged Shabtai; and tiny Matrona. Not to mention Erota and her newly pledged allegiance.

Yes, they would stand strong.

From ahead, he felt sudden wind resistance.

He identified, via monochromatic visibility, the crooked teeth of a ridge and realized he was going to be smashed into the rocks. He was still a few kilometers from his destination and his original host, which meant he needed to press on.

Desperate, he tried to snag a cross-draft. When that failed, he tried to hook onto a treetop.

It was no use.

At the mercy of the wind, Ariston's Collector was slammed against the cliff, his hazy presence mauled by great granite molars. The breeze died in the lee of the ridge, and he found himself spiraling into the forest below.

CHAPTER
FIFTY-ONE

Sinaia

"You. How *dare* you?"

"Gina, please."

"Where *were* you?" She drove a fist into Cal's arm. Cocked back and landed a second blow. "You were supposed to keep him safe. My *baby* . . . You said you would be there."

"I'm here now, aren't I?"

Gina's mind raced to the few times Cal had been around: the escape from Cuvin . . . the Borsa safe house . . . the conversation at Ruby Falls . . . the chat on the Tennessee River's bank.

At present, they were in the thickening darkness of snow-dusted mountains that loomed over this narrow valley. Cal had parked the charter bus outside the Sinaia train station, where silver tracks ran parallel to the turbulent Prahova River. A hillside of trees hid the station from the tourist village on the slope above, and the building was vacant, having serviced its last passengers for the evening.

Cal and Gina faced each other in the station's open entryway. She was already shivering in her spring dress.

"Jacob," she said, "is dead. We didn't even . . . Jed and I never even got one full day with our son."

"I'm sorry."

"That's all you can say?"

"What can I do but try my best to make things right?"

Faces were pressed to the bus windows, watching their exchange. Cal had explained to all onboard that their vehicle had been targeted by "local ruffians" and that he needed to consult with Gina since she was familiar with this region.

She ignored the spectators. "You lied to me," she said. "You failed me."

"I've failed a lotta people."

"Ohhh. So what's one more, huh? You are *pathetic*."

"I have to live with that fact every day."

Cal's eyes swam behind a liquid sheen, and briefly Gina thought he was going to shed tears. Like she cared. Then she realized it was only a trick of the moonlight stabbing down through windows in the depot's vaulted ceiling. Nearby, schedule boards and ticket booths stood at attention, as though awaiting the arrival of unearthly visitors. The nearby river seemed to murmur in conspiratorial tones.

This place was too much. Gina had been back in her homeland only a few months, and already her mother's old superstitions were pawing at her mind.

"Did *you* plant the bomb?" she hissed at Cal. "Was that *your* pack?"

He looked pained by her words. "Definitely not. Just ask around, and you'll find JanSport in thousands of stores. That trick of theirs was pretty rotten."

"Let me get this straight. You know what happened, but you weren't able to put a stop to it beforehand? Big help that was, Cal, buddy boy. Why're you even here?"

"I'm not." He winked and twirled an end of his mustache.

Gina was not amused. "You know what, right there in that bus, I've now got another kid to protect."

"Who you met at the Strand."

"Yeah, and . . . Hey, wait."

"The day of the choir performance," Cal said.

"You set that up?" Then: the realization. "You *knew* I would see the Letter. You knew I would care for him."

"Now you're tracking. Poor kid, he was in sorry shape."

"He was missing a toe. He was half-starved."

"Stories for another day." Cal removed his sunglasses and adjusted the brim of his hat. A pair of cars passed by, cutting north toward Brasov and Sighisoara, the birthplace of Vlad Tepes. "Main thing is, you are what that boy needs."

"Me?"

"Can't think of anyone better, Gina."

She swallowed down a cocktail of hope and indignation. Although she wanted to be angry, she couldn't deny the comfort of Cal's presence here in the Carpathian dusk.

"Hey," a muncitor called from the doorway of the bus. "When're we going to go? We're all tired and hungry, and the kids are getting spooked out here."

"Would you gimme a few minutes?" Cal snapped in his gruff driver's voice. He turned back to Gina. "Before you came along, Dov spent some time training with me, and he's got lots more to learn, but he has been hardened by over two and a half years of survival in the woods and on the streets. He'll be fine. A little love'll carry him a long way."

"He's not exactly the most receptive kid."

"Cut him some slack, and you just might come to like him."

"I do like him," Gina said.

"Not really. Admit it. Mostly, he's your chance to redeem yourself."

She threw another fist at Cal's arm. "Who are *you* to talk about redemption? You're the one who abandoned my baby boy. I don't even have enough fingers and toes to count the ways you misled me."

"There's still stuff that I . . . Listen, it's not all that it seems, Gina."

"Sure. Whatever."

"Man, we don't have time for this right now. There's so much I wanna tell you, but first we've gotta think about Dov. If we head into that town, we'll be walking into a trap. She knows he's coming."

"The Collector," Gina said. "The one I saw at Ruby Falls, that one?"

"Name's Erota."

"So she was there in Chattanooga. At the hospital."

Cal gave a grim nod.

"Was she the one you ran over on the road? You think it killed her?"

"There were two of them, and at best it delayed them a little. You ask me, she'll always be able to find more evil minions to throw in front of the bus." Cal coughed out a sour snicker. "We're talking about the undead, remember?"

"I'm still trying to wrap my head around that."

"She might get an arm broken off or an eye gouged, but she's gonna keep on coming, and there's not too much that'll stop her. Think the Energizer Bunny with fangs."

"That's just creepy and wrong."

"Tell me about it. And she's not the only one."

"Great."

"She's working under one named Ariston."

"How'd she find me?" Gina said. "How's she know about Dov?"

"That research you did on his family, it raised a red flag for Helene Totorcea, an archivist at Arad's city hall. You might've even talked to her on the phone or something. Helene's a Collector, as well."

"Totorcea. That's the family out by where Mrs. Amit disappeared."

"Tortocea is a front. Flavius Tortocea is really Ariston, their cluster leader. And, believe me," Cal said, "Dalia's dead, and they're all guilty. Since their release in '89, they've been wreaking havoc. The orphans across Romania, the thousands with HIV . . . Who do you think infected them?"

Gina pressed her lips tight, breathed deeply through her nose.

"That goes back," Cal said, "to their first stinkin' day in this country."

"And that wasn't enough for them? Now they want Dov too?"

"'The leech has two suckers that cry out, "More, more!"' Straight from the book of Proverbs, and if you ask me, it's a dead-on description."

"Will they *ever* be satisfied?"

"Not until they can drag down the Nistarim. Erota's got her household all riled up over that, ever since the attack in Chattanooga failed."

"Failed? How can you *say* that? She *killed* Jacob."

"It failed to usher in Final Vengeance. Guess she still thinks you're a key."

"Why?" Gina's fingers swiped at her brow. "My Letter's gone."

"I know. And, I'm sorry to say this, but my guess is you won't be having any more of your own children—not any of the Nistarim candidates anyway. But you've got a mother's heart, and there'll always be more kids for you to watch after." He angled a thumb at the bus, at the row of curious onlookers. "Not just the Concealed Ones, but the others caught in the crossfire."

Months earlier, this conversation would've had Gina's head spinning. Now, with animosity held in check, she began to bring things into focus. These Collectors, these vile creatures from the abyss, they were her enemy. Their basic objectives: blood, infestation, and destruction.

From here, it was a matter of choosing the most accurate end-game maneuvers.

"So," Cal said. "What's our next step? Fight or flight?"

She looked toward the bus and wondered if she could survive the heartbreak of another loss. She wrapped her arms around herself to keep warm. A diesel truck lumbered past, spewing fumes.

"How 'bout both?" she said.

"What've you got in mind?"

"You take the kids and hide them away. Don't tell me where. You just do it. Then we meet back up later, far away. Say, tomorrow in Bucharest."

"And what'll you be doing in the meantime?"

"I'll be up there." She gestured toward Sinaia. "Keeping the Collectors occupied."

"A queen sacrifice?"

"Just living up to my name."

"I don't like it."

"I think it's a fine name."

"Hah. You know what I mean. I don't like you facing these things alone. Sure, you're immortal, but what if they turn you to their side?"

"Can they do that?"

"None of us are without fault," he said. "But that's up to you, isn't it? The Power of Choice. Not to mention, they could just tear you apart and then bury you where I can't find you. Three days, that's it. *Sayonara* and *c'est la vie.*"

"Cal, I'm not asking your permission here. They've destroyed the lives of children all over Romania, and they took my own son away from me. That's all I need to know. They can take, take, take, and take some more, but eventually they're going to lose."

"The Immortal Game," Cal commented.

"The . . . What'd you just say?" Gina gave him a sidelong glance. For years she had wondered how she'd learned to master chess and all its intricacies, and his random comment seemed loaded with implications. "Are you telling me you're a chess player?"

"You know, you can be one uppity little girl. I mean, really. Who do you think taught you how to play?"

The Bucegi Mountains, Romania

The Collector was nothing.

He was particles of soot at the foot of a cliff, subject to the elements. He was swatches of shadow, overlapping, drifting, then disappearing, as the night's monstrous maw swallowed him into its collective black bosom. He had scarcely the wherewithal to dredge up the identity of his chosen host.

Ariston. Of Apamea. The House of Ariston.

In the Bucegi Mountains.

A niggling thought told him that his destination was the cool caverns up the mountainside. He had to get there.

A blast of cold air sent him hurtling in the opposite direction.

CHAPTER
FIFTY-TWO

Sinaia

"You were the one?"

"Yep."

"But . . ." Standing on the station steps, Gina shook her head. "I have no memory of that."

She was still rocked by the assertion that he'd been the one to instruct her in the art and warfare of chess. This meant he'd been there earlier, much earlier, in her childhood stages. It meant, too, he was older than he appeared.

"Since when does all of life get categorized by one person's memories?" Cal asked her. "Do you remember being taught how to walk? Or to form sentences? C'mon, that's just arrogance talking."

"You knew me when I was little?"

"Not as well as I woulda liked. Nikki was very protective of you."

"Tell me about it." Gina thought of her mother's overbearing ways and her disapproval of every boy Gina had expressed feelings toward. Still, she had the feeling there was something Cal was not divulging.

"Please," a female muncitor said from the bus. "It's getting late."

"Pass out snacks," Cal responded, more sympathetic this time. "Got a bag of licorice, plus some apples, in a box behind the driver's seat. That should keep the kids quiet for now."

"Thank you."

Gina's gaze climbed the neighboring slope, skimming over the stands of conifers and catching the glow of the alpine village that was just out of sight. It was a well-known destination, its streets clogged with vacationing families, beer-drinking tourists, and honeymooning couples. She imagined up there, somewhere, the Collectors were waiting.

"Okay, Cal," she said. "Since you claim you were my teacher . . . In the Immortal Game, what is White's subtle little move that sets up the final sacrifice?"

"Why is it you always need proof?"

"You haven't exactly been a rock of stability, you know."

"You sure tell it like it is, don't you?"

"What other way is there? And since you refuse to answer the question, I'm going to assume that—"

"Pawn to e5," he said. "White's nineteenth move."

Gina's mouth was left gaping. She bit her lip, then shook her head. "Whatever. It's a famous game. Sure, there's lots of people who could spit out that answer."

"Then think about this . . ."

"What now?"

"You: Regina." He tapped his own chest. "Me: Cal."

"Sorry. I don't get what you're trying to . . ." She threw her head back and laughed. She thought of the piese de șah, her stately pieces with their individual abilities and assignments. "*Cal.* In Romanian, it's the word for *knight.*"

"Always hopping into the middle of things. You know, e5's also a great spot for a knight."

"I can't believe it. Out of context, I just never put the two together."

"Here's something else to jar your memory." Cal reached into the inner pocket of his coat and withdrew a bundled object. "It's from your chess set."

Gina accepted the offering. She unfurled leather straps and found the sheath Jed had made her, accompanied by the antique dagger.

"Where'd you get this?"

"From Nikki."

"I thought I'd never have to see this thing again. What's she want you to do, bleed out a few more of my sins while you're with me?"

"No, I took it from her."

"And she let you do that? Said, 'Here, take this family heirloom.'"

"It was mine to start with, and now I'm giving it to you."

"I don't want it."

"What we want and what we need—sometimes those are two different things, Gina." Cal jerked his chin toward the hill. "And you're gonna need it. This is your chance to do all the things right that Nikki did wrong. Just don't reject the truth because of the lies she's added to it."

"The truth? Uh, run that by me one more time."

Cal rested a hand on the spot just below her throat. He said, "The answer dies within."

"And that means what?"

Waiting for his response, Gina told herself to remain aloof. She'd been overloaded with head-spinning information and nebulous legends, and she was already distressed by the walls that were crumbling inside.

Hold on. Just hold yourself together.

"Like we talked about in Chattanooga," Cal said, "it's all about dying to your own will each day, while keeping the spirit alive. Identifying with the Nazarene's suffering, while living for what really matters. It doesn't always mean happiness, but it does mean being content. Believe me, those two are not the same thing."

"Well, buddy boy. Thank you. Very profound."

"Hey, I try."

Gina moved her hand to Cal's, felt her heartbeat fall into rhythm with his. Though baffled by his rhetoric, she sensed meaning and experience pulsing through his words. Despite her reservations, her fears, she found that she wanted to hold on to that.

"So," she whispered. "Guess it's up the mountain I go."

"You sure you wanna do this?"

She looked at the children in the bus, even turned on a reassuring grin for the darling girl in the front seat, for the twins Petre and Pavel Podran, and for Dov Amit, whose face remained a blank mask of survival. His welfare was on her shoulders.

I'm not letting another one die.

She strapped the dagger to her thigh, let her dress fall back over the leather sheath, and said, "I'm sure."

Spurred along by her grin, young Petre came bounding from the bus. His good behavior had earned him a ride on this field trip, yet he now seemed intent on reaching Gina despite the muncitor at his heels.

"You get back in this bus, Petre," the man ordered. "You do it *now*."

"Gina, I gotta tell you something."

"Petre," the muncitor was calling.

"Gina, please." The twin arrived at her side.

Cal slipped into gruff mode again and gripped the kid's shoulder. "What're you doing, young man? Do you want a lashing for getting out of your seat?"

"See there?" the muncitor said. "Look at the trouble you're in."

Petre shot Cal a jealous look, then fixed round, black eyes on Gina.

"What is it?" she asked, taking his hand.

"My brother's scared. It's dark on the bus."

"Well, you go back and stay close by him then."

"Where's a bathroom?"

"It can wait," the muncitor said.

Petre shifted from one foot to the other, putting on a display that was obvious if not heartfelt in its deception. "But I really have to go."

"Or maybe," Gina said, "you just don't like me talking to other men."

"Pavel. He thinks you don't like him anymore."

"I like him, and I like you too." Gina touched his nose. "Now, go sit down. This is about to be over."

Over Petre's shoulder, she saw that Dov had now planted himself on the bottom step of the bus. He swept his gaze toward Cal, attentive to any commands, and said in a Hebrew-accented voice that was urgent but steady, "What should I do? Someone's coming toward us, through the woods across the road."

Gina's eyes scanned the trees but saw nothing out of place.

"Bring me my pack," Cal told Dov.

The boy ducked back into the bus, where gibbous light on the windows turned the occupants into pale, ethereal beings.

"What's going on?" the male muncitor huffed.

Cal removed his hat, slapped it against his leg, then snugged it back over his head. "Gather the children in the back rows, stay down outta sight, and keep all doors and windows closed. You hear me?"

"The local ruffians, you think?"

"Something like that."

"You're the driver. I say you take us to the police station. Surely there's one along the main stretch through town."

"We can't outrun them forever." Cal clapped an arm over the man's shoulder and steered him toward the vehicle. "Do as I say. Go."

Dov reemerged. He brushed past the muncitor, who drew the bus door shut behind him, then hefted the satchel he had fetched from beneath the driver's seat.

Cal stretched out his hand. "Time to split them up."

The fifteen-year-old reached into the bag, producing a bundle of crude, tapered spikes. His mentor withdrew a handful. The metallic sounds reminded Gina of medieval warriors suiting up for battle, and she felt primal courage well through her chest. She had a sudden sense of purpose.

Dov seemed to feel it too. On his forehead, the letter Tav gave off a faint blue iridescence through his black hair.

"What're those?" she asked, pointing at the spikes.

"MTPs," Cal said. "Metal tent pegs. My weapon of choice."

"Are you kidding?"

"Think of that guy in the Bible, the one who got his head hammered into the ground while sleeping. These things're nasty sharp. With the right leverage, a child could put one through a person's temple."

"Sometimes," Dov said, "you have to do the bad thing."

"The *right* thing," Cal said. "What's right isn't always easy."

"So, we're fighting zombies now?"

"Undead," Cal corrected her. "Zombies don't need blood the way these things do. You've got your dagger. Use it. It has its own symbolic power over the Collectors, or at least as much as they'll give it credit for. It's betrayed their kind before."

"This thing?" Gina said. She drew her weapon, noticed nothing particularly remarkable or supernatural about it, and she hoped it would do. At this point, what other option did she have?

"It's two-thousand-years-old."

"Not another one of your stories. Not right now, Cal."

"Once belonged to Peter."

"As in, the disciple?"

"He tried protecting the Nazarene with it, even cut off a guy's ear, but that wasn't part of the plan. Pete got scolded for it. Dropped the thing right there on the spot—the scene of the crime. Not that it mattered." A sardonic twinkle played through Cal's eyes. "There was no fingerprinting back then, so he didn't have to worry about them tracing it back to him."

"Hilarious. And it got here *how?*"

"Long story, Gina. Basically, Judas grabbed it off the ground and stuffed it into his robe. Lotta good that did him."

"So we're about to fight some vampires, and all I've got to trust in is an old knife and some crazy stories."

"It's not what you trust in. It's *who*."

Dov was tugging at Cal's arm. "Here they come," he said.

The Bucegi Mountains

He was drifting, running low on mental energy for this trek through the night. With limited sensory abilities, he was crippled by the blackness that pooled in this gorge. He had no idea where he was in relation to Zalmoxis Cave.

This was foolishness. Utter absurdity.

Partnered with the Collector within, Ariston liked to think of himself as a creature of urbane ways, comfortable with women, envied and emulated by men. His manner was smooth, his movements imperious and confident.

And now, his Collector was lost. Kicked about by unruly forces of nature.

Frantic to arrest his progress, he clawed at a shape ahead, found himself slipping between two sharp objects that were curved and . . . They were the horns of a sure-footed chamois poised here on the steep rock. Even as he tried to grasp hold, the goatlike animal swiped its head and tossed him off the way it would a pesky insect.

"Ariston."

To his vaporous ears, the voice sounded thin and waxy.

"Ariston."

Definitely his name. Or rather the name of his permanent host.

"If you can hear me, hang on a bit longer. Once the wind's died down, make your way back to the cave. Shalom and I will try to meet you there, after we've captured the woman and the boy."

He wrapped what little there was of his intangible form around the next thing he bumped into. Like the tattered flag of a beleaguered army, he found himself waving from the sharp point of a twig.

Then, to his great relief, a small gust broke him loose.

Sinaia

"They're right there," Dov said.

A briny odor swirled down the slope, followed by the emergence of a man and a woman from the stone path that cut between the trees. One was recognizable to Gina: the slender brunette from the bookshop. The other was a fatherly sort, grand and graceful. They were beautiful specimens. Humans, it would seem. And yet they possessed an aura wholly other, hinted at in their stark, emerald eyes that pierced the night.

Gina had seen that look before, years ago in Cuvin. Had Teodor's uncle been one of these things? Was that why he'd wondered if she bore the Letter?

So this, Gina realized, *is what Collectors look like.*

"The young woman's Shalom, and the man is Nehemiah," Cal said. "There should be a few more. I'd bet Auge's around somewhere, and she's been a weepy, unholy terror since the death of her husband. Listen, I'll deal with these two while you keep an eye on the bus, Gina. Guard that door."

"Where do you want me?" Dov said.

"Shouldn't you be in the bus too?" Gina checked.

Cal shook his head. "If he goes in there, he'll draw trouble to the others. Nope, he's staying out here with us."

From the doorway, the male municitor beckoned Dov to come onboard, but the boy refused to acknowledge the gestures or commands.

"You can go if you want," Cal said. "I'm not forcing you here."

Dov raised an MTP in his fist. "I want to help you fight."

Gina thought of the sorrows her tiny Jacob had seemed to bear even in the womb, and understood now the pressure Dov Amit must be under. She felt proud of this little man who had endured enough already. Though she detected the trembling in his hands as he grasped the metal spikes, she heard no wavering in his voice, and she felt her heart soften toward him.

"You position yourself between me and the bus," Cal instructed him. "If they get past me or try to circle around at Gina, it'll be on your shoulders to act."

Dov straightened. With his grimace of discomfort over unseen sorrows, the blue glow on his forehead intensified. "I'll be ready."

Gina believed him. She knew his training was minimal, yet it was more than she or the others possessed. Already, the boy had struck down a Collector with his own hands. Could she do the same?

"How 'bout you?" Cal asked her. "You ready?"

Shalom and Nehemiah were nearing, their arms swinging, razor-edged fingernails lengthening, eyes burning.

"You better believe it, buddy boy."

CHAPTER
FIFTY-THREE

Cal withdrew an MTP from the group in his left hand and flexed his fingers around the object, weighing it. Another set of cars chugged northward, bisecting the distance between the vampires and the empty train station. A bicycle rattled by as a peasant woman headed home for the evening.

Gina backed toward the bus, the blade of her own weapon glinting. She pressed against the door, confirmed that it was shut tight, and made sure there were no signs through the windows of any children onboard.

Good. All she had to do was hold her ground and rely on the dagger.

Cal's words: *It's not what . . . It's who.*

And, back on a Chattanooga riverbank: *If you choose to believe, that's all it takes . . . a chance at being cleansed.*

He made it sound so simple. Simplistic was more like it. Nothing in this world got handed to you on a platter. That was a fairy tale. A dream. Gina had known since this blade's first bite into her own skin that life was anything but simple. Look at her now, with a chance to turn against her enemies the very blade that had cut her as a child.

ERIC WILSON

Well, maybe there was some justice after all.

Across the pavement, Cal the Provocateur was setting his chin and advancing toward the pair of Collectors. He looked strong, light on his feet, and self-assured. She wondered how many others he had faced.

There's so much I wanna tell you . . . he had said earlier.

"Go back the way you came," he was barking at Shalom and Nehemiah. "I know why you're here, but you're not getting anything. Not tonight."

"Oh?" The man smirked. "And who are you to talk?"

"I think you know."

What was that supposed to mean? Gina wondered.

"I do," said Nehemiah. "And I'm not the slightest bit worried."

"Stop right there."

"We want the boy, the one with the letter Tav."

"Can't have him."

"Let us take him, and we'll leave the rest alone."

"Not gonna happen."

"At least let me have *her*," Shalom chimed in, aiming a curved finger-nail at Gina. Though her demeanor was demure, her eyes glowed with an insatiable fire.

Gina's throat tightened. She raised the dagger higher, thought of the angel tattoo on her back, and found herself praying for protection. A futile gesture, perhaps, but desperate times called for desperate measures. For a moment, she sensed the whisper of wings over her shoulders, then told herself it was her imagination playing tricks.

Just stay focused. Keep your eyes open.

Cal took advantage of Shalom's diverted attention and lifted the MTP in his hand. In a fluid motion that rocked him back on his heels and then forward again, he stepped into his throw and launched the crude yet significant weapon. It spun like a dirty icicle and would've split the young woman's skull, except that she sidestepped to the left.

She grinned, incisors showing for the first time as the sharp imple-ment disappeared into the foliage behind her. Her serrated fangs could've been stalactites in the ancient cavern of her mouth, formations that had

FIELD OF BLOOD   383

elongated over the ages. Like the earth, like the grave, she was ready to swallow and devour.

She took steps in Gina's direction.

Cal moved to cut her off, but Nehemiah circled the other way.

"Dov," he said.

"I'm watching."

"Come here, child," the paternal figure purred. "You're the one I want."

Dov squared his shoulders.

"Never mind the home for orphans and undesirables, the hideously infected. Is that what you want? You want to play victim to HIV, like the others?"

Gina thought she detected a slump in the boy's posture.

"Come home with me," Nehemiah urged. "I have a teen son, and I'm sure you and Shabtai would get along fabulously."

"If you want him," Cal said, positioning himself in the middle of the lot, "you get me too. Package deal."

"I'm a man of Jewish origin. You must know how I love a bargain."

"You're a body thief and a bloodsucker."

"I am rather thirsty, too true."

With that, the verbal sparring was over.

Nehemiah, despite the middle-aged legs of his host, broke into a smooth sprint, with deadly fingers raking the air at his sides. This time, Cal rocketed two tent pegs through the space between them, one after the other. As Nehemiah dodged the first, he moved into the path of the second, and it punched through his right eye, exiting through the back of his skull.

The spray of blood and brain matter turned black against the watchful moon—a blossom of death, emitting a gagging odor. The body slumped to the ground. Fell facedown on the near side of the road.

A freight truck roared around the bend and clipped the backs of his legs, never even slowing on its journey.

This, Gina thought, *was going to be easier than she thought.*

That's when she spotted a plump woman with short hair coming up from the riverbank. It wasn't Erota. Perhaps another from the Akeldama

Cluster? Hadn't Cal mentioned someone named Auge? A bereaved widow? The woman ascended the slope and stepped over the train tracks, becoming visible in sections as though rising from the soil itself. Bright green roiled through her eyes. Like a witch's brew foaming in twin cauldrons, some of it spilled over.

Or was that just Gina's mind embellishing the scene?

No, there were droplets oozing down the revenant's cheeks and dotting the earth at her feet. Tears of sorrow? Of anger?

To the side, Cal and Shalom were faced off in the parking area. Dov moved closer to Gina, still trembling, still wielding an MTP. She gave him an encouraging wink, and they drew a breath in unison.

"I won't let anything happen to you," he said.

Which plucked the very words from her lips.

Dov stepped forward, the spike gripped in his small fist. He raised it to shoulder level, ready to carve in either direction. The dagger's handle was sweaty in Gina's grasp, despite the chill of the mountain breeze.

"It has its own symbolic power . . ."

Cal had directed her to guard the entry to the bus, but a rush of motherly instincts told her to join the attack. The numbers were in their favor, three against two. Cal could hold his own. She and Dov could deal with this stout, weepy-eyed aberration before them.

A deep-throated growl cut through the night.

"What was that?" Dov asked.

The sound came from a stand of trees near the river's edge, and Gina ran through the possibilities. She knew her country was full of all sorts of wildlife, and the Carpathians—including these Bucegi Mountains—formed a topographic horseshoe that was home to the only dense carnivore population in central Europe. Wolves, hawks, lynx, and . . .

Bear. *Ursus*, in Romanian.

She couldn't bring herself to verbalize that fear. Local brown bears were not uncommon near Sinaia, and not particularly aggressive toward humans, but under the guidance of a Collector, one could be a fearsome predator.

Above, shear winds drew a curtain of cloud across the moon, and the inky shadows exploded with activity. Veering toward Gina's position, Shalom sprinted across the pavement, pursued by Cal, while the revenant from the river accelerated from the other side on stubby legs.

At the center, Dov and Gina stood guard before the charter bus full of hidden, yet audibly whimpering, orphans.

Tomorrow's Hope was under attack.

Weepy Eyes crested the riverbank, chin down, knees churning. Dov took three quick steps toward her, then ducked to the left and swung with his right arm as their paths converged. The MTP grazed the Collector's side, and the creature swiveled to respond to this threat.

Around the front end of the vehicle, Cal feigned a similar attack on Shalom, then spun round and slashed at her extended left limb. He took it off at the wrist, showering the pavement with her blood—the ingested life force of others, tapped and absorbed for her own vile existence.

Gina turned away.

Evil could not be endured. She knew these creatures, if not repelled, would keep coming, keep attacking, feeding and drinking to satisfy a need that could never be met. Still, it was hard to watch.

Don't even feel sorry for them, she reminded herself. *No mercy.*

Nearby, Dov stood and took another swing at his opponent.

The Collector snarled at him.

Not on my watch!

Activated by this new resolve, Gina looped behind Weepy Eyes, detecting salt and sulfur and the fetid odor of demonic rage. She wasn't sure, though . . . Would her dagger be more effective going through the head, the neck, or the heart? She was familiar with vampire legends, but they seemed upended by these Jerusalem's Undead.

She swung the blade, but the woman spotted her and pivoted with a backslash of tapered fingernails. Gina ducked beneath the blow as a lock of chestnut hair was clipped from her head. She stumbled forward, felt a knee hit the pavement.

A little lower, little faster, and that could've been lights out. Back to your feet. C'mon, get up.

Dov, to the rescue, grazed the stout woman's elbow with the spike. As she reared back in pain, he hurled it at her and impaled her flabby upper arm. The green tears splashed and sizzled on the ground.

She was still alive, though. If that word even fit.

"Through the temple," Gina shouted at Dov.

He brandished another MTP and took aim. The Collector looked from Gina to Dov, chose the smaller threat, and charged again at the orphan boy. Gina was a mother bear, intent on protecting her cub, but her attention was yanked away by a screech from a bus window. She turned and saw Petre Podran's swath of black hair as he squirmed through the opening. Despite Pavel's attempts to grab at his legs, Petre kicked at his twin brother and dropped to the pavement.

"No!" Gina shouted. "Back inside."

Petre scrambled to his feet. He had armed himself with a thick walking stick, probably taken from one of the older muncitors. He looked so small, only nine years old, and yet his eyes glowed with stubborn loyalty.

"No, Petre. Stay back."

"I can fight, too," he said. "Like Dov."

On Gina's left, Dov was in a deadly dance with the Collector. His every move was parried by the stout creature's slashing arms and brutal fingernails. He stumbled, slipped to a knee, and Weepy Eyes advanced.

With dagger raised, Gina ran to intercept and if possible blunt the attack, but the beast spun past her, past Dov, and instead targeted the smallest threat.

Petre stiffened.

To his credit, he never retreated.

Gina planted her left foot, halting her own momentum, and shifted back toward the Collector. Too late. She and Dov were still ten feet behind the loathsome thing, when Weepy Eyes propelled herself through the air and slashed both hands toward the nine-year-old. Though Petre took a swing with his heavy stick, the Collector's left forearm deflected the force and the right drove razor-edged nails into the child's chest.

Petre's eyes widened, and a gasp spurted from his throat as he smashed into the side of the bus. Impaled there, he lifted his gaze to Gina. The light in his eyes showed no fear, no pain, only deep regret for having failed to protect her.

Then the light went out.

Gina screamed, her chest torn apart by a rage and despair she had hoped to never feel again. She wanted to drop to her knees, to melt into the earth and never return, but Dov was still here and the beast had torn free from its latest kill to face the fifteen-year-old with the luminescent mark on his forehead.

Dov risked stepping into the enemy's reach, an MTP held high.

Through the temple . . .

Gina didn't hesitate. Corkscrewing all her force through her hips, she drew back the dagger and plunged it into the creature's side.

Once, twice. Deeper.

The effect was instantaneous. The Collector howled, weakening her grip. Her nails drew thin trails down Dov's arms, but there was no more strength there. The undead beast was doubly dead.

Gina removed her blade and rolled away the rotund corpse.

Dov stood, his breath ragged and his scratches beaded with red drops. He stared at his foe, touched her with his foot. In a need to be sure, he rammed an MTP into the Collector's temple.

He collapsed then, into Gina's arms—and sobbed.

She clung to him and felt something begin to break within her own chest. She found herself close to tears—for Jacob, for courageous Petre, for her damaged marriage, and for the loneliness that ached in her chest.

She released Dov and bent to the body of the fallen twin. She had failed him. Why was she even here? Was it her destiny to march children into the blades of death?

She lifted her chin.

No. This isn't over, not yet.

With Dov's assistance, she lifted the boy and fed him back through the window of the bus. The muncitors helped bring him inside, while Pavel pressed his face to the glass in obvious shock.

"Keep down," Gina urged the passengers. "Don't let them see you."

"You're on your own," a male muncitor said. "We will not stay for this."

"You can't leave. Cal . . . the driver . . . You need to trust him."

"Trust? Already, we've lost one of our orphans!"

Those words echoed Gina's own sorrow, her conflicted emotions. She wanted to believe, yet Cal had failed her before. And now, once again . . .

"Please," she said. "Just stay quiet and don't move."

The muncitor chuffed at that.

Another deep growl from the trees muffled his dissension and introduced the brown bear that lumbered into view. It rose on its hind legs, standing seven to eight feet tall and probably close to a thousand pounds. The claws on its powerful forearms looked four or five inches long, dull but deadly.

It dropped back to all fours and rumbled forward.

Gina released Dov and glanced back at the bus. Though the door was still closed, she saw a muncitor peek over the lip of a window. Gina jerked her head once, indicating to get back down out of sight.

Cal, oblivious to the bear, had two MTPs left, and he was still trying to deal a final blow to Shalom. Stripped of the facade, her true vampiric nature had been exposed, and the decorous beauty was now a ratty-haired, wild-eyed, one-handed creature. Losing blood, she was pale white, and her breath came out in foggy puffs as she bared her fangs and snarled.

Cal raised a metal spike, but stepped back when she lashed out with her lethal nails.

The bear was picking up speed.

Gina knew she was no match for this monster. Normally, she would've admired its strength and size without fear. Brown bears could kill a stag with a single swipe of a paw, yet they often sustained themselves on simple roots and sprouts and fish. Unless threatened, they were docile around humans.

But average bears didn't have luminous emerald eyes.

"Cal?"

He flicked his gaze her direction.

She pointed at the beast with her knife tip. To run away would only incite the animal's predatory instincts, yet the weapon seemed small, toylike, in the face of this approaching danger. She, who had been like a mother bear herself only moments earlier, now felt helpless. She pulled Dov around to her backside, lifted the dagger, and hoped, cursed, prayed for the Provocateur to act.

Don't just stand there. Cal . . . Cal!

If necessary, Gina decided she would stab at the animal's eyes to protect her young ward, but the chance of succeeding seemed no more likely than that of her flinging the blade across the river and having it lodge into a boulder.

"No, Dov."

He was trying to step forward.

"Wait," she said.

She saw Cal darting past the bus, angling to intercept the bear. He had a metal spike in each hand. The bear was also at full speed, its great mass of fur quivering with each step, rolling waves of grizzled brown beneath the night sky.

Dov was not to be denied.

Armed like his mentor, he broke free and trailed on legs that were quick yet hampered slightly by a missing left toe.

"No!" Gina yelled.

Cal feigned left, then planted his right foot and spun the other way, slipping past the monster's gaping maw. He tried to ram an MTP through matted fur, yet the bear was already past him in a collision course for the small fifteen-year-old boy.

This was not going to happen. Not while Gina was alive.

Though she tried to bolt forward, her legs failed her. She was telling them to move, but they were taking her nowhere. She remained stationary. Terror and guilt clamped an icy hand around her throat.

Dov!

The bear slowed as one of the boy's MTPs careened off its huge round head and peeled back a flap of hide. The animal seemed annoyed more than anything, rising to full height before Dov and Cal, bellowing between powerful jaws packed with sharp canines.

Gina tried again to move. She choked: "Get . . . back . . . here."

She realized then that the hand at her throat was more substantial than emotion, more corporeal than panic. From down past her chin, she nabbed a glimpse of a tapered fingernail as it curled and tightened its grip.

She was being strangled.

"Cal . . ."

She tried to call out his name, without success. How could she have been so selfish as to pull him away from his own life-or-death skirmish? She craned back to see her enemy.

Shalom's intense stare was locked onto her from behind. Gina tried to stab backward with her dagger, but the female Collector was already kicking at the back of her legs so that she dropped to the ground.

Gina landed hard. Felt the impact through her kneecaps, into her spine.

"You're coming with me," Shalom spit near her ear. "We have a nice, cozy cave for you, safe from the elements."

Gina reached back for a handful of hair, for the eyes, while using her other hand to slip the dagger back into its thigh sheath. When that failed to free her, she tried to smash her cranium into the creature's nose or lips, anything to loosen the iron grip on her neck. Instead the hold tightened further, and she felt her air shut off as she was lifted by the adrenaline-charged strength of this undead foe.

She was on her feet again—barely, wobbly. She was being dragged, half carried. Her windpipe was constricted. She heard the possessed bear's roars, as though from far away, then human yelps and a shriek of pain. Her sight was dimming, giving way to this pressure on her carotid artery. She couldn't breathe, couldn't see.

Maybe if she could just—

She was passing out. Stars were winking in the blackness above, winking good night.

Hi, my name is Gina. I'll be your guide as we descend . . .

CHAPTER FIFTY-FOUR

Zalmoxis Cave, Romania

Gina Lazarescu refused to verbalize her pain. Propped on weary legs, she tested the thick ropes that pulled her arms toward opposite walls. Her body was chilled, her thoughts as murky as the light seeping through the cave's mouth.

She had failed Dov. And Petre. Where was Cal?

Though she couldn't see her captor, she sensed someone was near. Was Shalom standing guard outside?

"I know you're here," Gina called out.

In response, a cold wind swept the subterranean chamber with a briny odor. Where had that come from? By her guess, she was a hundred kilometers from the Black Sea, trapped in the mountains over Sinaia.

The salty air stung her eyes. She blinked and detected movement at the base of the far wall. A man was curled on the ground, the collars of his jacket flapping in the breeze, small black wings beating at his neck.

Another prisoner? If so, why wasn't he tied up? Maybe he was dead.

Cal?

No, that wasn't his jacket.

Something trickled along Gina's skin and slipped down the curve of her armpit. She craned her head and saw roots tangled around her left bicep, hooked into place by curved thorns. Blood was leaking from the puncture points.

Drippp, drippp . . .

She was being drained. She thought of the leather sheath strapped to her thigh. She thought of ripping loose from the entanglement, but the result would be shredded flesh.

"You're letting it go to waste. If you want it, come and get it."

Her voice triggered action in the shadows. The sprawled man's eyes snapped open, and a preternatural green fire ignited in his pupils. He lifted himself from the ground, brushed pebbles from his stout legs, and patted at wavy, black hair. Then he faced her. One hand stretched, bridged the distance. He was there beside her in an instant.

Was this their leader? Cal had told her his name was Ariston.

Lord Ariston was glad to have made it back to Zalmoxis Cave. In the deeper reaches of these caverns, he had lain Eros and his own son Sol to rest, but that was not what interested him. No, not now.

As he reentered his host and stood to his feet, he was struck again by a splitting headache. He winced. Pushed aside that distraction. He was rewarded with a vision—a slight-framed captive, with unruly hair, bronze skin, and deep brown eyes.

Regina Lazarescu.

She was unaware of her pedigree, of course. Hampered by ignorance, she stood here docile and defeated.

Wasn't that always the way of it with these humans?

Of course, Shalom deserved some credit for Gina's capture. Ariston had spoken with his daughter earlier and heard of the confrontation in the valley below. She'd told him of Erota's shift into a female bear, of the deadly skirmish near the train station. He could only hope Erota made a safe return.

Ariston had also heard of Shalom's arduous trek up the mountain trail, of her bleeding stump and the effort to get the hostage secured. Though she'd wanted to drain Gina on the spot, to restore her core temperature, he had denied that request.

Shalom slunk off, seeking fresh blood to restore her core temperature. She would be back soon enough.

Until then, Ariston would enjoy his time with the captive.

Gina threw her head back and swallowed a scream. The Collector was tugging, almost playfully, on the tangle of razor-edged roots. He ran one finger up her rib cage, then touched the blood-stained tip to his tongue while she tried to harness the tremors of adrenaline that ran along her skin.

"Hello," he said. "I am Ariston."

"You are weak," she hissed at him. "You have to tie me up to have a chance, is that how this works?"

"You sound upset."

"I'm tied to the walls of a cave."

"Anger's often a disguise for other emotions."

"Why'd you bring me here?"

"So we could talk. Don't you see, Gina? You're my link to the Nistarim."

"Let me go." She could only imagine what this creature would do if he found her orphan children. She hoped Dov was still alive. "Please, undo my wrists. My arms are getting numb."

Her foe pulled closer. "We all endure pain, don't we?"

She met his gaze, saw tears sizzling down his cheeks, sketching oily trails. One by one, they fell to the dirt and exploded into tiny molten flames. With the toe of his shoe, he extinguished them.

"Why are *you* crying?" she mocked.

"I care about you, my dear."

"Then set me free."

"Would you be free? Really? Your pain is a foretaste, that's all. A chance to share what I feel every waking hour."

Gina's limbs turned rigid. If only she could reach her dagger, but her arms were trussed too tightly. One thing she knew: Cal wouldn't be coming for her. Either he was dead, or he would be waiting for her in Bucharest as they'd planned. She imagined joining him there, sipping espresso at an outdoor café while he told her of his escape from the bear and his rescue of the orphans.

Assuming any of that were true.

What else had he wanted to tell her? Would she die here, never knowing?

Focus, she told herself. She would have to deal with this on her own. She needed to keep her captor talking, to give herself time to think and regain strength.

"You're not human," she told him.

"Not entirely. I'd say I'm more human than a human. I'm—"

"White Zombie."

The Collector tilted his head. "Not quite."

"No, it's a rock group. They have this song about . . . Never mind."

She closed her eyes, broke the stare. She sensed the presence of something insidious and barbed, running along the left side of her neck. It was connected to the tangle around her arm. What had been done to her? She remembered the thorns Cal had mentioned. Were these the same thing? They were coiling from the scar on her neck, the place Nikki had cut and bled and infected with her twisted thinking.

Gina chuckled. Now wasn't this ironic? Her mother's attempts to purge her of impurity had only contaminated her with resentment.

"Why're you laughing, dear?"

Her breath caught.

"By all means, don't stop. It sounds nice."

Her eyes popped open. "Go to hell."

"Oh, yes, I'm sure your mother drilled that religious stuff into your head. Strange, isn't it, how those who feel the most guilty often point the longest fingers?" He touched his own fingertip again to his lips.

Could he taste Gina's bitterness in her blood?

"And what's my mother guilty of?" she inquired.

"The desire to be loved."

"Right. By living on the run and changing identities?"

"Humans—always running from their sins."

"Or trying to bleed them away."

"I could help you with that. A moment's peace—isn't that what you want, Gina? Rest from your turmoil?" His mouth brushed along her neck.

Her nostrils filled with his musk. Dizziness blossomed in her head. This was the same emptiness she'd always felt beneath the blade of the dagger, and her pulse was tapping at her temples in a soporific rhythm. His mouth—so tender, so warm. She hadn't expected that. This couldn't be how the others had died. She'd heard about their corpses, the manner in which they'd been eviscerated.

Along her skin, the Collector's lips parted.

Why'd it always start this way, with a kiss? She thought of that infamous betrayal two thousand years ago. There was also her own fateful kiss on that morning at Erlanger Medical—before she'd walked away from her baby boy.

A whimper caught in her throat. She leaned her head back, a sob welling within. "Jacob," she cried. "I'm so sorry."

"You can't blame yourself," the Collector said.

"What have I done?"

"We all cause harm to those we love. Your mother certainly knows that."

A squeal of anguish rose in Gina's throat. Like an animal flushed from its burrow, the sound bounced between stone walls on its dash off into the darkness. She didn't care what this creature thought. How could he possibly understand the love between a mother and child.

Between Gina and Jacob. Between Gina and Dov, even.

What about, between Nikki and Gina?

"Shhh," the Collector comforted.

She tuned him out. There was something important here.

The thorns . . .

She realized these barbs at her neck were a product of her own unforgiveness. Sure, Nikki had tilled furrows in her daughter's skin, yet it was Gina who had tended the seeds of bitterness and left them to grow. How could she put all the blame on her mother's distorted methods, when she, Gina, had nursed the vines? She'd wrapped herself in them, never considering the dark fruit of this corrupted harvest.

She had to break free. Could she be one of those Cal had talked about, one of Those Who Resist? It seemed impossible now. To make even the smallest movement would lead to more pain and eventual death.

The Collector's black hair tickled her chin as he nuzzled close. His head nudged the earring dangling from her left lobe.

What had Cal said?

A drop of His Blood . . . that's all it takes.

Gina recalled their discussion along the Chattanooga riverfront. She thought of these thorns rooted in anger, oozing from her neck and encircling her arm. Could one drop really free her? Could she swing that dangling orb into her mouth and bite down, ingesting the life force of the Nazarene.

Freedom. Forgiveness. Life.

Could it be that simple?

Then her thoughts turned to Jacob again. Where had Cal been when her newborn son needed him? When those nails exploded through the air? And why had Cal left her to her mother's insanity during all those childhood years?

Gina wanted to believe, she really did.

But how did any of that help her now, in the real world, with real scars and a real enemy?

She wasn't going anywhere until she dealt with these thorns of the past.

Ariston drew in the heady scent of his prey's fear and panic. The pounding of her pulse—so close, only a mouthful away—was intoxicating, and he took pleasure in this violent foreplay, drawing it out. By the time he dove in, her blood would be racing, ready to burst into the back of his throat.

If she only knew how easily she could break away.

Of course, she had no clue.

Like other humans, Gina was full of doubts that only lent themselves to the Collectors' goals. How easy it was to persuade and possess these quibbling, vomitous beings. It wasn't Ariston's style, however, to let hatred show. He preferred the finesse of flattery and gentle tones. Already, he knew she was susceptible, her memories a weak spot. He'd heard the stories of Chattanooga from Erota, and he'd just listened to Gina express her guilt over her son's death.

What now? Did she think Cal would come to her rescue?

Ariston wondered what had transpired earlier at the Sinaia train station. According to Shalom, Erota had been in a fight for her life—not only with the present but the past.

Dov Amit . . . the present.

Cal Nichols, or whatever his true name was . . . the sordid past.

Rumors from other clusters had filled Ariston in. Cal, they said, was one of the original Nistarim—a man Lettered long, long ago, then buried in Jerusalem, then raised again and given a task. For centuries, he had served in that role until the solitude drove him into a woman's arms.

Nicoleta. Nikki . . . She'd warmed him for a night.

Just that easily, Cal had violated the stipulations of his commission and lost his Letter. Another, for the sake of this dismal planet, had stepped into his place, but Cal still wandered the globe, trapped in his immortal frame, trying to right his wrongs.

On this one point, Ariston could relate to the miserable cur . . .

He and Cal, they were both fathers.

Nine months after Cal and Nikki's violation, a baby girl had been born. She was half-human, half-immortal. And, after years of patience, Ariston had hunted her down. She was here now, her arms tied to these walls of stone.

Gina was on her own.

Even if Cal and Dov had survived their ordeal, they wouldn't know where to find her. She could only hope they were alive and that Cal would guard the children of Tomorrow's Hope better than he'd done with Jacob.

If she died here, would Jed ever know what happened to her? Would Teo?

The Collector was whispering at her ear. "Your memories, my dear. They're encoded in your DNA, in your blood. I can draw them out in only a few mouthfuls. I give you my word." He slid along the scar at the nape of her neck, where her hair was pulled back in a clasp. "Why continue carrying those awful thoughts?"

His offer was alluring, his tones soothing.

But no, hadn't that already been the story of her life—jagged shards and jumbled pieces?

The Collector's lips were stretching wide, stiff against his gums, while serrated teeth combed her skin in search of a resting place. Without breaking through, his teeth clamped onto a tendon that ran the length of her neck. She gazed into the dark and found strange reassurance in that firm pressure, like a kitten held in its mother's mouth.

Yes or no. Which would it be?

The knotted tangle was pressing into her skin, stretched from her neck down along her arm. Her childhood, her bitterness—it was all there, holding her hostage to events she could not change.

I'm done. Time to let go of it all.

"You said only a few mouthfuls," she breathed. "Are you sure?"

"For what I have in mind, it's all I need."

"But I . . ." Gina closed her eyes. "I want . . ."

She wanted to be free. Her soul had been prisoner to Nikki's venom, to these thorns that Gina had watered with her own salty tears. She was so tired. Yet, in these limbs of hers, she still had a faint semblance of strength.

She still had the Power of Choice.

Gina Lazarescu braced herself for the pain, knowing, believing, it would be the first step on her path of escape. Her arms trembled. Blood traced a sticky pattern down her side, while sweat trickled from the sheath's warmth against her thigh. She told herself this was the only chance she would get. If she hesitated any longer, remorse would chase her to the grave.

Honor . . . duty . . . combat.

"What is it, my dear?" the Collector urged. "Tell me what you want."

"I want to feel you close to me. I want you to take it all."

Queen sacrifice.

CHAPTER
FIFTY-FIVE

Lord Ariston reveled in this moment. He leaned forward. He'd had fun toying with his prey, and now he was ready to feed. His head pounded with the tension of this pseudomortal existence, and he hoped a full partaking of Gina's blood would soothe the aching of his swollen gums where the fangs protruded.

"I want you to take it all," she told him.

He dipped toward her neck, that smooth bronze skin, and—

What was this?

Gina was moving with desperate bravado. Moaning between clenched teeth. Yanking with her left arm, rolling her wrist, and shredding her own skin in the tangled grip of the thorns.

The thick rope drew taut. With the torque that extended from her shoulder, she sawed the razor-edged brambles against the cord.

Tiny red spheres, spilling, spilling . . .

Ariston found himself hypnotized by this wasteful display, but he snapped back when he comprehended that she had severed herself free from the restraint. He leaned back in, planning to latch his mouth onto her throat, her lips, anywhere that would geyser warmth onto his tongue.

In her desperation, though, Gina was faster.

Her mangled arm swung down, and her fingers clawed at her thigh. She caught him with the flashing blade of the dagger just as his upper body weight edged in for his meal.

The dagger tore him open with fiery zeal. Gina seemed to find scant satisfaction as the sharpened steel tooth tasted from his side. No. She demanded that it feed on the deepest parts of him as well, stabbing it again, letting it bite through skin and ribs into the core of his undead being.

Just as she'd requested, Ariston was taking it all.

His scream shattered the cave's stillness and ran unobstructed through the damp granite corridors.

Gina's arm was sliced to ribbons, and yet—spurred by thoughts of Dov and Cal, of Jacob and Jed—she carved upward with the dagger, opening the torso of her enemy and scything the narrow space between them with crimson rain that splattered her face and ran down her lips.

She heard, in his cries, the sounds of swarming insects and beasts. Each voice, each bark and mewl and roar, each buzz and hiss and fluttering leathery wing, was an accusation—evidence of his abomination.

To the Collector, her weapon seemed to be a curse.

Apamea to Akeldama to anathema.

He staggered back, his eyes pools of shimmering agony. He was incapacitated, unable to see clearly. He wobbled. Dropped to his knees. Began to shrivel before her eyes.

The Restless Desert was a blistering sea of sand and mournful wails. The Collector was heading there now. Particle by particle, shadow by shifting shadow, he felt himself coming apart at the seams. His clothing was hanging loose over skeletal limbs and bare strips of sinew. He was being torn from his dying host, banished for a time undetermined: *facilis descensus Averno.*

In a final, blind, spiteful flail, he lurched forward in the withering body of Ariston and snapped his jaws at Gina Lazarescu, hoping to take along a fading memory of physical sustenance.

His right incisor scraped over her arm, failing to break the skin. He was left to feed on emptiness, on a wash of hot wind that worked over his cracked lips, his tongue, and down his throat.

Down, down . . .

Into arid, unquenchable sand.

Drenched with sweat, Gina was about to collapse. She reached to cut the rope from her other wrist, then switched the knife into her right hand. She curled unfeeling fingers around the ancient hilt and moved the edge to her scarred neck, where she cut away the bitter vine.

Weak and wobbly, she stumbled forward even as the creature on his knees began to shrivel before her eyes. She tore away from his last attempted bite, left him snapping on air.

Was that movement she detected from the mouth of the cave? Were others out there, waiting?

She was free, for now. The first step . . .

Journal Entry

June 29

The weather's still decent, but soon enough it's going to be another cold, soggy winter. I can't stay here. I've been stuck on this island too long, trapped by fear and thoughts of what others will think of me. How'll they react to the way I look? Will they think I'm disgusting?

It's time to face whatever's out there. Hiding from the dark won't make it go away, and Lummi Island will still hold its secrets—the ones I've tucked away for later.

Just thinking about leaving makes me weak, but I've got to do it. The lessons I found in Gina's last droplet will keep me going. Even though I'm starting to get an idea of my part in all this, it's almost too hard to believe. There's so much I don't know, and I'm really hoping I'll find Those Who Resist. Maybe they can explain more.

So here it is. I've written everything down. Who knows? Maybe it'll come in handy. Sometimes you do a bunch of work that never gets noticed, and other times when you think it's all over and you might as well just bag it all up for good . . . that's when the unexpected happens.

Death isn't really the question. I can see that now. I guess we all have our thorns, and they eat us alive—day by day, this slow digestion. I know as a fact I can't do this on my own. Some might call me weak, but I think true strength comes through confession. And, in this struggle against the Collectors, it seems to be the only way.

I'm going to take Cal's word for it. I believe the answer dies within.

ACKNOWLEDGMENTS

Dave Robie and BigScore Productions (literary agent)—for the belief and tenacity to represent my work.

Allen Arnold, Amanda Bostic, and Ami McConnell (Thomas Nelson's A-Team)—for bringing a dead dream back to life.

Leslie Peterson (Write Away Editorial), Amanda Bostic, Becky Monds, Jocelyn Bailey (Nelson editors)—for sharpening this story so that it would have teeth when necessary and only a soft nibble when that worked better.

Jennifer Deshler and Katie Schroder (marketing team)—for going the extra mile to spread the word.

Mark Ross (packaging manager)—for coming up with a cover that rocks.

Anne Horch (editor)—for early support of this novel and for bolstering my initial vision.

Carolyn Rose Wilson (wife)—for sticking with me through the thick and thin, the lean and the mean, and for giving lots of good loving.

Cassie and Jackie Wilson (daughters)—for sharing great music, scary movies, lots of laughs, and plenty of patience.

Mark Wilson (dad)—for that first trip to Romania in the early seventies, and for helping this technical ignoramus put together a website.

Linda Wilson (mom)—for recent travels together in Israel, and for a continual flow of ideas and prayer for this series.

Shaun and Heidi Wilson (brother and sister)—for sharing gypsy memories, hand-crafted chess sets, and experiences in then-forbidden countries.

Silvia Krapiwko (researcher) and Zvi Greenhut (archeologist) at the Israel Antiquities Authority—for allowing a surprise visit and for providing the details.

Joe Keleher and Ceridwen Lewin (friends, writers, and fellow travelers)—for joining my alleyway escapes from the vampires of Busteni and Bucharest.

Stephan and Angela Khuen (friends and fellow travelers)—for some funny moments together in Timisoara and Arad, and for more adventures to come.

John Hulley and Polly Seligum (gracious hosts from different cities)—for hospitality and transportation in Israel, and for the vigorous exchange of ideas.

Hillary Kanter, James Beardsley III, Vennessa Ng, Ellie Schroder, and Dana Baker (friends)—for facilitating my trip back to Romania after twenty years.

Gabriel and Estera Fira (my Romanian family in America)—for delicious meals, help with the language, and dreams of hiking together in the Carpathians.

Cristian Cazacu, Dennis Budnik, and Florea Romeo Tarcea (my hosts in Romania)—for hospitality, local insights and treats, and spiritual refreshment.

Valerie Harrell, Davin Bartosch, and Roosevelt Burrell (friends, coworkers at FedEx Kinko's)—for patience, lots of laughs, and research materials to sink my teeth into.

Daniel Silva, Bodie and Brock Thoene, and Morris West (novelists)—for the suspenseful Israeli-centered stories that first sparked my interest.

Sta Akra Writers, Storytellers Unplugged, The Council of Four, John B. Olson, Sue Dent, Tosca Lee, Ted Dekker, and others (novelists)—for encouragement, laughs, and prayers along this journey.

Kevin Kaiser (video producer)—for good friendship, and for coming up with a topnotch video trailer that makes my efforts look like child's play.

Sean Savacool, Rick Moore, and Matthew Champion (friends)—for regular fellowship, coffee, and creative stimulation.

Gary and Johni Morgan (pastors), and Mosaic Nashville—for spiritual covering and guidance, and for promoting art that's outside the box.

As I Lay Dying, Audioslave, The Awakening, Chevelle, Demon Hunter, Flyleaf, Killswitch Engage, Linkin Park, Plumb, Project 86, Radiohead, Red, Skillet, Smashing Pumpkins, White Stripes (modern rock groups)—for providing the loud music and piercing lyrics to keep this novelist up late into the night.

Readers everywhere (young and old)—for finding a place to bury these words . . . May they bring back to life things you thought were long dead.

I welcome your feedback online:
www.jerusalemsundead.com * jerusalemsundead@hotmail.com
www.myspace.com/jerusalemsundead

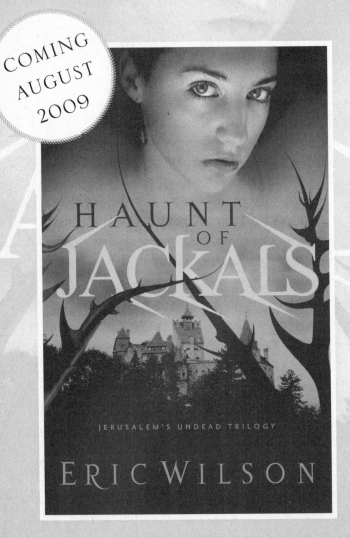

Thorns will overrun its palaces . . .
The ruins will become a haunt for jackals.

Isaiah 34:13

COMING AUGUST 2009

THE NEXT INSTALLMENT OF
THE JERUSALEM'S UNDEAD TRILOGY